A FULL RECOVERY

Sasha thrust the doctor's okay at him. "Here."

Nick took in her high color, the temper sparking in her gray eyes. Without bothering to reach for it, he glanced down at the paper she was all but jabbing into his chest. His eyes lifted once again to look into hers. "What's this?"

"What do you think it is, Vinicor?" She waved the paper under his nose this time. "It's my medical clearance."

"Uh-huh. Let's see that." He took his time looking it over before he finally returned his attention to her. "So you really feel okay?"

"Right as rain, bud."

"No lingering effects? No light-headedness, no weakness?"

"No." Without thinking, she cocked an arm and flexed a biceps at him. "Strong as an ox."

"Good." He reached out, curled his fingers around the proffered muscle, wrapped his other hand around the back of her neck, and pulled her into his room. Slamming the door with a raised knee, he crowded her up against it. "Because I've waited long enough for this."

Sasha was just opening her mouth to ask him what the hell he thought he was doing when his hands plunged into her hair and his mouth came down on hers. It was akin to being struck by lightning, something she should have remembered from the other time he'd kissed her.

Books by Susan Andersen

PLAYING DIRTY

BURNING UP

BENDING THE RULES

CUTTING LOOSE

COMING UNDONE

JUST FOR KICKS

SKINTIGHT

HOT & BOTHERED

GETTING LUCKY

HEAD OVER HEELS

ALL SHOOK UP

BABY DON'T GO

BE MY BABY

BABY I'M YOURS

SHADOW DANCE

ON THIN ICE*

OBSESSED*

PRESENT DANGER*

EXPOSURE*

*Published by Kensington Publishing Corporation

ON
THIN
ICE

SUSAN
ANDERSEN

ZEBRA BOOKS
KENSINGTON PUBLISHING CORP.
http://www.kensingtonbooks.com

ZEBRA BOOKS are published by

Kensington Publishing Corp.
119 West 40th Street
New York, NY 10018

Copyright © 1995 by Susan Andersen

All Kensington titles, imprints, and distributed lines are available at special quantity discounts for bulk purchases for sales
promotion, premiums, fund-raising, educational, or institu-
tional use.

Special book excerpts or customized printings can also be
created to fit specific needs. For details, write or phone the
office of the Kensington Special Sales Manager: Attn. Special
Sales Department. Kensington Publishing Corp., 119 West
40th Street, New York, NY 10018. Phone: 1-800-221-2647.

Zebra and the Z logo Reg. U.S. Pat. & TM Off.

ISBN-13: 978-1-4201-1717-2
ISBN-10: 1-4201-1717-3

First Printing: August 1995

10 9 8 7 6 5 4

Printed in the United States of America

For all the support you've given me over the years
This is dedicated, with love

To
Aunt Thelma
Whom I've gotten to know all over again

To
Martha McKenney
Who single-handedly raised the sales in
south King County

To
Doug Armitstead
Who is probably responsible for raising them
everywhere else

And to
Alda Hewes, formerly of Shipstads and Johnson,
for sharing her time and insider information of
the world of professional ice skating.
Many, many thanks.

PROLOGUE

The junkie shifted from foot to foot. He sniffed, swiped a grubby finger under his nose, and hitched his loose jeans to a more secure position on his thin hipbones. Eyes in constant motion, he glanced to the mouth of the alley where foot traffic passed by, reassuring himself that none of it was the law. Returning his nervous gaze up the shadowed passageway, he searched out the back door of the Thai restaurant, on the alert for any employee stepping out to have a smoke. He noticed, without actually registering, the dog that nosed through the spilled refuse next to the dumpster; then he felt his attention once again compulsively drawn back to his supplier's hands. Shuffling impatiently, he stared with ill-concealed hunger at the little plasticized bag of white powder and licked his lips.

The dealer noticed and gave him a smile of cool contempt. "A little anxious, big guy?"

The junkie ignored the jibe. It was his first contact with this particular supplier, but already he'd recognized that this was a vendor unlike any he'd ever dealt with before.

Unfortunately, as it turned out, this was also one of the ones who got their jollies out of making customers sweat. Disparaging eyes observed his every move and registered his physical distress, which took the form of trembling hands and facial tics; scornful lips curled slightly in derision. Narrow fingers first extended the bag of heroin to him and then twitched it out of his reach milliseconds before he could grasp it. "This what you want?" the voice taunted. "How bad ya want it, I wonder? Bad enough to bark like a dog?"

Asshole, the junkie thought when the supplier finally tired of tormenting him and got down to business. But he didn't say anything.

He didn't dare. If the transaction was cut short before the scag was his, he was gonna die, pure and simple.

As it was, he was drenched in sweat and shaking badly by the time he got back to the room where he flopped nights. Collapsing on the thin, bare mattress that had been thrown without benefit of frame or box spring directly onto the floor, he fumbled for his cardboard cigar box. Out of it he pulled a used hypodermic, a small bent and blackened spoon, and a cheap disposable lighter. Working as slowly and carefully as his shaking hands would allow, he tapped the heroin out of the bag and into the spoon and heated it over the butane flame. Within moments, he was drawing the liquid up into the syringe. Picking up a length of surgical tubing, he tied it off just above his elbow.

However, no matter how hard he pumped his fist or slapped at the inner bend of his elbow, he couldn't raise a vein. Finally, with an impotent curse, he removed the tourniquet and toed off his right shoe. Yanking off his sock, he pulled the tubing tight around his ankle, tied it off, and inserted the hypodermic needle into the one good vein he found on his foot. He depressed the plunger.

A rush of heat suffused his veins and he smiled euphorically. It lasted perhaps twenty seconds. Then like a flash of summer lightning, a brilliant white light seemed to expand in his brain and he closed his eyes, slumping sideways.

He was dead before his head touched the floor.

ONE

The huge bus had already rumbled to life outside the hotel by the time Sasha Miller finished turning in her room key at the desk. She paused to pour herself a cup of coffee at the courtesy table and then, juggling it along with her purse, train case, and overnighter, went outside.

The baggage compartment gaped open, a black hole just below the silver logo, *FOLLIES ON ICE*, lettered in cursive on the side of the midnight-blue bus. Sasha set her overnighter down next to the driver. "Good morning, Jack." Sipping her coffee, she watched him over the rim of the cardboard cup as he stowed and arranged luggage.

"Mornin', Sasha." He looked up with a smile, but a small frown tugged his brows together as he ran a familiar eye over her baggage. "Where's your skate case?"

"It's okay, Jack," she assured him. "After last night's show, I simply didn't feel like lugging it up to my room, knowing I'd only have to turn around and lug it back down again this morning. So, believe it or not, I actually left the darn thing in the compartment here." She thumped the side of the bus and shrugged, giving the driver a self-deprecatory smile. "I know, I know, not exactly my standard operating procedure."

"Well, variety is the spice of life they say."

Sasha laughed. "You'd probably know a lot more about that than I would, Jack. Heard tell you had yourself a pretty hot date last night."

He shook his head. "Good God," he commented mildly. "Not much passes by unnoticed in this group, does it?"

"Not much," she agreed. "And you know as well as I do that nothin' passes by unremarked. Follies is a lot like life in a small town that way." Only a hell of a lot more tolerant then the one where she'd grown up. She and Lon . . .

She purposely shrugged that thought aside. She didn't want to think about Kells Crossing or Lonnie today. The sky was blue, the air was clean; why dwell on matters that would only make her downhearted? "So, tell me," she demanded instead, "was it a fun date? Did you have a good time?"

"Yeah, it was all right," he retorted. "She was a real nice woman."

"Nice? Oh, Jack, my condolences. I'm real sorry to hear that."

"Get outta here, Miller." He took a mock swipe at her and obviously had to bite back a smile when she grinned at him with cocky delight as she hopped nimbly out of reach. "Damn fresh kids these days," he grumbled. "Got no respect."

"Hey, maybe you'll get luckier one of these days," she called to him as she boarded the bus.

Sasha exchanged greetings with other performers as she made her way down the narrow aisle; she bandied insults with the wardrobe woman and a couple of her favorite techies, who as usual were congregated in the back of the bus. But she joined none of them. Instead she took a seat by herself in the middle.

Connie would undoubtedly make her usual last-second appearance and she'd expect Sasha, as always, to have saved her a place. Sitting down next to the window, she stowed her purse under the seat, set the train case in the seat next to hers, and, opening it, began to apply makeup with a light hand.

She was cleansing her fingers with a premoistened baby wipe several minutes later when the bus door closed with a pneumatic whoosh. Head snapping up in alarm, she turned automatically to look toward the hotel entrance. Even as she watched, the portal was flung open and Connie Nakamura came flying through, bags banging awkwardly against her legs. The door of the bus wheezed open again when she reached the curb.

"I've got a schedule to keep, Nakamura," Jack informed the petite Japanese woman. "I'm not reopening the baggage compartment."

She climbed breathlessly aboard. "Wouldn't dream of asking, Jack."

With a disgruntled expression, he closed the door behind her and put the bus in gear, pulling out of the valet drive before she reached her seat. Staggering slightly with the movement, Connie regained her balance and continued down the aisle. She stowed the largest of her bags in the overhead compartment and then grinned down at Sasha.

"That was the closest call yet," Sasha commented, picking her train case off Connie's seat and setting it on the floor. "One of these days Jack's going to leave you behind."

"Nah," her friend disagreed. "Never happen. Then he wouldn't have anyone to play the game with, and where's the challenge in that?" A corner of her mouth quirked up sardonically. "Man, can't you just picture it: everyone on time and ready to go, day after day? Jack'd be bored silly in a week. I keep him young. Well, me and the occasional widow he takes out to dinner." Connie sat herself down, drew her right heel up on the seat, and finished tying the shoelace she hadn't had time to tie earlier. Turning her head she asked, "So where the hell did you disappear to yesterday afternoon?"

Sasha thought fast. "I, um, went out to the arena."

Connie gave her a doubtful look. "Yeah, right," she said skeptically. Then looking her straight in the eye she added softly, "I was out there, Saush, looking for you."

Tension stiffened Sasha's neck. "Were you? What time?"

"Four."

"Well, there you go. I finished checking out the ice about three-forty-five. We probably passed each other in transit."

Connie regarded her friend closely. "I don't know what the hell's going on in your life right now," she said quietly. "But I sure wish you could trust me enough to share it with me."

Sasha wished the same thing even as she was making conciliatory noises and changing the subject. More than anything else in the world she wished she could do that, for it would be wonderful to unload her burden onto someone else's shoulders.

But, oh, God, I can't, she acknowledged to herself. *I love Connie, and I do trust her. But she didn't grow up the way Lon and I did so she couldn't possibly understand.*

And she would never, not in a million years, ever approve, Sasha tacked on in silent admission. *That's a fact.*

Lon Morrison lay on his bunk trying to tune out sounds that were prevalent day and night in the confined area that defined his cell block. He daydreamed of skating. It was a surefire way to pass time, one he'd utilized almost daily for the several years he'd been incarcerated.

He thought of soaring across the ice with Sasha, of the lifts and the jumps. They'd always had a near telepathy when it came to skating together, it was an inexplicable phenomenon that contributed to making them the hottest up-and-comers the figure skating pairs circuit had seen in years. That, and the consistent use of sex and rock and roll in a world that, at the time, had still been chastely waltzing across the ice two-by-two to the well-mannered strains of Strauss.

They'd had one foot on the fast track, he and Saush, but then he'd gone and screwed it up royally. He'd been hungry after a lifetime of living on the wrong side of the tracks. He'd wanted more; he'd wanted it now; and for his trouble what he'd gotten in the end was . . . nothing. No money, no fame . . . just jail time. Not exactly the way he'd planned it.

Sasha had gone on to skate on the ladies' singles circuit. She hadn't exactly had a lot of options—the scandal of his arrest had rocked the ice-skating world and for a while she'd been tarred with the same brush of his reputation. It had made her a less than ideal candidate for prospective new partners. If she wanted to remain a skater, she had to go back to skating the way they all started out . . . solo.

But, hell, when it came down to it she'd done all right for herself; he hadn't destroyed her career along with his own. She'd made it to the Olympics, for Christ's sake, where she'd won the silver.

To hear her tell it, though, aside from the day when they'd indicted him, you'd think it was the most tragic time of her life. And granted, to miss out on Olympic Gold by two lousy tenths of a point was a bummer. But look at the job offers that had come her way since the Olympics. Nobody gave a rat's ass that she hadn't brought home the gold. She'd had more offers than she'd known what to do with and for an Olympic contender, professional skating really paid.

It was sure as hell a long ways from Kells Crossing.

Saush sent him *Skate* magazine so he could keep up with the industry news. There'd been a lot of changes in skating since he'd been away from it. Jesus, some Canadian guy was doing a quadruple toe loop. A *quadruple*. How he kept from breaking his frigging ankle on the landing was beyond Lon, but talk about an opportunity to haul in the big bucks. That achievement alone had garnered the guy a shot at the really big hitters—the power endorsements.

Well, big stinkin' deal. Lon wasn't bustin' his chops with envy. He was due to be released soon; then he, too, was climbing on the gravy train. It was all out there, just waiting for him.

All he needed was a little inside help. And for that he had Sasha.

* * *

Weary beyond belief, Mick Vinicor looked at the activity going on all around him. And felt ambivalent as hell. The good news was, it had been a successful knock-off. This raid, the tail end of which was currently being cleaned up, was the payoff for several weeks of deep cover and it was a beaut, resulting in the arrests of several high-ranking suppliers and dealers and one top drug czar.

The bad news was, he was surrounded by suits. And like most field agents, he despised suits.

He couldn't sit around on his butt and sulk about it forever, however, while other people did his work for him. Mick shot the cuffs of his silk shirt, dusted imaginary lint from the two-thousand-dollar jacket he wore, consulted his outrageously pricy Rolex, and climbed to his feet.

He was immediately shoved back onto the couch cushions and not with a gentle hand, either. "Stay put, asshole," the suit growled down at him. "I'll tell you when it's time to move."

The lines between the good guys and the bad guys had been growing increasingly blurred in Mick's mind lately and he didn't stop to think; he simply reacted. Before the suit knew what had hit him, the man he'd obviously taken for one of the big-money drug dealers was on his feet again. The agent's head was hauled back in a rough fist and he felt the cool press of blued steel against the carotid artery beneath his jaw. The pistol's barrel constricted his breathing as he involuntarily swallowed.

"That's *Special Agent* Asshole to you, cocksucker," Mick informed him, dangling his DEA shield in front of the bureaucrat's eyes. He turned him loose. "Jesus," he complained to the field agent over in the corner, who was trying his damnedest to restrain a smile, "where do they *get* these guys, anyway, Epcot Center?" Small wonder the field men joked the agency's initials stood for "Don't Expect Anything."

He heard about his actions when he came into headquarters the next morning, of course. Now there was a big surprise.

"You don't pull your gun on a fellow agent," ranted the head suit at the conclusion of his tirade, pacing back and forth in front of Special Agent Vinicor, who leaned his jean-clad hip against a battered wooden desk and, with arms crossed over his sweatshirt-covered chest, watched his superior add some additional wear and tear to the already played-out carpet.

Mick had been following the diatribe with a certain amount of cynical amusement, but that particular emotion disappeared quickly when he heard the phrase that triggered his own temper. "Fellow agent?" he snarled, pushing himself upright. "No pencil-pushing bureaucrat is my *fellow ag* . . ." He ground to a halt, forcing down the rest of the condemnation like a bitter tonic. It left an acrid taste that was hard to swallow, but he wasn't entirely suicidal when it came to his career. A harangue against pencil-pushing suits to McMahon, who was the biggest pencil pusher of them all, probably wasn't the wisest course of action he could take.

Swallowing his pride with great difficulty, he mumbled, "My apologies." God, that hurt. But he had no desire to end up humping a desk in Waaskooskie Peoria. He gave it a little more thought and then limped out a grudgingly tacked-on, "Sir."

"You called him a cocksucker, Vinicor!"

"Yeah, well, sorry about that, too. But in my own defense, sir, he called me in asshole. Now you know as well as I do that assholes are anyone who's *not* DEA, sir—and especially not a DEA street hump." Vinicor grinned crookedly. "Let's me out."

"Oh, what the hell," McMahon suddenly capitulated. "He was only FBI anyhow."

Mick swallowed a laugh. His butt was saved only because

he'd had the good fortune to threaten an FBI agent instead of one of the DEA's own. You had to love it.

The Drug Enforcement Administration and the Federal Bureau of Investigation had a standing rivalry. A 1982 attorney general's order directing a coordinated effort between the two agencies had set the tone when it required the DEA administrator to report to the AG through the director of the FBI.

It was an order that had never once been followed and one the attorney general was wisely considering rescinding. He much preferred that both agency heads continued to report directly to him anyway, having learned the hard way that day-to-day informal coordination worked much more successfully than any attempts at a formal arrangement. Even then it required the deputy attorney general to oversee operational matters and resolve disputes between the two agencies.

The supervisor had been shuffling through some papers on his desk. Finding what he wanted, he looked up at Mick. "So. You ready for a new assignment?"

Mick hesitated. The truth was he knew he was in serious danger of burning out. Deep cover required an agent to sleep, breathe, and eat his role twenty-four hours a day, for however many days were necessary to see an assignment through to its completion. A field agent, or hump as they were known in the lexicon, was out there all on his own with no one to back him up, and armed, more often than not, with nothing more substantial than a bullshit story and his acting ability.

That part Mick could live with. Hell, his own mother had once said he was such a good liar that he was bound to end up either a con artist or a politician . . . and of the two, she had added, she sort of hoped he'd opt for con artist. No, what really affected his general attitude these days was that even when he did make a righteous bust, it seemed the suits and the politicians were invariably standing in line just waiting for an opportunity to undo all his hard work. Mick's belief in actually making any kind of difference in the war on drugs had been wearing increasingly thin.

Then McMahon said persuasively, "This is undercover, Vinicor, not deep cover. Hell, it'd be like a day at the beach for you." He tossed a file on the desk.

Mick resisted the temptation to see what it contained for about forty-five seconds before he broke down and scooped it up. A loose snapshot slid from the folder and he plucked it off the desktop.

"Ice skaters?" Mick looked incredulously from the picture to his supervisor. "You want me to bust a coupla kid *ice skaters?*" Looking back down, he ran the side of his thumb over the woman in the picture. A definite looker—too bad she was only a baby.

"They're Miller and Morrison," McMahon said, coming around the desk to stand next to Mick. He looked down at the snapshot. "Sasha Miller and Lon Morrison. And they ain't kids no more; this was taken quite a while ago."

"So what's the history?"

"Several years back they were some big-deal, hotshot sensation on the amateur figure skating circuit. Won top prizes in about every competition goin', I guess. Can't remember the exact dates, but if you need 'em they're in here." He thumped his forefinger against the folder Mick still held.

Mick tore his eyes away from the woman's face in the photograph and looked up at McMahon. "What's any of this got to do with me?"

"Well, a funny thing began to happen around the ole ice rink, Mick. Everywhere Miller and Morrison competed, high-grade heroin began showin' up on the streets. Scag so pure it had junkies dropping like flies." McMahon rubbed his palm over his balding scalp and frowned. "We got Morrison in a sting, nailed him dead to rights for distributing. I'm pretty damn sure he was recruited by Quintero but we couldn't get the kid to flip, not even when faced with murder two. Actually, because he didn't show up in NADDIS—hell, didn't have any priors at all—in the end he got off fairly lightly: seven-to-ten in minimum security. The girl was never implicated and went her merry way without him. She's still skating. She won the silver at the Winter Olympics, then went professional. That shoulda been the end of the story."

"But?"

"But there were kilos of heroin never accounted for, Vinicor, and now the shit's turnin' up again. Gotta be the same stuff—it's knockin' off junkies like ducks in a shooting gallery. We've had reports from San Diego, LA, San Francisco, Fresno. You name it; if it's a city of any size in California, we've heard from them."

"So you want me to investigate Morrison."

"Nah, Morrison's due to be sprung soon, but at the moment he's still in lockup." McMahon thumped his finger against the woman in the snapshot. "I want you to nail Miller."

Mick felt a tiny pulse of excitement but sternly suppressed it. "If she checked out clean the first time around," he said, deliberately playing devil's advocate, "what makes you think she's got anything to do with it now?"

McMahon passed him a full-page advertisement from *Variety* for an upcoming engagement for *Follies on Ice*. He pointed out Sasha Miller's photograph. Leaning closer, Mick looked it over, studying it carefully. He read her name in bold print beneath the full-body shot and beneath that, in finer print, US champion and Olympic silver medalist.

"Now look at the itinerary," McMahon said.

Mick flipped to the next page and scanned the contents. "San Diego, LA, Bakersfield, Fresno, San Jose, San Francisco," he murmured. He looked up at his supervisor. "We've got a trail of dead junkies matching the dates the ice show appeared in these cities, I take it."

McMahon pointed a finger at him and cocked his thumb. He pulled the trigger. "Got it in one."

"How many kilos involved?" Mick inquired.

For the first time McMahon looked uncomfortable. "Uh . . . seventeen."

"Oh for . . ." Mick tossed the folder aside in disgust, watching as the advertisement floated to the desk in its wake. "Call the local Narcs," he advised flatly. The DEA dealt in cases where seizure of heroin and cocaine was counted in tonnage. It didn't say much for the American way of life that they'd come such a long way since the seventy kilos seized in the French Connection just twenty years ago.

McMahon shook his head. "Can't do that. The show stays in one town maybe three-four days before it moves on to the next one. In the bigger cities like LA and Frisco it maybe stays a week. It's due into Sacramento tomorrow and when it leaves there it crosses state line into Oregon."

"Let the FBI have them then."

McMahon just looked at him and Mick rolled his shoulders uncomfortably. The FBI always attempted to dismantle an entire drug trafficking organization in a single law enforcement operation. When they had identified principal members and gathered sufficient evidence to prosecute, they tried to arrest all the leaders and key members at one time. One little independent skater wasn't going to grab their attention, even if her product was killing off junkies faster than you could say habeas corpus. "Shit," Mick muttered in disgust.

McMahon was looking down at the picture of Sasha Miller on the desk. "Man, she had me fooled," he admitted. "Pure as the driven snow, I woulda said." He frowned and scratched at his scalp. "Well, no, that's not exactly right. You should see this girl skate, Vinicor. Babe's so hot I'm surprised the ice don't melt—hell, I didn't know they could get away with that kind of sexy stuff in a family ice show."

Shaking off the memory, he met his agent's gaze. "But I tell ya honestly, when it came to the scam I coulda sworn she was bein' straight about not knowing what her partner was up to. His arrest sure as hell seemed to knock her on

20 *Susan Andersen*

her pretty little butt." He swore softly and shook his head again. "Just goes to show ya, I guess. There's no fool like an old fool."

"Well, don't let it get you down," Mick advised, for once feeling a trace of empathy for a suit. "We all get conned one time or another and a pretty little honey with big baby blues and a patter that makes her appear vulnerable is a better reason than most of the excuses I've heard for an agent being rooked."

He rubbed his thumb back and forth over Sasha Miller's picture in the *Variety* advertisement on the desk, tracing the pretty curl of her lips with the edge of his nail. Then his eyes snapped up and met his supervisor's dead-on. "I'll promise you something, though," he flatly vowed. "If this is the woman responsible for distributing the tainted scag up and down the West Coast, I'll personally bring you her head. Hand delivered on a platter."

TWO

Sasha opened her eyes to a hotel room that looked just like a hundred others she had awakened to in her lifetime, and for the briefest moment she couldn't remember what city she was in. Um. Blinking sleepily, she rubbed long, narrow fingers over her mouth, trying to raise a little moisture to alleviate the cottony taste on her tongue. Sacramento, wasn't it? Yes, sure, of course. Sacramento.

She rolled out of bed, stretched luxuriously, and ambled on into the bathroom. When she emerged a few minutes later she felt much more alert. Climbing into a pair of tights and a leotard, she donned a threadbare pair of sweats and pulled a thick, hooded sweatshirt over her head. Once she had cautiously picked the snarls out of her thick and curly dark hair, she swept it to the top of her head with one fist and secured the high ponytail with a coated rubberband. Its weight caused it to tilt haphazardly to one side the minute she let go. Not particularly interested in making a fashion statement anyway, she ignored its lopsided disarray. Picking up her purse and skate bag, she let herself out of the hotel room.

On the taxi ride to the arena, Sasha watched the scenery go by and mulled over the confusion of the past few days. Henry Chambers, their business manager, had abruptly left the Follies. Without any prior notice, which was not at all like him, he had simply departed. Rumor had it there was some family emergency, but his unexpected departure had left a great deal of confusion in its wake. The scramble for rooms yesterday had been a regular free-for-all without Henry there with his ubiquitous clipboard in hand, to direct their arrival at a new hotel in a new city with his customary soft-spoken and calming efficiency.

Fortunately, the powers that be had already found a replacement; a new guy was due to take Henry's place later this afternoon. The chances of him being half as nice as Henry, who was sort of unassuming and sweet, were pretty slim, but she'd be happy to settle for someone half as capable.

And Henry, bless his heart, even in the midst of his own crisis had not forgotten about her. One of the last things he must have done before he'd departed was to arrange for someone to let her into the Sacramento rink where tonight's performance would be held. He'd left her a note to inform her that from 9 A.M. on there would be guards on duty who would be expecting her.

Henry understood the importance Sasha placed on being able to check out the ice in each new rink before she had to perform on it in front of thousands. And efficient as usual, he hadn't let her down. There was a guard to meet her and let her in when she arrived at the Arco Arena at nine o'clock sharp. That left her two hours to practice before the caravan of five forty-five-foot-long semitrailers was due to arrive with sets and scenery and the stage crews who assembled them.

It was cold and dark inside, and as she followed the guard down several corridors the hollow echo of their footsteps bounced back at them from the low-ceilinged concrete hallways. The moment they entered the arena proper, their voices took flight, resonating from the tiers of empty seats that rose up to the soaring ceiling.

The guard's escort ended just inside the arena's entrance and within moments, amid the clank of switches being thrown, the lights overhead began to come on one grid at a time. Sasha slid out of her sweatpants, sat down in a rinkside seat, and opened her skate case, pulling out her skates.

She toed off her street shoes and leaned over to don the

skates. It was second nature to exert steady, equal pressure to the laces, and in moments she had them secured and was on her feet, delicately shaking the tension from first one leg, then the other. Stepping onto the ice, she reached down to remove the rubber guards that protected her blade's sharp edges and placed them atop the balustrade separating the ice from the stands.

She started skating slowly around the rink, warming up her leg muscles and developing a feel for the ice. Every rink had its own distinct flavor, the ice in each different from any other. As she neared the culmination of her warm-up exercises, Sasha gradually began to increase her speed.

Skating to center ice, she stopped in a spray of ice chips and took her opening position. With phantom music playing in her head, she paced herself through her first number and when that went well, moved on to the next. For some reason the double axle was giving her fits today and finally, in frustration, she focused her concentration, pouring all of her energy into improving her execution of it.

The axle is the only jump in which a skater takes off while going forward. Sasha bent her left knee, arms stretched backward. With a single movement she brought her arms forward and her right leg close to her body, thrusting herself into the air. She pulled her arms in tight and crossed her ankles for speed, turning two and a half revolutions. Kicking back with her right leg, she landed firmly, gliding in a small arc.

Okay, good. She tried it again. It came off without a hitch. Feeling cocky, she decided to try a triple.

And fell on her butt.

Laughing, she picked herself up. What the hell, her act didn't include the triple anyhow; she'd just wanted to see if she still had it. She tried again and it went off smoothly enough, although the landing could have stood a lot more polish.

Sasha's mind wandered as she continued to practice her routine. Professional skating didn't call for the same degree of technical difficulty that the amateur circuit demanded when grading its performers, and if one didn't constantly practice it was easy to lose proficiency. Sasha tried to stay on top of it, to keep her skills honed. At the same time, she didn't deny it was a major relief to be skating solely for an audience these days—their appreciation tended to be uncritical.

The amateur circuit in her experience had been far from flexible, but the Follies was a different story, and she loved it. Unlike some of the other big name ice shows, Follies encouraged their performers to develop new routines incorporating innovative ideas, a concept that she, as a skater whose individuality on the ice had often been more of a detriment in competitive skating than an asset, dearly appreciated. She'd lost a lot of points in her competition days for being different, but no longer was she at the mercy of some judge who, before her program had even begun, had a preconceived idea of what it should all be about. And that was wonderful.

Skating had been her life for . . . God, forever, it seemed. It was what had enabled her to leave Kells Crossing.

It was the reason that her life there had been so difficult in the first place.

She'd grown up on the wrong side of the river in a place where such things mattered. There was a strict social order in Kells Crossing that one was expected to adhere to religiously. You were either Town with a capital T or you were from the poorer west side. Skating and Sasha's association with Ivan Petralahti had landed her somewhere betwixt and between.

It was a less than enviable position to be in at the best of times and especially rough for a teenager. She and Lon Morrison, or so it had seemed at the time, were the only two people in all of Kells Crossing who had never quite known where they fit in. Neither fish nor fowl, nowhere had they appeared to entirely belong. Except on the ice.

* * *

She met Lonnie when she was ten years old. They were both from the west side, children of millworkers, but their paths had never crossed.

Which wasn't that surprising. Lon was a year older than she and lived on State Street. She lived closer to the river on Fifth. They attended the same school but were in different classes. He was a boy, she was a girl; their interests up until the day they met were in different arenas. But then one Saturday afternoon Ivan Petralahti opened his ice rink to the millworkers' children, and Sasha and Lonnie were exposed to a brand-new world.

It changed their lives.

The social structure in Kells Crossing was for the most part defined by its economics. Doctors, lawyers, merchants, mill owners, and the mills' upper management lived in Town on the east side of the river and the wealthiest lived in the big houses that lined the Hill. The inhabitants of those huge, ornate houses were considered pretty big fish in the small pond that was Kells Crossing.

But Ivan Petralahti was the closest thing it had to a celebrity.

Ivan Boris Petralahti was an Eastern European who was well known and well respected in the world of international figure skating. Still a foreigner when all was said and done, of course—at least as viewed through the parochial eyes of Kells Crossing's first families—that didn't stop the social lions from inviting him to every social function the Hill had to offer. Inbred prejudice could be counted on to take a back seat to one-upmanship every time.

After all, Petralahti did train world champions and Olympic medalists in that private complex of his on the outskirts of town, the one from which famous people were known to come and go. Hostesses therefore vied for the privilege of his attendance. Having Petralahti make an appearance at one's soiree was considered quite a social coup, especially as he was wont, as often as not, to send his regrets to the numerous invitations he received. Ivan cared only for skating and considered the social structure in Kells Crossing narrow in scope and provincial in outlook.

Sasha Miller, a millworker's child, would never have expected to even meet the man. And in truth, she was much too young to care. His celebrity status meant nothing to her; all she knew about the man in fact was that he kept to himself, talked with a funny accent, and had a private ice rink on his property.

The latter was the only thing she considered to be of interest.

Sasha loved to skate. She lived for the winters when first Swenson's pond and then the river would freeze over and she could pull out her old hand-me-down skates. She was most particularly looking forward to this year, because for the first time ever she didn't have to stuff the toes of her skates with Mama's old cast-off nylons in order to make them fit. From the moment she heard about the opportunity to skate in a real rink—something she had yet to experience—she didn't get one decent night's sleep.

Like Christmas, it seemed as though the big day would never arrive. Ultimately it did, of course, and Sasha was among the very first to reach the Methodist Church on Seventh Street where the bus that would take them to Mr. Petralahti's rink was parked. She scrambled aboard and then was forced to wait in an agony of impatience for the rest of the children to arrive. By the time the last straggler finally took his seat, she was on the verge of screaming.

Too excited to indulge in small talk, she spoke to no one on the short ride across the river to the outskirts of town. She instead stared out the window, watching the scenery pass by as she silently willed the rickety transport to go faster.

The rink was everything she'd dreamed it would be and more. The ice was even and smooth, like nothing she'd ever skated on before. And safe. What a picnic it was to not need to keep an eye peeled for thin ice, to not have to identify the trouble spots that required avoiding. Filled with joy, she zipped round and around, weaving in and out of the more cautious skaters.

A boy in the center of the rink caught her eye. He was attempting moves she had attempted on Swenson's Pond last winter, and with about the same amount of success. Watching him pick himself up for the third time, she skated to center ice to join him. Silently, side by side, they attempted to make their blades perform in a manner which the two of them hadn't even the experience to name. When their skates refused to behave and instead tangled up and knocked them to their knees or on their butts, they grinned, picked themselves up, and tried again.

It was the best day of Sasha's life.

And it was over much too soon. Before she knew it, she was home again, peeling potatoes for dinner and prattling on in rhapsodic terms of her day at the rink. She had been discoursing nonstop for a solid twenty minutes when the doorbell rang and interrupted her excited monologue.

"I'll get it," her mama said with a fond smile for her daughter's euphoria.

Sasha hacked away at the potato in her hand and tapped her toes in an impatient tattoo against the worn linoleum floor. She hoped whoever it was wouldn't keep her mother at the door too long, because she still had lots more to share with her. She hadn't even told her about the boy yet.

Sasha realized she hadn't even learned his name. They'd skated together, bouncing attempts at fanciful footwork off each other, for the better part of three hours. But they'd hardly exchanged two words. It was kind of weird the way they hadn't really *needed* to talk, almost as if they'd understood what it was the other one wanted to accomplish without having to utter so much as a word.

"Sasha?" Her mama's voice, sounding kind of funny, interrupted her reverie. Sasha looked up to see her in the doorway. "Come on out here, please. There's someone here to see you."

Sasha followed her into the parlor but stopped in shock just over the threshold. Seated on the old, dilapidated easy chair was Ivan Petralahti.

Himself.

In her house.

Her mouth opened and closed several times, but no words emerged. Gripping the doorjamb for support, she finally squeaked out his name. "Mr. Petralahti!"

"Hullo, Sasha." He rose to his feet. "I haff come to talk to you of skating," he said.

"To me?" Her eyes got big. "You want to talk to me?"

"Yes. I watched you skate today and I see somesing . . . somesing special. No training. Rough, you understand. But you luff it, yes?"

"Oh, yes! More than anything."

"Then you will come be my student. Be at the rink Monday promptly after school. I will expect you no later than 4 P.M." He moved toward the door.

"Mr. Petralahti," Sasha's mother said anxiously, fearing he may have somehow overlooked the poverty of their home, "we simply can't afford—"

"Iss a scholarship." Petralahti turned back to assure her. "I am giffing out two and one will go to Sasha on a probationary basis. If she does as well as I expect, it will be hers permanently. The second iss earmarked for a young man named Lon Morrison." He turned to Sasha with a slight smile. "I sink you know him, eh? Four o'clock," he reiterated autocratically. "Do not be late." And as abruptly as he had arrived at their door, he was gone.

Sasha blinked in wonder at her mother. "Mr. Petralahti is going to be my teacher?" She laughed suddenly, that deep, affecting laugh she'd had since she was a toddler, and grabbed her mother by the hands, whirling her around. In the midst of their third spin, she suddenly pulled back to regard her mother with puzzled eyes. "But why did he say

I knew that person, Mama? I don't know anybody named Lon Morrison."

But, she did. More or less. For the first thing she learned on Monday when she walked into Ivan Petralahti's big, barn-like structure and saw him whizzing around the rink was that Lon Morrison was the boy from center ice.

She shook her head, coming back to the present with a start. Holy cow. Where had all that come from?

As if you don't know.

Sasha skated slowly over to the rinkside seats where she'd left her sweats and skate bag. She'd better hit the road. This little trip down memory lane was all well and good . . . but life did move on.

Then her head raised with stiff-necked pride. No, tell the truth, she demanded fiercely of herself. It wasn't well and good at all; actually, it was kind of disturbing. It brought back memories she'd just as soon forget, and while recollections of Ivan were all very pleasant, thoughts of Lonnie were just plain, painful.

She was tired of the pain. But her ties to Lon Morrison seemed to keep her perpetually bound to it.

Sasha pulled off her skates, wiped the blades dry, put the rubber guards back on, and packed them away. Pulling on her sweatpants and street shoes, she went in search of the office to call a cab and let the guard know she was leaving. Ten minutes later she was on her way back to the hotel.

A group of Follie's performers was just coming out of the coffee shop when she walked into the lobby. Connie was among them and, spotting Sasha, she peeled off from the group and crossed over to her. "Hi! Where've you been?"

"Checking out the ice at Arco Arena."

"Sasha, Sasha, *Sasha.*" Connie shook her head in mock

despair. "I have *got* to teach you to have a little fun." She nodded toward the coffee shop. "You hungry?"

"Starved," Sasha admitted. "I skipped breakfast."

Connie grabbed her arm and steered her into the restaurant. "Come on, then," she commanded. "I'll keep you company while you eat."

Connie all but danced in her seat with suppressed excitement while Sasha put in her order. "Hot news," she said the minute the waitress walked away. "The new manager arrived while you were out." She gripped the edge of the tabletop, straining closer. "And wait until you get a load of this guy, Saush." She pursed her lips, rolled her eyes to heaven, and flapped her fingers. "Um, um, um."

Properly incredulous, Sasha met her friend's eyes over the rim of her water glass, then slowly lowered the glass to the table. "You're kidding," she marveled, her gray eyes wide. "A babe? We've got us a manager who's good-looking, who's *hot*? Isn't there some sort of law against that?" Oh bless Connie's heart, this was exactly the sort of nonsense she'd needed. It beat the hell out of brooding about Lon. Nakamura was the best in the world at coming up with topics that were silly, frivolous, and fun.

But her friend had been mulling over Sasha's description, actually giving it serious consideration. "Good-looking?" she murmured doubtfully. She shook her head. "No. That's not exactly the way I'd describe him."

Sasha made a rude noise. "Well, if he's not good-looking what was this, Connie?" She pursed her lips, rolled her eyes, shook her fingers as if they'd been burnt. "I thought you were trying to tell me the Follies had gone out and hired us a honey."

"They did." Connie grinned. "The guy's not particularly good-looking, is all. But wait until you see him, Sasha. He's"—she searched for wording that would illustrate the man's impact but finally gave it up—*"masculine,"* she said. "Very, very masculine."

"Okay." Sasha nodded sagely. "Masculine is good."

"You don't know the half of it, toots. Mere words do not do this fella justice." Connie was silent while the waitress placed Sasha's order in front of her. As soon as she left she said, "On the minus side, he's already managed to seriously offend Saint Karen."

"Jeez." Sasha's sandwich was suspended halfway between plate and mouth, her expression a study in admiration. "He's only been on the premises—what?—three hours, tops?"

"Try about an hour and a half"

"Oh, even better. How did he manage to offend somebody so fast?"

"Not just somebody, Sasha . . . Karen. And it was profanity. The use of extreme profanity."

They grinned at each other. "That's bound to keep her hands out of his pants for a good week or so," Sasha commented dryly.

Karen Corselli was a fellow performer and a walking conundrum. Blond and deceptively fragile in appearance, she always dressed in trademark silver for her performances on the ice, looked like an angel, and favored numbers with a Christian theme such as the Lord's Prayer and Ave Maria. Known for her absolute refusal to tolerate rough language, she was always quick with an offer to lead a prayer.

And yet . . .

If one could believe the rumors, she was also very fond of the men. *Very* fond. There were those who insisted she was a downright slut.

Such an interesting contradiction was a source of endless entertainment and speculation for Sasha and Connie. They only saw the one side of her. With them, as with the other women in the troupe, she was basically nice enough, if a little distant and very stuffy. Frankly, she came across as a prude. A *preachy* prude, and try as they might, they couldn't quite picture her any other way.

According to the male population of *Follies on Ice,* however, at least the heterosexual division, a prude she was not. And when she invoked God's name with them, they insisted, it *wasn't* for the purpose of preaching.

"I always feel guilty when I say stuff like that about her," Sasha admitted now. "I've never seen her act with anything other than extreme virtue. I mean, it's entertaining as all get-out trying to imagine her doing what the men say she's doing, but I don't know, Connie; it's hard to credit. I've been ac-quainted with her for years. Not friends, maybe—she's so self-contained I doubt that anyone really *knows* her all that well—but we followed the same amateur circuit. The point is, she acts so pure all the time."

"I know what you mean. And most of the Bozos who claimed to know her in the good ole Biblical sense are full of shit more often than not, anyway," Connie agreed. "But . . . *all* of them, Sasha? Every damn heterosexual male in this company? Performers, lighting techs, roadies, stage crew? That's a lot of men all claiming the same thing."

Sasha looked at her friend across the table. "You know what makes me believe it might be true?"

"Henry," Connie stated with a grin.

"Yeah, Henry." Sasha's return smile was a little sheepish. "When I heard he'd been with her, I flat-out asked him but he refused to kiss and tell—like the very nice gent he is. But, God, Connie, he blushed so hard I was afraid he was going to spontaneously combust." She laughed suddenly, an unprompted robust sound that came from deep in her dia-phragm. As always, it caused people to turn and look at her, smiling reflexively at the sound. "Man, if it's true and she seduced *Henry,* she must be something."

Connie was still grinning. "Kind of boggles the mind, doesn't it?"

"I'll say." Sasha looked at her friend across the table. "So what was the deal with the new manager? What exactly did he say to her to put her back up?"

Connie repeated the string of obscenities and watched Sasha's mouth drop open in shock. "Yeah. To give Karen her due, the guy's got a mouth on him. It kind of took me by surprise when he introduced himself as the new manager, 'cause you know the powers that be and their reverence for the 'Follies' Family Image.' " Her fingers crooked quotation marks around the phrase. "Your act is about as R rated as we get. In Mick's defense, though, he didn't actually say it to her. I was running a little late coming down here for lunch—"

"Ooh, there's a surprise."

"Kiss my pretty gold butt." Connie had practice ignoring that knowing sort of quirk Sasha could give to her right eyebrow. "Anyway, I ran into Karen upstairs just as she was heading back to her room from God knows where. I told her that everyone was meeting in the coffee shop and she decided to come down with me. Mick, which you've probably figured out by now is the new manager's name, was standing outside his room. He was trying to juggle all this stuff he had in his hands and open his door, and we were just passing by when half of what he was holding fell to the floor. He let rip, and as you've already heard it was with quite a bit of creativity." Connie shrugged. "You know Karen. She stopped to let him know in no uncertain terms she found that sort of language intolerable."

"And did he take one look at her big brown eyes and fall all over himself apologizing?" They'd seen that reaction more than once.

"He was about two seconds away from telling her to f— off," Connie replied with a laugh. "He didn't actually say the words, but you could see them forming. He's gotta be one of the few men I've ever seen she hasn't managed to leave feeling about an inch tall by the time she's finished raking them over the coals."

Connie watched in silence as Sasha consumed her sandwich. Then she rolled her shoulders and continued, "It was kind of weird, though, Saush. One minute he's all arrogant male and you just know that nothing is going to make him back down. Then all of a sudden he takes a closer look at her and then at me . . . and it's like watching night turn into day. He didn't exactly fall all over himself even then, but he smiled, which believe-you-me is nothing to sneeze at." She grinned. "It about knocked my socks off. He says, 'Karen Corselli' as if he's known her all his life and gives me a nod. Well, okay, I'm a line skater, so he's not gonna know me by name. But that's when he introduced himself as the new manager. *Then* he apologized . . . and a pretty speech it was, too." Connie shook her head. "Man. This guy. I'm telling you, Sasha, he's got something and it is *potent.*"

Sasha studied the expression on her friend's face. She and Connie often cracked jokes that to an outsider would most likely make them sound as sex starved as convent-bred schoolgirls and twice as horny. But in truth each knew the other was mostly blowing smoke and would cheerfully admit to it if pressed. Connie viewed men and relationships with a broad sense of humor laced with just a hint of cynicism. Sasha's outlook equaled her friend's in humor, but was laced with something else. Something a little . . . darker.

Which was why the expression currently gracing Connie's face piqued Sasha's curiosity. For it held her usual humor as well as the edge of cynicism that Sasha was accustomed to seeing. But there was something else there also. Attraction, perhaps, but if so, it was one that appeared to repel almost as much as it enticed.

"Whew." Sasha propped her chin on her hand, finished chewing the last of her sandwich, and with unabashed interest observed her friend across the table. "I wish you could see your face," she said. "I don't think I've ever seen you look quite this way." She studied her a few moments longer. "No fooling, Connie," she finally said thoughtfully. "If he can pull this sort of response out of you, I most definitely look forward to meeting this guy."

THREE

Sasha missed out on having that particular opportunity granted by no more than fifteen seconds. Her introduction to the new manager, had he been just a heartbeat or two slower, would have taken place in her very own hotel room, where Mick was in the midst of installing a tap on her phone.

Utilizing an extensive if particularly vicious vocabulary to steadily berate himself under his breath, he hastily screwed the receiver back together and slipped from her room, fading from sight around a bend in the corridor just seconds—*seconds,* damnit!—before Miller and Nakamura stepped off the elevator. Leaning back against the wall, he shoveled his fingers through his hair and blew out a deep breath.

Christ, that was too damn close for comfort. He couldn't believe he'd nearly let himself get caught in the act like some goddamn neophyte. You'd thick he'd just fallen off the proverbial truck.

The close shave made his eyes narrow. Wouldn't it have been just too slick for words to have gotten trapped in her room like some rank amateur? Sighing, he pushed away from the wall and walked slowly back to his room. The mockery he perceived was most likely only in his own overworked imagination, but the sound of feminine chatter seemed to snigger as it followed him like a pointing finger down the hallway.

He must be losing his touch. If he hadn't left the door ajar, he wouldn't have heard the elevator reach the floor and Nakamura conveniently call Miller by name as the doors were opening. In which case, the game would have been over before it had even begun. Sheer blind luck had saved his butt, and depending on that in this business could buy an agent a quick and painful death.

So, okay, bugging had never been his forte, and ordinarily he left it to the techs. But that was no excuse. He had damn well better *make* it one of his strong points, because they hadn't bothered to apply for a Title 3 intercept. In other words they were foregoing the court order in this case and winging it.

That gave him a laugh, albeit a somewhat weary one. What they, Vinicor? Is there anybody here but us chickens? *He* was winging it, and no one else. Out in left field, all alone. Flying solo.

Again.

The point was, with a gig that moved around as much as this one did, he was going to have to go through this again and again in every damn city they moved to. Not that it should present a particular problem from this point forward. As the manager he'd be in control of room assignments and could therefore get to Miller's room before she even checked in. Theoretically.

The real problem here was his state of mind regarding this assignment: his attitude was in serious need of adjustment. He'd only been on the job two stinking hours and already he was mishandling it left and right.

Fuck up number one was . . . using language like that in public. He was so accustomed to scamming dealers and the big-money men who supplied them, so used to associating with other lowlifes of their ilk, that he forgot not everyone in the world peppered their language with casual obscenities.

On the other hand, neither had he realized there were still people in the world as tight-assed as that Corselli woman. Hell, even his mother had been known to utter the infamous "F" word once in awhile. Well, once anyhow.

Okay, okay. Mom would have snatched him by the ear and

dragged him to the nearest rest room to wash his mouth out with soap if she could've heard him this afternoon.

"Face it," he decided in self-disgust, "first day out and you screwed up big-time." Usually *A Closed Mouth Gathers No Feet* was his anthem, a credo to live by, and he just naturally kept his lips zipped in a new situation until he knew damn good and well what the lay of the land was. Once that was established, he blended seamlessly into his environment.

Instead he'd arrived at this assignment with a ready-made attitude, as if he didn't have to try as hard because these were only skaters that he was dealing with and—face it— how tough could they be?

He had always taken a great deal of pride in knowing that he was giving his very best to each and every assignment. But it was going to be a little tough maintaining his sterling record or even honestly calling himself a professional if he continued to coast on this one. Particularly in view of the fact that he'd be doing so simply because this was a case that didn't strike him as being as crucial as the jobs he was accustomed to handling.

Besides, ole Henry Chambers would be ashamed of him.

He'd waylaid Chambers in his hotel room on the last night of the Follies run in San Francisco. Pulling out his shield and ID, he'd held it up for the man to see the minute he'd opened the door. "Henry Chambers?"

"Yes?" The man had looked from Mick's face to the San Francisco operative who was with him, and then stared at the DEA credentials presented to him. After a painstaking study of each identification card, he'd handed them back, looked up, and met Mick's eyes once again, clearly perplexed.

"I'm Special Agent Mick Vinicor of the Drug Enforcement Administration. This is Special Agent Erik Bell." Mick had been at his most authoritative, knowing that it tended to intimidate people into doing what he wanted them to do. "We'd like to come in for a moment and speak to you."

He had to hand it to the man; Chambers hadn't been a

pushover. He'd let them in, and he'd listened to their abbreviated summary of the situation—with the suspect's name deleted—and the reasons therein why Mick needed to take over his position with the Follies. But he hadn't for one moment been placated when Special Agent Bell had tersely suggested that he, "Just think of it as a vacation for yourself with full pay."

It wasn't until Mick finally lost patience and snapped, "Listen, if you want to do this the hard way just say the word and I'll shut down the whole damn operation until I can finish conducting my investigation," that Chambers had caved in . . . and even then it had been with a few conditions of his own.

He had earned Mick's respect.

He'd also made it quite clear, when giving Mick a crash course in his job, that he had a particular soft spot for Sasha Miller. Mick knew Chambers wouldn't reciprocate the esteem in which he was held if he knew Mick was failing to extend Miller the respect that Chambers seemed to think she was due. But Mick could rectify that, and he would. From this moment on, he'd extend respect like it was going out of style.

Mick Vinicor was going to show her the same regard he would offer to any other quarry he was planning to bring down.

Sasha got her first good look at the much-lauded new manager that night. She ran into him at the arena just before her first evening performance and understood immediately what Connie had been trying to tell her about the man. His impact ranked right up there with being slugged in the solar plexus by a giant unseen fist.

She should have been clued in by all the talk that had spread like wildfire throughout the line women's dressing room. With time to kill before she was due on the ice for her first number, she had as usual been hanging out with the line skaters in their locker room.

As an Olympic medalist she was entitled to a private or semiprivate dressing room, but it was a perk she'd passed on her very first week with the show and she'd never seen a reason to go back on her refusal. She simply wasn't comfortable copping a star attitude, and besides, it could get very lonely being set apart from all the other skaters.

Since everyone paid their own room tabs, a few of the show's stars did elect to stay at more expensive hotels than the rest of the cast could afford. Not Sasha. On the contrary, the first year she had skated with the Follies she'd actually roomed with several other women. The lack of privacy had quickly palled and she had given that up, but still she preferred the closeness to be found sharing travel and accommodations with the rest of the cast and crew.

That night the locker room was abuzz. In retrospect Sasha realized Vinicor was the hot topic of the evening, but it hadn't sunk in immediately for she had barely walked into the room when she caught her costume on the sharp edge of an open locker door. A seam ripped, beadwork scattered, and her whispered impieties momentarily overshadowed the snatches of conversation that she heard but didn't actually assimilate until much later.

Connie went to get the wardrobe mistress while Sasha got gingerly down on her hands and knees to retrieve the tiny sequins, rhinestones, and small crystal beads that had bounced their widely separate ways across the grimy floor. Eventually the costumer arrived, declared the damage too extensive for a quickie repair, ordered Sasha out of the outfit, and trotted off to fetch an alternate costume.

The locker room had cleared out, the line skaters out in the arena for the opening production number, by the time Sasha had pulled everything together for the second time. Whispering a curse when she saw the time, she snatched up her skates in one hand, and dashed from the room.

And ran smack-dab into a solid wall.

She heard it say "Oof" as she bounced off its hard surface. Clutching the skates to her stomach before they could slide out of her grasp, she reached out her free hand not only to steady herself but as a characteristically tactile way of apology. It grabbed onto warm, hard flesh.

"I'm sorry," she gasped to the T-shirt-covered collarbone a scant inch from her eyes. "I should have been looking where I was going." Her hand squeezed the forearm beneath her fingers as her eyes began to rise. "Forgive me. I swear I'm normally not this rude but it's been the craziest damn night. My costume tore, I'm running late, and I . . ."

Her eyes reached his face and she felt as if someone had stomped the wind right out of her. Struggling to catch a breath, she stared.

This had to be Mick Vinicor and Connie was right, he wasn't handsome. He wasn't a frog or anything, but his features certainly were nothing to write home about. They were just sort of run of the mill . . . except for his teeth, which were orthodontia perfect and toothpaste-ad white, like something out of the glossies. She backed up a step in order to view him more clearly, her mind racing as she attempted to figure out exactly where his appeal lay.

Weathered and muscular—masculine wasn't such an inept description after all, she decided dazedly. He was a presence to be reckoned with, exuding something that was nearly . . . animalistic, even if she couldn't quite pin down its origin. His hair was brown, his eyes were blue, nothing spectacular about the shade of either. But there was an intensity about him that was palpable as a force field, and it radiated from his eyes, was hinted at by his posture, giving him a vitality that made him seem almost . . . dangerous. But that, of course, was patently absurd.

Wasn't it?

Well, whether it was or it wasn't, she couldn't quite see this guy as a business major, but then again the good Lord knew she wasn't always the most astute judge of character. Just look at her blind defense of Lonnie. She hadn't been able to see him as a drug dealer, either, and she would have sworn on a stack of Bibles that she'd known his character as well as she knew her own.

It felt as though she had stood there for an age just gaping at the new manager, but in actuality her assessment was made quite speedily. She noted his height, which was average, perhaps five eleven, maybe six feet. Then she noted his build, and it nearly stopped her heart for an instant. A ridiculous reaction, undoubtedly, but there it was; in spite of the multitude of athletic builds she had seen in her many years on the circuit, she'd never before come across anyone who'd made quite this sort of impact on her. He was wearing a plain old white T-shirt and a pair of charcoal Dockers, and while she wondered in a distracted corner of her mind how he kept from freezing to death in this drafty back hallway, his clothing was certainly nothing she hadn't seen a dozen times before on a dozen different guys.

Yet on him they somehow managed to look extraordinary. No two ways about it, the man was built. Wide shoulders, solid chest, well-developed biceps, muscular forearms. Her eyes skimmed past the expensive-looking watch on his wrist to his large hands.

Her gaze snapped back to the watch. She grabbed him by the wrist and turned it until she could see the face of the timepiece. "Oh, damn!" Dropping his arm she turned to sprint away. "Sorry again about barging into you," she called back over her shoulder and then laughed when it hit her how demented she must appear to him. First she'd practically bowled him over and then she'd just stood there like a dufus with her tongue all but hanging out while she stared at him. Wasn't chemistry a grand thing? Skates clattering against her hip, she raced down the concrete passage.

Mick stood in the middle of the corridor and watched her

until she disappeared. Then he slowly followed her down the hallway.

She wasn't at all what he had prepared himself for. He'd known she'd be pretty from her picture, but he had expected there to be a hardness about her in real life. Instead it turned out that the black and white photograph hadn't even done her justice.

In the flesh she was a warm golden color with touches of rose. Her eyes were pale gray rimmed with darker gray and they contained tiny flecks of gold near the pupils. Her hair was abundant, a black curly cloud that looked wild and soft.

And that laugh.

God, what a gut grabber that was.

Somehow all his expectations had gotten knocked for a loop, in the space of a few measly minutes. Where he'd expected a demeanor that coolly invited all comers to drop dead, she'd instead been all flustered apologies, soft hands, and big eyes.

Mick shook himself like a wet dog. So what? So she was pretty and had big, curious eyes. Big deal. Plainly the woman knew how to run a con even better than he did. That didn't mean he had to be first class A-I chump and fall for it, did it?

Arriving at the area that passed for the wings, he stood back out of the way, arms crossed over his chest, and surveyed Sasha's firm little butt in its skimpily cut, glittery red briefs while she was bent over tugging her skate laces into place. He watched her lift her head up to grin at something a stagehand said to her and told himself sourly that her apparent friendliness was probably all part of the scam.

"And NOW, ladies and gentlemen, PLEASE give a BIG WARM WELCOME to OLYMpic Silver Medalist, SA-SHA MILLER!"

Sasha tossed aside her jacket and the Nikes she'd just exchanged for her skates, slid her palm along Connie's as they passed each other when the line skaters streamed off the ice, removed her guards from her blades, and stepped up onto the ice. Propelling herself into the arena proper, she glided around the rink, head back, arms raised, and laughed with pure joy while the crowd applauded. God above, she loved this.

Every single show, it never failed that her initial appearance on the ice managed to provoke an identical response from her; and the musical director, who knew a commercial sound when he heard one, had been quick to cash in on it. He'd ordered a recording made of her contagious laughter and it played back now over the loud speakers, climbing to the topmost seat in the house, making people smile in reaction. Making men shift in their seats.

The opening strains of "Angel from Montgomery" poured out of the loudspeakers and Sasha launched into her routine. Mick left his post against the wall and came up to the arena entrance to watch her performance.

Because the music in Bonnie Raitt's song was too slow throughout to sustain a long program, the musical director had recorded it in abbreviated form. Sasha glided with lazy ease, swooping and spinning languorously.

Then the music changed. It segued into Richard Marx's "Playing with Fire" and the tempo and style radically altered. The little fringed scarf tied around Sasha's hips came off, exposing the almost thong-cut panty of her costume, and she began to move her hips and shoulders in subtle rhythms to the music. Mick, watching from the wings, found himself swallowing dryly before the song was halfway through.

Connie Nakamura came up to stand beside him. Interested as always in catching people's reactions the first time they saw Sasha perform, she studied his features carefully. Vinicor's face was perfectly expressionless, but she noticed his Adam's apple make several slow slides up and down his throat.

"She's something, isn't she?" she finally demanded with typical enthusiasm. "It's funny, because there are only so many moves a skater can make, so hers shouldn't look all

that different from what everyone else is doing. And yet"—
her eyes on her friend's performance, she pursed her lips and
shook her fingers as if they'd been scorched, a gesture with
which Sasha was very familiar—"when Saush does it, it's
pure sex appeal." Then she turned her attention back to Mick
once again.

"You should've seen her with her old pairs partner," she
said. "I saw them once at a Pan American competition and
they were so hot I kept expecting steam to rise up off the
ice. I have never seen a program like it . . . before or since."

"Yeah?" Wondering how much she would willingly volunteer, Mick raised an interested brow in her direction before
his attention was drawn once again to the woman in the
arena. "So where is this partner now?"

Connie's smile faded and she shifted slightly away from
him. The space she opened up between the two of them was
infinitesimal in distance, but Mick recognized it for what it
was: a sudden mile-wide gulf. If he hadn't already known
about Miller and Morrison, her posture would have alerted
him that there was a story here and caused him to go digging
for it.

"He's . . . retired," she replied repressively and turned her
attention back to the performance out under the lights. Sasha
Miller was her closest friend and there was no way on God's
green earth that Connie was going to resurrect that old scandal for the delectation of some guy she'd just met this afternoon—macho babe or not. If the new manager wanted to
know about Lon Morrison bad enough, she wasn't fool
enough to think a dozen different people around here
wouldn't be more than happy to supply him with all the sordid details. But it wouldn't be from Connie Nakamura's lips
that he heard it.

The music reached a crescendo and Sasha exited the rink,
flushed and happy. There wasn't anything quite as stimulating as performing in front of a receptive crowd and she was
flying high. It had been a dream of hers to skate for *Follies*

on Ice since she was a young girl and she still had to pinch herself sometimes to accept that the dream had actually come true. The downside—the unrelenting pressure of constant travel, the occasional fatigue—simply didn't matter once she hit the ice.

Connie was standing by the new manager and Sasha flashed them a smile as she got out of the new act's way. Stopping to apply her blade guards, she stepped off the ice, gathered up her Nikes, and slipped into her wool-and-leather letterman's jacket.

She loved this coat. It represented everything she'd missed out on back in her Kells Crossing high school days. She used to watch the girls who wore their jock boyfriends' jackets—or better yet, the ones who had earned their own—and she'd always felt so envious and excluded. She hadn't had time for extracurricular activities back then; her schedule had been devoted exclusively to skating. She'd loved it more than anything in the world, but it made her different from the rest of her classmates—and being different is not a lot of fun for a teenager. Particularly in a small town.

More important than having an adolescent wish realized, however, this coat was significant to her because she'd bought it the day her mother died. Carole Miller was in her thoughts every time Sasha put it on.

Connie was responsible for the purchase. Sasha had been knocked flat by the news of her mother's death, and unable until the following morning to get a flight out of the city they were currently playing, she'd nearly climbed the walls, not knowing how to deal with her grief. She'd holed up in her hotel room, alternately crying and staring into space, until Connie had come knocking at her door.

"C'mon," she'd insisted the moment Sasha had opened it. "You know those jackets you're always raving on about? We're gonna go downtown and get you one."

"Maybe another time, Connie," Sasha had retorted listlessly, starting to close the door again. "Today's not a good day to go shopping."

Connie had blocked the closing door. "Ah, now that's where you're wrong," she'd disagreed firmly, barging in and bundling Sasha into a coat. Gathering up her friend's purse and room key, she'd placed them in Sasha's hand and then held her off at arm's length, her hands gripping Sasha's shoulders while she looked her straight in the eye. "Today is the best possible day to buy yourself something you've been wanting to buy forever. I think your mom would get a real kick out of knowing you were treating yourself to something special in her honor."

And so Sasha had bought this deep red wool jacket with its camel leather sleeves. Two cities later, Connie had found an athletic supply house and bought her a thick wool letter S, arranging to have it applied to the front. For her birthday a bunch of the skaters had gone together and custom ordered a woolly silver FOLLIES ON ICE to put on the back. Jack the bus driver had bought her a skating patch for the sleeve. It was like no other coat anywhere in the world and she loved it.

She loved the woman who over her protests had dragged her out to make the purchase. It had been possibly the worst day of her life. But warm memories, which the coat inspired every time she slipped into it, was like an ongoing healing process, so she was grateful she'd allowed herself to be coerced.

Pulling the coat closed against the backstage chill, she joined Connie and Mick. Connie gave her a one-armed hug and whispered, "Good program." Then Sasha turned to Mick. Thrusting out her hand she smiled up at him. "Hi again. I didn't stop to introduce myself when I ran into you earlier," she said. "I'm Sasha Miller."

Mick gripped her hand, giving it a firm shake. "Mick Vinicor."

His fingers were hard skinned, dry, and warm, and Sasha

blinked at the jolt that went through her at their touch. "Yeah, I . . . uh . . ." She cleared her throat. "I know." She gathered her wits. "That is, Connie told me about meeting you this afternoon." She realized he was still holding her hand and slipped it free. Unconsciously working her fingers, she opened and closed them at her side.

Jeez, what was this? She suddenly felt and was acting like a damn high school girl. But he was standing very close, giving her his undivided attention, and for some odd reason she couldn't seem to draw her eyes away from his.

She cleared her throat again. "Uh, listen, sometime before we leave Sacramento I need to sit down with you for a few minutes and go over a few things."

"Sure." Mick nodded agreeably and took a step back, giving her a little space. "What sort of things do you have in mind?"

She drew a deep breath and quietly expelled it, feeling on safer ground with some distance between them. "Just the usual business stuff that Henry used to take care of. Like making arrangements for me to have first day access to the arenas where we perform. It's important to me to be able to check out the ice in a new place and I'm hoping you'll continue where he left off."

"No problem." Without warning he once again closed the gap between them. Standing close, eyelids developing a sudden carnal heaviness, he looked down at her. "I'm in room 415; stop by anytime. We'll . . ." His gaze fastened on her mouth, his tongue slipped out to touch his lower lip. Then his eyes rose to meet hers. ". . . talk."

Connie choked. When Mick turned his head easily in her direction and Sasha, with a little more effort, dragged her gaze from Mick's to look at her, she coughed a few additional times and waved a hand at them. "Swallowed wrong," she explained, pressing the tips of two fingers to the hollow of her throat. "Well, hey!" she said brightly the moment she got herself under control. "I'd better go change my costume.

I'll, uh, talk to you two later." Without awaiting a response, she turned to go.

"Wait, Connie, I'll go with you." Sasha turned to Mick. "See you, Mick; I look forward to working together," she said and moving as fast as her delicate blades would allow, hurried to catch up with her friend.

Connie flashed her a sidelong glance but waited until they reached the locker room before saying anything. Then she turned to face Sasha, fanning her cheeks with her fingers. "I've said it before and I'll say it again. That man is potent," she declared.

Swallowing, Sasha nodded her agreement. That was the God's honest truth—more potent than anything she'd ever before come across.

"At first when he was standing so close and looking at you—the way he was looking at you—I was a little jealous. I mean, I saw him first after all."

"Yeah, but you didn't say dibs."

Connie laughed. "Yeah. And just as well, I think, too. I have a feeling that fella is way more man than I'd know how to handle."

Sasha grabbed Connie by the wrist and dragged her over to the frayed couch in the corner of the room. "And you think I can?" she demanded, collapsing onto the dusty cushions. "Even supposing that I wanted to . . . God, Connie, he probably comes on like that to every woman he comes into contact with."

"No, I don't think so, Saush." Connie sat down next to her. "I stood there talking with him for a while and there wasn't so much as a *hint* of anything like that. Not with me, not with Karen this afternoon, and not with Brenda, Lois, Mary, or Sara, all of whom came up for introductions about the time you were coming off the ice. God, when he said 'we'll . . . talk,' I about swallowed my tongue. I think what he was really saying was, 'come to my room and I'll rip all your clothes off and do stuff to your body so nasty it'll make you scream.' "

Sasha licked her lower lip. "It wasn't just in my mind then," she said slowly. "I thought maybe I was exaggerating the . . . vibrations." She rubbed her hands down her thighs and gripped her knees. "Wow," she whispered. "He's good. I mean, I'm used to those guys who drool all over me after they've seen me perform, and I know how to handle them. But he's a lot more subtle—which makes him about a hundred times more effective." She turned her head to look at Connie. "I take it it's safe to assume he watched the 'Playing with Fire' number?" Dammit, how many times had she been through this, through the multitudinous come-ons from men who thought she was what she skated?

"Yeah, he did," Connie acknowledged. "And I'm as sure as I can be, without having checked to see if there was any action going on behind his fly, that it turned him on. But I think you're seriously underestimating the man if you think he's the type to allow himself to be led around by his hormones. Y'ask me, if he's decided he wants you, it's got nothing to do with having watched one performance on ice."

"Maybe. But in a way, Connie, that's an even scarier scenario, don't you think? Because, I mean, you're right." She leaned over and tugged at her laces, working them loose to take off her skates. Finally, she looked up at her friend. "He *is* potent and you're not the only one who wouldn't have a clue how to handle him. There'd be no staying in control with that guy."

"So you're going to just let an opportunity for a romp with a man like that one pass you by? Ah, Saush, tell me it isn't so."

Sasha's laugh was involuntary and nervous. "Well, at the very least I think I'll exercise a little native intelligence for once in my life and arrange for any future meetings between the two of us to be conducted in the hotel coffee shop." Her eyes held confusion when they met Connie's. "Maybe if we didn't have to work with this guy for God knows how long . . ."

She blushed and gave Connie a sheepish smile. "You know I'm not a big fan of one-night stands, but I'm telling you, Connie, it would be a real temptation if this was just someone who was going to be left behind when we move on." Then she shrugged and shook her head. "But that's not the case; he'll be coming right along with us when we leave. So, yeah, I believe I'm gonna steer clear. Who needs the aggravation? No," she mused, and Connie wondered just whom she was trying to convince here, "I really don't think it's smart to complicate a working relationship with sex."

Mick had different ideas on the matter. Restless and edgy, he stalked the corridors of the arena trying to burn off the synapse of hot energy that pulsed along his nerve endings and arced between his cells. Mixing sex with business sounded like a fine idea to him. It sounded just about right in fact. Mixing a whole lot . . . of both.

Okay, so it wasn't what had been in the game plan when he'd set out on this assignment. But she'd changed the rules tonight when she'd stood there staring up at him with that fraudulent wide-eyed uncertainty. He didn't like being played for a fool.

God, he had to hand it to her, though, she was good. Mick unknowingly echoed the same sentiments Sasha had expressed about him. Hell, she had to know how good she looked, yet she was smart; she hadn't played that angle at all. Instead she'd worked it casual and friendly and then had stood there all but trembling when he'd turned up the heat a little. Those big gray eyes had told him all sorts of contradictory stories. They'd seemed attracted but uncertain. Come closer, they'd said; stay away.

Hell, yeah. She was *damn* good.

He'd never in his life played the whore for an assignment,

no matter how important it was. Well, call him a slut, but this was one instance where he was more than willing. He'd spent most of his time the last few years hanging out with the dregs of the earth. But they at least were halfway honest about their unrelenting avarice. Most of them owned up to it; they didn't pretend to be something diametrically opposed to what they actually were. Just who did this little honey think she was fooling? No one who sold product that killed off half the junkies on the West Coast was saving it for marriage.

But if that's the way she wanted to play the game, then he would, by God, play it right along with her.

FOUR

Mick never got an opportunity to play it one way or another. Sasha Miller managed to avoid him quite handily for what remained of the Follies' Sacramento run. Only once were they alone together and even then "alone" was a relative term. She requested a meeting to discuss the arrangements she'd previously mentioned, but insisted on holding it in the hotel dining room. They were alone in the sense that nobody bothered them, but it was in the midst of a roomful of diners.

And just to add to his general frustration, even her phone remained mute.

He knew better than to expect instantaneous results on any assignment but found it aggravating nevertheless in this instance. For the first time in his career he was impatient, anxious to rush a case, unwilling to let it unfold at its own pace. In all his years of doing covert work, he had never felt the pull of an unwanted attraction involving the subject of an investigation, and be it involuntary or otherwise, the fact that he was battling such an attraction now made him competitive in ways he'd never before encountered.

Dammit to hell, it took more than a pretty face and a great body to distract Mick Vinicor from his given goal. True, his quarry were generally men. But he'd been offered the favors of innumerable girlfriends, whores—hell, even the occasional sister or wife—in the course of previous investigations. Sometimes, if the woman herself was willing and not simply the chattel of some drug czar, he'd availed himself of those offers. More often he hadn't. But never had the potential for sex possessed the ability to distract him from his objective.

And he wouldn't permit it to distract him now. The attraction for Sasha Miller might be stronger than any he could remember in a long, long time, but he didn't give a damn how sweet faced this little skater dolly was; he'd blow her out of the water before he'd allow her to lead him around by the gonads.

His mood was decidedly dark the last few days of the California run.

Further opportunity to advance the investigation into the next phase didn't arise until the end of the week. When the skaters left for the upcoming leg of the tour they were transported by air, Follies policy stating its performers were to be conveyed by bus only if the ride could be accomplished in four hours or less.

At the conclusion of the final show in Sacramento, the road crew packed up the semis and hit the road early the following morning. The skaters, however, were given a rare day to sleep in, a few hours to themselves in which they could catch up on their laundry, simply be lazy, or go out and explore the city before they had to leave to catch the afternoon flight for Eugene, Oregon.

Thinking this would be a good time to begin the seduction of Sasha Miller, Mick went to her room. She wasn't there and he was unable to track her down before it was time to catch the bus that would take them to the airport. Cursing both himself and the suits who'd assigned him to this case, Mick's intention when he turned in his room key was to grab the seat next to Sasha on the bus. He needed to begin insinuating himself into her life and was anxious to get on with it. The sooner he wrapped this business up, the quicker he could get back to the type of cases he was accustomed to.

However, he hadn't calculated Connie Nakamura into the equation. On time for once in her life, she outmaneuvered him as they jostled for position in the bus's narrow aisle. Knocked out of the way with one economical movement of the petite Asian woman's hip, he took a seat in the row behind them and openly eavesdropped on their conversation. It garnered him absolutely nothing in the way of new knowledge that could advance his case.

He vowed to do better on the airplane, but his assistance was required in his role as manager and by the time he untangled the problem, the two women had boarded the plane and were once again sitting together. Mick stood in the aisle, hands on his hips, and stared at them a moment with barely concealed irritation. Jesus, were they joined at the hip or something?

As if knowing exactly what she had thwarted, Connie grinned at him knowingly. Gritting his teeth, Mick gave her a feral grin in return and moved on. To add insult to injury, the only available seat on the plane was next to Karen Corselli. Ah, hell. That was *all* he needed to round off an unproductive and exasperating week.

He half expected to spend the flight being forced to listen to another lecture regarding the foulness of his language. But Karen pretty much ignored him as she stared out the tiny porthole window.

Until the turbulence struck.

They hit a pocket of bad weather just as they were passing over Roseburg. The plane took a pounding as they bucked head winds, causing it to shudder and shake a bit.

At first Mick merely assumed Karen was a nervous flyer. The airplane took a little swoop and she gasped and grabbed for his leg, nervously clutching him just above the knee. The next bit of turbulence had her gripping his thigh. Mick patted her hand reassuringly.

Two minutes later, her fingers were softly groping the denim of his fly.

"Jesus Christ!" Mick jumped a foot. Head whipping around to stare at her, he felt himself gaping like an idiot.

God Almighty. He had long ago ceased believing there was anything left in this world that could shock him.

Only to discover in that moment that he was mistaken.

Was this the same young woman who just three days ago had read him the riot act for using obscene language in her presence? When it came to shock value, not much could beat having her grab his crotch out of the blue. It did the trick, absolutely, stunning him nearly speechless.

Heads turned at his involuntary exclamation and Mick did something else he hadn't done in years. He blushed. Karen's head was still averted, but it was turning in his direction as he grasped her wrist and yanked her hand away from his lap. Her fingers stretched to administer one last surreptitious stroke even as she instructed him coolly, "Kindly don't take the Lord's name in vain."

"Holy shit, lady," he whispered hoarsely. "What're you, crazy?"

"Mr. Vinicor," she reprimanded him frigidly, "I will not tell you again. Watch your language." Then in an undertone, as the plane's engines whined with the change of altitude, she murmured without even bothering to turn her head in his direction, "You're the man in charge of room assignments so I assume that means you know what my room number will be." Her head turned briefly to meet his astounded blue eyes and she passed a delicate tongue over her lips. Her voice was contrastingly crisp when she instructed, "Come see me."

Mick was jumpy and unnerved the rest of the flight. He'd been an agent with the DEA for nearly twelve years and had dealt with many diverse personalities. It was an aspect of the job he'd always taken for granted; it simply came with the territory and was an accepted part of the job description. Hell, he'd broken bread with sociopaths and conned psychotics; he'd partied with conscienceless killers and out-lied pathological liars, all without breaking a sweat. Bringing one small-time dealer to justice should be a piece of cake in comparison.

So then why did it feel as if this were shaping up to be the screwiest goddam case he'd ever had the misfortune to be assigned to?

It was edging on six by the time Mick had straightened out all the room assignments and distributed every last hotel key to the Follies' performers and other personnel. Whose bright idea had it been for him to take over the managers duties anyway?

There was more work to this job than he'd expected. He couldn't neglect it or people were going to wonder why he'd been hired in the first place, and the objective here was to bring as little attention to himself as possible. Yet he wasn't quite sure how he was supposed to keep an eye on Sasha Miller, worm his way into her confidence, and deal with all this shit, too.

He pretended not to notice when Karen Corselli pressed discreetly up against him as he handed her the key to her room. Having failed to elicit a reaction, she stood looking at him a moment longer, an invitation in her eyes, before she finally stepped aside to make way for the next person in line.

Karen let herself into her room, slung her overnighter on the bed, and kicked off her shoes. She rummaged in her bag until she found her little night-light, plugged it into the socket next to the bed, ordered up room service, and then searched the television for something not totally vulgar that she could watch while she ate. After dinner she took a long bath, freshened her makeup, and donned her most alluring nightgown.

By ten o'clock that evening it had registered that Mick Vinicor wasn't going to come knocking on her door.

Prowling the room, she whispered furiously to herself, frustration burning hot in her veins. Unbearably familiar, a sense of powerlessness infused her, and like an irritant lying just below the surface of her skin, like an itch beyond her reach, it mocked all her accomplishments. *Drat* him. Drat *all* men.

She stood in the center of the room, chest heaving with the deep breaths she took in an attempt to regain control. Okay. All right. It wasn't as if she were a stranger to this feeling of impotence. But that of course was the very problem, and, oh, how she hated it.

She had grown up in a fundamentalist Christian home where she was expected to be seen but not heard, unless specifically called upon to sing a hymn or recite a lesson from the Bible. And woe be to her if she forgot or stumbled over her words. The common punishment for misbehavior in any of its guises was a stay of up to as many as three days in a dark, damp, seven-by-four-foot cubicle in the cellar.

Usually after Father had taken his birch stick or his belt to her.

It had never grown less terrifying in that unlit chamber, filled with its musty smells and skittering noises, no matter how many times she was put in there. It had always imbued her with such feelings of hopelessness and rage that she had feared she would burst with them. So she'd sung every acceptable gospel song she'd known, recited Bible verse after Bible verse, and swore repeatedly that someday she would have influence and authority. No one—no one!—would ever be allowed to inflict pain on her then . . . or make her spend time in a small, dark space again.

She'd discovered the power of sex when she was seventeen years old. Up until that time, in compliance with her austere relatives' demands, she'd kept her nose in her Bible and her feet on the straight and narrow, bound for Glory. She had gone to school; she'd gone to church; and any free time left over was devoted to skating—but only after her coach had assured her rigid parents that she would never be subjected to any material that didn't have good, clean values.

Which, of course, was as it should be.

It was at skate practice that she'd first began to notice the way boys acted around her. If she quite properly dressed them down for using unseemly language, they would hang their heads. But when they looked at her their eyes were avid; and if she moved a certain way, bent in a certain manner, used her tongue to moisten her lips, a bulge would appear behind their zippers. She was pretty and her body was beautiful, and she discovered she could control boys with it.

Power. It was so sweet, and for the first time in her life she had access to the real thing.

Over the years her power base had enlarged until these days there was little she couldn't accomplish or obtain. Most of the time it was simply a matter of placing herself in the right place at the right time. Of knowing how to manipulate the right man. Clearly, the airplane this afternoon hadn't been the right place for Mick Vinicor.

Or perhaps it was the timing that was off.

Well, the time was always negotiable. As for the place . . . she didn't doubt for an instant that she would eventually find a spot that he would find eminently suitable for their purposes. Heavenly days, it would be rather ludicrous to harbor doubts about her eventual success, wouldn't it? Why would she want to do that?

She hadn't failed yet.

It was after midnight when the taxi let Sasha off in front of the Eugene hotel. She strode through the lobby doors and headed straight for the lounge. She could use a stiff drink.

Damn Lonnie anyhow. How on earth had she allowed herself to be talked into this?

Tossing her evening bag on the table, she slid into a U-shaped booth in one of the darker corners of the dim bar. It seemed like an eternity before the cocktail waitress sauntered over and took her drink order. Sasha fiddled with a book of matches as she watched the waitress walk away, turning it end over end between her slender fingers while she brooded.

What difference did it make why she'd caved in—what counted was that she had. She'd listened to Lon's arguments and she had agreed to his plan, however reluctantly. She could have said no. She *should* have said no. But . . . no. Instead she'd gone ahead and dated that old geezer, flirting on the thin edge of feeling like a whore in order to get Lonnie a place with the line skaters when he was released from prison in a couple of weeks.

She thought she was probably a better friend to him than he was to her. He knew how it would affect her to be petted by some stranger; he knew better than anyone else in the world, and yet he had asked it of her anyway.

But then again, to be fair . . . he was desperate. Lon wouldn't have asked it of her if he wasn't and that was something she understood.

God, more than anything she would like to be able to talk it over with Connie—why she was doing this stuff she didn't want to do and how it made her feel—but how could she? Connie wouldn't understand. Hell, she barely understood it herself. Acting the tease, playing these stupid games, made her feel like a cross between a high-priced hooker and what's-her-name in that old TV spy spoof—Agent 99. She didn't know whether to be ashamed of herself or fall over laughing at the absurdity of it all.

At the moment she didn't feel much like laughing.

On the disgraceful side of the scoreboard was her behavior with J. R. Garland, who was the talent agent responsible for most of the performance hiring for the West Coast branch of the Follies. She'd been doing her damnedest to sweet-talk him into promising Lon a job when he was paroled from prison, vamping the old guy to beat the band. It was a balancing act of flirtation and letting it be subtly understood that she didn't intend to compromise her morals any more than she was currently doing simply to ensure her friend's employment. There were definite limits here. She might be linked to Lon by a lot of years and even more shared history, but she wasn't sleeping with any man for his benefit. And Lon knew better than to expect it of her.

On the comic relief side were the moronic espionage games of Lonnie's that she'd been playing. Calling him from a pay phone when there was a perfectly good telephone in every hotel room she'd ever stayed in; burning his letters as soon as she'd read them. For heaven's sake, who did he imagine would possibly care what the two of them talked or corresponded about?

Well, she'd done her part and she had honestly believed she'd never again have to lie to Connie if queried as to her whereabouts at any given time. When the Follies left San Francisco where J.R. was based, she had thought she'd seen the last of her role as the intelligence-impaired coquette.

Which is why she'd about died this afternoon when she received the telephone call from a jovial J. R. Garland, telling her he was in town for business and insisting that she join him for a late supper.

Sasha shuddered, tugged on the microscopic skirt of her black cocktail dress in an attempt to obtain a little more coverage for her thighs, and tossed back a slug of the Baileys Irish Cream the waitress placed before her. She didn't feel particularly good about herself at the moment, and she *swore* that this was the end of it. No more. Tonight had been the very last time she was putting herself through this bullshit. If Garland opted not to hire Lon after this, that was too damn bad. Lonnie'd gotten himself into trouble without any help from her; he could darn well . . .

"Hi, I thought that was you," a voice, soft and low, interrupted her thoughts. "Mind if I join you?"

Sasha's head jerked up. Standing in front of her booth was Mick Vinicor, looking too damn energetic for words. God above, where did he get all that vitality he perpetually exuded? It made her weary just looking at him. She opened her mouth to tell him yes, she did in fact mind, that she would just as soon be left alone; but he was already sliding in next to her, sitting much closer than was necessary. "Make yourself at home," Sasha said dryly and took another sip of her drink.

He grinned, flashing those impossibly white teeth at her. "Thanks, don't mind if I do." A waitress appeared as if by magic. Must be nice to be a virile male sometimes, Sasha thought sourly. Mick ordered a beer, flirted with the waitress a moment, and then leaned back so he could view Sasha from head to toe.

Her coat was tossed behind her, carelessly spread open across the banquette, and she was wearing a little nothing of a lace dress that was cut low in a sweetheart neckline between her breasts. The garment was lined from bust to hem but her shoulders and arms glowed lightly golden through the tight black lace of the long sleeves, and scallops of sheer lace edged past the sheath lining to play teasing games on her thighs. Christ. You'd think the impact would have lessened after watching that face and body for the past several hours. And yet . . .

Mick swallowed dryly but forced a cocky grin and an insouciant tone as he sprawled back, arms stretched out along the banquette. "Killer dress."

"What, this old rag?" Sasha retorted, and both her voice and her face were entirely void of expression. She watched him coolly over the rim of her cocktail glass.

Okay, so she wasn't going to give an inch. He'd already pretty much acknowledged that she would be a formidable opponent. "Yeah, it's a beaut. You just get back from a date or something?"

He knew where'd she'd been, of course. He'd retrieved the call from the recording in time to follow her to that restaurant downtown where he'd watched from the bar as some old fart had pawed her all night long. It made him grit his teeth every time he thought of the way she'd just sat there and let him.

Hell, not only let him, but had smiled while she was allowing it. Smiled and laughed.

"I don't really want to talk about my evening, Mick, if you don't mind." She drained her drink. "This hasn't been the best night of my life."

That caught him by surprise. He hadn't expected her to admit to any weakness. But before he could take advantage of what might be the only moment of vulnerability she'd ever display to him, she was already getting ready to leave. She pulled her coat off the banquette to drape over her shoulders and collected her purse; then she began to edge around to the far side of the banquette. Due to her skirt's propensity to climb into the indecent zone with every incautious movement she made, that was necessarily a gingerly process, and Mick took advantage of her creeping progress to reach across the table and wrap his fingers around her wrist. "Wait," he said, staying her. "Don't go."

Sasha froze in place, experiencing that same zap of awareness she'd felt the night he had held her hand too long backstage. She gazed at him warily. "Why?"

"Why?" His thick brows drew together. "Hell, I don't know." And he didn't. He knew he wasn't going to get any more out of her this evening. She was gun shy and not at all receptive to sexual advances, and it was for damn sure she wasn't going to tell him squat.

And it wasn't as if he required her assistance anyhow. He could get all the information he needed on the old sleezebag she'd met without holding his breath waiting for her cooperation. Hell, that part was child's play: he'd sent the son of a bitch's name in to be processed the minute it had come off the recorder, and by tomorrow afternoon whatever secrets the old guy possessed would be in Mick's hands.

Yet still he retained his light grasp on her delicately boned wrist. "You're pretty," he finally said. "You look like you've had a rough night. I'm lonely." He shrugged as if to say, take your pick. "So what do ya say you let me buy you a drink?"

His fingers relinquished their grip but lingered to stroke the table next to where her hand rested. "I'm not on the make, Sasha," he assured her. "I just want someone to flirt with for a few minutes." When she stiffened slightly, he held up his hands, palms out in entreaty, and hastily added, "Or if you don't feel much like flirting, I'd still like someone to talk to."

Sasha sagged back in her seat. "All right." She was wired up and unlikely to fall asleep any time soon, anyway. Why go up to her room when she'd only end up tossing and turning for the next several hours? She straightened and gave Mick a slight smile. "You must think I'm crazy," she murmured as she tossed her coat off her shoulders. Mick signaled the waitress and Sasha gave her order. When they were alone again Sasha turned back to Mick.

"I did something tonight I'm not very proud of," she admitted, "and it's left me feeling a little raw. I'm sorry, though, if I've taken it out on you."

Again she caught him by surprise . . . and left him confused. He didn't understand this. He had her pigeonholed as a conscienceless bitch. She might *look* soft as a satin boudoir pillow, but she had to be cold as death and harder than diamonds to deal poison the way she'd been doing without batting an eye. He'd be mighty interested in learning how the old man she'd met tonight fit into all this. He must be some piece of work to have this little operator running scared. Mick forced his voice to be low and empathetic when he said, "Don't worry about me; I've got a hide like a rhinoceros. You want to talk about it?"

Sasha swallowed an involuntary snort of laughter. "God, no. I've already made up my mind I'm not ever going to get sucked into a situation like tonight's again. All I want to do now is forget it ever happened."

Mick obliged her by changing the topic, but he was about as disconcerted as it was possible to get. What the hell was going on here? She wasn't acting at all the way he'd expected and it left him consumed with curiosity. He wanted nothing more than to learn all her secrets. He *would* learn all her secrets; he planned to seduce them out of her one by one.

Maybe not tonight.

But soon. Perhaps tomorrow, because by then he should have the leverage he needed to start prying them out of her.

Just as soon as he got the information he'd requested on J. R. Garland.

It didn't turn out to be quite that simple. In point of fact, the information he received merely added to the confusion. Jesus, what a screwed-up case this was shaping up to be.

Garland was a damned talent scout. Period. He had no arrest record and there was absolutely nothing that connected him to the drug world. So why had Sasha Miller sat there and allowed him to put his hands all over her, to pat and stroke her like some damn pet Pekinese? Garland wasn't a drug czar to whom she had to toady up, and clearly she hadn't allowed it for its entertainment value.

Or, hell, maybe that's exactly what she'd done. What did he know about the way she got her kicks, when it came right down to it?

He needed to know more about her in order to figure out what made her tick. So far she hadn't done one damn thing that fit into any mold he was accustomed to seeing. So he sought information in the good old time-honored street hump way.

He broke into her room again.

Except for the one communication from Garland, she hadn't received or made a single telephone call since he'd first placed a tap on her phone in Sacramento. So today he ignored the phone—he'd done his work there already—and went straight to the closet.

Her luggage, stacked on the shelf above the hangers, was empty. Mick checked for false bottoms, but the dimensions were the same inside and out on all the pieces. He felt for false linings.

It was just plain old standard issue baggage.

He riffled through the clothing on the hangers, checking pockets, running his hands swiftly over the fabric, feeling for concealed hiding places. Nothing.

Same with her shoes; there was nothing stuffed in the toes, and the glittery little evening bag tossed in the corner of the closet held only a forgotten lipstick and some change. He swiveled the lipstick open and sniffed it.

Then promptly swiveled it closed again and replaced the cap. Why was he wasting time? She was only down to lunch with some of the other skaters; he didn't have a hell of a lot of time here. He crossed over to the dresser.

His hands wanted to linger in the lingerie drawer but he sternly refused to allow them. Swiftly, he moved from drawer to drawer, perusing the contents without disturbing their order.

When the dresser failed to yield any secrets, he checked under the bed, felt between the mattress and the box springs, patted around the television set in the enclosed armoire. He examined the backs of the hotel artwork and inspected the carpet for loose spots that may have been pried up.

Clean as a freakin' whistle.

He was in the bathroom, poking with his pen in a jar of some kind of cream, when he heard a key in the door.

Son of a bitch! Wiping off the pen, Mick stuffed both it and the Kleenex in his jean's pocket and looked around. Jesus, he was never going to live this case down—if it wasn't one fucking thing it was another.

He climbed into the bathtub behind the white curtain and pressed up against the enclosure under the showerhead. It was just the frosting on his cupcake that the damn thing had a leak. Throughout the next several tense moments, maddening drops of water plopped with the regularity of a metronome onto his forehead and then slowly rolled down to drip off the tip of his nose.

Sasha and another woman entered her hotel room. Mick could hear their feminine voices as they walked straight past the bathroom.

"It's here somewhere," he heard Sasha say as drawers rattled open. "I know it is. The last time I wore it was . . . ah! Here it is." There was a muffled thump. "What do you think . . . will it work?"

"Oh, Sasha," the other voice breathed. "It looks perfect."

"I want to see it with your dress. What do you say we take it down to your room so you can show me?"

Yes, yes, yes, Mick silently urged. Do that. Go to her room. *Go.*

"I've gotta pee first," the other voice said. "Mind if I use your bathroom?"

"Help yourself."

Mick flattened himself against the wall. He heard the rustle of clothing and the sounds of her doing her business, and he didn't breathe again until the toilet flushed. The water ran in the basin and then stopped, and he figured she was finally about through. *Get out of here,* he silently urged. *Get. The hell. Out of here.*

And he thought she had, but suddenly her voice was just on the other side of the shower curtain. "Oh, you've got a bathtub," she exclaimed and he watched in dismay as female fingers wrapped around the edge of the curtain and started to move it back. "My room only has a shower."

Then Sasha was in the room, too. "You prefer baths?" The other woman must have nodded, because Sasha continued, "You oughtta speak to Mick Vinicor about it. I bet he could make sure you get a tub in your future rooms."

"Ohh, Mick," the other woman murmured. "God, is he a babe, or what?" she demanded and her hand dropped away from the curtain. Mick heard her footsteps on the tile floor as she walked away. "How'd you like to climb into that guy's pants?"

And just when he would have liked them to stay in the

room, so he could hear Sasha's reply, they walked out in a burst of laughter, slamming the hallway door closed behind them.

Eking out a thin breath, he waited a moment and then eased himself out of the tub. Noting the placement of the towel, he pulled it off the shower rod, rubbed his head dry and placed it back where he'd found it. Quickly completing his inspection of Sasha's toiletries and cosmetics, he checked inside the toilet tank, felt around behind it, and then walked back into the bedroom. He stood in the middle of the room, looking around.

Well, this didn't make a damn bit of sense. A messy explosion of lingerie from a half-opened drawer caught his eye and he crossed the room. Picking up a minuscule pair of leopard-skin print satin panties from where they'd fallen on the carpet, he stood pulling them through his fist, thinking about the result of his search as he stared down with unseeing eyes at the rest of the jumbled lingerie, scarves, and costume jewelry that spilled out of the drawer.

Usually, the only people who came up this clean when their room was tossed turned out to be . . . innocent. But hell, he knew that wasn't the case.

No, either she used the hotel safe or there was a key somewhere, most likely one that she kept on her, which would open a safety deposit box. Or a locker. Or *something*. He just had to get closer to her.

And he would, dammit.

Absentmindedly tucking the minuscule panties into his hip pocket, he looked around to make sure he hadn't left anything behind that might alert her. Then he let himself out of her hotel room.

FIVE

All of a sudden Sasha couldn't seem to turn around without tripping all over Mick Vinicor. He was everywhere she went.

How he had managed to get himself included in every damn social situation going these days was beyond her, but the man definitely got around. If she joined the ever-fluctuating group of skaters, techs, and stage crew who met for lunch daily in the various hotel coffee shops, he was there . . . and somehow always managed to end up seated right next to her. A group of them went out on the town after the show one night . . . and Mick was there. They played poker in Connie's room another night . . . Mick was there. They arrived in Portland Friday night and when six of them went together to rent a car to drive to the Saturday Market on Sunday . . . Mick was one of them. It was making her nuts.

God, she was so aware of him, and the methods he used to enhance that awareness were so subtle she was hard pressed to identify exactly what he was doing to make her feel this way.

Not that she had dared to even *speculate* as much aloud, of course. Her mama hadn't raised no fool, and Sasha didn't voice her suspicions to a soul—well, except to Connie—because she knew darn good and well that it made her sound paranoid beyond belief. The determined way he was pursuing her was already grist for the rumor mill and it appeared to amuse the hell out of a lot of people. She refused to contribute to their entertainment by suggesting that there might be something calculated in that pursuit.

Sasha nevertheless recognized that Mick was acting deliberately. She didn't know how she knew and it didn't make a lick of sense . . . but she couldn't quite grant herself permission to trust him all the same. She could lust after him a little, but she would not trust him.

After wasting too much time thinking about it, she decided her skepticism over his motives had to do with the appraising look in his eyes that she had chanced to see more than once when she'd looked up unexpectedly to find him watching her. At the same time—and this was the confusing part—not discounting the chilling calculation she saw when he trained those assessing eyes on her, there was also a very real heat in the cool, blue depths that she found equally undeniable.

It was too damn confusing for words. Just admitting she experienced this rampant sexual curiosity in the first place was enough of a shock. Her public skating style to the contrary, Sasha had always thought it was one of life's little ironies that she actually wasn't a very carnal person. Privately she found sex to be highly overrated.

She had been deprived of her illusions on that subject at an impressionable age. Like young girls everywhere, she'd had her share of crushes on members of the opposite sex. Unlike other young girls her age, however, before her social skills had even had a sporting chance to properly evolve she'd already become the social pariah of Kells Crossing's west side.

Had she not, she freely admitted she most likely would have been too busy for much socializing anyway. Her life at that point had been a continuum of school, skating, homework, and bed. But it would have been nice to be granted a chance to test her wings. Just possibly she might have found a way to squeeze in a social life between her responsibilities. She had never had the opportunity to find out. Instead it was necessary for her to rush off from school the moment the last bell rang, and her association with Ivan Petralahti contributed to her alienation. Add to that the traveling she'd done to various competitions held in far-off, exotic locales, and it was enough to render her an outsider on her own side of town.

And therefore to be considered fair game.

She had been teased in less than friendly tones from practically the moment it was first learned Ivan had chosen to give her private lessons at his compound. Millworkers talked at their dinner tables and the general gist must have been that Carole Miller's girl was getting above herself, because when their children came to school they had plenty to say to Sasha about the way she thought she was so much better than everyone. They were equally quick to point out that they considered her nothing but a stuck-up snob. Even the friends she'd had before Ivan Petralahti entered her life subscribed to a similar theory once her free time was curtailed by her new skating lessons.

It had hurt; she couldn't deny it. But she'd had Mama and Lonnie, who was going through an identical displacement, and perhaps even more importantly, she'd had her skating lessons with Ivan. The skating made up for almost everything else.

And so it went for several years. She and Lonnie were different than the usual millworker's kids and as such were gruffly excluded. The average west-side worker had to struggle just to put enough food on the table—never mind extras—and there was an overt resentment that transferred from parent to child regarding the obvious expense being poured into their development as skaters.

Then Sasha began to fill out physically, and the less-than-subtle ostracism she'd previously been subjected to began to develop even darker overtones.

At close to sixteen years old, Sasha had arrived at puberty quite a bit later than most of millworkers' daughters. She'd always been on the small side, with a thin and gawky appearance, and had tended to look younger than her age. Until shortly before her sixteenth birthday she'd been all sharp shoulder blades and knobby knees, all big eyes, wide mouth, and wild hair.

I'm so ugly, Mama, she'd frequently lamented in disgust. *I'm always gonna be a freak.*

No, sweetie, her mother would invariably reply, sweeping Sasha's thick, soft hair away from her face and smiling down at her. *Trust me on this, baby; someday you're going to be a swan.*

But Sasha knew that all mothers thought their daughters were beautiful; it made their judgment an iffy thing at best.

Then overnight, everything she had previously despaired of as being either too awkward or ungainly seemed to rearrange itself into a new configuration that was altogether pleasing. No longer did she have so many protruding bones; there was a new feminine softness overall. It was in the delicately curved but freshly rounded hips and buttocks; in the peach-sized, satisfyingly ripe little breasts; in her rounder thighs and calves; in her softer shoulders and arms. She was suddenly the proud possessor of a contour that, far from voluptuous, made her feel feminine for the first time in her life.

To cap it off, she also finally grew into her eyes and mouth. It, too, seemed to evolve overnight. She went to bed one evening convinced that while her body might finally have developed into something resembling a female's, her face was never going to be anything but mutt-ugly. She awoke the next morning to discover that not only was Sasha Miller no longer homely, she was actually becoming downright . . . pretty.

She should have been allowed to thrill in the discovery for at least a short while. The rancor of her schoolmates, however, seemed to pick up apace with her budding beauty.

She never knew how the rumors got started, but along with her new looks she'd suddenly gained a reputation. It was commonly accepted that Sasha Miller was the west side's new good-time girl. Whispers circulated that she put out at the drop of a hat. The first she heard about it was the night she went out on her one and only Kells Crossing date.

God, how the idea of that date had thrilled her. And it had been everything she'd hoped for, too . . . right up until the moment when she'd had to fight like a demon in the front seat of a parked car, on a dark, deserted road, in order to retain custody of her virtue. She'd had a crush on the boy forever; she might have been willing to surrender her virginity to him on some eventual date if he'd treated her with care and respect. She was *not,* however, about to let it be taken from her by force.

With a determination that she failed to realize was quite exceptional, Sasha refused to allow school to become the nightmare it could have been following that incident. There was no denying, however, that it became decidedly uncomfortable. Boys she'd barely even spoken to before were suddenly claiming to have known her in the Biblical sense and making kissing sounds when she walked down the hallway; a hush fell over the girls' rest room when she entered.

Lonnie waded in on more than one occasion when he spotted some high school lothario pinning Sasha to a locker while his hands trespassed where they had no business being, and a few other brave souls also attempted to buck the social order and befriend her.

But Lonnie had problems of his own. More than once he was slammed up against a locker for his efforts while a furious face was thrust close to his and a venomous voice, filled with small-town prejudice, warned, "Keep out of this, faggot! The day I need some dickless wonder's advice on how to deal with a round-heeled slut is the day I'll join you in puttin' on a tutu and prancing around some rink!"

And Lon, being Lon, had always given just as good as he got. Shoving his tormentor aside, he'd jeer, "Isn't inbreeding a wonderful thing, Saush? It promotes such intelligence, as you can see by this fine specimen here." Whirling on the redneck, he'd suggest, "Why don't you go on home and screw your sister, Bubba? I hear the line's real short this afternoon."

Except for Mary Sue Janorowski, the only girl in school whose reputation was worse than Sasha's, the other students who'd attempted to go against the flow and befriend her invariably found their own lives made so miserable they soon gave up the attempt. Mary Sue, who had earned every bit of her reputation, breezily flipped people off when they threatened to ostracize her as well, or she stared them in the eye and coolly rattled a skeleton or two. She knew where every single one was buried. Having her as Sasha's only female defender did absolutely nothing to enhance Sasha's already black reputation, but Sasha didn't care. Mary Sue was the only schoolmate she remembered with warmth.

In her senior year, life on the west side of the river in Kells Crossing developed a nightmarish quality. It was in February that the mills effected a massive layoff, and it turned her neighborhood into a walking horror show. Hollow-eyed men, smelling of stale beer and defeat, loitered outside the ubiquitous street corner taverns at all hours of the day and night.

It got so that Sasha dreaded walking past the taverns on her way home from school each day. To these men she seemed to represent the affluence that thrived only on the east side of the river. A new desperation prevailed and she became a handy scapegoat. Out-of-work men regarded her as a daughter of the enemy—the mill owners who controlled their economic survival—instead of one of their own. Sasha could have told them the citizens of Town looked down on her every bit as much as they looked down on anyone else from her side of the river, but it didn't matter. She was representative of something the millworkers couldn't have. She was a safe target, and their hands would reach out as she walked by; their mouths would open and tongues would wag at her with lascivious suggestiveness.

Perhaps because she couldn't remember her own daddy and so tended to revere the father figure, it struck her as ten times more disturbing than what their sons were doing. She crossed streets to avoid them, yet still it seemed she had to contend daily with the feel of rough hands sliding off various portions of her anatomy, as with head held high, she sailed past with as much dignity as she could muster.

Ivan caught her crying about it at practice one afternoon. Usually able to disguise her feelings more adroitly, this was one instance when it simply proved too much work to dissemble.

"What iss this?" he demanded in concern, coming across her in the back of the rink where she had gone to be alone until she could get a grip on her emotions. "What iss so bad that it makes my Sashala cry?"

Sasha swiped at her tears and attempted a smile. "It's nothing, Ivan," she assured him stoically. "Really."

"The *hell* it's not," Lon's voice interrupted. He came out of the shadows where he'd been watching her in brooding silence. Turning to Ivan he snarled, "Maybe it's got something to do with the fact that she was nearly raped on her one and only date in this godforsaken town. Or maybe it's because men old enough to be her father make filthy suggestions and put their grubby hands all over her every goddam time she tries to walk down the street. She can't step out of her house without being molested." Lonnie had seen it for himself one day and had nearly gone ballistic. He'd been walking her home ever since.

Twitching now with a too-long-suppressed rage, he glared at Ivan, transferring his belligerence to the one man he knew would allow him to vent his feelings.

Ivan paused to give the boy's shoulder a comforting squeeze before he sank down on the bench beside Sasha. He reached out to rest his hand upon her head, its warm weight penetrating the thickness of her hair to lend a feeling of security. "I'm sorry, my dahlink girl," he said gently. "There's no excuse for such behavior."

"It's criminal, is what it is," Lonnie said with cold finality.

"Ya," Ivan agreed. "It is." Looking down at Sasha's averted face he said slowly, "I sink, Sashala, that the people on your side of the river, well, I sink they live desperate lives. And when they look at you, I sink they feel a double measure of hopelessness, because they can see that there iss a specialness, which is yours, that they will never have."

And Lonnie, considering Ivan's words, thought that was probably the truth. Sasha did have something special—she all but shined with it. Hell, for years now she'd been the target of all this unrelenting bullshit. The brunt of it was aimed directly at her, and yet somehow she managed to remain untainted by it. How many times had he seen her backed into a corner with some redneck's meaty, unwelcome hand on her breast? She never screamed or swore—she usually just stared at her tormentor with those big gray eyes, and if the last of their humanity hadn't already been chiseled away by small-town prejudices drummed into their heads from the cradle, it pricked at their conscience. He'd watched it with his own eyes, seen it make them shift in shame, make their hands fall away, make them feel like the dog shit they were. She handled everything that life dished out to her with ten times the grace that he did.

"I'm tired of this crappy longhaired music," he said with sudden restlessness and hopped up. Skating over to the dual cassette player, he pulled a cassette from his jacket pocket and popped it in. He cranked up the volume and skated back to where Sasha and Ivan still sat. Pink Floyd's "The Wall" blared out of the loudspeakers, and he could feel the bass thumping beneath his skates as he stopped with a flourish in front of them. He held out his hand invitingly. "C'mon, Saush," he yelled over the music. "Let's show Ivan what we can do with some real music."

"That iss not skate music," Ivan roared, "that iss an abomination!" But it was an argument he'd been steadily losing over the past year. He'd allowed it in the first place only because he was not blind to the problems that faced his two young protégés in this unforgiving little backwater town, and practicing to their raucous music seemed to him a safe enough outlet for blowing off steam.

But then six months ago, without his permission, they had substituted it for their scheduled program at Nationals and now they had actually begun to build a reputation in international competition for their innovatively sexy brand of skating.

Watching them grin at each other as they did a side-by-side double lutz and then smoothly segued the movement into an overhead lift, he shrugged and settled back. Oh, what did it matter? It was one of the few things these days that didn't seemed destined to break their hearts.

For the past several years it had been nearly impossible for Sasha to reconcile her feelings for Lon. Given all that they had shared, she thought it should have been fairly simple but it wasn't. Instead, where he was concerned her emotions constantly shifted, an ever-changing pattern whose basis was a confusing snarl of contradictions.

For the longest time he had been her closest friend, her fellow outcast. Her big brother, almost. He had been, when everything else was said and done, the boy who had taken an awful lot of abuse on her behalf in a never-ending attempt to protect her. And God, how she loved the boy he had been in those days.

But there was a new hostility underlying her old feelings, a subterranean animosity she had to constantly struggle to overcome whenever she thought of the way he had thrown it all away. It arose, bitter as bile, every time she remembered how, in a world *finally,* blessedly free of the taint that had haunted them all those years in Kells Crossing, he had willfully saddled her with a brand-new reputation to live down.

It didn't matter that she hadn't sold drugs, just as it had never mattered that she wasn't a snob or a whore or a piece of meat for some rednecked lout to manhandle. Once again, not because of anything she had done but this time in response to her partner's actions, she had found herself the target of suspicious, unfriendly eyes.

And once again she had overcome the stigma by resurrecting an attitude she'd found successful in the past. She had closed her ears to the innuendoes and her eyes to the sidelong glances that were cast her way. She'd refused to talk about Lonnie or what he had done. Most of all, she had worked her tail to the bone.

Lon's request that she cozy up to J. R. Garland to secure him a place in the line hadn't helped her conflicted emotions, but Sasha now tried to shrug all the confusion aside. She waited in a drafty back hallway in the Portland Coliseum, clutching a phone receiver to her ear as she waited for the penitentiary bureaucracy to grind with its usual excessive slowness through the act of processing her call to Lon.

It wasn't as if getting her feathers all ruffled did her a damn bit of good anyway. Most of the stuff she tended to brood about was over and done with a long time ago, so what was the point? As for the rest . . . well, she could have exercised her options and God knows she'd had every opportunity to tell Lon no.

Except . . . that was something that had always been very difficult for her to do.

Suddenly the receiver on the other end was picked up. "Sasha?" Lon's excited voice came down the wire. "Is that you?"

"Hey, Lonnie."

"Hey yourself, sweet thing." There was an infinitesimal pause and then a sudden burst of exuberant laughter. "I don't know what you did, kiddo," he said excitedly, "but it came down through the warden's office yesterday that I got the job. Saush! I got the job! I'm gonna skate again."

Sasha sagged in relief. She had planned to stand tough on the issue of J. R. Garland . . . and she would have, too. Still, she was just as happy that the need to fight it out had been eliminated. Lon had a way of talking her around, from time to time, until she found herself doing things at his behest that she'd truly just as soon not be doing. "That's good, Lonnie."

"Damn straight it's good, toots. And I owe it all to you." He hesitated and then continued in a more sober tone, "Listen, Saush, my parole is effective on the fourteenth. I can catch a flight that lands me at SeaTac in Seattle at around 1 P.M. and meet you in Tacoma. That is . . . that *is* where the schedule you sent me says you're gonna be that week."

"Yeah, we've got three days at the Tacoma Dome," Sasha confirmed.

"Do you think it would be possible for me to schedule some rink time while we're there and then again in Seattle?" Sasha could almost feel his shrug drift down through the wires as he continued, "I don't actually start performing with the line skaters until the first show in Spokane on the twenty-third, but let's face it, babe, I'm five years, two months, and seventeen days out of practice. That about qualifies me for the Rusty Blade award."

"We've got a new manager," Sasha replied and then responding to a warm spot on the back of her nape, turned to find the aforementioned manager standing directly across the hall from her. She jerked in surprise.

Mick was lounging with his wide shoulders and the flat of one foot propped casually against the wall at his back. Muscular arms crossed over his T-shirt-clad chest, he stared at her.

Sasha turned back to face the wall-mounted pay phone. "Speaking of whom, he's right here. I'll talk to him for you; I'm sure something can be arranged." Unaccountably, her heart began to thud against her ribs as she looked over her shoulder and met Mick's eyes. "I've, uh, gotta go," she murmured into the phone. Curling her fingers over her mouth and the receiver to provide a little pocket of privacy, she turned her back to Mick once more and whispered, "This is good news, Lon . . . the best. I'll see you on the fourteenth." She replaced the receiver in its hook and slowly turned back to face Mick.

"So, tell me," he inquired, dropping his foot from the wall and pushing away to stand upright. "Just what is it you're going to ask the new manager and for whom?" He stood facing her, his clenched fists jammed out of sight in his Levi's jeans pockets. This, then, was how she'd been managing it. Jesus, he was a chump.

He'd almost decided he was on the wrong trail after all, and all because her phone lines had been clear and her room had come up clean when he'd tossed it. *And, hell, admit it,* he prodded himself fiercely, *because that's what you wanted to believe.*

That was the part that really fried his ass.

"Could we discuss this later, Mick?" Sasha interrupted his thoughts. "It took me longer than I expected to get my phone call put through this time, and I need to get some practice time in before the roadies show up."

"Oh, by all means," Mick muttered, following her down the hall into the arena proper. "Far be it for me to cut into your precious practice time."

Puzzled by his tone, she shot him a curious glance over her shoulder but then shrugged and charged into the rink ahead of him. Mick forced back the scowl he could feel pulling his eyebrows together. Christ! How did she get away with looking so damned innocent anyhow; how did she get away with that scrubbed face and lopsided ponytail that made her look like some goddam teenager? What she was ought to show. It bloody well ought to show in some discernible manner.

Which was a damned odd thing for a man to be thinking when he'd run as many cons on the criminal element as Mick had.

Well, it was time to bring out the heavy artillery. He was through letting things slide. Sitting down next to the seat where Sasha had piled her skate bag, letterman's jacket, and pants, Mick leaned back and crossed one ankle over his knee. He propped his elbows on the armrests, steepled his fingers over his nose, and stared out at Sasha as she ran through her routine on the ice.

Usually, when he wanted to insinuate himself into a suspect's life, he labored to make them like him. Not far beyond like is trust, and no seduction will work without trust. And in the end, undercover work was, no matter what the media tried to make of it, just that. A seduction.

In this case, all his labor wasn't paying off quickly enough to suit him. He'd tried to be patient but he was growing itchy. So he was going to turn things around a little.

He was going to bypass the like part and jump headlong into the seduction.

Eyes narrowed, he observed Sasha out on the ice. He never tired of seeing her skate, and little by little, due primarily to watching her every chance he got and asking a ton of questions of anyone who'd take the time to answer, he had begun to pick up a modicum of knowledge about figure skating.

That thing she was launching into now was called a Bielmann spin. With one leg bent up behind her and her head tilted way back, she bent backward at the waist and reached back with both hands to grasp the blade's toe pick. Then she lifted her arms toward the ceiling, bringing the skate along in its wake and, while spinning in place, raised and lowered her leg from the middle of her back to a full extension that was nearly a standing, vertical split. She let go of the skate and went into a fast layback spin, her head and arms bent as far back as they could reach.

The woman was agile.

And he was going to show her new ways to apply all that agility the first opportunity he got.

He was sprawled out in his seat, blocking Sasha's access to her skate bag and jacket when she came off the ice at the conclusion of her practice. Standing at the balustrade, sawing her blades back and forth as if she were on a Nordic Track machine, she stared down at Mick and couldn't help but notice that even in a relaxed state, that rude energy of his was apparently innate. It practically emanated from him in waves; it burned in the back of his steady, unwavering eyes when they met hers.

"If you aren't going to get up could you at least hand me my blade guards," she demanded impatiently when he displayed no inclination to move aside his wide spread legs so she could reach her stuff unassisted. "I can't step off the ice without 'em."

He took his sweet time complying with her request and regarded her all the while with that unnerving gaze. She was the first to drop her eyes.

His jeans, she observed as she slipped on the guards and climbed off the ice, were worn and faded nearly white except for faint streaks of indigo along the seams and in the folds radiating out from his fly. The material was thin and soft, and *boy* did it faithfully cup his . . .

Oh God, oh God, it was changing, straightening out, growing thick. Sasha had an insane impulse to laugh out loud, but her throat was too dry. Sudden heat prickled her cheeks and the desire to laugh collapsed entirely. She *knew* she should look away, that she was asking for trouble if she didn't, but it was almost as if her eyes had developed a life all their own. She continued to avidly watch as the object of her scrutiny realized its full potential.

"All right, by God," Mick growled, "that does it!" He shot out of his seat, gripped Sasha by the waist, and hoisted her onto the waist-high balustrade that separated the spectator seats from the rink. Roughly kneeing her legs apart, he insinuated himself between them and reached behind her to wrap her ponytail around his fist, forcing back her head.

For just a moment he stared down into her eyes, taking note of the lambent excitement that blazed back at him. Then his lids grew heavy and he lowered his head, rocking his mouth over hers. His free hand came up to spread across her arched throat, thumb and index finger wedging beneath the angles of her jaw to fetter her completely, keeping her face tipped up to his.

Sasha's awareness of Mick was almost painful in its intensity as he pressed up against her, put his hands on her, kissed her. His lips were dry and rough, but the interior of his mouth was all slippery heat as his tongue plunged with slow, suggestive rhythm against hers. She felt surrounded by him—his taste on her tongue, his scent in her nostrils, his heat all around her, inside her.

And, oh, God, she liked it.

With a little yearning sound slipping up her throat, Sasha widened her thighs to allow him nearer, clutched fistfuls of Mick's T-shirt in both hands, and hung on while she kissed him back. All thought processes shut down and she simply *experienced.* Experienced the press of his chest hard against her breasts; felt his hands a little rough in her hair, against her skin; felt his mouth, hot, a little wild, demanding total compliance.

She did more than comply. Her lips clung to his, following his lead exactly. Loosening her desperate grip on his T-shirt, her arms slipped up to wrap around his strong neck, her slender fingers plunged into the soft hair at his nape. Her legs spread yet wider and she tried to haul herself a little higher, to fit herself more exactly to his contours. She knew just the place to harbor that hard . . .

Mick made a guttural sound deep in his throat. Relinquishing his grip on her head, his hands skimmed over her shoulders and down her back until they reached her round little butt. God, she was so warm, all steamy and damp from her workout. He curved his fingers to scoop his hands under her, tilting her hips up and jerking her forward in one economical motion. Had they been without clothing she would have been impaled to the hilt. As it was, his erection aggressively nudged the soft cleft between her thighs. Pressing hard, he rotated his hips.

Sasha breathed in sharply. Her thighs gripped his hips, her calves clamped down on the backs of his thighs, and her pelvis tipped forward to maintain contact. With a muted roar, Mick ripped his mouth free. He dragged it across her cheek to her ear, teeth worrying the lobe like a puppy with a knotted rag before his lips burrowed into the hollow behind it. He breathed raggedly through a slightly opened mouth.

"Ah, God, you feel sweeter'n honey," he said in a hoarse voice and Sasha shivered in reaction. The hands gripping her bottom slid to the backs of her upper thighs, pulling them wider apart, and his fingertips flirted with the elastic leg opening of her leotard. "How do we get you outta this thing?" he demanded impatiently. "I've gotta . . ."

Noises they should have heard sooner suddenly intruded. Still distant but coming closer were the sounds of raucous insults being traded by roadies, the deep-throated rumble of semis being backed up to the loading docks, the heavy footsteps and squeaking wheels of the scenery haulers and their cargo. Mick cursed, untangled himself from Sasha's legs, and stepped back, sprawling once again onto his seat. Staring up at her, seeing her all flushed, damp, and tousled, he palmed his erection where it strained behind the fly of his jeans and pressed hard. "God," he said through gritted teeth. "I hurt."

You could have knocked him over with a feather when Sasha averted her eyes and blushed scarlet right up to the tight little ringlets that clung so damply to her hairline. Mick experienced a queer pitch in the pit of his stomach. Oh, man, what the hell was going on here? Staring at the top of her bowed head as she struggled with her skate laces, he tried to analyze his unease.

Well, all right, it had been a mistake to allow himself to get so caught up in the feel and taste of her that he lost track of everything else around him. It was unprofessional—he knew that—but, c'mon, the woman was good.

Yeah, she is. But is she actually all that experienced?

The question came out of nowhere and he didn't like it or the impulse of . . . fairness—or whatever the hell it was—that prompted it. What? he demanded in silent disgust. Are you suddenly developing a conscience here, Vinicor? Becoming a bleeding heart, maybe? Kind of late in the day for that, ain't it? And, hell, this is no Little Miss Innocent we're talkin' about here, anyway. You've seen her skate; you know what she does for kicks in her off time. Miller's no virgin—believe it.

I buy that. And I ask you again. Do you really think she's all that experienced?

Ah, shit. Mick abruptly sat forward in his seat. "Just how many lovers have you had?" he demanded.

Sasha's head snapped up. "I beg your pardon?" Her spine slowly stiffened. "Really, Mick. I fail to see where that's any of your busi—"

"Answer the damn question. How many?"

"Two." The retort was given sulkily, for she was furious with herself for responding to that autocratic tone at all . . . let alone with such promptness.

Two? Mick sank back, staring at the heated color on her face and throat as she dropped her eyes and went back to removing her skates. *Two?*

He rolled his shoulders uneasily. Well, okay, fine. It sure as hell didn't fit in with the usual profile or any of his theories, but . . . fine. No, this was good really; he could use this. Definitely; it could be made to work in his favor.

He'd reel her in with sex. In this one aspect of her life, at least, she didn't have much knowledge and he had plenty;

so it ought to be a piece of cake. Hell, it was the oldest method in the history of mankind when it came to procuring information.

He would simply use his body to get her so damn enthralled that in no time at all her secrets would be his secrets. And the minute they were his, bam! He'd slam her pretty little ass in jail. He'd be killing two birds with one stone, really: working her out from under his skin and making the streets a safer place for your everyday garden variety junkie. Yeah, this was good.

So why was he suddenly so disenchanted with himself? Life was a goddam melodrama, but get real, what they *wouldn't* be dealing with here was an evil-hearted villain taking ruthless advantage of the little orphaned Match Girl. Sure, there was an added benefit in it for him. He could slake this runaway lust he'd been feeling ever since he'd first clapped eyes on her. But, hey, really, when all was said and done . . .

He would merely be doing his job.

Six

Karen Corselli saw the new manager with Sasha Miller in the corner of the lobby, and it stopped her in her tracks. The longer she stood there watching them, the more fuel it added to her slow-burning annoyance. Really, the way Mick crowded Sasha every time he talked to her was so *obvious*. Just look at them. She had half a mind to go over there and tell him what a spectacle he was making of himself. People were beginning to talk about it in the crudest ways.

He'd followed Sasha to the Coliseum yesterday. Karen knew—she rented a car as a matter of course in every new city they played and seeing him leave the hotel, thinking to surprise him, she had followed his cab to the east side of the river.

Some surprise. It had been on her, not him; and it certainly hadn't been a pleasant one. Drat him, anyhow. It didn't take a lot of guesswork to figure out why he was at the Coliseum; everyone knew who had a standing arrangement to test the ice in every arena they played. As soon as Karen had realized where his destination was taking them and just whom it was he was chasing after, she'd peeled off in the opposite direction in a cloud of burning rubber.

Why on earth was he pursuing Sasha Miller? What could he possibly see in her? For all her vulgar, spurious displays of sexuality on the ice the woman was actually rather dull.

And spurious was exactly what those displays were, too. The truth was, little Sasha Miller didn't have any appreciation for what a judicious use of sex could accomplish, an ignorance Karen found incomprehensible.

And inexcusable. She failed to understand *anyone* who exhibited such total disregard for the game. Life, when it came right down to the nuts and bolts that made it interesting, was simply one ongoing quest for power. Personally, Karen had no use for anyone who failed to take full advantage of their potential.

Flaunting a beautiful body just for the sake of it certainly had no worth in itself. Heavens above, it was just plain common, and it gained a woman nothing. A gorgeous face and spectacular figure were assets to be utilized in order to achieve one's desires. Determining an aspiration and then manipulating events until you realized it, *that* was the only thing that counted.

But apparently no one had ever bothered to tell Sasha Miller. As far as Karen could determine, Miller had never attempted to wile so much as the teensiest favor from a man by using the promise of her body. Aside from that one young man back in the amateur circuit days—what was his name again, Tim Something-or-other?—Sasha never seemed to indulge in sexual activities, period.

There had to be a story behind her failure to do so, but that was the one secret Karen had never been able to pry out of Lon Morrison. To her eternal annoyance.

Karen *liked* learning secrets; it was yet another rich source of power. Apparently, however, Sasha had never shared that particular confidence with Lon or with Tim What's-his-name either, because while Tim, during the aftermath of sex with Karen, had been more than willing to denigrate Sasha's capabilities in bed, he hadn't been able to answer her cautiously worded queries.

Karen hadn't been interested in hearing how superior her sexual performance was to Miller's. That had never been in question. She'd wanted the dirt, but unfortunately it was not to be.

Which of course was neither here nor there. What she really wanted to know was why Mick Vinicor was wasting his time with Sasha when Karen had given him innumerable opportunities to take his best shot at her?

That man was turning out to be the preeminent challenge and luckily for all concerned, Karen loved a good challenge. The more difficult it was to capture his interest now, the more absolute would be the rush of power when she ultimately did.

So, let him flirt with Miller. When that cloying sexual shyness of hers cranked his frustration level up to an unbearable degree, Karen Corselli knew that Mick Vinicor would be darn grateful to turn to a real woman for relief.

"Give us a kiss then, luv." Mick crowded in close to Sasha. He'd caught up with her in the lobby and hustled her over to the corner. It provided a feeling of privacy as people came and went, even if they were actually only half hidden from casual view by the dusty fronds of a huge palm. He flashed his white, white teeth at her in what his mother used to call "Micky's charm-the-birds-outta-the-trees grin."

Sasha refused to be charmed. "Mick, for heaven's sake," she said in exasperation, "will you back off?"

"Sure . . . just as soon as you give me a kiss."

"I'm not going to kiss you, Vinicor, so get used to it. And I'm sorry if I gave you a different impression yesterday, but I'm not going to go to bed with you either."

He rubbed the side of his thumb over her cheekbone and down the softness of her cheek to the full swell of her lower lip. Sasha had to concentrate hard to keep herself from squirming beneath his touch.

"Ah, now, that's where you're wrong, Miller," he was retorting smoothly when she dragged her focus away from the rough feel of his skin against hers. "I *am* going to be lover number three." He thumbed her lip down and rubbed the callused pad along its slick interior membrane. "Maybe not today. Maybe not tomorrow. But it will happen."

"You think so, huh?" Sasha batted his hand away. "Well, that just makes you sound pretty damn cocky, if you ask me." And *not* without good reason. "Saying so doesn't make it so," she insisted.

Mick shrugged and gave her a gentle smile. "C'mon. You know you think I'm a handsome devil."

She snorted. "You're not even close to handsome, Vinicor."

"Cuter'n a bug's ear, then."

"If you want to do animal analogies," she said with a sweet smile, "try 'rat's ass.' "

That big self-assured grin was back. Propping his hands on the wall behind her, he brought his face down to her level. His chest brushing the front of her shirt, his lips at her ear, he breathed, "Sexy, then," and his hot breath traveled the whorls of her ear to leave a rash of cold goose bumps in its wake. "I betcha think I'm sexy."

Her eyes began to close. *"Yes,"* she agreed helplessly.

Mick's entire body jerked and the easy grin fell apart. "Oh, *Gawd,* Sasha. Let's go up to my . . ."

Before he could finish articulating his demand, he found himself being shoved back and she was sliding out of the corner he'd backed her into. She turned to face him, her hands curled at her side.

"You don't get it, Mick," she said earnestly. "Yes, you're a sexy guy—that's been apparent from the first night we met. But *I'm* not a sexy woman." She slicked her hair back off her forehead and stared up at him intently. Racking her brain for the right words, she finally gave up, shrugged one shoulder, and simply came out with it. "Don't let my performance on ice fool you," she urged. "I'm actually not all that big on sex, if you wanna know the truth."

There. It was out. It hurt to say it, but she didn't ever want to see the disappointment in this man's eyes that she'd seen in the eyes of her other two lovers. They'd both made it pretty damn clear that she should have come with a truth-in-advertising guarantee, because as far as they were concerned she might be one hot number on the ice but she was a bust in bed. And they were right. She hadn't had any experience with the tricks they'd expected her to perform for their pleasure; she'd been stiff and self-conscious, and it hadn't been very good. Still, their assessment of her abilities had hurt terribly.

It would kill her if Mick thought the same.

"Oh, yeah," he was agreeing with easy amusement, "I could tell by the way your skate blades were digging holes in the back of my knees out at the Coliseum yesterday that you were just humoring me." He took a step closer and his voice dropped. "I could see you weren't big on sex by the way you wrapped your arms round my neck and tried to climb up onto my dick."

"That's enough, Mick!"

"Sorry," he promptly apologized. "I've been hanging out with the wrong kind of people the last couple of years and I guess I can be pretty crude sometimes." He reached out to cup her flushed face in his hard-skinned hands. Leaning down he kissed her gently, briefly, then pulled back and looked her straight in the eye. "But get used to the basic premise here, darlin'," he advised peremptorily. "Because I *am* gonna be number three. Count on it."

For the second night in a row, Sasha cautiously stepped into her skimpy costume, pulled it up, and had beads start clattering onto the floor. "Dammit!" she snarled.

Two times now that her costume had threatened to fall apart for no apparent reason? My God, if she didn't know better, she'd think someone was trying to sabotage her, but that, of course, was patently absurd. More likely it was a bad spool of defective thread or something. Still, she didn't look forward to taking it to the wardrobe mistress. The woman was overworked as it was, and counting the one Sasha had snagged on the locker door, this made three extra jobs she'd created for the woman in much too short a period of time. She gingerly removed the costume and bundled it together, blowing out an aggrieved breath. This was simply one more instance of how her life seemed to be escaping her control these days.

She'd had her ducks all in a row for the first time in her chaotic life, and now it felt as if the little beggars were slip-sliding all over the damn place.

Perhaps she'd never be accused of being overly conventional. Sasha freely if somewhat despairingly admitted that her life to date had been anything but. But did she have to pay for it forever? It wasn't as if it had been a conscious decision on her part to begin with—the circumstances had been more or less thrust upon her.

And, dammit, for the past several years her lifestyle *had* been pretty ordinary. Maybe it wasn't exactly traditional, but big deal. She liked it; it suited her—at least being different wasn't a punishable offense and her emotions weren't bombarded on a daily basis, as they'd been under the good old mill-town mentality that ruled back home. She'd overcome Kells Crossing. She'd overcome the stigma of being the ex-partner of a convicted heroin dealer. She'd made a few good friends and had a job she loved. Comparatively speaking, life had been almost mundane.

Yes, all right, she had a few little sexual hang-ups. It didn't take a psychotherapist to figure out why. But she was young; she'd deal with them all in her own good time.

Or so she'd always thought . . . until the advent of Mick Vinicor into her life.

The way he made her feel—all crazed and scared and itching for something she'd never had—made her confront the realization that she'd been lying to herself. She hadn't been dealing with it at all—she'd been ignoring the problem.

And if she had her choice, she'd just as soon continue to ignore it.

That was the thing, though. The choice seemed to have been removed from her hands. Mick had determined a course and no two ways about it, the man's will was formidable. She could feel the two of them, like newspaper-crafted sailboats in a fast current, heading pell-mell toward the destination he'd ordained.

She, too, had free will of course. She tried to keep that in mind; but it was difficult when the damn thing seemed to go flying out the window every time he got within touching distance.

"It's one thing to joke about it," she admitted to Connie the last night of their Portland run. "But the truth is, the outcome really does scare me silly."

Connie was still reeling from Sasha's confession of life in a small town. She couldn't conceive of the type of harassment her friend had undergone . . . and couldn't imagine keeping it to herself for all these years if something of that nature had ever happened to her. "I've known you, what, Sasha, almost three years?" she finally said and then demanded incredulously, "Why the hell didn't you ever tell me any of this stuff before?"

Sasha didn't pretend to misunderstand. "I don't know," she said and then added with stark simplicity. "I was ashamed, I guess."

"Oh, Saush, no!" Connie inspected her friend's expression carefully. "Please, tell me you didn't blame yourself for the actions of a bunch of jerk-off rednecks."

"No, no, it wasn't like that . . . exactly. I'm not entirely neurotic." Sasha kicked off her shoes, pulled her heels up on Connie's bed, and hugged her thighs to her chest. Resting her chin in the little divot where her kneecaps pressed together, she gazed at her friend solemnly. "For over two years on practically a daily basis I had some ham-fisted yahoo putting his hands on me. And most of the time I could honestly just divorce myself from it, pretend it didn't bother me to be felt up by boys and their damn *fathers*. I thought I was okay with it, Con, but I don't think I was, really, not way down deep inside. It left me . . . I don't know—scarred. Maybe if I could have talked it over with Mama . . ." Her shoulder inched up in a helpless shrug. "But I was afraid to, afraid it would throw her right in the middle of the whole darn mess. The people in my part of town apparently kept the way they felt about me separate from the way they felt about my mom, and I was terrified of upsetting the balance. So I buried what I felt. But it's prevented me from having a normal, healthy sex life and I'm ashamed of that."

"Have you ever had a sexual experience that was positive?"

"Well, . . . not really." Her lips curled up in a forlorn little smile. "Isn't that pathetic? I mean, I've had sex and everything, several times with two separate guys, but I can't say that I liked it much. It sure wasn't the stuff you read about in books. Not awful or traumatic or anything—just something I sorta wanted to get over."

Connie quit prowling the room and sat down next to her. "So if you've decided it's inevitable with Vinicor, why does the thought of doin' the deed with our good manager scare you so much? I mean, it's gotta be an improvement that he turns you on, doesn't it?"

"Yeah, you'd think so, wouldn't you?" Sasha turned her head to look her friend in the eyes, resting her cheek against her updrawn knees. "But I've got this need to be good at the things I do, and I'm not good at this. It's not even a matter of being *kind of* not good; I'm really lousy. I mean, Connie, here's this guy, he looks like he invented this stuff and it terrifies me when I think of the way he's going to look at me once the shoutin's all over. I've seen this look and believe me, it hurts. And jeez, Connie, if that isn't enough to send me into a spin, then there's Lon." Her bark of laughter was tinged with hysteria. "Two more days and I'm going to be seeing him face-to-face for the first time in over five years. I still don't have the foggiest idea what my reaction to *that* is gonna be."

She remained uncertain of her response right up until the moment she opened he door to her hotel room and saw Lonnie standing in the hallway. Then it was as if the five-year separation, the constant vacillation between feelings of hostility and remembered good times, had never been. Fingers pressed to her lips, all she had time to say was a trembly, "Oh," before he hauled her out in the hall and into his arms to give her the granddaddy of all bear hugs.

"Hey ya, sweet thing," he whispered into her hair. "Miss me?"

"Lon." Sasha clutched him tightly for several moments. His hug, his scent, took her back, was a reassurance of things familiar. Finally pushing away, she held him off at arm's length. "Let me look at you," she demanded.

Lonnie held his arms out from his sides, presenting himself. As she inspected him he inspected her in return, slow and thorough, looking for changes, noting things that had stayed the same. "Well, you're sure a sight for sore eyes," he said with a grin. "Prettier'n ever, I see."

"And you're still as full of sh . . ."

"Now, now." Lonnie slung an arm over her shoulders. "Aren'tcha gonna ask me in?"

"Oh. Yes. Please, c'mon in." They stepped into her hotel room and she closed the door behind them. Turning back to him, she was quick to assure, "No, really, Lon, you're lookin' good. I was half afraid you'd be all pale and skinny."

"Nah. I got a little weather in the exercise yard. And I kept in shape with regular workouts—weights and stuff. Prison life does come with a few amenities."

There it was, said out loud, the bald reminder that Lonnie's long absence from her life hadn't been the result of something simple or easy . . . like living in another state. Sasha looked away.

"Hey." Lon reached out and pulled her chin back around with his fingertips. When their eyes met once again, he asked, "Is my incarceration gonna be a problem between us, Saush?"

"No, of course not," she assured him quickly . . . too quickly. Her eyes slid away. Then she forced herself to meet his gaze once again and her chin tipped up fractionally as she shrugged. "Maybe. It's not the imprisonment so much; it's all the stuff that went into putting you there." She hesitated and then admitted, "I've still got a lot of hard feelings, Lon."

"Yeah, I s'pose you do. And I suppose you've got a right to them. But I'll tell you something, Sasha." His eyes held a hardness she'd never seen in him before. "Things are *never* gonna be one hundred percent the same again, so you might as well get used to it. I just spent the last five years of my life locked away—that's a fact we can't tiptoe around."

"I never suggested that we should," she replied stiffly.

"No, you didn't. You'd just like me to avoid saying the word out loud instead, so you'll feel more comfortable."

"Comfort be damned," she snapped, furious that he should choose to put that interpretation on it. "Every time I'm reminded of where you've been, Lonnie, and *why,* my comfort zone's not the first thing that pops into my head."

"Yeah? So, what *is?*"

Feelings she'd been suppressing for years surged to the fore. "You really want to know?" she demanded. "I'll tell you what the first thing is." Then she drew herself up, tamped those feeling down. She shook her head, taking a small step backward, as if to remove herself from the conflict. "No," she said through tight lips. *"No.* I'm not going to do this. I am *not* going to fight with you."

Lon ground his teeth in frustration. "Dammit, Saush, I hate it when you do that! I hate it when you get all prissy and controlled on me, like Sasha Miller's just too goddam angelic to brawl with the rest of us sinners." He stuck his face close to hers. "Tell me what the first frigging thing that comes to mind is."

She remained silent.

"Prison," he taunted, thinking of her previous reaction to the word. "The Pen, the Big House, the Slam—"

"Anger," she screamed and thumped him one on the chest. "Okay? You wanna know what my first reaction is when I think about what you did? It's pure, undiluted *anger.*" They were standing close, nose to nose as they battled in the old familiar manner, a habit that had its origins way back in the days of their very first arguments. "Damn you, Lon, I'm so mad at you I could spit!" Her chest heaved with the force of her emotions as she stared up at him. "We had a *place.* For the first time in our lives, we had a place where we were accepted just for ourselves; where we didn't have to explain to anyone what makes us tick . . . or *apologize* for our very existence. And you screwed it up!"

"I screwed it up for *me!*"

"Oh, and you think it didn't reflect on me? You think people believed I didn't know all along exactly what you were up to? God, I can't tell you how sick I got of being the goddam outsider again." She placed her palm on his chest and gave him a furious shove. He was bigger and stronger than she; it merely rocked him back a step, and her control slipped another notch. "It was Kells Crossing all over again, you self-absorbed sonofabitch. The only difference was that this time nobody tried to grab my ass or feel me up!" Tears welled up in her eyes and spilled over, and she struck out at him blindly. "Damn you, Lon Morrison. Damn you, damn you, DAMN YOU!"

He stilled her pounding fists by the simple expedient of grabbing her wrists and manacling them in one hand. With his free arm, he snagged her around her shoulders and hauled her up against him. "Holy shit," he muttered, pressing her face to his chest. She shook with great, wrenching sobs. Holding her tightly, wordlessly, until the worst of the storm had abated, he finally pulled back a little and inquired, "So why the hell didn't you ever tell me any of this back then, Sasha . . . back when I was going through the arraignment and trial?"

"I don't know." She wiped her nose against his shirt. "'Cause you had enough on your plate without heaping my problems on it, too, I guess."

"Yeah, that's the Sasha we all know and love, all right," he agreed with a humorless bark of laughter. "Wouldn't want to bother anyone with anything as inconsequential as fuckin' up her life."

She dashed a hand under her eyes and glared up at him. "Would it have changed anything, Lon? Would it have kept you out of jail, or turned me into a damn Homecoming Queen?"

He looked down at her red-rimmed eyes and runny nose and dragged her over to the night stand by the bed. Pulling out a Kleenex, he extended it to her. "Here," he commanded, "blow your damn nose. Jeez, you got snot all over my new shirt." Watching to make sure she complied, he then pressed on her shoulders until her knees buckled and she collapsed onto the side of the bed. He squatted down in front of her and reached for her hands.

"No," he answered seriously, staring up at her. "It wouldn't have kept me out of prison. And it was probably too late by then to win you any popularity contests. What it might have done, though, Saush," he told her soberly, "was save your stomach more than five years' worth of wear and tear. Or are you gonna try and tell me you haven't been letting it eat at you all this time?"

She knuckled her eyes and scowled at him. "Don't flatter yourself, bud."

Lon laughed. "You're right," he said. "The Sasha Miller I know wouldn't have sat around brooding about it. Hell, you rebuilt your life, snagged the Silver at the Olympics, made friends and influenced people, and generally got on with it, just the way you've always done. It was probably only in the odd moments that it ate a hole in the lining of your gut."

One corner of her mouth tipped up. "Yeah, that just about covers it."

He rose to his feet and then sat down on the mattress next to her. Slinging a brotherly arm over her shoulders, he gave her a little squeeze. "I can't change what's gone before," he admitted. Turning his head to look at her, he added, "What I can do, though; what I *will* do, Saush, is keep my nose clean from this day forward. I won't let you down again . . . I swear."

His intentions were the best and he was totally sincere as he made the vow. He just didn't realize how hard it was going to be to keep that particular promise.

The phone was picked up on the third ring. "Hullo?" The greeting was offered in Ivan Petralahti's usual abrupt, *telephone-calls-are-a-nuisance* tone.

"Ivan?"

"Sashala!" His voice warmed by several degrees. "It hass been too long since we last spoke, my dahlink. How iss everysing with you?"

"Pretty good," Sasha replied. "And how about you? I've missed you."

They spoke in generalities for a while, catching up on the latest developments in both their lives, exchanging gossip from the figure skating world. Finally, knuckles whitening as she tightened her grip on the receiver, Sasha hesitated and then said, "I, uh, wanted to let you know that Lon is here. He's out of jail." There was a frigid silence on the other end of the line and she rushed to fill it in. "He was paroled on the fourteenth and I got him a job with the Follies. In the line, that is—he'll be skating in the line." She knew she was babbling, but her nerves were on edge, fearing his reaction.

Not without good reason. "Lonnie iss dead to me," he said, and there was no doubting the finality in his tone. "I haff told you this before."

"Ivan, *please* . . ."

"No, Sasha. I saw him through the trial but I told him then, as you well know, that that wass the end." He was quiet for a few seconds and then burst out, "He had a bright future . . . and he threw it away. He sacrificed everysing—including, almost, *your* future—to make money from z'filthy drugs. No! He iss no more to me. We will speak of somesing else."

And that was that. Sasha felt a sick clenching in the pit of her stomach. She needed so badly to be able to talk of Lonnie to Ivan; he was the only other person in the world who understood how it had been for the two of them in the old days, the only one who could possibly understand her conflicted feelings where her old friend was concerned. And what was that old saw about a problem shared being a problem halved?

But Ivan, whom Sasha secretly believed had to be similarly conflicted by the same opposing emotions that tore her apart, absolutely refused to discuss it. It was nothing new; she shouldn't be so disappointed. He had cut off that particular conversational avenue the day Lon was indicted, and clearly he was no more willing to reopen it now than he had ever been.

In a way, she even understood his hard-line attitude. Ivan was Old World, possessed of a rigid code of honor, and he held firm views and strong beliefs. But understanding didn't make it easier to accept. It would've made a world of difference to her if he'd been willing to at least listen while she worked through her own confused feelings. His frigid refusal to discuss it at all punished her right along with Lonnie.

She could feel him waiting for her to change the subject,

and she knew that if she didn't the conversation would have to be terminated. Out of nowhere a bone-deep loneliness struck and she blurted, "I miss Mama."

She hadn't known she was going to say that, but suddenly her sense of loss was overwhelming. It hit her the way it used to in the early days right after her mother's death, and she had a sinking feeling that the emotions were embarrassingly evident, coloring her voice.

Ivan's voice gentled. "I know you do, Sashala. She wass a good woman."

"Ivan, do you think . . ." she faltered but then came out with a quetion that had been on her mind quite a lot lately ". . . do you think she knew what was going on with the millworkers? Do you think they took their dislike of me out on her?" *Do you think I should have asked her about it myself instead of being such a coward and waiting until it was too late, the chance forever eliminated?*

"No," he immediately replied. "Remember when you won the Silver and the networks broadcast those signs in your hometown that said, 'We Love You, Sasha Miller'?"

Her voice was bitter. "Do I ever." She could still recall her shock when a sports announcer had thrust a mike in her face and asked how it felt to have the support and love of an entire town behind her.

It had felt like the worst sort of hypocrisy.

She could remember going back to her room in the Olympic Village and watching with cynical disbelief the coverage of Kells Crossing millworkers marching through the streets with banners that stretched from sidewalk to sidewalk. Banners that proclaimed their love for her.

"Well, I sink that was for your mama. I sink that when she bragged about you at the mill, they separated their jealousy of you from their respect for her. You were never accepted as one of their own, but your mama wass, and I always sought those banners were their way of showing her their support during the games."

It was what Sasha had always assumed, also, what she'd *wanted* to believe, so she accepted Ivan's explanation. It was too late to make a difference now, anyway, and she preferred to believe that her mother had remained ignorant of the mill-workers' true feelings for her.

There didn't seem to be much to say after that. She appreciated his reassurance over the matter that had been nagging at her for some time, but what Sasha truly needed from Ivan he was unable to give. Shortly thereafter they said their goodbyes and hung up.

Sasha grabbed her skate bag and left her room. No sense brooding; life was full of disappointments. You got used to it.

Besides, she'd promised Lonnie she'd go out to the Dome with him.

Mick pulled the headset off his ears and punched the rewind button on the tape. Swell. Another conversation that raised more questions than it supplied answers.

He packed away his equipment and backed out of the closet where he'd been sitting on the floor while he listened to the recorded phone tap. Well, one thing he did know now was how J. R. Garland fit into the picture.

Sasha had been whoring for Morrison's job. A simmering anger burned deep in Mick's stomach. She'd had him all but convinced that she was the closest thing to a virgin and all along she'd been whoring for that heroin-pushing son of a bitch.

I've done something tonight I'm not exactly proud of. The memory of her expression that night in the bar, of her tone as she'd said those words, floated across his mind.

Okay, maybe not whoring exactly. But it was damn sure the reason she'd let that old goat put his meaty paws all over her.

The tiny corner of his mind that noted absurdities had no

sooner whispered a mocking caution against mixing meta-
phors than it was snarled into silence by a rage ten times
more dominant. Anger rode like a green demon on his back,
but he forced it into submission by pure strength of will. He
had a job to do here and this wasn't helping.

What was all that stuff about the millworkers being jealous
of Sasha and her not being accepted as one of their own?
And how the hell could a mother not know that? Maybe he'd
better have her background checked more thoroughly. Often,
events that happened yesterday affected events of today—it
might give him a handle on what made her tick.

I miss Mama. Mick glanced at the telephone sitting on
the night stand next to his bed. That was the one sentence
in the whole conversation he would just as soon not dwell
upon right now. Just remembering the grief in her voice
kicked at something deep in his gut. There'd been such deso-
lation there, intimations of things too late to rectify.

I miss Mama. He might not want to hear it, but the words,
the tone, kept replaying in his brain. Truth was, lives could
change in the blink of an eye. You never knew when you
might lose someone.

Mick crossed over to the night stand, picked up the receiver, and punched out a series of numbers. Flopping onto
his back on the mattress, he snagged the body of the phone,
plunked it down on his stomach, and tapped out a tune on
the plastic between the disconnect buttons while he listened
to it ring on the other end of the line. Then suddenly it was
picked up, and his face split into a huge smile.

"Hi, *Mom?* It's me, Micky."

SEVEN

A thin envelope was delivered to Mick by special messenger seconds after he hung up the phone. Looking up and down the hallway, he searched for prying eyes, watched the messenger until he disappeared from view, and then closed the door. Hefting the envelope's weight in one hand, he checked his watch for the time on the other. He really didn't have time to go over whatever the agency had sent. Lon Morrison was hitting the ice in twenty-five minutes, and Mick planned to be there. Then again, if its size was anything to go by, this didn't appear to be a missive that would be particularly time intensive . . .

He ripped open the tape-reinforced envelope.

A few minutes later he let the single sheet of paper drift to the table and sat back in his chair. Well . . . that was unexpected. He didn't know why it should catch him by surprise; however—it wasn't as if anything else concerning this damn case had made a great deal of sense so far, so, hey, why start now? He reached forward and picked up the paper to read it through one more time.

With the exception of one dead addict, discovered the day after Mick joined the Follies in Sacramento and believed to have made his purchase from an unknown dealer sometime during the day *preceding* said discovery of body, the string of drug-related deaths connected to this case had come to a halt. The sale of heroin was assumed to have ceased.

Why? Mick wondered on his way over to the Tacoma Dome. And perhaps more importantly, for how long?

His whole career had been one long association with people involved in the sales, distribution, smuggling, or prevention of drugs. He knew the species from one end of the spectrum to the other, from those who profited to those who busted their humps trying to put a stop to it; from drug lords, the top money men who controlled the trade; to mules, the couriers used for smuggling; to Border rats, the Customs and DEA agents who worked the Mexican border. And if there was one thing that was guaranteed, it was that nobody shut down a profitable operation for long. Not without a damn good reason.

It was his job in this case to figure out what that reason was. Well, either/or. Either he figured it out, or he just hanged tough until the operation started up again—and it would. But he was a bottom line kind of guy. And the bottom line was that one way or another he planned to put a halt to it.

He wasn't exactly knocked on his butt with astonishment when he walked into the arena a short while later and discovered that he wasn't the only one harboring an itch to learn more about Lon Morrison. The old scandal had been resurrected right along with the discovery that Morrison had been hired for the line, and Mick must have heard at least a dozen different people in the past few days hashing it over in all its gory detail. A goodly number of the Follies' skaters had turned out today, apparently to judge for themselves whether Morrison could still skate after more than five years away from the ice.

He could. Even Mick, who was admittedly nobody's idea of an expert, could tell that the man had something.

After watching for a few minutes, he pulled his curious gaze away from the skater going through his paces out on the rink and scanned the arena until he located Sasha in the small crowd seated rinkside. He made his way over to the cluster of skaters.

Through sheer force of personality he cleared a path to his objective. Staking out the seat next to hers, his shoulder jostling her as he settled himself, he nodded to her and to Connie on her other side, but held his silence as he leaned back and gazed out at the man on the ice.

Morrison's hair flashed with golden highlights beneath the overhead lights as he skated backwards, his chin tipped into his shoulder to spot where he was going. He whipped along the perimeter of the rink with respectable speed, then launched into a double toe loop.

"He's gonna screw it up," Sasha muttered. Surprised, Mick turned his head to look down at her. Her hands were clenched in her lap, her gray eyes fastened on the ice and he looked back in time to see Morrison land on his ass. For no good reason, Mick experienced a little spark of satisfaction.

Connie leaned forward to peer into Sasha's face. "How did you know that?" she demanded.

"He lost his concentration," Sasha retorted without taking her eyes off the ice. "It always happens when he gets full of himself. Okay, Big Shot," she muttered to herself as Lon climbed to his feet and shoved off, slowly building up speed once again. *"Focus."*

There was an intimacy in knowing someone as well as Sasha apparently knew Morrison, and it was a familiarity that didn't sit well with Mick. It made him uneasy in a way that he couldn't quite pin down, and it gnawed away at a spot in the depths of his stomach. Whatever the emotion that caused it, it was unwarranted and unwelcome and sure as hell not one he particularly cared to examine too closely. He sternly relegated it to a far corner of his mind.

Morrison's next landing was not perfect but was nevertheless much smoother. "Better," was Sasha's assessment. She turned to Connie. "He needs work, but not nearly as much as I feared," she remarked. "I really don't know many who could do so well, having been away from it as long as he's been." Reaching out with a tactile gesture that was typical of her, she brushed her friend's arm with her fingertips. "Listen, Con, you wanna help?"

"Sure."

"Good. Go on out and show him the combination for the first number. If I know Lonnie he's gonna be itching for something specific to practice before he's even got his basics nailed down again."

Connie changed into her skates and climbed to her feet to comply. She met Lon out on the ice and spent a few minutes conferring with him. The moment they understood what she was up to, Brenda and Sara jumped into their skates and joined her. Lonnie and the three women spent several moments in consultation. He watched them demonstrate a series of movements and then all of them skated in slow time through the routine the women had been illustrating.

Sasha's neck was stiff with tension as she watched. She really could have done without the audience here today; this was awkward enough as it was. Witnessing Lon back on the ice after he'd been away from it for so many years was an emotional milestone, one that she couldn't help but feel should have been private between the two of them. Then she rolled her shoulders in an impatient little shrug. Well, as those old philosophers The Stones were so fond of saying, you can't always get what you want. And a damn shame it was, too.

Awareness of Mick beside her, his shoulder warm, pressing against hers, his legs sprawled out, left knee within brushing distance of her right, added to her edginess and served to divide her attention. She kept anticipating, now that Connie was gone, that at any minute he would say something, would crank up the heat he invariably generated whenever they were in contact these days. But he sat quietly.

Crowding her as usual in the physical sense, he nevertheless left her a little mental distance.

And the fact that she was so pathetically grateful for an act of thoughtfulness that for all she knew might be entirely accidental served as a pretty good indication of the kind of shape she was in. What was obviously needed here was for her to take a giant step backward, to put some distance between herself and the events that had been unfurling these past few weeks.

The fact did remain, however, that whether he deserved it or not, Sasha did experience a spurt of gratitude toward Mick for having the sensitivity not to push her today. In truth, she didn't think she was up to coping with his high-energy expectations on top of everything else.

Shoot, the real truth here was that she didn't want to have to concentrate on anything beyond her yearning to skate with Lon. It had been so long since they'd skated together and it used to be one of her very favorite things to do. They had a connection on the ice that she'd never experienced anywhere else. With anyone else.

Watching him skate with the three line women, she observed the progress that evolved in the very short time that they advanced from several walk-throughs of the routine to a creditable rehearsal complete with taped music. It was all she could do to simply sit still and watch. She wanted to be out there and if it had been just the two of them, just she and Lon, she would have given him some time to reacclimate—say, ten minutes—and then hit the ice with him.

As it was she felt constrained by all the watchful eyes.

Lonnie apparently labored under no such constraint, for suddenly he bellowed her name.

Sasha jerked in surprise, pushing her shoulder hard into Mick's. "What?" she croaked, in a tone so low she was surprised he even heard her.

Evidently he did. "Get your skates on, sweet thing," he

yelled at the top of his voice, "and get your butt on out here."

"What am I, your pet dog?" she yelled back. "If you've got something to say to me, Lon Morrison, then come on over here and say it properly!" But she was already toeing off her street shoes and digging through her skate bag.

Seconds later, he stopped with a flourish in front of her. "C'mon, Saush," he commanded impatiently. "There's a song on this tape we gotta skate to. It's got our name written all over it."

"Yeah?" Bent over to tighten her laces, Sasha raised only her eyes. She cocked an eyebrow, appraising him with mock coolness. "You harboring the illusion that you can keep up with me?"

"In my sleep, babe."

"So what are we waitin' for?" Without so much as a glance in his direction, Sasha clambered over Mick's legs and joined Lon on the rink. Mick watched them skate to center ice. He watched them put their heads together, occasionally using hand movements, a sweep of an arm, or tiny steps to pantomime an action.

Connie flopped down next to him. "This should be good," she said with cheerful enthusiasm. Casting him a glance out of the corner of her eye, she pondered how he was taking this big reunion but was ultimately forced to shelve her curiosity. His face didn't offer any clues and she conceded defeat with a shrug. What Vinicor didn't want known clearly wasn't revealed.

Out on the ice, the huddle broke up. Lon's head lifted and he called out, "Hit it, Sara. And pump up the volume."

Drums, hot and heavy, pounded out of the speakers. Sasha launched off, skating fast as she swung her hips and ran her hands seductively up her body, outlining thighs, hips, skimming her waist, lightly cupping and lifting her breasts, before extending her arms out in front of her as she rocked her shoulders. The drums were joined by horns and then Don

Henley's hoarse tenor asking how bad do you want it, and Lon took off after her in heated pursuit. The song had a driving beat. It was rhythmic, sexy, and Morrison and Miller played it for all it was worth. Lon pulled Sasha up from a fast Death Spiral and hooked an arm around her waist, jerking her close. Their pelvises thrust and bumped, rocking in time to the music with exaggerated sexuality before she broke away once again to lead him on another chase. When he caught up with her, he wrapped his fingers around the back of her neck, crowded up close behind her, and they both bent and swayed in unison. Then she was gone again.

Mick leaned forward in his seat and watched. So this was the much-vaunted Morrison and Miller sex-on-ice act he kept hearing so much about. It was hot enough to generate steam, no question.

Not that he personally gave a damn.

It was a sentiment that probably would have played a lot better if he hadn't ambushed Sasha when he came across her on her own a short while later. Most of the onlookers had drifted away by that point and Mick was himself on the verge of leaving when he crossed paths with Sasha in one of the corridors that led off from the arena.

He had a hot, leaden feeling deep in his gut, and he didn't stop to think matters through when he came abreast of her; he simply reacted. Reaching out, he snagged her by the back of the neck and slammed his body up against hers. "God, you're makin' me crazy," he said hoarsely, staring down at her. Pivoting on one foot, he backed her into the wall. Then, before she had time to react one way or the other, he was kissing her to within an inch of her life.

Sasha barely knew what hit her. One minute Mick was approaching down the hallway, the next he was all over her. His body was heavy against hers, his mouth was hot and damp and demanding, and so fierce it drove her head into the hand cupping the back of it and then ground that hand in turn into the cement wall. Her sense of self stood up in outrage. Dammit, he couldn't treat her like this.

Yet she was simultaneously compelled by his very aggressiveness. It wasn't civilized and mannerly. It wasn't wooing with sophisticated settings and witty repartee. It was pure animal attraction, tinged with a sense of desperation, and the truth was she felt equally attracted, equally desperate. Most likely she should be fighting it tooth and nail. Instead, she felt a tightening deep between her thighs.

She had just begun to kiss him back when Mick suddenly ripped his mouth way. Breathing raggedly, he demanded, "Was Morrison one of the two?"

"Huh?" She stared up at him with dazed eyes. "Two what?"

Mick's head dropped and he licked into her mouth with a lascivious sweep, sucked hard on her full bottom lip, and then pulled away. "Don't toy with me, Sasha," he said in a harsh voice. "Of your two lovers . . . was Morrison one of them?"

She had been blinking lazily as she'd peered up at him, not putting any particular effort into collecting her scattered wits. But his abrupt interrogation was like being splashed in the face with a bucket of cold water, and her eyes narrowed. "I don't know why you're so damn interested in my pitiful sex life," she began, only to be immediately cut off.

"Has he kissed you the way I do?" Mick growled, his face close to hers. His hand reached up between them and spread over her breast. "Has he put his hands on these beautiful little tits?" Insinuating a hard thigh high up between hers, he watched her face and demanded, "Or spread your legs and buried—" His voice dwindled away at the sudden change that came over her expression.

It was as if a sheet of bullet-proof glass had suddenly dropped down between them, sheer but impenetrable. He couldn't pinpoint the exact moment but he knew he'd made a serious tactical error. She froze beneath his hands and raised a face to his that was as cool and shuttered, as calm as a nun's. There was a strength, a dignity, in the depths of her clear, gray eyes as they stared into his, and shame, scalding and complete, flooded him.

Jesus, what was the matter with him? His mother had taught him better than this. Mick retracted his thigh; his hand started to slide away from her breast and he took a step back. Good God, since when had he needed to resort to molestation to get what he wanted? "Sasha," he said with sincere contrition. "Jesus, I'm sorr—"

There was a roar of rage directly behind him and suddenly he was gripped in strong hands and whirled around. Two seconds later he slammed into the wall.

Instincts honed over the past eleven years erupted and Mick propelled himself away from the bulwark at his back. Crouched low and leading with his right shoulder, he plowed into the body of the man standing in front of him and drove Morrison across the hall into the opposite wall. The impact echoed in the narrow corridor.

Mick welcomed the chance to brawl; he wanted to use his fists, to pound on Sasha's precious Lonnie until he was nothing but a smear on the concrete floor. But it was a wish not destined to be granted, for he made the mistake of looking into Morrison's face at the same time he was cocking back his fist, and he saw that Lon wasn't even looking at him. He was staring at Sasha and there was something tortured in his eyes.

"Has it never stopped, then?" he demanded hoarsely. "Good God, Sasha, do you still have men pinning you down to cop a feel?"

The strength left Mick's arm and it fell to his side. He craned around to stare at Sasha also, not at all liking the connotations of what Morrison was asking her. And he heard the echo of Sasha's voice saying, *I'm actually not all that big on sex if you want to know the truth.*

"No, Lon, it's not like that," Sasha assured him earnestly.

"Really. I know what it must have looked like, but Mick is . . . different." Face flushed, she risked, before returning her attention back to Lon, a quick glance in Mick's direction. It was really hard for her to admit to any such thing right in front of him, especially in view of the way she'd been trying to hold him at arm's length, but she didn't want them fighting because of her. Besides, it was the truth, in its own way. Her relationship with Mick, such as it was, did differ from any other she'd ever had, even if, for just a second there, the feel of his hand on her breast had been like a time warp sending her reeling back into the hometown mode of defense.

Mick released Lon and stepped back, but the two men eyed each other like two tomcats facing off over a boundary line. "You do anything to hurt her," Lonnie promised in a low voice, "and I'll serve her up your balls for breakfast. On toast points, Vinicor—count on it."

Only professional survival instincts prevented Mick from retorting that *he* wasn't the one who'd asked her to play the whore to secure him a job. Which, if she had a goddam history of being molested, was an even shittier thing to have demanded of her than he'd originally believed.

But he bit down on his tongue. Sasha just might begin to wonder how the hell he knew she had vamped old Garland into giving Lon the job; and somehow he doubted that explaining he was tapping her phone and following her every move would earn him any points. Blowing his cover wasn't in the game plan.

But he was damned if he'd just walk away and leave this bastard with the last word. Thrusting his face aggressively close to Morrison's he said softly, his voice full of insinuation, "Hurting her is not in my plans. Wearing her out with my *lovin'* maybe . . ."

"You sonofabit . . ." Lon threw a punch, which pleased Mick no end. Before the swing was complete Mick had already ducked under it and grabbed Morrison by the shirt front, slamming him back against the wall.

"You heard the lady," he murmured in the same soft voice, one that was pitched too low to be heard by anyone other than the man whose face was mere inches from his own. "I'm *different*. You keep pressing it and I'll show you just how different I can be."

"Stop it, both of you!" Sasha was suddenly there trying to get between them. She grabbed one of Mick's wrists in both her hands and tugged. When his grip didn't budge, she sank her nails in. Hard. "You're causing a scene, damn you both, and I won't have it."

The combatants turned their heads to look at her. Mick then looked beyond her to the small group standing at the end of the corridor. It consisted of Connie, Brenda, Karen Corselli, and Jack the driver, and they were all watching with unabashed interest.

Son of a bitch. *Real professional behavior, here, Vinicor.* He looked back at Sasha and noted that her face was pale except for the two bright splotches of color that burned high across her cheekbones.

"Take your claws outta my wrist, darlin'," he said gently. As soon as she complied, he released Morrison and stepped back. Cocking an eyebrow at Sasha, he inquired, "So. You ready to go then?"

"In your dreams, Vinicor," Lon snapped. "She's riding back with me."

Sasha damn near exploded. Taking a giant step backward to distance herself from both men, breathing deep to keep from screaming, she said through clenched teeth, "If the two of you were going up in flames, I wouldn't cross the street to spit on either one of you. The next time you want to make a spectacle of yourselves, you damn well leave me out of it. I've had enough of this shit to last me a lifetime." She hated men, hated, hated, *hated* them.

Turning on her heel, she stalked down the corridor. Seeing Karen open her mouth as she drew near, she snapped, "You say one word about my language, Corselli, and I'll flatten you. C'mon, Connie," she commanded in a more moderate tone as she passed her friend, "let's go back to the hotel."

"Why do they *do* that kind of stuff?" she demanded on the short ride back to the inn. "I don't understand men at all; I swear I don't. I mean, what's it to Mick whom I've slept with? I don't ask him about his prior love life . . . and you can bet it's a whole lot more extensive than mine could ever hope to be." She noticed the driver eyeing the two of them in the rearview mirror, listening to their conversation with obvious interest, and dropped her voice. "And, jeez, Connie, where on earth would he get the idea that I've slept with Lon? That would be like having sex with my *brother.*"

"Ah, finally, a question I think I can answer." Connie gave her friend a tender smile. "Sasha, it was obvious from the way you talked about Lonnie at the Dome earlier that you know him very well. One might even be forgiven for assuming you know him quite intimately. Add to that the image the two of you project when you skate together, and it's really not such a surprising conclusion to jump to. And, hell, it's not like you've ever told Mick anything about your relationship with Lon. So he simply drew his own conclusions based on what he observed, and it gave him a case of the green-eyed monster."

"All right," Sasha conceded slowly. She was reluctant to relinquish her fury but ultimately forced herself to acknowledge the logic of Connie's words. "Yeah, okay, I suppose I can understand that. But what's Lon's excuse?"

Connie shrugged. "That I don't know. By the time I got there, Mick had him rammed up against the wall. Well, I guess he did that twice, didn't he? The first time, then. Perhaps if you reconstruct the events you'll have a better understanding of Lon's reasons. Just what started the whole thing, anyhow?"

"Oh," Sasha whispered, suddenly remembering. "Okay, so maybe Lonnie thought he had cause." She filled Connie in on the incident that started the brawl. "I kind of regressed for a minute there when Mick put his hand on my breast. But all that fighting and posturing . . . You know, when it comes right down to it, Con, I swear men get off on this kind of thing."

"Yeah, it's one of those male deals that women never quite comprehend. I sure as hell don't understand what they find so appealing about the prospect of getting their teeth kicked down their throats."

"Me either. While I think it started off being about me, in the end I think it was really about them. Some territorial muscle flexing thing." She sighed. "Oh, hell, let 'em duke it out if it makes them happy. For once in my life I'm going to use my brain and just steer clear of both of them."

If everyone else was vastly entertained and highly amused to see Lon Morrison and Mick Vinicor fighting over Sasha Miller, Karen Corselli was not. She was perturbed.

Seriously perturbed.

She was very unhappy with the way events had been unfolding of late. Mick had turned down her freely offered body . . . while actively pursuing little Miss Butter-Wouldn't-Melt-in-Her-Mouth's. *Why,* for heaven's sake, when he could have her? She didn't understand it; she truly didn't. And she and Lon had been "such good friends," as the saying went, once upon a time; yet he hadn't so much as looked her up or even said hello since his arrival yesterday. His only interest seemed to be in namby-pamby Sasha. Karen was getting heartily sick of the sound of that name.

Although she would perhaps admit that she'd been just the tiniest bit impressed when Sasha had warned her with such fierceness against issuing a lecture concerning her language . . . not that a reprimand wouldn't have been well deserved, for it had been most improper. Few people had ever deterred Karen from objecting to anything she felt strongly about—and heaven only knew her feelings regarding the inexcusable use of such language were strong and pure. Yet, in spite of herself, she *had* been deterred. For just the merest instant, she had caught a glimpse, an intimation, of such power in Miller's eyes . . .

Karen's backbone snapped erect. Well, she was certain it was an aberration; for if there was one thing she'd determined a long time ago, it was that little Miss Miller wouldn't know what to do with real power if it came right up and tapped her on the shoulder. Besides, even if it had been the genuine article it was a puny thing compared to her own.

Karen wouldn't countenance interference in her plans; she simply would not. And, oh, what plans she had . . . big plans. They included Mick Vinicor *and* Lon Morrison.

They did not include Sasha Miller.

Ultimately, Karen was convinced, everything would work out in exactly the fashion she intended. It invariably did; she was quite diligent about seeing to it. As always, of course, she would say her nightly prayers, with perhaps just a bit more fervor than usual.

But meanwhile Sasha Miller had better just stay the heck out of her way.

EIGHT

The final Tacoma show was performed in front of a near-sold-out crowd. The Dome was darkened except for professional lighting that highlighted the set designs and brought out the glittering colors in Sasha's costume. When her number changed from slow and languorous to fast and sexy, the lighting director switched to different colored lights, accenting the shift in moods.

Down on the ice, Sasha feared that she was in very deep trouble.

She'd felt the slight wobble in her blade on that last camel. God, why had she left her skate bag on the bus last night? She was always careful to check her equipment following a show, but she'd still been upset over that mess earlier in the day with Lon and Mick and she'd figured to hell with it—why schlep the damn thing up to her room just to turn around and schlep it back down again tomorrow? Nobody else was quite so compulsive with their gear, and when it came right down to it, *what* exactly could happen to the stuff in the baggage compartment of the bus?

Well, for starters, it felt suspiciously as though the blade on her left skate was loose. But what were the chances of that? They were screwed and glued on; they didn't simply come undone on their own. Oh, sure, screws did drop out with regularity and moisture rot did invariably set in, but she'd checked them just the other day and they'd been in good shape.

And even if the blade was merely clinging to her custom-made boot by a thread what could she do about it in the middle of her performance?

She skated flat out because that was the only way she knew how to skate. She couldn't stop to check for a defective blade halfway through her act, and she couldn't cheat the audience by tippy-toeing through her performance. She could merely deliver her best and hope to heaven she was wrong about the blade.

She wasn't.

It all blew up in her face when she touched down from the double axle. She didn't hear or see the blade snap free upon landing; all she knew was that one minute she was performing a truly fine landing from what had been a nice, high turn, and the next her leg had buckled underneath her and she was spinning and sliding across the ice to crash headfirst into the barrier that separated the rink from the spectator seats.

She registered the collectively indrawn gasps of the horrified crowd a millisecond before an immense pain exploded in her head. A gray mist swam inward from the outside edges of her eyes and her ears began to ring. Then everything went black.

When she came to, the walls of the backstage corridors were rushing past and her stomach nearly revolted. She narrowed her eyes in an attempt to focus, and swallowed hard against the nausea that persisted in rising up in her throat. Conquering it, she ultimately realized that she was being wheeled on a gurney down the hallway.

A door banged open and the bright lights overhead dimmed as she passed from indoors to out. A cold, misty breeze blew over her and she shuddered; the next instant she was being lifted into the back of an ambulance and a blanket was being tucked around her.

"I'm coming with her," she heard a male voice say and wondered vaguely who it was.

"Not in here you aren't," the attendant replied. "You'll have to follow in your own car." He turned to the other attendant. "Get the doors, Kenny."

The next thing Sasha saw was hands, in the periphery of her vision, reaching in and grasping the young man by his lapels. He was hauled past her, sputtering protests all the while, and out into the street.

"Listen," she heard a low, authoritative voice say through gritted teeth, "I'm the manager of *Follies on Ice* and I don't have a car. Now, you've got an unconscious woman in there and I'm stuck out here for God knows how long before I can get a taxi. What the fuck are you planning to do? Leave her lying around in some hospital corridor until someone from the show can get there with the information you know they're gonna require just to check her in? Use your head, kid."

The response was resigned, if a little sulky. "Get in."

Ah. Mick. Sasha turned her head toward the sound of the two men climbing into the back of the ambulance. The doors slammed and her stomach lurched again as the ambulance pulled out.

"Hey, you're awake." Mick squeezed into a space next to her and picked up her hand. "You're gonna be okay, Sasha," he assured her gently as he studied her eyes. The pupil of her right eye was pinpointed, while the left was dilated so wide its iris appeared to be black instead of gray. She focused on him with a fuzzy, trustful sort of intensity, and something about that look caused his stomach to flip-flop.

"I don't know how much you remember," he said to her in a soft voice, "but you lost a blade off your skate and you hit your head pretty hard. Looks like you've got a concussion but you're on your way to the hospital to be checked over. How you feelin'?"

"Pukey." She started to lift her hand up to touch her throbbing head, but Mick intercepted it. He brought it back down and stacked it on top of the one he already held, stroking both of hers between both of his. "Head hurts," she murmured fretfully.

"Yeah, I know it does, Saush. We're almost there, though, so just hold on; they're gonna get you fixed up." He turned to the attendant and said in a low, fierce undertone, "We *are* almost there, aren't we?"

"Five minutes."

They were at the hospital for hours. It was early morning by the time Mick carried her past the hotel's deserted front desk to the bank of elevators at the side of the lobby. Sasha had halfheartedly protested when he'd scooped her off the seat of the cab and into his arms, mumbling that she could walk perfectly well on her own. When he acted as though he'd suddenly gone deaf, however, she didn't bother to repeat herself. The truth was, although she felt better than she had a few hours ago, she still felt a long way from great.

As the elevator doors swooshed shut, enclosing them in the small, mirrored area, Mick looked down at her. The top of her head lolled against the bottom of his throat, she was limp in his arms, and in spite of her assertion that she was feeling better, she sure as hell didn't look it. "I don't imagine you've got your room key secreted anywhere in that little costume, do you?" he inquired without a great deal of hope. He couldn't see much of it, swallowed up as she was in his jacket, but he was pretty sure it didn't boast any hidden pockets.

Sasha didn't bother to open her eyes. "Huh uh." Then tightening her left-handed grip on her skates—which had still been on her feet when they'd arrived at the ER—she tried to pretend, for about two seconds, to more alertness than she actually possessed. She pried her eyelids open and blinked up at him.

"Z'in my bag at the Dome," she said more comprehensively and then yawned. Her eyes, feeling weighted, slid closed again. "Sure hope Connie grabbed it," she tacked on in slurred tones. Mick's chest and arms were warm, the sway when he walked and the elevator's movement as it rose to her floor was soothing, and the lure of slumber was more than she could resist. She could feel its effects wrapping her up like a down comforter.

"Sasha." It felt as if no more than five seconds had passed when she found herself being cautiously shaken awake. "Sasha, can you hear me?"

She hunched her shoulder out from under the hand that was gently rocking it. "Go 'way."

It came right back again, warm and persistent. "Come on, baby, wake up."

"Miiiick, leave me alone. I'm tired."

"I know you are, darlin'." He pulled her up into a sitting position, smiling wryly when her head promptly flopped forward. He hooked a finger beneath her chin and tipped it up. "But you've got a concussion," he informed her, "and the doctor said you need to be awakened once an hour."

"Y'ask me, the doctor's full of . . ."

"Shh, shh, shh." There was laughter in his voice and Sasha pried an eye open. "Having an interrupted night's sleep beats the hell out of slipping into a coma," he assured her. When he saw that she appeared to be a little more fully awake, he leaned back at arm's length, his hands still firmly gripping her shoulders, and looked her over. "How about getting a little more comfortable, now that you're awake? You want to change out of that costume into something less restrictive?"

Sasha looked down at herself, surprised to discover that she was still in her red spangled and beaded "Playing with Fire" costume. Cut low between her breasts and high on her hips, it was a wonder she hadn't frozen to death. "Oh, my gosh, Mick, my jacket!" At the sudden recollection that everything had been left behind in the Tacoma Dome and that they were leaving for Seattle tomorrow, panic began to surface.

"It's okay." Mick didn't have a clue what made her jacket so special to her, but he was nevertheless quick to reassure.

"I called Connie when we got back to let her know how you were doing, and she said to tell you that she's got all your things in her room."

"Oh. Good." She gave him a sleepy smile. "I would like to change," she decided. "Grab my blue nightie, will you? It's in the second drawer on the right."

He was gone and back in seconds. He handed her a big, soft T-shirt. It was maroon. Sasha looked down at it in puzzlement as he cupped a palm under her elbow and helped her to her feet. "What's this?" Eyes raising, she slowly inspected her surroundings. "Where are we? This isn't my room."

"No, it's mine."

"Oh. Okay." Holding her head very carefully she shuffled into the bathroom and closed the door behind her.

When she came out, Mick threw back the covers and helped her into bed. "Scoot over," he ordered. She did as he said and he snapped off the light, shucked out of his jeans and shirt and climbed in beside her.

"Hey." Sasha started to raise up on one elbow but her head pounded too viciously. She subsided onto her hip, resting her head on her upper arm. "Whata you think you're doing?"

"Getting an hour's sleep," he replied.

"Not here you're not." When he played deaf for the second time that night, she reached out her free hand and gave him an indignant poke. "Vinicor!"

He rolled onto his back. "For Christ sake, Sasha," he said irritably. "What do you think I am, an animal? This might come as a shock to you, Miller, but it really isn't necessary that a woman's head be bashed in before I get her into my bed."

"But it probably helps," she shot back without thinking.

Mick laughed. "Oh, if you weren't so hurt, you'd pay for that," he said. Then he rolled over again, presenting her with his back.

He woke her continually the rest of the night, and in the process grew heartily sick himself of the sound of the alarm going off every hour on the hour. When it went off for the last time at nine in the morning he groaned and pulled the pillow over his head. Oh, God, not again. Five minutes. That's all he asked . . . just five more minutes. Between the covers and Sasha's warm little backside curved into his lap, it was so nice and cozy in here, and he didn't want to move.

Sasha's . . . ? Oh, shit. Slowly he pulled the pillow off his head. He twisted from the waist and slammed his hand down on the alarm button, shutting off the irritating noise. Then shoving up on one elbow, he turned back.

They had both gravitated toward the middle of the bed in search of the most convenient heat source, which had turned out to be each other. He was curved, spoon fashion around her back from the waist down, and now that he was more alert he had a vague recollection of being plastered to her from the waist up as well, his arm wrapped around her middle, his face buried in her hair, before the alarm had sent him groping for his pillow. The T-shirt she wore had worked its way up around her hips and his morning erection was snugged firmly between her sweet little cheeks, only the thin cotton of his jockey shorts separating them.

I'm not an animal, Sasha. His brain played back his words for him. But he could be. Oh, God, he so easily could be.

He eased his hips away. Rolling out of bed, he walked with stiff discomfort to the bathroom. He was back out in seven minutes, shaved and showered.

Dropping the towel to the floor, he stepped into clean underwear, pulled on his jeans, and jerked a white dress shirt from the closet, slipping it on and buttoning it up. He tucked, zipped, and rolled the shirt's sleeves up his forearms, then crossed back to the bed.

"Sasha." He squatted down next to the bed and briskly reached out to awaken her. "Saush, come on. Time to get up."

* * *

Sasha leaned her cheek against the cool glass of the bus window and watched the scenery go by. Connie sat quietly beside her, thumbing through a magazine. Normally it was a reasonably quick ride from Tacoma to Seattle but traffic was very heavy today. There was some sort of multicar pileup just this side of a place called Federal Way, causing them to creep along and turning a forty-five minute drive into something much longer.

Sasha tended to doze off at the drop of a hat, and Connie would poke her awake if she appeared to be sleeping too deeply. During moments such as this between doze and poke, her thoughts, like rats in a maze, were inclined to dash to and fro without discernible results.

She was dealing with some major perplexities and her thought processes felt as mushy as her head. In part, the dead-end walls that she kept mentally running up against had to do with that perpetually confusing man/woman issue. Now there was a puzzle she had yet to figure out. However, the majority of her confusion stemmed from her accident, and trying to make sense of *that* was like hitting the wall going ninety.

If there was any way to avoid it, in fact, she'd opt in a heartbeat not to think about it at all today. She'd much prefer to put off any speculation concerning what had put her in this condition until she felt a hundred percent up to snuff again, for her thoughts left her feeling uneasy and alone. Made her feel almost isolated. But it was not an easy matter to ignore. Because it shouldn't have happened.

She had assumed, last night, that she'd had a moisture rot problem in the sole of her boot. Serious skaters had their boots custom made from individual forms of their feet and the blades were glued and screwed on, as opposed to the riveted blades on skates that were sold off the rack to beginners in sporting goods shops. Eventually the waterproofing wore off, however, and moisture got into the plates, dissolving the glue. Screws dropped out with great regularity, which could be a real hazard on the ice. The sole around the blade plates softened from the constant bombardment of ice spraying up beneath it and eventually gave way. So when she'd felt the wobble, she'd thought, Oh God, Harlick sure doesn't make as good a boot as they used to. But this morning, when she'd looked at her skate . . .

She'd had to make her silent apologies to Harlick, for the soles were in perfectly good condition. Yet every damn screw had come out at the same time.

And that simply wasn't possible. There were six screws holding the blade to the toe and four securing it to the heel. Now, maybe it was conceivable that a few could have loosened and perhaps, if you stretched credibility to the limit, even simultaneously on both heel and toe. But all of them at once out of an undamaged piece of leather?

Yet . . . what was the alternative here? That it had been done deliberately? That someone had just happened to know that her bag had been left in the bus on that particular night and had snuck into it to loosen the screws on her skate? Good God, talk about stretching credibility—her head must have been banged up even worse than she'd thought.

Who would have any reason to hurt her? And *why,* for God's sake? Even supposing she had some heretofore unknown enemy lurking in the shadows just dying to dump her on her ass, what kind of wussy method was that to harm someone? It was too uncertain. She might have checked the blades before her performance, and truly it was just bad luck that her double axle had been performed on the periphery of the rink. It could just as well have been executed in the middle of the rink where the worst that would have happened to her would have been to spin around the ice on her face in front of thousands. Embarrassing, sure. But hardly the stuff of a mad assassin.

And yet the uneasiness persisted.

It was a relief to finally pull up to the hotel that afternoon. Sometimes the lack of privacy that was so much a part of this life got to her. Usually she thrived on it, but her defenses were down today and she just wanted to get into a room where it was quiet and calm and she wasn't surrounded by constant chatter. She slapped on her softly structured hat, yanked it down to her brows, and climbed to her feet.

Mick looked up from his clipboard when Sasha stopped in front of him. With a gesture lacking her usual animation she held out her hand for her room key. He ran a critical eye over her face as he handed it to her.

Despite the jaunty little cloth hat she wore, with its cheerfully feminine garden print and its big silk flower pinning the floppy brim back to the crown, she looked wan. Her hair exploding out from under the hat's restraint was just as lustrous as always, but her cheeks, normally so rosy in her warm, golden-skinned face, were pale, her complexion sallow.

It wasn't his place to be bugged by it.

"You have that release?" he inquired crisply as he passed her the room key and marked it off on his master list.

"Yes," she replied coolly. She patted a couple pockets and then shrugged, too lethargic to search any further. "I'll bring it to you in the morning."

"See that you do, Miller. Without it, you don't get back on the ice."

"So you said this morning." Sasha turned away before he could see the tears that rose to her eyes. She never cried. Hardly ever. Her armor was just a little thin this afternoon; that was all. She'd be back in fighting trim by tomorrow.

But she would never, not until the day she died, understand the rules in this damned man/woman game.

Now granted, her brains were pretty scrambled last night. But she could have sworn that Mick hadn't begrudged taking care of her. No one had asked him to, after all; he'd just sort of taken it upon himself to take charge. And he'd been patient and gentle and, truly, for a man of his temperament, pretty downright sweet actually.

This morning though . . . Well it wasn't as if he'd suddenly turned into a snapping, snarling adversary or anything. In a way she would have understood surly, because taking care of someone who's ill is not exactly a laugh a minute and he'd probably gotten even less sleep than she had. But it hadn't been like that. There'd simply been this . . . wall. This lethally polite, impenetrable wall.

She'd never seen him distant like that, and it was amazing how authoritative a little aloofness could make a man appear. She'd gotten the strongest impression he wanted her off his hands, as if she were a stranger he'd accidentally knocked down in a train station and now all he wanted to do was to pick her up, brush her off, and send her on her way. He'd checked her eyes for pupil reactions with cool, impersonal professionalism, declared the worst of the concussion over, and as soon as was decently possible had passed her off to Connie with strict instructions that she be taken back to the hospital to have her neuro signs checked.

When she'd tried to demure, feeling, if not one hundred percent better, then at least worlds improved from the night before, he'd looked at her without an iota of the previous night's gentleness and demanded, "You want to skate again, Miller?"

"Y-yes, of course," she'd stammered, feeling unaccountably betrayed by his abrupt coldness.

"Well, you're not going to do so without a doctor's release."

"Yes, sir," she'd snapped out smartly in response, drawing herself up, damned if she'd allow him to see that it mattered to her how he acted. She'd stood there feeling vulnerable and exposed in his oversized T-shirt; then, with a dignity she'd taught herself years ago and pretending she wasn't buck naked underneath a piece of cloth that suddenly felt insufficient, she'd gone quietly around the room gathering her scattered belongings. She'd turned to Connie, who had been standing silently, looking from her face to Mick's. "Do you have my room key?"

"Yeah." She'd produced it and handed it over to Sasha, who had turned once again to Mick.

"Thank you for your care last night," she'd said quietly. "I appreciate it." She'd turned and walked out of his room without a backward glance.

She didn't glance back at him now as she walked to the elevator. But Mick watched her. His jaw tightened as he saw Morrison run to catch up with her, solicitously helping her aboard the car and bending down to murmur something in her ear. He watched until the doors closed behind her . . . and that son of a bitch Morrison. Then he turned back to the next person in line.

Lon had intended to stay away from Karen. It was a promise he'd made to himself the minute he'd found out that she, too, was skating for *Follies on Ice*. And what a little bombshell that discovery had been.

The skating world was a small one—he'd known that—but this almost bordered on the ridiculous. Good God, small was one thing . . . but who the hell would have expected it to shrink to these proportions?

Well, shrunk it had and it didn't matter whether he was prepared for it or not. The basic fact couldn't be changed: he and Karen Corselli were skating for the same company. So, looking at it realistically, avoiding her entirely was probably out of the question. The next best thing, he had determined once he got past the shock, was to simply steer clear of her.

No ifs, ands, or buts. He wasn't about to put himself in the way of temptation, and that was the beginning and end of the matter. Jesus, especially not that temptation. Karen Corselli was one lesson he'd learned the hard way. He was keeping his distance.

But he had forgotten the strength of her will when there was something she wanted. At the moment, apparently, that something was him. And she was certainly one enticing woman. He was as fascinated now by the contrasts in her personality as he had been several years ago.

Sasha had never known about his association with Karen, and Lon would just as soon keep it that way. She had never thought to ask who had turned him on in the first place to the fast money to be made in drug trafficking, and since he'd actually been caught because of his own stupidity, he'd been careful not to bring Karen into it.

The woman had a real flair for intrigue; she loved the sneaking around and meeting on the sly; she got off on presenting one image to the public while displaying something entirely different in private. Way back when, her two different sides had drawn him in. They continued to tug at something inside of him today.

He found it amazing that her public persona wasn't some hypocritical display put on simply to fool the troops. She had a sincere abhorrence of hearing anything that smacked of taking the Lord's name taken in vain, and her fight to combat smutty language wherever she encountered it was a genuinely held conviction, one that she lived by. You wouldn't hear obscenities passing Karen Corselli's lips in public or in private.

But, ah God, the other uses that woman would willingly put those lips to behind closed doors was enough to raise the dead.

He looked down on them now, unpainted and innocent looking, engaged in an act that was anything but innocent. His hands clenched in her hair, his eyes closed, and his head fell back as he groaned. Call him weak; call him a fool. He'd known how good it would be and in the end just hadn't been able to stay away.

But there always seemed to be some kind of payment required when it came to sex with Karen, a hidden cost, which when the heat and need were upon him he tended to forget about. Afterwards, however, lying depleted in sweet postcoital bliss with Karen's head nestled on his shoulder and her fingers strolling lazily up and down his chest and stomach, he was forcibly reminded of it.

"That was nice," she murmured. She twirled a curl of chest hair around her finger. "Turn on the night-light, will you? It's getting dark."

He complied, amused as always by her irrational fear of the dark when she was so fearless in every other way. But he knew better than to comment. Karen had no sense of humor whatsoever when it came to that particular little frailty; she refused to speak of its origins, and he had wisely learned to keep his amusement to himself.

They lay quietly for several moments. Then she inquired casually, "How are you set for money, Lon?"

He shrugged. "It's tight, but I'll get by until payday."

"How would you like to earn a nice little nest egg?"

Lon raised his head up and tucked his chin into his neck to stare down at her. "Doing what?" he asked flatly.

"Nothing you haven't done before, doll." She smiled up at him, her hand stealing down to stroke him to hardness once again.

"Uh-uh, no way." He reached down and removed her hand, determined that this time at least she wouldn't use that particular method to make him do what she wanted. "Where'd you get scag to sell, anyway?" he demanded. "I thought you got out of the game when they sent me up."

"Um-hmm."

He jerked up on one elbow, dumping her off his chest and onto the mattress. "Jesus, Karen—"

"Don't take the Lord's—"

"Yeah, yeah, sorry. You did give Quintero the seventeen kilos I gave you to give him back, right?"

"Ummm."

"Right?"

"More or less."

"More or less?" He felt like shaking her. "What the hell does that *mean,* more or less?"

"It means I cut 'em with a little sugar and held a teensy bit back, kind of in reserve for a rainy day." She'd done it for the power of knowing she could do it . . . and get away with it.

"Karen." He stared down at her. "How much is a teensy bit?"

She shrugged coolly. "About a quarter."

"You held back *four and a quarter kilos?"*

"Uh-huh."

"Jeez." Lon whistled through his teeth. "You've got nerves of steel, girl; I gotta hand you that." Then he frowned. "But what about when you contacted the dealers in all the cities? It had to have gotten back to Quintero."

"Do I look stupid, Lon? I didn't contact his dealers."

"So who's pushing the product?"

"Me . . . when the mood strikes me. And now that you're here, you."

"No. Not me. If that's your plan, you can just get it out of your head right now."

"Yes you. I want you to."

"Too bad, baby, because I'm not getting back into that shit."

"Lon," she warned sternly, but he overrode her interruption.

"Don't tell me not to use that language, Karen, because sometimes it's the only thing that fits. I just spent five years of my life in a correctional institute—*five years,* babycakes, and I ain't never going back. Besides, I promised Sasha . . ."

Too late he swallowed the rest. Ah, damn it to hell.

He really wished he hadn't brought her name into this.

NINE

Even back in their amateur circuit days, Karen had displayed a curiosity regarding Sasha's sexual proclivities that Lon had found difficult to comprehend. She was messing around with *him* for God's sake, so why all the interest in Saush's sex life? What was it to Karen who Sasha did or didn't sleep with?

The way she used to hound him, though—Karen simply could not resist digging up the dirt. She wanted to know every little detail about every single person she came into contact with. What possible use that information was to her once she'd gotten her hot little hands on it was anybody's guess, but the minute she decided she needed something she was like a damn pit bull with its teeth sunk in and its jaws locked tight, shaking, shaking, shaking until it was hers.

Lon had caved in on a number of her demands, mostly because it was easier than arguing about a bunch of stuff not worth fighting over. But he'd never caved when it came to Sasha's personal business. Sasha was his best friend; he didn't sell her secrets for even the best blow job in the world.

Which surely most folks would agree was all very noble and heartwarming of him. He still wished to hell he hadn't brought Saush's name up now.

Karen had grown very still, but she slowly pushed herself up first onto one elbow, and then to a sitting position in the middle of the bed. Unmindful of her nudity, she swept her blond hair out of her eyes. "What did you promise Sasha?"

Shit. Well, there was no dancing around it now. Lon looked her dead in the eye. "I promised her I'd stay away from the drug scene and most particularly that I wouldn't sell again."

The look Karen gave him was incredulous. "Why on earth would you do that?"

He wasn't about to attempt an explanation of those tempestuous small-town teenage years to Karen Corselli. Mind racing, he snatched a partial truth out of the air. "Because she put her neck on the chopping block getting them to hire me."

"Yes, Lon, who exactly *did* she sleep with to secure you this job?"

"Maybe she prayed for it, Karen," he drawled, knowing that would bug her. She considered praying her forte, arrogantly assuming that because not everyone made as big a production out of their faith as she did they must therefore somehow be lacking in it. Reaching for his pants, he rolled to his feet and climbed into them.

Karen watched in frustration. She was losing control here and she didn't like it. Moreover, she absolutely refused to tolerate a loss of power for a moment longer than she had to. Men did *not* walk away until she was darn good and ready to let them go.

Yet from the very beginning, Lon had been different. Some of the time she had been able to dominate him with the same ease as other men. But there were other times when he was as recalcitrant as a Missouri mule. Unlike the majority of the men she was accustomed to dealing with, men whom for the most part she could master simply by displaying her displeasure or withholding her sexual favors, Lon thrived on adversarial situations. He enjoyed arguing and putting her back up and would do so whenever the mood struck him, just for the sheer thrill of it.

And from the beginning she'd let him get away with it because there was something about his attitude that she found extremely . . . stimulating. She watched now in silent mental and sexual frustration as, without so much as a further glance in her direction, Lon slid into his shirt, gathered up his socks and shoes, and sat down on the side of the bed to put them on.

She squeezed her thighs together. How dare he deny her wishes and then simply ignore her this way? Who did he think he was? Needing a scapegoat and disregarding Lon's active penchant for doing the opposite of anything he was commanded to do, she petulantly decided she knew precisely where to lay the blame for this most recent little display of independence.

Squarely on Sasha Miller's doorstep.

For as long as she'd known Lon, he'd been protecting Sasha Miller's interests, and frankly Karen was tired of it. Sasha had entirely too much influence over him, and *that* was a source of power Karen would not countenance. Between her interference in Lon's decisions and this business with Mick Vinicor, she was really beginning to get on Karen's nerves.

Something would have to be done about her and that was a fact.

Something a bit more conclusive than that pansy little accident on the ice the other day.

Sasha thought that by knocking on Mick's hotel room door, she was probably asking for trouble. As a last resort, however, having exhausted every other resource and unable to locate him anywhere else, she didn't see what other option she had. There were only three hours until tonight's performance and he'd made it painfully clear that she wouldn't be part of the program without a clearance from her doctor. Then—and she perceived this to be an act of deliberate malice on his part—having laid down the law, did he make himself readily accessible? Oh, no. He was nowhere to be found when she tried to hand the damn thing over to him.

Her knock went unanswered. *Damn,* not here either, apparently. Slamming her palm against the door panel in frustration, she turned away and was two steps down the hall when the door suddenly opened behind her. Sasha turned back.

Her heartbeat threw in an extra little thump and then picked up speed as she stood there looking at him. It was obvious she had interrupted his shaving.

Barefoot, wearing a white T-shirt tucked into olive-drab Dockers, he was using the towel draped around his neck to wipe creamy foam off his throat, and his cheeks and jaw were shiny in that way that only freshly shaved skin can be. His hair was slicked straight back from his forehead, still damp enough to show the track marks of his comb.

Sasha thrust the doctor's okay at him. "Here." Okay, so she sounded a little surly. But damned if she was going to stand around and pump up his ego by admiring his manly charms.

Mick took in her high color, the temper sparking in her gray eyes. Without bothering to reach for it, he glanced down at the paper she was all but jabbing into his chest. His eyes lifted once again to look into hers. "What's this?"

"What do you think it is, Vinicor?" She waved the paper under his nose this time. "It's my medical clearance."

"Uh-huh. Let's see that." He took his time looking it over before he finally returned his attention to her. "So you really feel okay?"

"Right as rain, bud."

"No lingering effects? No light-headedness, no weakness?"

"No." Without thinking she cocked an arm and flexed a biceps at him. "Strong as an ox."

"Good." He reached out, curled his fingers around the proffered muscle, trapped his other hand around the back of her neck and pulled her into his room. Slamming the door with a raised knee, he crowded her up against it. "Because I've waited long enough for this."

Sasha was just opening her mouth to ask him what the *hell* he thought he was doing when his hands plunged into her hair and his mouth came down on hers. It was akin to being struck by lightning, something she should have remembered from the other times he'd kissed her.

In a fuzzy, faraway corner of her mind was a thought knocking to be heard. She shouldn't allow him to get away with this. She was going to regret this lamentable lack of willpower and she really ought to put a stop to it. Reasons to do just that, *good* reasons, at the forefront of which was a nebulous feminist rhetoric that tried to insist he couldn't just grab her and kiss her whenever he damn well pleased, got jumbled together in her brain. She couldn't seem to formulate one complete, coherent thought.

Which was probably just as well since her senses refused to get caught up in anything that might cause her to call a halt to this anyway. Not when it felt so good. Not when those self-same senses were being overwhelmed with all these hot urges.

God, his mouth. It . . . felt . . . so . . . *good.* His lips were strong and his tongue was aggressive, and Sasha raised up on her toes to get more of both, sliding her hands up to frame his cheeks. She reveled in the feel of his flesh, so warm and smooth beneath her fingertips.

Mick made a noise deep in his throat and widened his mouth. Then he dragged it closed, sucking at her lips, licking at all the sleek, hidden hollows. It wasn't until quite a bit later that he finally raised his head to look down at her.

Sasha was slower to open her eyes and Mick observed her passion-induced lethargy with satisfaction. Her skin was flushed and her eyes were heavy-lidded and dark as pewter when she finally dragged them open. Her hands still clung to his cheeks as she stared up at him in a daze.

"Damn, you're pretty," he said in a rough voice and bent his head to hers once more. By the time he raised it again she was making little sounds in her throat and moving against him with unthinking sexuality.

Mick picked her up and carried her to the bed. He laid her down, ripped his shirt off over his head and came down on the mattress next to her. Propped up on one elbow he looked down at her; then unable to stay away from her mouth, he bent his head and kissed her again. Kissing him back with equal fervor, Sasha's arms reached up to wind around his neck, and Mick smoothed his free hand up her ribs to palm a small breast.

A strangled moan exploded out of her throat. Arms still clinging to his neck, Sasha ripped her mouth out from under Mick's and arched into the hand molding her breast. Eyes closed, head thrown back and rolling restively from side to side, she panted for breath through parted lips. Mick watched her as his forefinger and thumb came together on her nipple, gently squeezing it, tugging it to its full distention beneath the double layers of cloth that comprised her T-shirt and bra.

"Mick?" Her eyes flew open but lacked focus as she stared up at him; her fingernails anchored themselves in the bare skin of his shoulders. Against the mattress her hips executed a small bump and grind. Mick stilled.

Except for the thumb and finger that held her nipple. "Damn," he muttered, lavishing it with more of the same attention just to see more of her reaction. "Ah, *damn,* Sasha." Then he came out of his paralysis and burst into action. One-handedly, he wrestled her shirt out from under her waistband and up over her breasts until it was bunched around her chest. Thanking God her bra had a front closure, he finessed open the hook between her breasts and peeled back the sheer cups of her bra. He looked down at her. "Oh, God. That's beautiful."

Sweet as peaches, was his first thought. That's what her breasts reminded him of. They were small, golden, round. And ripe; God they looked so ripe. He could visualize biting into them, could almost taste the juice that would explode against his palate, slide down his throat. Lying on her back the fullness was flattened slightly, but her nipples were blush-pink, long as the tip of his little finger, and poking arrogantly skyward.

He brought one hand up to gently stroke the delicate curvature. Then he cupped the underside of her breast with hard-skinned fingers, pushed it up, and lowered his head to lap one of those uppity nipples into his mouth. Lips closing around it, tongue applying suction under it, he drew strongly.

Sasha's vaginal muscles pulled tight. "OhGodohGodohGodohGod," she crooned frantically. "Mick?" Her hips writhed and she thrust her breast more fully into his face, aching for, dying for . . . she didn't know what.

Mick did. Her responsiveness was so damn hot, he could feel his restraint slipping. God, he wanted to chew these sweet little morsels right off her breasts, wanted to bury his face between her legs and slather and slobber and to generally go at her like a damn animal. He pulled back, on the edge of control, his breath sawing at his lungs like a long-distance runner's.

When his touch left her and didn't come back, Sasha opened her eyes. Mick was braced over her on both hands, head hanging, only her arms around his neck connecting the two of them. "What?" she whispered and the confusion in her voice caused him to bring his head up to stare down at her. Then a stricken expression crossed her face. "Oh, my God, I'm not doing anything for you. I'm sorry; I should be reciprocating, shouldn't I?" She started to disentangle her arms from around his neck.

But Mick expelled an ironic little snort of laughter and reached a hand up to still her movement. Sliding it up the smooth skin of her arm to cup his hard palm around her elbow, he forced her to tighten her grip around his neck again and then stroked his cheek against her upper arm. "No," he said and was surprised at how rusty his voice sounded. Clearing his throat, he reiterated more firmly, "No." When she simply stared at him as if trying to gauge whether he was just being polite, his mouth twisted into a wry smile and he said honestly, "That won't be necessary, trust me."

"Oh, but—"

His patience slipped a notch. "Sasha, I'm hotter 'n a pistol; I really don't think reciprocation's such a good idea." He watched it sink in and then added more temperately, "Seems I've got a hair trigger where you're concerned, so believe me when I tell ya: you touch me and it's gonna be all over but the shouting." His hand left the soft tangle of arms around his neck and stroked down her side, fingers teasing at the side of her breast. Unconsciously, Sasha turned into his touch.

"I'm afraid I'm not very good at this," she admitted and to Mick's amazement he could see that she really believed it.

"Ah, now that's where you're wrong, darlin'," he disagreed. "I'd say you were made for this." He kissed her hard, then raised his head up to grin down at her. "But I'd be happy to walk you through it."

His expression was so full of himself that Sasha couldn't help but grin back. "Yeah? You'd do that for me?" She laughed that sexy laugh of hers and untangled her arms from around his neck. Extending them as far down his back as they'd reach, she scratched her way back up to his shoulders, then stroked her hands around from there to the swells of his chest. She rubbed her palms back and forth, back and forth, across small pebbled nipples and smooth, rounded muscles. "That's mighty big of you."

Mick shivered. "Trust me, honey, you don't know the half of it." Grabbing her hands, he pressed them to the mattress on either side of her head. Then sitting back on his heels, he reached for her shirt and eased it over her head. He tossed it aside. After staring at her breasts for several moments, he suddenly hunched over and caught one protruding nipple between his teeth. He tugged at it, sucked it hard for an instant, then let it go with an audible pop. Then he kneed her legs apart and bent forward to brush his chest against her bared breasts. His mouth fastened to the side of her throat at the same moment his pelvis suddenly lowered to surge fully between her legs.

Sasha's breath sucked in sharply and she arched her back, thrusting her breasts more solidly against him. She drew her knees back to experience more of the erection that strained between them. "Oh, God, that *is* mighty big of you," she tried to joke as her head tilted involuntarily to the side to allow his lips more freedom.

Neither of them was in the mood for laughing, however—the time for playfulness had passed. Even through the layers of clothing separating them, sensations were taking over and they moved against each other in an ageless, urgent rhythm. Her hands slid off his pectorals, under his arms, and down his bare back to the crisp cotton that covered his muscular buttocks. She clutched the rounded muscles there and pulled him even tighter against her.

"Ah! That's it." Mick moved his hips several times before he started easing back. "I want you naked. Now."

She was reaching between them to scramble out of her pants even before he finished speaking. Mick vaulted off the bed, kicked out of his Dockers and Calvin Klein's and pulled the drawer open in the night stand next to the bed. He fished a box of condoms out from its nesting place between the Gideon's Bible and a pair of satin leopard skin panties. With a glance over his shoulder he slid the panties under the Bible and closed the drawer. Flipping open the cardboard top he grabbed a condom out and tore its wrapping open with his teeth.

When he'd finished putting it on, he looked up to find Sasha watching him with big eyes. She was kneeling in the middle of the bed, her arms crossed at the wrist and braced against her upper thighs. Her pose might have been designed to preserve her modesty, but her eyes were anything but chaste or shy. They stared with unblinking, outright fascination at his erect penis.

He dove across the mattress and tumbled her onto her back. "You like what you see?"

She looked up at him, all flushed cheeks, tumbled dark hair, and moist, red lips. "Yes."

He reached for her right hand and brought it down between their bodies, holding it by the wrist a fraction of an inch from where he strained between them. "Wanna get your hands on it?"

Excitement burned in her eyes. *"Yes."*

He let go of her wrist and her fingers wrapped around him, gripping him tightly. She squeezed him through her fist, first to the root, then to the tip.

"Ahh!" Mick's breath exploded from his lungs. His fingers raced down her belly to the soft thatch of hair between her legs. Separating slippery folds of flesh, they headed like heat-seeking missiles directly to her clitoris, where they feathered gently back and forth. She whined softly and opened her thighs.

"Oh yeah, you like that." His throat was so constricted it was an effort to squeeze out the words. Still, he demanded, "What else do you like? Tell me what you want."

"You," she said without hesitation. "Inside me." Her hips twisted in his direction and she pulled on his erection, trying to bring them closer together. "Oh, Mick, please, I want you inside me!"

He grabbed one of the pillows and punched it down, sliding it beneath her hips. Bracing himself over her, he reached down to guide himself into her.

She was tight, very tight, and sucking in a deep breath he entered her carefully, going two steps forward and one step back, sliding forward a couple inches and pulling back one, then sliding forward a couple more.

"Oh please, oh please," Sasha began to chant in a whispery voice, concentrating on the thunderous pleasure that was building deep between her legs. "Oh, Mick, please . . ."

"Look at me." He planted his hands on the mattress and stared down at her, hips plunging forward, easing back, in shallow strokes. "Open your eyes, Sasha, and look at me." He wanted to be damn sure she knew it was him and not that sonofabitch Morrison.

She did as he commanded. He looked so powerful looming over her, with those wide shoulders, the strapping chest and tightly muscled stomach. His eyes were bluer than usual and they blazed down at her fiercely. "Wrap your legs around my waist and your arms around me anywhere you want," he said. "I want you to hold me."

She complied, and only then did he complete the penetration, sinking into her until he could go no further. Air hissed through his teeth, and they gleamed whitely in the gathering gloom as his lips curled away from them in a grimace of pure pleasure.

Sasha was caught unprepared for the sudden violence of the orgasm that overtook her the moment he was entirely inside her. Eyes clinging to his, her nails dug into his flesh and raked slowly down his back. "Oh, Mick . . ." She sucked in a sharp breath. "Oh, pleeease . . ." Hard, undulating contractions imploded around that foreign rigidity stretching up inside her, and her eyes locked on his in blind wonder. Except for a long, barely audible shuddering whimper, she rode the sensations silently, concentrating on how they felt and the way they seemed to go on.

And on.

And on.

"Christ." Mick watched her face, felt her nails scoring his back, her inner muscles clamping down and squeezing him as she came, and he gritted his teeth so hard he could feel the tension in his temples. He had to force himself to continue the gentle in and out motion. She sure as hell didn't require a lot of movement on his part and he feared if he suddenly began slamming into her like a renegade pile driver—which, oh God, was sure his inclination—he'd bring an end to her orgasm.

He couldn't prevent his hips from picking up a little speed though; he simply could not. Sasha didn't seem to mind. Still obeying his edict to look at him, her gaze continued to cling to his. Her mouth rounded and she breathed an ecstatic, "Oh, oh, oh, oh." Her nails dug deeper; those interior muscles squeezed harder, and Mick went over the edge.

He grabbed her wrists and slammed them onto the mattress above her head. Staring down at her while his hips went berserk, he saw the liquid eyes, the red, parted lips, the cloud of black hair corkscrewing all over the bedspread. Saw the golden upthrust breasts and long, pink nipples. "Mine," he growled, thrusting, pounding. "You're *mine* now."

Then he groaned, loud and long, and ejaculated in scalding pulsations, buttocks clenched tight to keep him deep, thighs spread wide.

And collapsed atop her several moments later, feeling boneless and satiated . . . and very, very uneasy.

Je-sus, where had all that emotion between them sprung up from? He'd like to tell himself it was no big deal, to convince himself that, hell, he'd been hot for plenty of women in his lifetime. But the truth was he had *never* reacted to anyone quite like this before.

And what the hell was all that "you're mine" bullshit? Mick became aware of Sasha's breath wheezing in and out of her lungs from his weight on her chest, and he pushed up slightly on his forearms to allow her to draw in some air. But he kept his face buried in her hair, breathing in its fragrance, and he kept her pinned in place with his hands and his body. Man, he'd love to laugh off that rush of possessiveness. He'd love to be able to look himself squarely in the eye in the mirror and say, "Yeah, well, sure I meant it at the time. But then I got off."

Hell, the truth was, at the moment he'd simply settle for

the ability to roll off her and walk away. But he couldn't. Neither could he formulate a single question to hit her with while she was pliable, couldn't think of one pertinent piece of information to demand from her that would advance this damn case.

Shit. This was not in the game plan.

Sasha was sensitive to the sudden tension in the air and experienced an abrupt rash of qualms where only moments before she'd been filled with certainty. He'd gone so quiet and still on top of her.

Tentatively, she tugged at the fingers manacling her wrists. Mick slowly released them and she slid her arms down from their crooked position above her head and wrapped them around him. Maybe if she just held him for a minute . . .

As soon as she smoothed her hands down his back, however, she felt the welts and raw grooves her nails had left behind and was immediately mortified. Dear God in heaven, what had she done? She could feel places where she'd actually removed strips of his skin!

Now she didn't know *what* to do with her hands. So she moved them lower and palmed his hard, round buttocks, but where five minutes ago that would have seemed a perfectly natural thing to do, it now felt too personal.

Which should have been patently absurd, dammit, given the way her touch set him to pulsing several times inside her. But it seemed obtrusively intimate nevertheless. If only he would say something . . .

She wanted to talk to him about the way she felt. Connected. God, so connected to him—in a way that she'd only ever felt before when she'd skated with Lonnie. And even that was like trying to compare night-lights to floodlights. The connection she felt here in Mick's arms far surpassed the one she felt when she skated with Lon.

They were clearly only her sentiments, though. His stillness, the way he hadn't said a word since he'd said she was his now . . . Well, that had been nothing more than sex talk obviously, and she had the feeling that he now regretted ever opening his mouth.

Not a woman who would ever willingly outstay her welcome, she inquired bluntly, "Mick? Do you want me to go?"

He reacted without thinking, rearing back so abruptly his hands, which were tangled in her hair on the mattress, tugged free several roots from her scalp. "You want to *go?*"

"No, that's not what I said. I asked if *you*— "

But he wasn't listening. "Jesus, you got a hot date with Morrison or something?" His face lost all expression as he reached down to yank the pillow out from under her hips. He pulled out and started to push up off of her. "Well, certainly, by all means—don't let me hold you up."

Sasha recoiled as if he'd thrust a handful of worms in her face. Mick watched it, saw the withdrawal that followed on its heels and only then did he replay her original question . . . and realize how badly he had skewed it.

Ah, shit.

"I'm sorry." He dropped back over her, gathering her hair gently into one fist and piling it out of harm's way above her head. He stroked gentle fingers down he sides of her face and throat. "I didn't mean that, Saush—I don't even know why I said it, except that I heard what I thought you were saying instead of the words that were actually being said." He rolled his shoulders uneasily. "I guess I'm a little unnerved here."

"You're a little unnerved?" She shoved at his shoulders. "Get off me, Vinicor."

"No, I don't think so. Not until we get this . . ."

"Get off me!"

Mick didn't have to be hit upside the head to recognize the signs of incipient hysteria when he heard them. "Okay, okay. Shh, easy now; I'm going." He rolled to one side.

Sasha scrambled out from under, not pausing for breath until she was off the bed. She searched frantically for her clothes, moving from spot to spot, gathering pants here, a

T-shirt there, until Mick came up behind her on silent feet and wrapped his arms around her. He held her against his naked warmth and buried his face in the cloud of curls against her neck. "I'm sorry," he repeated. "I know I acted like a chump, but give me hell, Sasha. Don't just run out on me."

Sasha went very still as his warmth began to penetrate to the nucleus of her jangled nerves. She stared at the far wall without actually taking in what it was she was looking at. "I never felt anything like that before," she said in a low voice. Her hair shifted against his collarbone as she shook her head. "Never. Lon is like my brother; I've never *slept* with him. My God, Mick, that would practically be incest. And those two guys I did sleep with . . . ?" She struggled for words and then shrugged in defeat. "I just never knew."

She licked her lips. "God, when you were inside me, it was so— But then it was all over and you didn't say anything and I could feel your anger. And I'm *sorry* about your back, but it's not as if I meant to do it; honest to God I didn't . . ."

Mick grinned into her neck. This was giving him hell? The one thing he could count on forever, apparently, was that Sasha Miller never reacted in any way that he might rationally expect. "So, basically, what you're tellin' me then is that you liked it, right?"

"Oh, *yeah*. It was—so—" She shrugged helplessly, digging her shoulder blades into his diaphragm. Words just failed her.

But then she pulled away and turned to face him. "But it's gotta be a one-shot deal, Mick. I mean, I thank you and everything . . . but I don't think it'd be a good idea to make a habit of this."

Mick felt his mouth drop open. "You're kidding, right?"

"Of course I'm not kidding!"

"What? Is it because I came so fast? Usually I can last longer than five minutes, I promise you. You just had me a little on the hot side and . . ."

"My God, it's not that." She was standing there stark naked in front of him and it was his choice of topics that caused her to blush. She wasn't even aware of their lack of clothing. "I didn't need you to last longer than five minutes, you may have noticed, and—dammit, Vinicor, we're getting off the track here!" Her posture grew very erect. "I think perhaps that drug Prozac was invented for people like you, Mick," she said stiffly. "You could use a personality pill."

"That's a helluva thing to say!"

"Yes, well, I'm sorry. But you're different people at different times and I never know from one minute to the next who you're going to be or how you're going to react to anything—especially how you're going to react to me. And this"—her hand twirled expressively at the bed—"well, I'm not saying it was a *mistake* exactly . . . I'm just saying we shouldn't do it again, is all."

"This," he said through gritted teeth as his larger hand imitated her gesture at the bed, "has damn well been building between the two of us since we first clapped eyes on each other. Admit it. And I'll tell you somethin' else." He stepped close and when she backed up, he just kept right on coming until her bottom pressed against the dresser. Fingers groping behind her to curl around its edge, she gripped it tightly and thrust her chin up at him. He leaned over until they were nose to nose.

"It's going to keep on happening," he promised her in a hoarse whisper. Slapping his hands down next to hers, he leaned back and looked her up and down. "Over and over and *over* again until we damn well get it right!"

"I thought we got it right the first time!"

"All right, then, until we perfect it. As for my personality"—he drew himself up and his eyes blazed down at her with affronted pride—"I was jealous of your goddam good friend Morrison, okay? This is not exactly an emotion I'm accustomed to feeling or anxious to admit, Sasha, so cut me some slack."

"That's it? That's the big apology?" She quit leaning away from him and stood up straight. "So what are you saying here, Mick? That it's *Lon's* fault you've been acting like Yay-hoo the Yo-Yo Man?"

Mick rammed his fingers through his hair as he stared down at her. "Christ, you're a hard sell!"

"What is it you're selling, precisely?" She shoved him aside and snatched her panties up off the floor. Stepping into them she then located her bra, but merely let it dangle from her fingers as she turned her head to glare at him. "I haven't seen you exactly knocking yourself out to convince me you feel bad about behaving like a jerk, Vinicor. But maybe I've got it all wrong; let me see now." She ticked off his trans-gressions on her fingers. "You cop a feel in the back hall of an ice arena and then pick a fight with my oldest friend."

"He started the fight, Sasha, not I."

"You take care of me when I'm injured, and Lord you're so gentle and nice. But then the next morning you turn from the man I thought was my friend into the Manager from Hell. And today you make love to me and then treat me as if I'm a two-dollar whore."

"That's not fair; I never—"

"You had sex with me, the likes of which, incidentally, I have *never* had before," she interrupted. "But once it's over, do we get to bask in the postcoital glow? Oh no. Before we're even finished, practically, you're knockin' me loose and accusing me of wanting to rush off and do the same with a boy I've known—"

"Morrison's no goddam boy!"

"—since I was ten years old!" Her voice kept raising, until she practically screamed, "But, because that *boy* gave you a little twinge of jealousy, that makes it okay, right?"

"A twinge?" Mick's voice was contrastingly quiet as years of iron-clad self-control went down the tubes. "Is that what you think it was, a friggin' *twinge?*"

"What else would you call it?"

"Christ, Sasha, look at me!" He waved a hand at his erection. "What you're basically telling me here is that I'm an asshole, and I must be, honey, because I'm hearing it but I've still got a hard-on for you that won't quit. Jesus, I see Morrison put his hands on you and I don't care how innocent it is; I want to knock him on his ass, kick his fuckin' teeth down his throat. I said it before but maybe you weren't listening. You're *mine* now." Mick forgot that possessiveness was not professional. He stalked over to her.

"So you tell me," he said in a low, rough voice, leaning over her. "Was I supposed to be in a big time rush to open myself up like some goddam sacrificial virgin by just *handing* you that kind of power?"

"So what then?—you just figured you'd hurt me first and beat me to the punch before I could hurt you?" His sincere emotion had taken a lot of the sting out of her ire, and she touched her fingers to his chest. "Mick, don't you honestly know me any better than that?"

"No, that's the whole point. I don't." He gathered her hair in one fist and held it away from her neck. His eyes roamed from her toes to the top of her head. "I mean, I know I crave your body. And I know I want to learn everything about you there *is* to learn: who you are, what you think. But I don't really *know* you at all." And what he thought he knew scared the hell out of him.

Sasha just looked at him for several silent moments. She knew what she wanted and if the thought of it frightened her a little, well . . .

"Then, I suppose," she finally said, "we had better get started working on that."

TEN

Sasha spent more time in Mick's room then she should have. Now the clock was ticking down; she was due on the ice in seven minutes. Still she sat in the line women's dressing room, very carefully checking out the attachment of her blades to her skates. She went over them screw by screw and ascertained that each and every one was screwed and glued on tight.

Then, grabbing them up, she raced down the corridors to the back stage area. God, she was such an idiot. It had been one of those freak things; that was all. It was ridiculous to think anyone she knew could have loosened them purposefully. Why would anyone want to hurt her?

They wouldn't have; they didn't. But, squatting down to carefully adjust her laces, she couldn't shake the feeling that she was nevertheless going to be checking and rechecking her skates for a long time to come.

Connie went to Mick's room later that evening when she failed to find Sasha in her own. There wasn't much doubt that Saush would be there; hell, it had been the talk of the troupe all night tonight that he'd finally stopped circling around her and moved in for the kill. So to speak. Connie knocked authoritatively.

Minutes later the door was yanked open and Mick, breathing heavily, his hair disheveled and his collarless denim shirt half unbuttoned, its left front shirttail pulled free of his pants, stared down at her. *"What?"*

Connie just grinned, enjoying his frustration. She thought that Vinicor probably got his own way much too often; it wouldn't hurt him to put his hormones on ice for a few minutes. "I was going to ask if Sasha's here but one look at you and it's kind of a redundant question, isn't it?" she said cheerfully and pushed him aside, stepping past him into the short hallway. She heard a scramble of bed springs and called out, "Make yourself decent, Saush; I need to talk to you for a few minutes."

Rounding the wall, she flashed an ironic smile at her friend who was sitting primly, fully dressed, in the middle of the bed. Sasha cocked one eyebrow at her inquiringly. The pose would have been a lot more effective, Connie thought wryly, if only her cheeks weren't flaming and her mouth wasn't all swollen from Vinicor's kisses.

"I won't keep you," she said with a knowing smile. "I just wanted to know if: one, you're going to Dave's big spaghetti feed tomorrow night, and two, if we're still on to see the troll under the bridge in the morning."

Having tucked in his wayward shirttail, Mick sat down on the mattress next to Sasha and rubbed a possessive hand up and down the instep of her bare foot while he eyed Connie challengingly. It was precisely that sort of claim-staking behavior at the arena tonight—not to mention Sasha's tactile responses to it—that had set the line women's locker room and the back stage crews to buzzing. "What the hell's she talking about?" he demanded, not taking his eyes off Connie.

"You know Dave DiGornio—"

"The set crew guy?"

Sasha nodded. "He's from Seattle and whenever we're in town his family invites everyone over for a huge pasta dinner."

"Okay, we'll be there," Mick told Connie decisively. He turned to Sasha and raised a brow. "That all right?"

"You kiddin', a chance to eat a home-cooked meal? You bet we'll be there." Seeing the next question forming, she explained, "As for the other, well, Seattle's one of the most interesting cities when it comes to public art, Mick. Their sense of humor's a little different here. We've been hearing about the troll for months now from Dave. It's under the Aurora bridge, he said, in a district called Fremont, where there's this other piece called "Waiting for the Interurban" that Connie read about in *Sunset* magazine. We wanted to see this stuff while we were here." She looked at Connie. "I still do. Have you rented the car?"

"Yeah. The only problem is, I can't find any Aurora bridge on the map. There's like seven bridges in this town but none of them are named the Aurora." She shrugged. "We'll just have to ask Dave, I guess—I'll see what I can do about tracking him down tonight."

Mick said, "I want to go too, okay?" Knowing Sasha would probably defer to Connie's wishes in this instance, he turned to her and added persuasively, "Include me, Nakamura, and I'll do the driving." He remembered from their trip to the Saturday Market in Portland that the women were ruthless in their attempts to avoid driving. They liked to sightsee without having to worry about traffic and directions.

"Fine with me," Connie said. "Brenda and Sara are going, too. There's room for one more, and, hey, if you're willing to drive . . ." She shrugged and stood up. "Well, I'll let you get back to . . . whatever." She flashed them a smile that said she was cognizant of what that "whatever" would entail. "Let's meet in the lobby at nine. Dave said there're some good restaurants and cafés in Fremont where we can get breakfast."

Sasha walked her to the door. When she came back Mick was standing at the side of the bed unbuttoning his shirt. He shrugged it off and tossed it over a chair and then moved to loom over her. Sliding a hand beneath the fall of her hair at her nape, he lowered his head, lips parted. But just centimeters before his mouth would have touched hers, he drew back. Changing the angle of his head, he came at her from another direction but did the same thing, stopping just short of kissing her. Sasha watched, mesmerized, as his tongue came out to slick across his lower lip. Gripping his bare shoulders, she stood on tiptoe to reach his mouth.

"Now, where were we?" he murmured with a crooked smile, holding his head just out of her reach.

"Dammit, Vinicor," she growled, "don't you mess with me." She dropped back onto her heels and peered up at him through narrowed lashes. "Unless, of course, you're anxious for me to toddle off down the hall and visit with Connie for the rest of the night."

He growled back. But she made note of the threat for future use. For it didn't escape her notice that he promptly left off teasing and gave her what she wanted.

"Mick?" It was late, but even though he'd been quiet for some time, Sasha didn't think he was asleep. She rubbed her cheek against the smooth swell of his chest and felt his arm tighten around her.

"Hmmm?"

"Do you have any family?" She raised her head up to peer at him through the darkness. Felt him stiffen and then relax again. But then his heart began to beat a little more heavily beneath the hands she'd stacked upon his chest to prop up her chin, and she frowned. "What's the matter with you?" she demanded, shifting her palm to lie flat against his sternum, registering its deep thud. "It's an easy enough question, isn't it?"

"Yeah, sure." But one that drove home the reason he was here in the first place, a reason that, with an uncharacteristic lack of professionalism, he'd been shoving to the back of his mind all day long. Mick sat up, dislodging Sasha from her indolent drape across his front. Face composed and utterly unreadable, he sat back against the headboard and gazed down at her. "I've got folks in Billings."

She scrambled to sit up. "Montana?"

"Yeah. My mom and dad."

Sasha sat cross-legged, pulling the sheet up to tuck under her arms. "Are you an only child too, then? So am I. Did you always wish for a brother or sister the way I did?"

Mick could feel his features growing stiff. "I had a brother. He's dead now."

"Oh, Mick, I'm so sorry." Her sympathy was immediate and genuine, and she scooted over to curl up against his side, wrapping her arms around his middle to hold him tight. "Tell me about him."

Part of him wanted to peel her off of him and shove her away. Violently. It was because of people like her that Pete was dead. But a larger part wanted to do exactly what she said and tell her. Tentatively, he put one arm around her.

"His name was Peter," he said and was surprised by the hoarseness of his voice. He cleared his throat. "Pete. He was eight years older than me."

"I bet you idolized him, huh?"

His arm tightened slightly around her. "God, yeah. He was golden, my big brother. Smart and funny, good-looking. And nice, you know? I mean, I was a pest, always wanting to hang out with him, and he'd actually take me along with him sometimes and just laugh when his friends objected."

"What happened to him, Mick?"

"Vietnam."

Her head snapped up. "That's how my dad died. I was just a baby, so I never knew him, but . . ."

"Pete didn't die there, Sasha," Mick interrupted her. "He got hooked on drugs there."

"Oh, Mick." It was said with true compassion. But a spear of ice seemed to find her heart and she withdrew just a tiny bit. Why was it every time she turned around she seemed to be confronted by the specter of drugs?

Her subtle withdrawal wasn't lost on Mick and he was filled with a wave of contempt so fierce he nearly choked on it. Unable to vent it by lambasting her with his opinion of drugs and the sleaze who dealt it, he vented it in another way. "That fuckin' war took Pete away from us and sent home a stranger," he said bitterly. "By the time he died when I was fourteen, he weighed one hundred and seven pounds and he'd steal the fillings from your teeth if he thought they'd buy him his next fix of scag."

"Scag?"

Oh, *please,* like you don't know, babe? Mick's posture was absolutely stiff within the circle of her arms. "Heroin."

Sasha, too, stiffened. Oh, damn it. Damn it clear to hell and gone. What was it about her life that seemed to lead all roads straight back to that same corrupt substance, over and over and over again?

Did she dare tell him about Lon? Chances were that he'd likely already heard via the grapevine anyway. Which, even more than the jealousy he claimed regarding her relationship with Lonnie, would go a long way toward explaining Mick's antipathy where her oldest friend was concerned. But she could still tell him about how it had affected her, couldn't she? It gave them a great deal in common. Why not tell him how just hearing the name of that narcotic these days was enough to make her teeth grow tight with rage?

But, no, better not. Judging by his rigidity, tonight was not the time to give vent to her pet revulsion. Merely trying to hold Mick at the moment felt like hugging Plymouth Rock.

He obviously wasn't in the right frame of mind to listen right now.

Mick was fed up to his eye teeth with all the bullshit and hypocrisy. Sasha's, that was, not his own. As far as he was concerned, his lies and half-truths were merely a matter of doing his job.

From start to finish everything about this case had differed from any other he'd ever handled. The main difference of course was that he was accustomed to ingratiating himself into the lives of known dealers. The question, when dealing with them, was not were they or weren't they. The question was: would they buy his scam. Everybody just sort of automatically assumed that everyone else was as big a crook as the next guy, or they worried that the next guy was a narc. But this . . .

He'd screwed up royally last night. For God's sake, you did not tell someone who dealt a particularly toxic drug that their narcotic of choice had killed your beloved brother—a move like that was strictly amateur. It wasn't as if he hadn't known it perfectly well at the time, either; he sure as hell didn't have the excuse of ignorance. Still some dominant voice had kept whispering in his ear, insisting he had to tell this woman the truth.

Bullshit like that was going to get him killed if he didn't watch his step.

He could not believe what he had done, couldn't believe he'd actually hamstrung this operation by divulging that particular slice of family history. Just how likely was she going to be to confide in him now about her little sideline?

Not bloody likely, that's how.

As far as he could see that left him with only one alternative. Now he had no choice but to take the scam public. Unless word that he was interested in heroin got spread around a little, this case was never going to move. Instead it would stagnate, for he was getting absolutely nowhere with it as it presently stood. But taking it public could be risky.

Damn risky.

The Follies was a microcosm of society as a whole. Damn near every personality type could be found represented within the framework that comprised the company. Mick was adept at ferreting out those who used—he had a real nose for it—but there was a fine line to be walked here.

For one thing, while being manager had gained him entree into *Follies* and had given him access to personnel files; it was also the factor most liable to hinder any dealings with the hard-core drug users. He possessed the authority to fire them, which was not a situation likely to make them anxious to admit to their habits, let alone share with him the name of their supplier. Add to that the small-town aspect inherent in having close contact day and night with a select group of people and he was treading a very thin line. It would take only one wrong step for the entire cast to learn of his interest.

He wanted certain people to believe he was a part of the drug culture. He did not, however, want everyone to think so.

What he debated, as he allowed the chatter of the women to drift in one ear and out the other on their drive to Fremont the next morning, was whether or not he wanted Sasha to think so.

As the women took pictures of the troll, a monolithic presence that crouched beneath the bridge, hair obscuring half his face, one protruding eye glaring out at the world, the crumpled body of a Volkswagen Beetle clutched in one long-fingered hand, he had to wonder just how inclined she would be to believe it if he *did* choose to go in that direction.

At least he had vented his spleen on Vietnam last night and not narcotics, so perhaps he could convince her that Pete's addiction had induced in him a burning desire to control the trade.

"Oh, God, aren't they wonderful?" Sasha interrupted his thoughts a short while later. "Mick, go pose with them."

He looked at the statues that comprised *Waiting for the Interurban*. Life-sized commuters, they huddled together under a bus shelter in the middle of Fremont Avenue. The waitress at the café where they'd had breakfast this morning had informed them chattily that the residents of Fremont loved to dress them up and would use any reason to do so. The statues were great, but still . . . "You're kidding?" he said in horror. "You want me to stand out there and *pose* with them?" The narrow sidewalks supported a pretty healthy foot trade and there was no way in hell . . .

"Yes, come on. Don't be a poop."

"Yeah, come on, Vinicor," Connie added dryly, and then Sara and Brenda added their persuasion.

"Tell you what," he said a little desperately. He was not going out there in the middle of the street to simper with a bunch of statues, and that was that. "Why don't you, uh, ladies go pose with them and I'll take photos for you on each of your cameras?"

That was greeted with enthusiasm and they loaded his hands with Minoltas and Nikons. While they posed with unabashed exhibitionism, Mick's attention returned to his problem.

Hadn't he just been bemoaning the way he'd mishandled the situation last night? Actually, what better way was there to get her to confide in him than by letting her hear of his interest in her favorite drug from another, presumably disinterested, party? Hey, who knew, maybe Morrison would even be the one to give her the news, and wouldn't that be poetic justice.

For the first time all morning Mick perked up. This could work.

He shoved aside the thought that it would mean an end to his relationship with Sasha and concentrated on the women's antics as they mugged with the statues, grinning as he clicked off several frames for each of them on their cameras. If his smile was perhaps a little forced, well . . .

All things came to an end and few knew that better than he. Sure, there was something about her that grabbed at a vital part of him when they were together, but that was only sex. And, hell, it wasn't as if he hadn't known already that *that* wouldn't last forever. There were plenty of other women in the world.

The important thing here was that maybe this damn case would finally start to go somewhere.

His plan succeeded more spectacularly and with much greater speed than he could have dreamed. The result, unfortunately, was not at all what he expected. It turned his whole life upside down instead and left him scrambling to save the relationship he'd been perfectly willing to toss aside just a few short hours ago.

Used to concocting elaborate lies when dealing with this element, Mick outfoxed himself in this instance. Had he simply asked outright, the hard drug users could have saved him a lot of time and trouble, for as he'd surmised earlier, the Follies was a lot like a small town in the respect that everyone basically knew who would and wouldn't do what. It was common knowledge that Sasha Miller disdained anything or anyone connected with drugs. She'd established that beyond a shadow of a doubt upon first joining the troupe, when people who knew of her connection to Lon but didn't know *her* had approached with requests for drugs. Consequently, she would be the last one with whom anything pertaining to that particular subject would be discussed.

It was purely by chance that Sasha even happened to overhear the conversation that changed everything.

Dave DiGornio's family home was an immense sprawling structure in an elegant neighborhood on Lake Washington, and the DiGornios were hospitable hosts. Their party hit on all cylinders following dinner.

It was cold and dark outside and rain came down in sheets, but all the doors had been cracked to alleviate the stuffiness generated by so many bodies. The crowd was loud and transient, shifting from room to room and spilling over onto the patio to stand beneath the eaves for a smoke, a breath of fresh air, or simply to admire the lighted swimming pool, whose surface was dimpled by the pounding rain. This was hardly the group to be put off by a little chill.

Standing in the kitchen near the back door, Sasha sipped a glass of wine as she looked at the mob that stood between her and the arched doorway to the dining room. Seattle was a coffee lover's mecca, and the crowd gathered around the gleaming chrome expresso machine appeared to be serious coffee lovers indeed. Sasha grinned into her wineglass. This probably wasn't the place to lecture on the perils of caffeine.

Not that she was of a mind to lecture anybody. But the sheer number of people pretty much eliminated any hope of getting through to the dining room where she'd last seen Mick. She slipped out of the house through the door at her back.

Once away from the lighted back porch it was dark as pitch for a short stretch, not even the weakest of moonlight penetrating the heavy storm clouds. Luckily, the brick path that curved around the house stayed close to the walls and was partially protected by the sheltering eaves. Sasha managed to keep reasonably dry as she moved quickly but cautiously toward the lighted patio that fronted the house and overlooked the lake.

The low voice that came out of the shadows stopped her in her tracks and made her slap a startled hand to her heart to contain its sudden racing pulse. Eyes trained on the group of people standing within the glow of lights reflecting off the pool, she hadn't even noticed the two men sitting in the open doorway of the cabana.

She recognized them as John Beggart and Marty Roth. Neither were men with whom she had much contact and she would have moved right along if the mention of Mick's name hadn't caught her attention.

"Vinicor?" Roth was saying. "You're full of shit, brother. No way I believe that."

"Hey, I didn't believe it either, man; not at first. But he shows up at the 211, and I'm tellin' ya, he's like some surprised to see *me* there shootin' some pool." Beggart paused and Sasha heard him sniff a substance up his nose. Her stomach started to churn with an unspecified dread that turned all too specific with Beggart's next words. "He shoots a few games with me and after I get back from a little trip to the john he says he heard tell someone in the troupe was dealin' H, and he asks me, do I know where he can score some?"

"Bullshit. *Vinicor?*"

"Yeah, man, I'm tellin' ya!"

"The dude's too healthy and besides, he's screwin' Miller. She'd never . . ."

Oh God. Sasha didn't wait around to hear the rest. Hot rage burning in her veins and cold sickness like a chunk of dry ice eating away at her stomach, she raced blindly past the group of skaters and techs on the patio, not hearing—let alone responding to—the greetings, one of which was Mick's. *Oh God. That sonofabitch,* was all she could think. The words chanted in time with the heavy pulse beating in her temples.

Mick caught up with her in the upstairs bedroom, where she was pawing frantically through the pile of coats heaped on the bed. "Hey," he said just as she unearthed her letterman's jacket from the middle of the stack. The face she turned his way was wiped free of expression and dead white. Filled with immediate concern, he reached out a hand. "What's going on, Sasha? Are you all right?"

Her arm snapped back in an abrupt movement that pulled it out of his reach. *"Don't,"* she said with great precision. "You. Touch me."

"What the—" He reached for her again but then at the look that flashed across her face, hastily retracted his hands, spreading them wide of his body in entreaty. "Talk to me," he demanded in his most authoritative tone.

She promptly complied. "I want you out of my life."

Mick's heart slammed up against the wall of his chest and acid poured into his gut like water over a spill gate. But he'd learned long ago to function through stress and so managed to respond calmly enough. "You want me out of your life," he reiterated with quiet equanimity. "Might I ask why?"

It wasn't the best time for quiet equanimity.

"My God, you're a cool one, aren't you," she demanded furiously. "You truly are one frosty son of a bitch." Hugging her coat to her middle she considered him with hostile eyes. "Tell me, Mick, just what did you hope to gain from all of this, anyway? Did you think if you *slept* with me, if you gave the little country girl a sexual thrill, that I'd be able to provide you with drugs? With—what did you call it now—*scag?*" She shook her head wildly and her laughter was too loud and bitter. "Honey, you aren't the first man to assume that because Lon 'n me are friends, I must have access to the stuff, too. You're just the first who thought he had to screw me for it."

Her gray eyes locked with his as she futilely attempted to wrestle her way into her jacket. She was too upset to notice that one sleeve was turned inside out. "I want you to stay the hell away from me," she said with fierce conviction. "If you don't," she promised grimly, "I will turn you in to the authorities so fast it'll make your head swirl—and you can take that to the bank, Vinicor. Lonnie's involvement with your filthy drug almost brought me down once; I will be *damned* if I'll allow you a shot at bringing me down, too."

From the very beginning Mick had recognized that Sasha didn't fit his usual drug dealer's profile; yet still he had ignored all indications to the contrary. Now knowledge of her innocence burst through him like a huge multicolored pyrotechnic and he was suffused with a joy so pure he nearly sang with it. The next instant he was swamped with terror. His only concrete thought was, *if you don't want to lose her, bud, you'd better damn well start talking.*

All his life, lies had come as easily to him as breathing and faced at this moment with explaining himself, he didn't even consider telling the truth. Well, he considered it. But then he rejected the idea. Not that he was going to *lie* to her, exactly; he just wasn't going to tell her the entire story. Total candor in this particular instance could well slit his throat.

He could tell her he was DEA, of course, but leave out the part about her being his primary target. Except . . .

If she told just one person, the odds were high that one person would find it too juicy not to tell someone else. And once word spread the case was burned.

Shit.

"Exactly what is it I'm supposed to have done?" he questioned cautiously.

"Damn you, Mick, don't you play the innocent with me!" She quit wrestling with the sleeve of her coat and glared up at him. "You know perfectly well what I'm talking about."

"Yeah, I think I do. But I'd like to hear it all laid out, if you don't mind, so we know exactly what we're dealing with. I don't want any misunderstandings."

"Okay, understand this. John Beggart says you asked him where you could score some heroin."

Mick's face was noncommittal. "He told you that personally." The flatness of his tone indicated this was not a question.

Sasha gave him a look that was filled with loathing. "Don't be a fool—everybody knows how I feel about drugs. I overheard him talking to Marty Roth."

Oh perfect, he thought with self-disgust. *Everyone knows . . . except you, Vinicor. Fool is the word for it, all right.*

"It's not what you think," he said. "It's part of my job description . . ."

"Oh please!"

"Listen; just hear me out. It's come to management's attention that heroin is being trafficked through the Follies. The reason they hired me in the first place is because they know how I feel about drugs—the subject of my brother came up at my interview and we discussed some of the training I'd taken in college for dealing with this sort of thing. Anyhow, in today's economy business degrees are a dime a dozen and getting this job was pretty much contingent upon working with them to see if I could find out who's responsible."

"I don't believe you," Sasha said flatly.

Yeah, it sounded weak to him, too. "Call Dello and ask him," he retorted without hesitation and made a mental note to call the Follies' CEO first.

"Don't think that I won't, Mick."

"I'm counting on it, honey. He'll confirm that I'm here to help stop drugs, not to traffick in them. Listen, Saush, would I have told you about Pete last night if I thought you had anything to do with drugs? It would've been incredibly stupid, don't y'think?" And so he had thought just this morning. Right now it seemed like the smartest move he had made since beginning this case.

He stepped forward to remove her jacket from her hands. "And I'll tell you something else, darlin'," he added, glad to be able to divulge something that was one hundred percent honest. "If there was a sexual thrill to be had here, it was all mine. I never once made love to you for any other reason than—"

The bedroom door slammed opened and Amy Nitkey, one of the lighting techs, burst into the room. She stumbled to a stop just over the threshold when she saw Mick and Sasha standing there. Discomforted by the palpable tension surrounding them, she stammered, "Oh, hey, sorry. I didn't know anyone was in here."

"Yeah, do you mind?" Mick inquired politely. "We'd like just a few more minutes' privacy."

"Sure. Just let me grab my coat, okay? I gotta run out to the car for a pack of smokes and it's coming down cats and dogs out there."

Mick looked at the stack of coats nearly three feet deep, saw by Sasha's face that she was maybe seconds away from getting ready to cut and run, and tossed her letterman's jacket to Amy. "Here, use this. There's an umbrella over there by the door, too."

Amy took one look at the expression in his eyes and shrugged. "Yeah, sure. I'll get this back to you in just a few minutes, Sasha." Then she was gone.

Mick immediately turned back to Sasha, not waiting for her to lambast him for that, too. "You gotta believe me, Sasha. I do not take drugs. Call Dello. Talk to my mother. Come with me to a doctor and I'll piss in a bottle or get a blood test. Jesus, I can probably get you a dozen affadavits by tomorrow afternoon."

Then, stepping close, he squatted slightly to bring their faces on a more equitable level and reached out to brush her hair off her cheek with the backs of his fingers. "I'll understand if you need more proof than my word before you can trust me on that," he said. "But if you take nothing else on faith, believe this. The *only* reason I've ever made love to you is because I can't be near you without wanting it so bad it nearly rips me apart. I swear that to you on my mother's life."

And Sasha believed him because she had to. No one else had ever made her feel the way Mick Vinicor did. She was a highly disciplined woman who before this man entered her life had never known it was possible to be reduced to a being who was all nerve endings and instincts. It would simply destroy something inside of her to believe it had all been a sham, a deliberate attack on her senses.

She nodded.

"I don't suppose you want to stay with me tonight, though, huh?"

She was opening her mouth to tell him he supposed correctly when they became aware of a horrendous commotion breaking out downstairs.

ELEVEN

Only a short while ago, Connie had been searching for Sasha. Not for any particular reason, she simply hadn't seen her in a while and wondered where she'd gotten herself off to. Consequently, when Connie entered a new room at the party she'd ask around to see if anyone had seen her.

"Find Vinicor," Lon Morrison advised somewhat sourly from a stool at the bar in the family rec room where he was watching a game of pool in progress. "She seems to be firmly attached to his hip these days."

Connie cocked an eyebrow. "Sour grapes, Mr. Morrison?"

"Not at all, Miss Nakamura. Just a statement of fact."

For the first time, Connie looked at Morrison through eyes not biased by previous knowledge. She knew her opinion of him had a tendency to be less than rose colored—it was sort of a knee-jerk protectiveness of Sasha. Connie felt that for a supposedly very good friend, Lon had treated her friend shabbily.

It seemed sort of dog-in-the-mangerish, however, to hold it against him when Sasha didn't. And Saush had gone out of her way to relate Lon's fierce defense of her back in their high school days. Returning his steady gaze, Connie came to the conclusion that perhaps it wasn't up to her to sit in judgment of him.

Before she could do more than nod curtly to acknowledge something of what she was thinking, however, Greg Lougynes, a huge, ponytailed roadie, twisted around to look at her over one massive shoulder. He was bent over the pool table, where he prepared to sink the four ball. "I saw Miller a coupla minutes ago," he said in his hoarse, gravelly voice. "She was headed out to her car."

Over by the fireplace, Karen Corselli's head came up. Rising casually to her feet, she tucked her purse under her arm, excused herself from the group she'd been visiting with, and, picking up her empty glass, left the room.

"Her car?" Connie echoed after a moment of blank surprise. Her slender black eyebrows drew together in perplexity. "Whatever for?"

"Smokes, I think she said." Lougynes sank the four ball and his gaze on the felt, walked around the table setting up his next shot.

"But Sasha doesn't smoke."

Greg's big shoulders moved in an indifferent shrug. "I'm just telling ya what I heard, Nakamura. I looked up when I heard someone say they was going out in this rain, and I saw Miller walking out the door. Ain't no mistakin' that coat of hers."

"Well, that's odd." Connie's eyes met Lon's across the room, and the looks they exchanged were equally bewildered. Then she shrugged and gave the man at the pool table a weak smile. "Thanks, Greg. I didn't mean to jump all over you." It wasn't his fault if she couldn't make sense of it.

"No problem." He sank the two and six balls in rapid succession. Straightening, he frowned in thought while he chalked up his pool cue. "You know, now that you mention it, the hair didn't look like Sasha's. I just saw that wooly 'Follies on Ice' on the back of the red jacket and figured—" His big shoulders rolled uncomfortably. "But come to think of it, her hair wasn't as dark as Miller's and I don't think it was as curly, either."

Connie shrugged. "Then I imagine Sasha must've lent her coat to someone." That made more sense than Saush going out in this weather for cigarettes that she'd never smoke.

Connie decided to check in the kitchen for her friend; perhaps she'd find her there.

She had barely cleared the rec room door when a woman outside began to scream.

It was a sound guaranteed to draw a crowd, and it did exactly that. Every single party-goer rushed outside.

Dave DiGornio and his father ran toward the street and the woman who had screamed was huddled on the patio under the eaves, pointing after them with one quivering hand, the other clamped to her mouth. Trembling uncontrollably, she tried to answer the barrage of questions that came like bullets from all sides. The volume from so many people all talking at once rose to cacophonous levels.

"What the hell is going on out here?" Mick's authoritative voice cut through the babble, leaving a momentary silence in its wake. Dragging Sasha behind him, he plowed through the crowd and stopped in front of the trembling woman. He dropped Sasha's wrist and reached out to grip the woman's shoulders in firm hands. "Are you okay, Cathy?"

She made a reply, but he couldn't hear it over the voices that had resumed their excited chatter. The decibel level had once again escalated and he impatiently jerked around to face the people surrounding them. *"QUIET!"* he roared.

A sudden silence fell, and he turned back to the trembling woman. "Now. Are you all right?"

"Oh, God." She pointed a shaking finger at the arterial that divided the expensive, sprawling homes from the lake. "A woman was h-hit by a c-car out there." Tears poured down her cheeks. "It hit her so h-hard she *flew*, Mick. And then it just k-k-kept on going!"

"Is anyone out there checking her condition?"

"Y-yes." She nodded her head and then couldn't get it to stop. She had to reach both hands up to hold it still. "Dave and Mr. DiG-Gornio and I were talking out here and they . . . and they're . . ."

"Okay, Cathy, you're doing fine." He looked up. "Somebody grab her a cup of coffee, please. And put some sugar in it." He looked at the crowd gathered around them. "Someone needs to call an ambulance." His gaze traveled swiftly from face to face; it stopped on the third one it saw. "Morrison. Call nine-one-one."

"Gotcha."

"People," Mick ordered. "Get out of the rain." He reached out and snagged Sasha's wrist again, pulling her near. "Take care of Cathy," he said. "She needs to be wrapped up and kept warm to combat any shock she may be in. I'm gonna go see what I can do for the woman who was hit." Mrs. DiGornio arrived just then with a large mug full of steaming coffee, which she extended to Mick. He took it and handed it to Sasha. "Get it down her." Turning back to Mrs. DiGornio, he briskly requested blankets, umbrellas, and a tarp if she could lay her hands on one quickly.

Their hostess conscripted the services of several of the people standing around and the items he required were promptly rounded up. Within moments, Cathy, wrapped in a blanket and clutching the cup of coffee in both hands, was being led indoors, and Mick, hugging a tarp, an umbrella, and two blankets, was jogging down the gradual, grassy slope to the street.

Dave DiGornio and his father were squatting on the sidewalk in the pouring rain. They were soaked to the skin. Except for one camel-colored leather sleeve and a pale hand with short, narrow fingers that curled toward the sidewalk on which she lay, Mick's view of the woman sprawled facedown in front of the two men was blocked by their drenched backs. He walked around Dave and stopped dead in his tracks.

This wasn't the stranger he had expected. The woman on the ground was wearing a jacket that was very familiar to him. Of deep red wool with a silver wooly *FOLLIES ON ICE* in cursive across the back and a skating patch on the camel leather of its left sleeve, there was only one jacket like it in the world and it belonged to Sasha Miller.

"Ah, Jesus," he said hoarsely. "It's Amy Nitkey."

Without interrupting his gentle search for broken bones, Dave DiGornio shot a glance up at Mick over his shoulder. "Whataya, blind, man? It's Sasha Miller."

"No," Mick retorted firmly, squatting down next to him. "It's Sasha's jacket, but that's Amy." He popped open an umbrella, set it up to shelter the fallen woman's head, then reached out to gently pull her hair away from her face. Even with her head turned away from them the identity was clear.

"I'll be damned," Dave murmured and helped Mick set up the tarp to form a rough shelter over the fallen technician. "It is Amy." He looked over at Mick. "She's got a weak pulse, but to tell you the truth that's about all we've been able determine—that she's still alive. She's getting soaked here, but we're afraid to move her in case she's got a spinal injury. Oh, good, you brought blankets," he added as he watched Mick snap one out and cast it over the injured woman. He pulled off the coat that had been covering her and tossed it to his father. "Dad, put this back on before you catch your death."

"What the hell happened, Dave?" Mick demanded. "Cathy said it was a hit-and-run?"

It was his father who replied. "It happened so damn fast I'm still reeling," he said. "The three of us were out talking on the patio and we heard the car accelerate, but our view of it was blocked by the laurel hedge. And I don't know about Cathy and Dave but I didn't give it much thought—I assumed it was just another car going too fast. That's been a growing problem in our neighborhood. Then, too, we didn't know that there was anyone in the street."

Mick looked at the thick, lush hedge. It was a good ten feet high and had probably been grown for that express purpose, to muffle traffic noise and provide privacy.

"We all looked down there, though, at the sound of a car gaining so much speed." Dave picked up the narrative. "And the next thing we know, there's a muffled thump and this woman's literally flying through the air. Cathy started to scream, but even over the noise she was making we could hear the car pick up speed again." He shook his head, incredulous that anyone could be so coldhearted as to mow someone down that way and then simply flee. "Dad and I moved, let me tell you. Even so, by the time we got down here the car was already gone."

"Can you describe it at all?"

"No lights, medium sized, and I think it might have been dark red, but I'm afraid I'm not positive about that," Dave supplied unhelpfully and his father nodded. "Had to have been a drunk."

Probably. But Mick looked down at Sasha's jacket on the rag-doll stillness of Amy Nitkey's body and shivered.

Sasha folded the heavy plastic bag that held her jacket over her arm and shivered. She looked up at Mick, who had just handed it to her and now stood on the other side of the threshold of her hotel room doorway. "How is she?" she asked.

Mick rubbed a weary hand over his chin. "Let me come in, Sasha."

She was all cool poise when she replied, "I don't really think that's a good—"

"Please."

She stepped back, holding the door open for him.

He walked straight to the little table situated near the window and collapsed into its nearest companion chair. Sitting there with his elbows on the table and his head in his hands, he dug at his scorched eye sockets with the hard-skinned heels of his palms. Sasha took a moment to detour into the bathroom to hang her jacket from the showerhead so it could drip into the tub and then sat down at the table opposite Mick, reaching out to graze the back of one of his hands with her fingertips. "How's Amy?"

He straightened up and reached for her hand. Gripping her fingers, he rubbed his thumb over her knuckles. "She's in ICU, but they're 'cautiously optimistic' . . . whatever the hell that means." He scrubbed his free hand over his face and then let it fall to the tabletop, staring through bloodshot eyes at Sasha. "I contacted her parents and they're on their way from Oklahoma City. Hopefully, by the time they arrive her condition will have been upgraded from critical to serious or maybe even stable."

He looked so discouraged that Sasha couldn't help herself, she reached out to brush his hair off his forehead with gentle fingertips. "What a mess."

"You got that right."

"So, what's next? Do they have any idea who did this to her?"

"Well, I talked to a detective from the State Patrol Accident Investigation Unit. He took all her clothes to the Washington State Crime Lab in Bellevue to be checked for transfer of fibers, paint chips; that sort of thing."

"But . . . my jacket."

"Yeah, well, I, uh, sorta held that out." At her look of horror, he assured her quickly, "They have enough without it. Amy was struck about thigh level. That means any fabric impressions and paint chips from the impact itself are going to be found primarily on her pants." And that would just have to do. He'd learned how much this jacket meant to Sasha and it might be months before she ever got it back. "Unfortunately, the heavy rain may have washed away much of the trace evidence, but the cop said the crime lab does wonders finding anything there is to be found. All it takes, apparently, is one tiny paint chip and they can tell what model, make, and year of car it came from."

"Yeah, but what good does the information do them once they've got it?" Sasha wondered. "Say they learn it's from a silver Honda Accord or a blue Buick Skylark. There must be thousands of either in Seattle alone."

"True, but an impact like this does some damage to the car and the driver's first inclination is going to be to get it fixed. The investigators will put out a bulletin to all the auto body shops in the greater metropolitan area and its environs, and they'll also lean on all the local illegal operations they know of. Patrol cars will be alerted to be on the lookout for a silver Honda Accord or blue Buick Skylark, such and such a year, with a bashed-in grill or whatever. The smokie I talked to said their case closure rate is pretty decent."

"Sounds like you got a lot of information."

"I had a lot of time on my hands waiting to hear how Amy was doing, and so did the cop assigned to the case. We talked." Then, to alleviate the small wrinkle still pulling her dark eyebrows together, he added, "He gave me a number to call tomorrow for a little preliminary information. If the crime lab comes up empty of trace evidence on Amy's other clothes, we can still volunteer your jacket."

"Oh, Mick, good." She relaxed. "I'd feel so awful if I thought I was withholding the one piece of evidence keeping them from solving her case."

And this is the woman you thought was running lethal heroin? Mick looked at her across the table and wondered why it had taken him so long to get a clue. "Leave it in the shower tonight with the plastic bag under it, and if you need to move it, put it back in the bag." He thought about Amy, crumpled on that sidewalk wearing Sasha's jacket. "I want to stay here tonight," he said and it wasn't so much a request as a statement of intent.

"No." Sasha pushed back from the table and rose to her

feet. Shaking her head, she stared down at him. "No, Mick. Forget it."

Mick curbed his impulse to grab her wrist and yank her back down. "I can't forget it," he said. "I want to stay."

"Too bad. I wasn't just blowing smoke when I said I was checking out your story, Mick. I meant it. When it comes to drugs I'm not taking anyone on faith ever again."

"I'm not asking you to. And neither am I planning to slap the moves on you, Sasha, if that's what you're worried about. I'll keep my hands to myself. I just don't want to leave you alone tonight. Hell, baby, *I* don't want to be alone."

Sasha thought of Amy wearing her jacket when she was hit by the car. It was absolute foolishness, the threatened feeling it gave her, because it was an accident, nothing more. That's what everyone was saying, that it must have been a drunk who ran Amy down like that and then simply continued on his way.

And yet . . .

It left her with an odd, uneasy sensation at the base of her neck. She didn't much care for coincidences and here were two accidents that shouldn't have happened, occurring within a week of each other. One impacted her directly, the other peripherally. And Mick was so darn capable. "Are you willing to sleep in the chair?"

Mick looked at the small chair and then down at his long legs. A small smile curved one corner of his mouth. "No. But as I said, I'll keep my hands to myself."

"Very well." Sasha nodded. "But don't make me regret it."

The bed was queen size and there was really no reason why they couldn't both occupy it, each on their respective sides. When Mick climbed in a short while later, however, he immediately rolled to the middle, hooked his arms around Sasha and pulled her over to occupy the same space. He wrapped himself around her, tangled his legs with hers, and pressed her head to his bare chest. His hand lingered to stroke her hair. "Night," he rumbled.

So much for keeping your hands to yourself, she almost protested. But she held her tongue, because truthfully she felt too secure to complain. For the first time since she'd heard about Amy being struck while wearing her jacket, the possibility of some deliberate malevolence in the action ceased to torment her. The possibility had been remote to begin with, yet an unease had still persisted. Here in the warmth and comfort of Mick's arms she finally saw the notion for what it was.

Entirely ludicrous.

TWELVE

Thou shalt not kill; thou shalt not kill. It was a feverishly repeated refrain in Karen Corselli's brain.

She wielded the foaming brush and high-powered sprayer at the coin-operated car wash, applying extra care around the front bumper and the undercarriage of her dark red rented Taurus. *Thou . . . Shalt . . . Not . . . Kill.*

Oh, merciful God, I know that You understand the necessity of removing Sasha Miller from this world and forgive me that un-Christian spurt of satisfaction when I hit her. You must have. Otherwise You surely never would have infused me with Your light, never would have allowed me to taste of the Glory and the Power. Karen scrubbed and sprayed, scrubbed and sprayed, warmed for a brief instant by the recollection of that raw infusion of savage gratification.

Then a cold chill rolled down her spine. It was Amy she had struck. Feeling complacent, she had blended back into the aborted party without anyone even realizing she'd been gone, and that's when she had heard who had been hit. *Oh dear, merciful God, forgive me . . .* Not Sasha at all; it was AMY.

Thou shalt not kill.

Falling to her knees on the wet cement, Karen scrubbed furiously at the backside of the bumper and underneath the front wheel wells, scoured the ridges of the steel-belted radials. How had this come to be? She had seen that coat; it was indisputably Sasha's. And Greg had said it was Sasha who had gone out to the car. Her face had been blocked by the umbrella, of course, but why would she need to see it when she'd already known whom it would be? It wasn't her fault. It should have been Sasha.

Amy would be okay. Yes, Amy would heal just fine; the Lord would provide. Karen could leave her fate in His hands and concentrate on other considerations. Like returning this car to Avis without being subjected to all sorts of inconvenient questions. There was no way on earth she could avoid owning up to some kind of accident, but the trick, clearly, was to provide a red herring to divert their attention. She finished blowing the suds clear with the powerful sprayer and stood back to assess the damage. Panic fading, her mind began to tick over with cool precision. She climbed in the car and drove away.

Fifteen minutes later she found exactly what she was looking for. Idling in the shadows of a rain-swept, twenty-four-hour Super Safeway parking lot, she adjusted her seat belt and eyed the small cluster of cars parked over in the far corner.

Then, giving the gas peddle just the barest touch of acceleration, she rolled straight into the white Ford station wagon.

It was barely past 9 A.M. the next morning when Sasha hung up the phone. She stood looking down at it for a moment before she turned away. Looking up, she found Mick propped up on one elbow in bed, watching her. "Mr. Dello confirms what you told me," she informed him solemnly.

"Yeah?" He rubbed long fingers over his bare chest while he studied her expression. "So how come you don't you look any happier about it?"

"I don't know." She came and sat down on the edge of the mattress. Running one slender finger back and forth over the bedspread, she studied its pattern of carnivorous-looking flowers as if it were the most interesting thing she'd ever seen and then finally admitted, "Partly, I suppose, I'm a little embarrassed to have been so wrong—"

"Hey, given what you overheard, Sasha, you had every reason not to trust me."

Her clear, gray-eyed gaze raised from contemplating the bedspread to meet his. She was still troubled. "Yes, well, that's pretty sporting of you, Mick, considering there's another part of me that can't help but feel you've still got some hidden agenda of your own that I've yet to find out about."

Oh, shit. Only years of practice kept the little zap of shock that trilled along his nerve endings from being revealed in his expression. For a brief moment he was tempted to tell her everything, to just lay it all out and see what she made of it. Hell, she might even be able to shed some light on the identity of the person running the drugs.

Then he immediately shelved that idea. *Yeah, and she might also send you packing, Jack—you wanna risk that?*

No.

Far better to come clean later when his position in her life was more firmly entrenched, when the sex he'd once thought he could use to pry her drug secrets out of her had been more aptly used to ensure she remained his. Besides, confiding in someone outside his field of work contacts was contrary to every professional precept he practiced. So, looking her squarely in the eye, he charmed her with some of his most creative lying to date.

And dismissed an uneasy nagging sensation that insisted he was going to pay for it later on.

Karen Corselli was also on the telephone early that morning. By the time she'd concluded her conversation with the car rental people she was feeling restless . . . and contemptuous. That was just too easy.

She still had to turn the car in, of course, but she didn't

anticipate a problem; the groundwork of having hit another car in a supermarket parking lot had been thoroughly laid. She would simply flutter a little and dither on ever so apologetically. Goodness, gracious, oh silly me, she didn't know *how* her foot could have slipped off the brake that way.

People were so easily led.

She felt a need to go out and flex some muscle. Crossing to the bed, she knelt down, reached beneath it, and pulled forth a metal strongbox. Opening it, she fastidiously selected a small plastic bag of white powder and then remained kneeling there with a small smile curving her lips for a few additional moments. She had been such a good girl for the past couple of weeks; she really was due the opportunity to exercise a little power.

An hour later she had turned in the car and if the people who worked the desk at Avis could have seen the pure steel in her expression as she stood outside the health department's needle exchange, they hardly would have recognized her as the same woman. She was on the corner of Second and Pike, two blocks up from Seattle's famed Pike Place Market. Having learned about this place by eavesdropping on the conversation of a couple of drug-savvy techs, she'd known as soon as she heard about it that she would undoubtedly find a reason to visit it some day. Opening the door, she went inside.

The small downtown corner facility saw a brisk trade; Karen sat quietly in a corner for a while and watched as junkies dropped off as many as fifty used syringes and picked up fresh ones. It was not precisely a tourist attraction widely touted by the Seattle Downtown Association.

But it was certainly one that was well suited for her purposes.

THIRTEEN

Much to Sasha's relief, when queried by Mick the Washington State Crime Lab reported they had collected sufficient trace evidence from Amy's clothing to run their tests. They were not forthcoming on what those tests revealed, but just knowing they had the necessary evidence to proceed was enough for Sasha's peace of mind. She had been willing to give up her jacket if it would mean providing the authorities with a place for their investigations to begin where none had before existed, but in all honesty she was just as happy it wasn't necessary.

That was one problem off her mind. Now if only there weren't so darn many others, all eager and willing to take its place.

She'd thought she had already settled her paranoia regarding the coincidental timing and happenstance of her and Amy's accidents, but there remained an uneasy little twitch deep in her stomach whenever she thought of them. Instinct was a thing she'd learned long ago not to dismiss out of hand, for nine times out of ten it seemed to be dead on the money. But where was she supposed to go with it in this instance? She didn't for the life of her see how she could lend credence to these niggling sensations. They were so nebulous they could hardly even be called suspicions and they simply didn't make sense.

Nevertheless, they persisted.

She went looking for Connie because Connie was a great

one for talking matters through and helping her put her problems into perspective. But she wasn't in her room.

Damn. Sasha turned away from her friend's door and walked slowly back down the corridor. Connie was probably off somewhere doing something fun with someone else. She tried not to let it bother her. After all, she'd been spending so much time with Mick lately she could hardly expect her friend to just hang around and wait for her to have a free moment. But what did she do now?

She finally decided to take a cab to the arena where Lon was practicing. Like Connie, they hadn't really talked much since she and Mick had started sleeping together, and she missed him.

Lon was tickled to see her . . . at least part of him was. Another part was almost annoyed that she had suddenly chosen to show up. What, she didn't have anything better to do today?

Things hadn't been working out the way Lon had envisioned. Okay, it had only been a few days but that was one character trait prison hadn't managed to kick out of him—he was as impatient as ever.

He'd put a lot of thought into what his future would be like during those endless days before his release. How he'd skate again, be with Sasha on a daily basis again. Like the old days. The one scenario he hadn't in a million years anticipated was having to compete for her attention.

Oh, sure, maybe occasionally with one of her girlfriends. But not with some solidly built roughneck who seemed to take great delight rubbing Lon's nose in her sexuality. That wasn't a subject he had ever cared to think about too closely. It had been easy enough to ignore with the only guy he'd known about, the one she'd lost her virginity to back in their competition days. Oh, he'd been aware of the substance of the situation, but he hadn't had to deal with the details. No one had ever thrust the knowledge that she was sexually active in his face.

Vinicor thrust it at him with both hands, making it impossible to ignore. Lon detested it. He'd spent too many years trying to keep men off her and the fact that she welcomed this guy in particular left him feeling helpless.

"I've got to get some sort of balance back in my life," she told him as they skated side by side, languidly performing an old routine. "I've been so enthralled by all this great sex that—"

"Jesus, Sasha, do you mind?" Unconsciously Lon put a greater distance between them. "I hate to be the one to have to break this to you, doll, but your taste in men really sucks, you know? What do you see in him anyway? The guy's hostile. Not to mention he's so goddam arrogant it's enough to make you gag."

"Arrogant to you, maybe. He makes *me* feel safe."

"Okay, I'll buy that." And for all that the guy irritated him, it was something he truly could understand. Vinicor did seem extremely capable . . . and dead determined to put himself squarely between Sasha and the rest of the world. "All the same, let's just leave it at that, huh? I don't think I wanna hear about your sex life with him."

Sasha snorted. "Since when? Aren't you the guy who always used to bug me for all the details?"

"Yeah, but that was when I knew it was safe to do so because the whole world knew you didn't *have* a sex life."

She cut her edges into the ice, coming to a halt. "You nasty little beggar! Just for that I think I'll supply you with all those steamy little details that sure shocked the heck out of me at first, like how he likes to hold my ankles in his hands when we make love—"

"Knock it off, Sasha! I mean it." He shuddered. "Jesus, this is like having to hear some guy brag about screwing my sister."

She watched for a moment in utter enjoyment as, with a flush climbing up his neck, he looked everywhere except at her. Then she abruptly sobered. "He wants me to move in with him, Lonnie," she said.

He muttered an obscenity, then met her gaze with narrowed eyes. "You gonna do it?"

"I don't know." She wanted to tell him about her conflicting emotions, how part of her ached to do exactly that, to move in with Mick lock, stock, and barrel, because she'd never felt this way about a man before and she wanted to see where it would take her. But there was another part of her that kept standing back to study the situation, afraid to trust that this man whom she was falling in love with wasn't operating under false pretenses on some unknown level. There was no factual basis for the latter suspicion, but there was *something* Mick wasn't telling her, something that she sensed but couldn't quite put her finger on. And it scared her to death to think she might be putting her heart on the line for him, when maybe on Mick's part it was all just a . . . joke or something.

She longed to lay it all out in front of Lon, but in the end she kept her own counsel. What would be the point? He'd made no bones about not liking Mick, so she could hardly expect impartial advice from that quarter. And when it came right down to it, this was simply a matter she needed to work out for herself.

So she simply repeated, "I don't know."

And later wondered if that was the point where Lon began to pull away from her.

Mick knew it had taken him too long, now that Sasha was no longer the primary suspect, to get around to wondering just who did have access to Lon Morrison's never-recovered heroin while the man was still in prison. It should have been the first question to pop to mind once Sasha's innocence was established, but instead it had taken him an entire day to narrow down the field. Damn. He was beginning to distrust his own professional acumen when it came to this case.

But then he stacked it up against the combined intelligence of the suits and he felt like the DEA's great white hope once again. The organization was going downhill fast and he was beginning to give some serious consideration to making this his last case. He'd threatened it before, more frequently in the past few years as bit by bit he had slowly grown disenchanted, but deep down he'd never really believed he'd ever see the day.

This was no way for a grown man to make a living, though, not as the agency was currently being run. It wasn't enough, apparently, to simply do his job. Increasingly, he had to work around grandstanding brass and bureaucratic posturing, and now, to top it off, they were sending out smooth-cheeked boys to deliver their messages. His most recent visitor seemed to have a difficult time distinguishing his ass from a hole in the ground.

Jesus, he'd *strutted* across the lobby, shiny black shoes, close-buzzed hair, constipated gray flannel suit and all, as conspicuous as a whore at a Baptist christening. Mick, half afraid the kid would walk right up to him and address him as Special Agent Vinicor, had hastily murmured a glib excuse to the line skater whose problem he was trying to straighten out and melted around the nearest corner. Two seconds later his arm whipped out of a shadowed alcove near the elevator to yank the junior G-man away from the brightly lighted lobby.

Mick had him up against the wall, with his forearm rammed against the young man's Adam's apple, before the kid knew what had hit him. Efficiently, he relieved him of his gun and stepped back, tucking it into the waistband of his Dockers at the small of his back. "What the hell do you think you're doing coming here bold as brass?"

"I was told you weren't in deep cover."

Mick stared at him in disbelief. "Does the word *covert* mean anything to you?"

"Hey, they're just a bunch of ice skaters." The contemptuous curl of the other man's lip told Mick his opinion of that.

"Jesus, kid, are you an example of what they're graduating these days? If so, it's a scary thought." Mick got a quick mental flash of his own opinion upon first joining the Follies in Sacramento; it hadn't been that dissimilar. But, Jesus. At least he'd employed the full contingent of professional responsibility.

His eyes were hard as he leveled them at the younger man. "There are basics you should've learned your first month in the academy," he said coldly. "Foremost being that you don't burn a hump's cover because *you've* determined the degree of danger his target constitutes." He saw that his lecture's only result was to have the young man clench his sphincter a few degrees tighter, and Mick shook his head, rolling his shoulders in disgust. He thrust out a preemptory hand. "What have you got for me?"

Sulkily, the young man passed him a small manila envelope. Ignoring him while he ripped it open, Mick scanned the contents. Then he swore with soft-toned, vicious creativity. His head snapped up and the heat in his blue eyes impaled the young bureaucrat where he stood. He crowded in, aggressively thrusting his face close to the other man's, invading his personal space with impunity. "You trot your skinny ass back to McMahon," he said furiously through his teeth, "and you tell him—" Abruptly he bit off his words, took a step back, and straightened. "No. Never mind; I'll tell him myself. You'd probably just fuck it up." Pulling the confiscated pistol from his waistband, he set it on the floor, used the side of his foot to sweep it beneath a snack-vending machine in the far corner of the alcove, and then turned and walked away.

Letting himself into his room moments later he was glad,

for the first time since he'd put the suggestion to her yesterday morning, that Sasha had refused to give up her room and move into his. At the time he'd been tempted to keep pushing until he got his way, but now he thought it was just as well that she wasn't waiting for him in his room. Because for once in his life he was simply too angry to dissemble, and the phone call he planned to make needed to be placed from a location where total privacy could be assured. Twisting the lock that flipped up an OCCUPIED sign above the dead bolt on the outside of the door, he crossed to the phone. He reread the memo, crumpled the flimsy stationery in his fist, and flung it onto the bed. Sitting down, he read the accompanying report with more care than he'd given it down in the alcove, but upon reaching the end, tossed it aside with equal disgust. Nothing had changed. It still didn't come close to justifying the memo.

Those bastards. Mick snatched up the receiver and punched out a number. Snarling at the intermediaries between himself and his objective, he was ultimately put through to McMahon.

He skipped past all the niceties and went straight to the meat of the matter, snapping, "What the *hell* is the meaning of this memo?"

"And hello to you, too, Special Agent Vinicor," McMahon said evenly. "Which part of it, exactly, don't you understand?"

"The part where some asshole in a three-piece suit, who has never laid eyes on the principals involved in the case, decides he knows better than I do about the facts I've gathered," Mick promptly responded without a care to what his supervisor thought of his language or his attitude. Let McMahon fire him; it would save them all a lot of time and trouble. Hell, he'd make the lie he'd told Sasha a reality and inform the Follies of the full scope of their drug problem, then get himself hired on as a consultant to show them how to get rid of it. As a civilian, there was a very real probability he could actually make a difference, something he had a difficult time doing in the DEA these days. "I requested information on current Follies' employees who had a connection to the amateur figure skating circuit during the year preceding Morrison's arrest. Seems simple enough, but what do I get instead?" His voice lowered in disgust as he snatched up the crumpled paper, smoothed it out, and read, " 'Continue covert investigation of Miller. Not convinced she has been cleared of suspicion.' " He had to pause to take a deep breath, surprised anew at the strength of the rage that coursed through him. "You want to tell me what you based that conclusion on?"

"The report *you* yourself requested on Miller's background, Vinicor."

"I've read the report, McMahon, and I don't see a damn thing here that justifies having my recommendations disregarded or my request for additional information overridden." He flipped through the pages slowly. "It says she was an average student who spent nearly all her free time at Ivan Petralahti's compound. No trouble in school, no arrests, not so much as a freakin' parking ticket."

"It says she was a slut."

A vein swelled in the side of Mick's throat as his back teeth clenched tight. "No," he disagreed coolly, forcing his jaw to unlock. "What it says is that she was *rumored* to have slept around—a rumor that's entirely unsubstantiated from all I can see. There's not so much as one confirmation here, not even one affidavit from a Kells Crossing male to give the rumor some teeth. Everyone appears happy to say she rolled onto her back at the drop of a hat, but—funny thing— no one admits they rolled with her. And, let's see"—Mick flipped to the page he wanted—"a Mary Sue Janorowski states the rumors were so many sour grapes started by a handful of students who were eaten alive with envy over the attention that skating brought Miller in a little town with a depressed economy."

"Janorowski's the town pump."

"Then she doesn't have a damn thing to lose by telling the truth, does she?" Mick plowed his fingers through his hair. "What's the deal here, McMahon? Even if Miller was the hottest thing since the Happy Hooker, what has it got to do with us or the operation? The only possible value she could still have to this case would be publicity wise . . ." His voice trailed away.

Ah shit.

"Bingo," he said quietly. "That's it, isn't it?" The question was purely rhetorical, given the charged silence on the other end of the line. "How did you envision the headlines, sir? Something along the lines of OLYMPIC SILVER MEDAL-IST'S REIGN OF TERROR ENDED BY DEA? Or maybe you foresaw something with a yellower tinge. Wait—I've got it: SLUT SKATER ENDS SLAYING SPREE, SURRENDERS TO DRUG ENFORCEMENT ADMINISTRATION. WEST COAST ADDICTS BREATHE EASIER." Anger was an ice-cold knot in his chest. "Give me the information I requested," he ordered through gritted teeth. "And don't send that snot-nosed kid to deliver it."

"You can be replaced, Vinicor."

"Yeah, so I can. I can also cause a stink so severe it'll take the agency years just to live it down. You know damn well I don't like drug dealers, McMahon. But you know what I like even less? Seeing an innocent woman railroaded in order to make some ambitious suit look good."

Mick replaced the receiver with gentle care.

Then he sat back and chewed on the fact that he'd just made an irrevocable decision concerning the future of his career in the Drug Enforcement Administration.

He was feeling aggressive by the time they reached Spokane. "Here." When Sasha reached the head of the line awaiting room assignment, he reached into his pants' pocket and pulled out a key, thrusting it at her. "This is to my room. You're staying with me."

She studied his expression in silence for a moment, then took the key and turned away without a word. He watched her walk away until Connie's impatient, "Vinicor, do you mind?" dragged his attention back to what he was doing. Finding Connie's place on his roster, he passed her the appropriate room key.

He didn't know what to expect when he got to the room. He wouldn't have been surprised to see the occupied sign flipped on above the doorknob, in which case he'd be shit out of luck, because not even a key would get him in then. Luck was on his side, though. This hotel didn't boast that particular security feature and the key turned smooth as silk when he inserted it. He stepped inside and closed the door.

Sasha's framed photographs and personal stuff were already scattered around and the shower was going in the bathroom. Mick tossed his suitcase on the bed and snapped open the clasps. Pulling out her purloined panties, he stuffed them in the hidden compartment containing his DEA equipment, gun, and ID and closed it back up again. He started to empty his suitcase but the sound of the shower lured him. Looking at the closed bathroom door, he kicked off his shoes and began pulling off the rest of his clothes.

Sasha jumped when the shower curtain abruptly swished open with a click of its rings, her right hand slapping in sheer reflex across the top of her left breast. "Jeez, Mick, you scared me half to death!"

He climbed in the tub, jerked the curtain closed behind him, and turned to her. She was staring up at him with big eyes, her hair in an unwieldy topknot that was listing heavily to one side and precariously anchored in place by a pair of rhinestone-studded, enameled black chopsticks. He made a sound deep in his throat and bent down to kiss her.

One minute Sasha was all alone; the next she was up against the tub-enclosure wall, with Mick's back blocking all the spray from the showerhead and his mouth moving on hers with an urgency that was only minimally in control. As approaches went, it had all the finesse of a Stone Age courtship ritual. If only she could think straight, she was sure she'd decide that this was just too Neanderthal to be the least bit arousing.

But all her analytical circuits were blown, so all she could do was respond. And what she responded to most strongly was the neediness in him. Mick was not a needy man by nature, but he seemed to require something from her right now that she was, by God, going to give to him. Ignoring the too-tight grip of his arms, the almost painful roughness of his mouth, Sasha simply hung on and kissed him back as best she could.

"God." Mick ripped his mouth free and stared down at her, breathing raggedly through his mouth. "I'm sorry; I'm hurting you." He started to release her but she tightened her grip around his neck.

"No," she said. "You're doing just fine, Mick. Don't stop holding me."

"Ah, Jesus." Then his mouth found hers again and emotions that had cooled down for a brief moment escalated out of control once again.

Seconds later he was blazing a hungry path down her throat. Then his hands were on her waist, lifting her against the wall. "God, I love your nipples," he muttered, worrying one with his teeth, his tongue, his gaze snapping up to lock on hers as he sucked it into his mouth.

She felt the heat of his look, watched his cheeks flex. Felt the resulting tug like hot lightning shoot from breast to loins, and whimpered helplessly. Her thighs spread apart and he was there between them suddenly, sliding into her, solid and intrusive, reaching high.

"Oh, Micky." She wrapped her arms more tightly around his neck and pressed her face into his neck. Her ankles locked behind his waist. Mick reached up with one hand and yanked the chopsticks out of her bun. They clattered to the tub floor as her thick hair tumbled down around them, spilling over his left shoulder and down his arm and back.

"Love your hair," he muttered and then he was silent as he gripped the underside of her thighs in hard hands and surged into her with deep, emphatic strokes. It wasn't until he felt her begin to climax that he spoke again.

"Love *you,*" he breathed into her ear, his voice guttural as he listened to her pant and sob for release, her arms a stranglehold around his neck. "Love you, love you, love you, Sasha . . . Ohh *God.*"

She couldn't have said afterward how they got from the bathroom to the bed. They must have remained locked together when he carried her in because her first conscious thought was when he pulled out and rolled to his back, snagging her with a brawny arm to pull her near. And then it hit her. "Oh, God, Mick," she breathed in horror. "You didn't wear a condom." Aware of the rush of moisture on her thighs, she automatically counted on her fingers, scrambled through a mental calendar. Then she relaxed. What was she doing? She didn't have to sweat the remaining days until her period. Like a lot of female athletes, her periods, due to the intense level of physical activity and perhaps the constant travel as well, were sporadic at best. The last one had been about twenty-one months ago. But Mick didn't know that and his actions had been foolhardy. So had her own, come to think of it, if she had even subconsciously counted on that for birth control.

"Shit!" He reared up on one elbow and stared down at her. "God, Sasha, I'm sorry. I've never been that careless in my life; I swear to you." He shook his head. "I don't know what got into me." He'd been like an animal marking his territory. Jesus, talk about primal. "What's the timing like? Christ, if I got you pregnant—" He smoothed the wild corkscrews of her dark hair away from her face. "I'll take care of you, darlin', I swear I will."

How? she wondered. He'd said he loved her. She hadn't expected that, but she couldn't deny it thrilled her to the marrow. But, how did he plan to take care of her? Pay for the abortion and hold her hand? Pay child support and make arrangements to see his kid on alternate weekends and six weeks every summer? Marry her? She knew she ought to question his intentions, demand some concrete answers, but in truth the prospective reply scared her to death. "No, I think it's an okay time," she said instead. *Oh, God, Sasha, you're so spineless.*

They were both silent for several moments, lying curled together on a bed they shared with his open suitcase. Finally, she said, "Mick?"

"Uh-huh?"

"I've never lived with a man before. What do we do when we're not making love?"

"We talk." Except there were so damn many things he couldn't talk about. He was just beginning to realize the tight little corner he'd painted himself into in this situation. If he had only one honest bone left in his body, however, he swore this on it: he would never lie to her again, no matter what. He might have to skirt around the edges of the truth at times, but he would not tell her an out-and-out lie. "Like, for starters, you tell me what it was like giving up your entire childhood to become a professional ice skater. And I'll tell you about growing up in Montana."

The Follies was such a tight little society that nothing escaped its notice, or comment, for long. As soon as someone heard that Amy Nitkey had been discharged from the hospital and was going home with her parents to recuperate, the word spread. And it didn't take more than a few hours for the news that Sasha had moved in with Mick Vinicor to reach Lon Morrison's ears.

He felt betrayed. The logical part of him knew perfectly

well that situations in life were never stagnant, but a stronger, more stubborn, corner of his mind insisted she owed it to him to always be there for him, to always be the same. When Sasha tracked him down and invited him to have dinner with her, he simply stood there staring at her with flat eyes that gave away no hint of his emotions. Eyes that had lived through incarceration. "Sure you wouldn't rather eat with lover boy?" he asked her insolently.

"Uh-oh. You've heard the news, I take it." She threaded her arm through his and tried to tug him toward the hotel dining room. "I wanted to tell you myself, but I guess I can't honestly say I'm surprised that someone beat me to the punch."

"Yeah, well." He disentangled himself. "My felicitations," he offered stiffly. "I hope you'll be extremely happy."

"Ooh, such sincerity." She hooked arms with him once again. When he simply stood there so unyieldingly, she snapped with the impatience of years of familiarity, "Oh, get the stick out of your rear, Lon, and c'mon. You'd think I was out to swindle you out of your last buck. It's a crummy dinner and I'm buying."

"Damn right you are," he agreed sourly as he allowed her to maneuver him toward the dining room. "My last buck is about what I'm down to."

She smiled at him as they seated themselves. "I could lend you some money if you'd like."

"I don't need your fucking charity, Sasha!"

"And I'm not offering you any, you dipshit!" she snarled back. "Jeez, Lon, if you were any stiffer you'd be an ironing board." She forced a smile for the waiter who stopped by the table to hand them each a menu. The minute he'd recited the daily specials and departed, however, she leaned over the table and said through gritted teeth, "I didn't offer to give you any money, you jerk; I said I could lend you some. But if you're too proud for that, then be broke. Just do me a favor and don't whine about it. If you had ever saved a dime in your life you might not be in this predicament."

"Yeah, okay; I'm sorry," he muttered. Rationally he knew she was right. But emotionally he thought, what the hell did she know about it, anyway, when it came right down to it? She was so goddam perfect she never seemed to feel the same impatience the rest of the world struggled with. Where most people could barely tolerate the wait to get their hands on a certain possession, Sasha quietly saved and abided. Christ. It was enough to make you gag.

Well, he was tired of waiting. He'd given it a shot her way. But he was merely a sinner, not some goddam flawless angel like Saush. He didn't understand how she'd turned out the way she had, given the way both of them had started from the same place. He admired and loved her more than anyone else in the world. But he wasn't like her. He didn't want to scrimp from pay check to pay check. He wanted stuff now, not a month, a year, two years from now.

And he knew just how to get it.

FOURTEEN

Not that she'd taken the time to apply much rational thought to the matter, exactly, but in some unacknowledged corner of her mind Sasha must have expected that it would be difficult getting used to living with Mick on a full-time basis. Instead, she found herself taking to it like a cat to its creature comforts.

She'd known the sex would be good but had been more than a little leery that they would get in each other's way once they rolled out of bed. Mick, however, turned out to be thoughtful in ways she hadn't anticipated. He didn't require round-the-clock entertainment. He steered clear of the bathroom until she was finished with it in the mornings, and the night a line skater with man problems had shown up with tale of woe and a pint of cheap vodka seeking female advice and comfort, he had discreetly made himself scarce.

Most days they each went their separate ways much as they had when occupying separate rooms. Mick was usually out and about doing managerial stuff all day long, and she still spent the usual amount of time testing the ice in various arenas and exploring with Connie. And even if they'd been tripping all over each other in the worst way possible, the unadorned truth was she probably *still* would have labored like the devil to find a way to make it work. For Mick possessed two traits that Sasha found almost impossible to resist. He was physical in ways that owed nothing to his sexuality and he spent a great deal of time simply talking to her.

Except for her mother, no one in Sasha's life had shown her much physical affection. She was a toucher by nature, and Mick fulfilled a need she hadn't even realized she possessed when he hugged her, or pulled her onto his lap, or toyed with her hair, or guided her along as they walked, one of his warm, hard-skinned hands wrapped around the back of her neck beneath her heavy fall of hair.

Little by little, she was learning about him. He had strong opinions on selected subjects, the most important of which she tended to agree with, a few of which they had argued to a standstill. He was verbal, tactile, and sometimes a shade too possessive for comfort. He said he loved her, and she refused to say it back until she was absolutely certain it wasn't just the novelty of great sex that she loved.

But deep in her heart she knew she was merely marking time. The man was beginning to own her, body and soul. And eventually she broke down and told him so.

Fairy tales really did come true.

Oh, Jesus, he was in a whole lot of trouble. He'd always thought love was for other people, never for him, but he'd fallen like a ton of bricks for a pretty little skater with big gray eyes and a mass of curly black hair. The feelings she could induce so effortlessly stripped him of every single protective layer he'd ever owned and he didn't even have the good sense to give a damn. This was the genuine article, all right, Love with a capital L. And no matter what, he was hanging on to it tooth and nail.

The question was, how?

He'd never had a relationship that had lasted more than six goddam hours in his life, but in his arrogance he'd actually thought he was doin' okay, thought he had it all under control. All he had to do was treat her the best he knew how, show her how he felt, use this time to entrench his position.

Then last night she'd told him she loved him.

God, he could see her still, going to pieces in his arms, breath coming fast, eyes luminous, whispering, "I love you, Mick; oh God, Micky, I love you." It wasn't until then he'd realized just how precarious his hold on this relationship really was. *Sooner or later,* his conscience taunted at the very moment she was making all his dreams come true, *you're going to have to tell her the truth, chump. You're gonna have to look her in those big trusting eyes and tell her you lied to her from the beginning.*

And that was going to be the death of all his dreams.

For he'd gotten to know what was important to her. She revealed a new detail of her private life daily. It never even occurred to her to hold anything back, and the minute she realized how defenseless she'd left herself she was going to hate him for it. More than anything he wished there was some way he could reciprocate, some way to hand her a few weapons against him to bolster her defenses, but there were too many aspects of his life that he simply couldn't share with her, at least not yet. Hell, the way he'd made his living for the past decade pretty well *was* his private life, and God knew that cut down fairly dramatically on the number of conversational topics that were safe to discuss.

So he'd talked to her instead about the things that were important to him. What he thought, how he felt about things, what he could live with, what he couldn't.

And knew without being told that it wasn't going to be enough. Not even close. After all the dishonesty that had poisoned her life, finding out he'd lied to her too was going to be one transgression too many.

He knew in his gut it was going to be the one she absolutely would not tolerate.

Lon rolled off Karen and stretched out on his back, smiling in satisfaction. Now this was more like it. It was restful to be in the company of someone who didn't expect him to be so damn good all the time. When Karen looked at him she saw him for exactly what he was. She wasn't forever conjuring up some friggin' boy scout who never had and never would exist outside of a sweet woman's wistful imagination.

He wished more than anything that he could be that boy scout. At the same time he was eternally weary of struggling to be what he damn well wasn't.

Karen rolled onto her stomach. She draped herself across him, scratching her fingernails lightly across his stomach. Lonnie wrapped a friendly arm around her shoulders and stroked her hair where it rested against his chest. He waited for her to once again bring up the subject of distributing her bootleg heroin. He was finally ready to be convinced—his days as a choirboy were definitely coming to a close.

This postcoital interval was generally when she started bossing him around, but she'd been strangely reticent ever since Seattle. He would much prefer that she think he was giving in to her demands, but her continued silence had the effect of making him restless. Now that he'd finally made up his mind he wondered what the holdup was. If she didn't bring the matter up soon, he'd have to throw it onto the table for discussion himself.

He was gearing himself up for the best approach when the little night-light that shed the room's only illumination blew with a sharp pop. They both jumped, then Lon laughed. He squeezed Karen, reaching out with one hand to grope through the soft darkness for the lamp on the nightstand. "Sounded like a gunshot for a minute there, didn't it?"

She didn't respond and it wasn't until her failure to do so became noticeable that he also noticed how rigid she had become against his side. She began to gasp as if she wasn't drawing in enough air, a high-pitched *hee* growing louder at the apex of each successive inhalation. Abandoning his search for the lamp, he turned back to her. "Hey, baby, what's the matter? Karen? You all right?" Her struggle for breath grew louder. "Jesus. Take it easy, now. You're all right; you're just hyperventilating. Christ, I wish we had a paper bag. Shh, now. Shhhhh."

For once she failed to hear the blasphemy. "Turn-on-the-light-turn-on-the-light-turn-on-the-light," she wheezed. "Oh please, I'll be good; turn on the light."

Once again he fumbled for the lamp and finding it, snapped it on. Immediately, most of the tension that held her in its grip left her rigid muscles. Lon spied a sack on the table and slid his arm out from under her, rolling to his feet. Snatching it up, he dumped its contents on the tabletop and brought it over to Karen. "Here. Breathe into this."

She did as he said, using both hands to clasp it to her nose and mouth. Within a few moments her breathing had resumed its normal cadence. She lowered the bag and lay staring up at the ceiling.

Lon studied her pale face. "You wanna tell me what that was all about?"

"No," she said through lips so stiff they barely moved.

"Okeydoke." He pulled the bedspread up, tucking her in, and then sat beside her quietly for several moments. Briefly, strictly in the interests of making conversation, he considered bringing up his newfound willingness to go back to his larcenous ways. But in the end he held his tongue, for he knew Karen too well. She was going to be royally pissed that he had witnessed her in a weak moment and would most likely feel compelled to pull a power play on him just to show him who was still the boss. If he said he was willing to do now what he'd refused to do before when she had demanded it of him, her most probable response would be to say: too bad, the timing's not right for *me* now.

Oh well, no big loss. This was Idaho. There were probably more neo-Nazi skinheads in this state than the type of customer she catered to, anyway.

*   *   *

Sasha spotted Lon sitting by himself in the far corner of the hotel coffee shop when she and Connie went in for lunch. He glanced up at her but then immediately returned his attention to the magazine that was spread out on the tabletop next to his plate. Sasha stopped so abruptly Connie bounced off her back.

Why, that lousy faker. She knew perfectly well he'd seen her but for some reason he was pretending he hadn't. Feeling perverse, she dragged Connie over to his corner table. "Hi!" She pushed Connie into a chair, tossed her wallet on the tabletop, and took a chair herself. "Mind if we join you?" Without awaiting reply, she snatched up a menu and shoved it in her friend's dainty hands. Connie grinned at her and flipped it open.

Sasha turned her attention back to Lon. "So, whataya reading?" She craned her head sideways. *"Playboy,* huh. You always did have intellectual tastes." She started thumbing through the magazine in search of the centerfold.

Lonnie jerked it out of her reach. "Saush, do you mind?" Scowling, he smoothed the pages she'd rifled, and in that moment she knew beyond a shadow of a doubt that he really was pulling away from their friendship. She'd suspected as much, given his recent attitude toward her, but had hoped she was wrong.

Dammit, though, she wasn't. Her old Lonnie could have been counted on to make a facetious comment about reading the magazine strictly for its articles, and then with his usual sarcastic humor would have plunged right in to help her trash the centerfold's good name, intellectual prowess, and flawless, perky, airbrushed figure.

This Lonnie looked at her as if she were a pushy tavern moll encroaching on his sermon preparation time.

Still she kept trying. "I'm going out to check on the ice at the arena after lunch," she said, hoping the good cheer in her voice didn't sound half as forced and phony to him as it did to her. "You wanna come with?"

Come with. It was an expression he hadn't heard in years—not, in fact, since they'd finally left Kells Crossing behind them for good—and Lon's heart constricted. His facial muscles wanted to give her a big old lopsided smile, but he sternly put the constraints to them. "No, Mother, I do not," he said flatly. And fisted his hands under the table at the hurt that flashed across her face.

"Excuse me, won't you?" she murmured breezily and pushed her chair back from the table. "I just remembered I . . . uh, forgot something." She turned and strode swiftly from the room, her head held high.

Not, however, before her companions caught the sheen of moisture that reflected the overhead light in her large, gray eyes.

There was a heartbeat of silence in the wake of her departure. Then another. Jon looked up to find Connie still sitting there, leaning back in her chair with her arms crossed under her diminutive breasts, watching him with a set expression. "What the hell are you gawkin' at?" he snarled.

"You son of a bitch," she said in disgust. Then her eyes narrowed, her arms dropped to her sides, and she leaned forward. "No. That's probably doing your Mama a disservice. You prick."

Lon ran his eyes up and down her insultingly. "You think about my prick a lot, Nakamura?"

She turned pink and made a sound of distaste. Nose in the air, looking him dead in the eye, she suggested, "Why don't you kiss my pretty gold butt, Morrison."

"I'd like that, dollface. Like to kiss *all* your delectable pink parts." Which was nothing short of the truth but he stated it as offensively as possible. He'd known from the first little pulse of sexual awareness that she wasn't for him. Connie Nakamura was another nice girl, like Sasha, and nice girls sure as hell weren't for a loser like him. He reached across the table and ran an insolent fingertip down the subtle slope of her right breast, scratching his nail back and forth over her nipple. "Whataya say we go up to my room, get naked, and get down to it?"

Slapping his hand away, she shoved back from the table and rose to her feet. She stared down, blistering him with the contempt that blazed out of her exotic dark eyes. "You make me sick. For reasons I will never comprehend, Sasha loves you. But instead of thanking your lucky stars for a friend like her you're so damn jealous of the fact that she's finally found someone who'll take care of her the way she deserves to be taken care of that you don't know whether to pee or go blind. Well, let me tell you, bud; you don't deserve her. She's worth a dozen of you." Then she, too, turned and walked out on him.

"You got that right, my little Far Eastern beauty," Lon muttered. "You are fuckin'-A, one hundred percent correct. St. Sasha is too good for the likes of this sinner." Then he shrugged, picked up his sandwich, and forced his attention back to his *Playboy.*

Sasha was nearly blinded by her tears, but she saw Mick through the blur talking to a man outside their room. She was blearily aware of the stranger shoving a clipboard at Mick and of Mick scribbling on it. Then a small manila envelope exchanged hands and the man smiled, spoke softly, and sketched a finger salute off his forehead before he walked jauntily down the hallway in the opposite direction from her approach. The tune he whistled floated back in his wake.

Mick was still standing in the hallway waiting for her when she reached the room. "Hiya, sweetheart; I didn't expect to see you again so soon." He broke off when he got his first good look at her and his smile of greeting faded to a frown of concern. "Sasha? What's the matter, baby? Are you all right?" He reached an arm out to wrap around her shoulders and she walked straight past it into his chest, burying her face in the crisp, laundered smell of his shirt and inhaling deeply the scent of soap, water, and man beneath. Clutching his spare waist, she held on as if her life depended on it, and the tears she'd been holding back by sheer determination overflowed.

Mick's arms tightened. "What is it darlin'? What happened?"

She started mumbling rapidly into his shirtfront but only one word in five was even remotely coherent.

"What?" Mick maneuvered them into the room and closed the door behind them. Rubbing his hands up and down her back, he leaned back from the waist and ducked his head in an attempt to see into her face, but she refused to relinquish her position against his chest, apparently entrenched for the duration. Once again she mumbled.

"Darlin', I can't understand a word you're saying." He backed her over to the chairs, sat her down in one and squatted on his heels in front of her. Reaching up, he used his thumbs to wipe the puddles from beneath her eyes and then swiped them like windshield wipers across her tear-streaked cheeks. When it appeared as if the flow may have been staunched, he picked up her hands, which rested so limply in her lap, and rubbed them between his own. "Start over again, Saush. And this time speak more slowly."

She told him everything she could recall concerning her past several encounters with Lon. When she'd finished, Mick remained on his haunches in front of her for a few silent moments, intently studying her eyes, trying to gauge exactly how she must have been affected. Finally, he merely said, "I'm sorry, sweetheart. I know it must hurt like hell."

His eyes dropped to where their entwined hands lay in a tangle on her knees while he considered for an instant what he could do that would be of practical assistance. Watching his thumbs rub back and forth across the backs of her hands, he finally looked back up and gave her the barest suggestion of a smile. "I could always beat him up for you. You want?"

An involuntary snort of laughter escaped her. "Yes! I think that would be most satisfying." Then her lips wobbled for a second before she got them back under control. Eyes locked with his, she confessed, "I'm scared to death he's getting back into the drug thing, Micky."

His professional instincts went on red alert, and even as he petted her and murmured reassurances his mind was analyzing ways to utilize this newest data. He was dying to pump her for further information. The portion of him that was her lover, however, was more empathetic.

It was no secret he thought Morrison was a worthless son of a bitch. He also knew, however, how Sasha felt about the guy. He'd learned a lot about her life since they'd been living together and a guiding force in it was that Morrison had been damn near the only friend she'd had growing up. And he'd protected her; Mick had to give him that. Morrison and Saush had been as close as two people can get, and now she was faced with the prospect of being forced to witness him toss his life away again, and all for the sake of the promise of the easy life that had ruined him once before.

Mick figured that what she was feeling had to be an equivalent to the frustration, rage, and bone-deep sorrow he used to feel back in the days when he'd known his brother was about to go out on the prowl in search of a new score. When he had known there wasn't a damn thing he could do to prevent it.

He pulled her up out of the chair and led her over to the bed. Tumbling them onto the mattress, he pulled her into his arms. And he talked to her.

He tried to prepare her for the eventuality that maybe she couldn't save Morrison. That maybe nobody could.

"But he promised me he was through with this shit for good!" she insisted.

"Baby, he could hardly tell you otherwise, could he? We all know your feelings on the subject. You would've wrung his scrawny neck for him."

"Damn it, Mick, don't patronize me. He *promised* me and I'm telling you I know when Lonnie's slingin' the bull and when he isn't."

Mick shrugged. "Okay. Then chances are there's someone else out there who's encouraging him to backslide." He hesitated, but finally decided there was no real reason why he couldn't comfort her *and* do his job—the two weren't necessarily mutually exclusive. "You have any idea who that could be, Saush?" he inquired. And held his breath.

"Not a clue," she promptly replied. "I can't imagine anyone even attempting such a thing. Well, maybe John Beggart or Marty Roth. But Lon would never go along with a suggestion from either of those idiots." She shoved up on an elbow in order to see Mick better. "Lonnie is mule stubborn, Mick. Suppose someone did offer him an opportunity to make some really big money. Financially it would appeal to him and he'd be tempted; I'm not denying that. But I also know Lon, and he would say no, flat out—at least at first."

"What makes you so damn certain?"

She looked him dead in the eye and repeated what she had told him already. "Because he promised me."

Mick felt a prickling at the back of his neck. For the first time he was beginning to get an inkling . . . and he didn't like what it was suggesting. Incidents, which up to this point had seemed senseless, were beginning to suggest a pattern that made a convoluted kind of sense. "Would he be likely to tell the person that he was refusing because of a promise he made to you?" he queried her without apparent emphasis.

Sasha shrugged. "Who knows?"

"Okay. Let me approach this from another angle. If he made you a vow—and clearly you believe that he was sincere when he did so—then why the hell change his mind now?" Sasha merely widened her eyes at him, her expression suggesting "think about it," and Mick nodded. "Ah. Sure. You and me."

"It's gotta be."

She laid her head back down on his chest and they were both quiet for a moment. It wasn't until then that she remembered the man with the clipboard. "Mick, who was that man out in the hall?"

"Who?" He raised his head up to look at her, but then settled back down again when he realized to whom she was referring. "Oh, the overnight express courier. I'm working on a project for someone and he brought me some information that I need. Or, at least I hope he did."

"Oh, Mick, I'm sorry." Immediately Sasha tried to push away. "I ought to let you get back to work," she insisted guiltily, but Mick tightened his arms around her, preventing her from leaving.

"Hey, it's not a problem," he said. "Trust me, babe, another five minutes one way or another isn't going to make all that much difference to anything I've currently got going. You know how it is." He gave her a self-deprecatory grin. "Nine-tenths of the stuff I do around here is straightening out the crew's or cast's personal messes."

He did a lot more than that, but she understood what he was saying. Mick had an undeniable air of authority about him and he got things done. The combination was irresistible to those who didn't boast similar capabilities and it hadn't taken long before people with problems began bringing them to him. Most were minor; a few were not. Regardless of the severity, he invariably solved whatever predicament was brought to him and he did it confidentially and without fuss. Not even with her did he discuss other people's troubles unless the person requesting help launched into the details of his dilemma in front of her. It was a trait she found admirable.

Luckily for Mick, it was also a trait that provided a convenient explanation for the sporadic missives from his true employer.

Sasha was a great respecter of privacy, but he hadn't stayed alive in a dangerous profession for as long as he had by taking unnecessary chances. *Don't Tempt Fate* were words to live by. He waited until she had tracked down Connie and they'd once again left to take a second shot at their aborted lunch before he sat down and ripped open the manila envelope the DEA courier had delivered.

And about damn time it had shown up, too. McMahon had taken his own sweet time delivering the information, and Mick knew a power play when he saw one. This was a little chest thumping on McMahon's part, his way of saying Mick's threats neither intimidated nor impressed him. Game playing of this ilk was just the sort of bullshit the suits loved best.

Looking on the bright side, though, at least the courier had been a total professional.

He studied the list of names of people connected to the Follies who had been on the amateur circuit at the time of Morrison's arrest. Sara Parsons. Karen Corselli. Jeffrey O'Brien. And seven names from the technical support portion of the Follies personnel. That sort of took him by surprise until he remembered what a closed little society the skating world was and then he felt foolish for jumping to an assumption that wasn't scrupulously thought through. He ought to know better. Of course it wasn't only the performers who moved around in this business.

Given a bit of consideration, as a matter of fact, skating was actually a rich kid's sport. Sasha and Morrison were the exception, not the norm. He'd learned enough since he'd been with the Follies to realize that on the whole it took a great deal of money to support years of training and cover expenses needed to compete on the amateur circuit. Hell, skate boots alone ran eight hundred to a thousand bucks a pair and they didn't even last that long given the moisture they were continuously exposed to. He sure as hell didn't rule out any of the skaters on the list, but they were less likely to need the money. And most of them had an athlete's respect for their bodies, which made it more difficult to imagine them pushing a substance guaranteed to destroy it.

On the other hand, Morrison hadn't hesitated to do it, and

for all Mick knew the motive had nothing to do with money. He had to start somewhere, however, and he chose—his finger ran down the list and came to a halt a short ways down the page—Jack Berensen. The bus driver.

Jack struck him as a stand-up sort of guy. But this wouldn't be the first case he'd come across where behind closed doors an apparently stand-up guy turned out be the nastiest son of a bitch a person would ever care to encounter, and in Mick's estimation the bus driver warranted a closer examination. His occupation alone was enough to arouse Mick's inbred suspicions. Driving a bus from town to town presented a world of opportunity to anyone with a larcenous bent.

Who the hell knew if it would lead anywhere; it was a working supposition at best. At least it gave him a place to start. Mick filed the list of names with the rest of his private paraphernalia and gathered his wallet and room key. He let himself out of the room.

When he returned to it several hours later, he was whistling softly between his teeth. His afternoon had been productive. He didn't have a clue yet where the information he'd gathered today would lead him or what it was going to yield in the form of tangible evidence. But it had felt good simply having a concrete goal to pursue. From the word go this damn case had been so far from the standard it was ridiculous. And face it, the fact that his mood was this elevated simply because he'd reestablished a little normal procedure back into his routine was nothing short of pitiful, but there it was. He'd done his job this afternoon as it should be done and he felt great.

Opening the hotel room door, the first thing he saw was Sasha sitting on the floor of the closet. A spontaneous smile lit his face and he reapplied his efforts to jiggling the key free of the lock. In the next instant he became aware of the exact nature of the mess surrounding her and nausea swelled up his throat.

His DEA identification was flipped open and resting on the rug. His gun was next to her thigh. She was holding her satin leopard-skin panties in one hand and the headset to the recording device dangled around her neck.

He didn't need to see the look of shattered fury in her eyes or the stamp of betrayal on her face to know that his entire future had just gone down the tubes.

FIFTEEN

Sasha didn't purposely set out to invade Mick's privacy. All she'd wanted was to find her "Skate the Dream" sweatshirt.

Like so much of the performing arts, AIDS had hit the skating community hard. There was a significant number of gay males in their midst, and too many had succumbed to the disease in the past several years. *Skate the Dream* was an exhibition that had been put on in Toronto some time back to benefit Canadian skater Rob McCall. It was one of the very first performances Sasha had participated in as a professional skater, and she treasured the sweatshirt that had been presented to her in commemoration of her contribution to the effort.

When it occurred to her that she hadn't seen it since Spokane, well, she didn't panic, exactly . . . but its disappearance did make her anxious. Left on her own with time to kill, her anxiety grew worse and finally she decided to mount a full-scale search. By the time she got around to Mick's suitcase it had become her last avenue of attack and her very last hope.

She dragged it off the top shelf of the closet and dropped it onto the carpeted closet floor, really hoping, as she knelt in front of it and popped the latches, that he had picked the sweatshirt up from one of their previous hotel rooms and stuffed it into his case, because she'd hate to lose it. She flipped open the lid of the case.

Oh, thank goodness. Relief flooded her when she found the sweatshirt neatly folded in the bottom of his suitcase. Pulling it on over her head, she dragged the heavy weight of her hair out from the neck opening and turned back to the case, fully prepared to close it up again and put it back where she'd found it. But a small black leather case, which the removal of her sweatshirt had uncovered, snagged her attention and she stared down at it, her curiosity aroused.

Her well-developed respect for other people's privacy knew exactly what the proper thing to do was, of course. No question about it, she should leave it undisturbed. It belonged to Mick. He'd never offered to share whatever was inside it with her, and it was really none of her business.

But . . .

He'd never offered to share whatever was inside it with her. Why not? Her slender index finger rubbed back and forth along the box's leather-encased top edge; then dipped down to stroke the small golden lock that was mounted on its front.

No, really, she shouldn't. Her hand dropped away.

On the other hand . . .

If it wasn't actually locked then it probably wasn't really *private* private. Her fingers returned to the clasp to fiddle and poke. She pressed down with her fingertip.

It was locked.

Damn. Now she was really curious. Why did Mick keep a locked box in his suitcase, and why had he never mentioned anything about it to her? She felt along the pockets that lined the inside of the big suitcase and then searched the lining itself, looking for a key.

Then abruptly she caught herself and went very still, with one hand braced on the closet floor next to the large suitcase, the fingers of her other hand flat against the padded sateen material that lined the bottom of the luggage. *Shame on you.* Good Lord, the case probably held a few of Mick's valuables, which he simply hadn't had a chance to deposit in the hotel safe.

Oh God, Sasha, what on earth are you thinking of, digging through his personal stuff like some cut-rate secret agent while his back is turned? She was ashamed of the answer. Somewhere in the back of her mind had lingered a persistent little suspicion that Mick was involved in something he shouldn't be. The idea of it scared her because if something happened to him she didn't know how she'd survive.

But to do this! She was all alone and no one would ever be aware of her momentary transgression, but she was nevertheless deeply embarrassed. Because *she* was aware. She was well aware that she'd been this far from attempting to pick the lock with her trusty nail file. Her mother had certainly raised her better than this, and if Mick should ever find out she would die.

It was in the middle of this melodramatic bit of self-flagellation that she noticed the discrepancy in height between the hand she had braced on the closet floor and the hand that was still flat against the bottom of the suitcase's interior. They were on two distinctly different levels.

A false bottom? All her doubts rushed back. *Oh, God, Mick, what are you involved in?* Her heart dropped and her stomach lurched up to meet it, for she was very much afraid she knew. She simply could not think of one good reason why a man would need a suitcase with a false bottom—certainly not a reason that was in any way legitimate. She began to feel carefully along both the interior and exterior of the luggage in search of a latch that would access the concealed compartment.

She found it during a span of time that could have lasted five minutes or could have lasted forty.

Feeling betrayed, feeling duped, she fully expected to uncover evidence that Mick was involved in drugs after all—all those heated protestations of innocence that had so easily persuaded her to the contrary notwithstanding. The first item she laid eyes on seemed to confirm her worst fears. Gingerly, she picked up the black-gripped, blue-steel-nosed handgun. Its heavy weight made her wrist droop and she hastily set it down on the carpet, careful to point the barrel away from herself.

Oh God, she didn't feel so hot all of a sudden. She doubted, in fact, that it was possible to feel any worse. Or so she thought until she picked up the scuffed leather wallet, and before she even had a chance to flip it open, noticed the leopard-skin-patterned satin panties that were folded into a tiny little triangle beneath it.

Her panties.

She wasn't even aware of the sick moan that crawled its way out of her throat. Oh sweet Jesus, when was it she had first noticed they were missing? She'd assumed she must have left them behind at one of the hotels in . . . was it California? Oregon?

Long before she'd become involved with Mick Vinicor, at any rate.

He'd been in her room. Gone through her stuff. Sasha's eyes burned dryly and goose bumps stood up on her arms and legs. He said he loved her, but long before he'd even kissed her for the first time he'd been pawing through her underwear drawer.

She was going to be sick.

Rinsing out her mouth a few moments later she braced her hands flat on the bathroom counter and slowly raised her head. She looked at her pale reflection in the mirror, distantly aware that water dripped from her nose and chin and noting in an indifferent corner of her mind that her skin looked almost jaundiced.

She didn't want to go back in there. But she had to. Her gray eyes, so large and vulnerable, narrowed and grew hard, and she slowly straightened, taking a deep, calming breath. She slicked the remaining moisture from her cheeks with both hands.

She should be accustomed to this kind of betrayal, to these never-ending lies by now. Hell, it wasn't as if this were a first or anything . . . not by a long shot. She attracted this sort of treatment as effortlessly as a pretty coed gathers Sigma Phi pins. Either she gave off some sort of scent or there really was a fundamental flaw in her.

The pity feast, however, would simply have to wait. She needed to finish what she had begun.

She picked up the wallet she had dropped in her mad dash for the toilet bowl and sank back down on the closet floor. For a moment, she merely sat and stared at the worn leather in her hand. Finally, she flipped it open.

And simply stared numbly at the contents.

It was a picture ID and a badge of some sort. She read the words, but they seemed to float in front of her eyes and scramble before they reached her brain. She wasn't making any sense out of them, so she read it again. And again.

A . . . policeman? Mick was some kind of *cop?* She gave the picture a closer examination. No, she must be mistaken. It looked more like a mug shot than a . . .

But the words insisted he was a special agent for the Drug Enforcement Agency. Administration. Whatever. He was a cop.

But why would a cop go through her underwear drawer?

To look for some sort of evidence apparently, she realized a moment later when she held in her shaking hands a report that detailed every sordid rumor ever to dodge her footsteps in Kells Crossing. She read and reread the bouncing words; then, letting it fall to her lap, stared blindly into the distance.

It appeared they'd covered just about everything, damn them to hell and gone, except for maybe her bra size. There was no way to verbalize the sense of violation she felt reading about herself, no way to measure how exposed and raw it left her feeling. She . . .

No. She couldn't think about this now. Reaching for a folded sheet of paper in the hidden compartment, she shook it out. It said the following was a list of the names Mick had requested. Scanning it, she recognized Follies' people who had been around clear back when she and Lonnie were following the amateur circuit. She checked the date, saw it was today's, and remembered the express delivery man. *Well, you gotta give the devil his due,* she thought bitterly. *Mick didn't precisely lie about the guy.*

For just a second, looking at the list, she felt a ray of hope. Maybe there *was* an explanation, after all. Maybe Mick was investigating one of the names on the list. Maybe . . .

Oh, get real, girl. Marvin Braverman? He hates drugs even worse than you do. Karen Corselli? Sasha shoveled her hair away from her face so ruthlessly the outer corners of her eyes stretched. *Yeah, right. How bloody likely is he to investigate one of those paragons when he's got the Slut of Kells Crossing right at his fingertips?*

Letting the list fall to the floor, she reached for the next item, a small black and silver box. It was next to pieces of gadgetry she could only assume were some kind of electronic equipment, none of which she recognized. The device she picked up at least held a little cassette, so she figured labeling it a tape recorder was probably a safe bet. She rewound the tape partway, put the headset on, and pressed the play button.

"I know you do Sashala," she heard Ivan's voice say. "She was a good woman . . .

"NOOOO!!" She ripped the headset from her ears and let it dangle around her neck. Tinny voices squawked out of the earpieces and she punched blindly at the stop button. Dry sobs heaved in her chest and her eyes felt seared. "No," she repeated in a whisper.

No.

She had believed she'd found something so rare and wonderful at long last—a relationship based on honesty. Someone in this world for her to love, who would love her in return. She picked her panties up off the floor and stared down at them. Now . . .

All her dreams were dust.

A key rattled in the lock and Sasha went very still. She stared through scorched eyes at the door, watched while Mick got it open, watched him jiggle the key to loosen the lock's grip on it. Was still watching when he spotted her. She saw the white, white smile that spread oh so spontaneously across his weathered face.

You liar. You lowlife, goddam liar.

She saw the realization hit him and watched as the smile dropped away and the color left his face.

"I can explain," Mick said hoarsely. But then he just stood there because he didn't know if he could, really, not to her satisfaction anyway. Closing the door behind him, he leaned—with arms crossed over his chest and hands tucked into his armpits—back against its sturdy surface and stared at her, afraid to take so much as a step in her direction. She looked about one nudge away from detonation.

"You wanna hear something funny, Special Agent Vinicor?" Sasha asked in a husky voice as she climbed to her feet. "I used to think Lonnie was paranoid beyond words because he insisted on playing the most moronic spy games you've ever heard of. He had all these asinine rules. I was supposed to burn his letters as soon as I read them. I was never to call him from my room, always from a pay phone. This was when he was still in prison, you understand. But, hey, why am I telling you? I'm sure you already know all this stuff. It must have driven you crazy, when you were listening in on all my telephone conversations, that not a single one of them was from ol' Lon. Is that when you decided to fuck the truth out of me instead?"

"Sasha—"

"You shouldn't have done that, Special Agent Vinicor. You never should have fucked the suspect—"

"You're not a suspect."

"—But then again, why not, right? After all, the report said I'm a slut, so that makes it okay, I guess. Hey, the government probably said it's all right to fuck the whore of Kells Crossing, because whores don't deserve to be treated with respect. It's not like they have feelings or anything. The only thing a whore really understands is a good, hard fuc—"

"SHUT UP!" he roared and she flinched. He was still afraid to touch her, but he pushed away from the door and moved as close as he dared, staring down at her. Jesus, she was in so much pain. "We make love, you and me," he said softly. "We don't fuck."

"Sure we do." She gave him a bright, superficial smile. "You don't have to lie anymore, Vinicor. I mean, really, how many times have I heard you say it yourself?" She mimicked him in the throes of a sexual encounter. "I want to fuck you, Sasha . . . Oh, God, I wanna fuck you so deep and so hard, it's killin' me!"

He couldn't stand to hear her turn his words into something obscene when that was the furthest thing from what they had been. "You liked it when I used sex words!" he snapped in frustration, then saw from her expression that that was what shamed her now. Sex talk was okay, was kind of exciting, when she'd thought he loved her. But now she believed he'd merely been using her.

Her expression smoothed out and she shrugged with a show of indifference. "Yeah, well, what more can you expect from the Slut of Kells Crossing? You know what they say— Once a whore always a whore."

Mick loomed over her. "You call yourself that one more time and I'm gonna . . ." His voice trailed away. Oh good, Vinicor. You're gonna what? Slap her? Tap her phone maybe?

And naturally Sasha picked up on his hesitation. Her chin jutted ceilingward. "You'll what?" she demanded coolly. "Is there something you haven't done already? Something you've actually overlooked?"

"I know you're not a whore," he said softly. "Okay? Maybe better than anyone else in the world, I know that."

"That's not what your report says."

"It's not *my* report, Sasha; it was sent to me. And, Jesus, am I the only one who clearly read what's in the damn thing? It says that a lot of guys professed to have slept with you but that not a single one of them could offer a shred of evidence to support his claim." He shook his head, staring at her. "I can't believe I'm arguing this with you, too. The goddam report doesn't say you're a whore. Jesus, how many times do I have to say it? Fighting with my supervisor over this very issue probably put an end to my career."

Sasha's eyes iced over. "Oh, hey now, that's tragic news. I'd sure hate to think I might be the cause of your potential unemployment." She bristled clear out to the curly ends of her abundant black hair. "My God, you've invaded my privacy, you've probably trampled my civil rights. Am I supposed to *apologize* because your boss doesn't think you've done a thorough enough job of it?"

Mick rammed his hand through his hair. "No, of course not. I'm just trying to tell you that when they wanted me to continue investigating you even after I'd told them you were clean, I refused, which led to some harsh words between . . ." His voice trailed away, since she obviously wasn't listening. Instead she was pulling her own suitcase off the shelf and before he could say a word she'd elbowed past him and was in the main body of their hotel room where she'd tossed the case on the bed and flipped it open. Going to the drawers she started pulling out her clothing, twisting from the waist to throw it haphazardly into the luggage.

"What do you think you're doing?" It was obvious, of course, but the words were wrenched from him anyway.

"Packing." Sasha strived for searing contempt when she looked up to meet his eyes, but she didn't have any idea how successful her attempt was. It felt so pitifully feeble. For no matter how many recriminations were backed up on her tongue, no matter how hot the rage churning in her stomach, there was a little voice inside of her crying for Mick to be able to explain, just like he said he could.

Just like he hadn't even attempted to do.

And that she should so cravenly desire any such thing made her grow angrier still. "I'm moving out," she snapped and might as well have added, "as any idiot can plainly see," for that was what her tone of voice suggested.

"No!" His denial was instinctive and from the heart, but he immediately caught himself. *That's not the way to go about it, you jackass.* His face lost all expression, and mind clicking furiously, he backtracked. "I'm sorry," he stated with cool, professional authority, "but I'm afraid I can't allow you to do that."

Bent over the bottom drawer, Sasha slowly straightened. The face she turned in Mick's direction was a study in regal displeasure. "Excuse me?" Glacial gray eyes met shuttered blue.

"Come over here and sit down," he commanded and the authority in his voice was such that she obediently rose to her feet before she could think it through. He reached out to assist her, but she jerked her arm out of his grasp, shoulder pivoting away and hand snapping up like the lever on a one-armed bandit to escape his touch. His hand dropped to his side. Sasha walked stiffly past him and took a seat at the table. Mick sat down in the chair facing her.

She met his eyes disdainfully. "You can't keep me here against my will."

"Well, actually . . . I can." And he was going to, by God. If he let her walk out on him now it was unlikely that she would ever give him a second chance to make things right between them. He was in love and he'd fight like Satan himself to hang on to her and the life they'd had for the past few weeks. His one and only hope to do that, as he saw it, was to keep her here with him where he could work on repairing the damage every single chance he got. "I'm putting you under protective custody," he informed her.

"What?" She snapped upright. "Protected from what? You can't do that."

"Yeah. I can. Listen—" he reached out and captured her clasped hands in one of his, hanging on despite her attempts to pull them away. "—I'm not doing this to bust your chops, darlin'. I think you're in danger."

She made a sound of derision and rolled her eyes.

"I'm not kidding, Sasha. Wasn't there anything that struck you as the least bit unlikely about your accident?"

"Don't be ridiculous," she started to say, but then her voice trailed away. God, she desperately wanted to hold her silence, but after a minute she reluctantly admitted, "There was no moisture rot in the sole of my boot."

Mick's eyes were intent. Dammit, he'd known it—his instincts very rarely failed him. "Explain," he demanded, and she did.

He scratched at his upper lip with the edge of his thumbnail. "So what you're saying is that screws drop out frequently and skates do lose their blades . . . but only if their soles have been softened to the point of rot by the constant spray of ice?"

"Yes."

"And your boot hadn't reached that stage yet?"

"No. The leather was still actually in pretty good condition. It shouldn't have happened."

Mick simply gazed at her for several silent moments before he said softly, "Amy Nitkey has hair the color of yours and she was wearing your jacket when she was struck by a hit-and-run driver."

"No!" Sasha sat rigidly, her hands cold beneath Mick's, staring at him across the table. He seemed to be all massive shoulders and fierce blue eyes. "It's a coincidence," she insisted. "There's no reason for anybody to wish me harm. No. You're just saying this to scare me."

Mick's grip tightened. "I hope to hell you are scared; a little fear is a good thing if it keeps you cautious. But you know damn well that's not the reason I'm bringing this up."

"Bull. Your sick little spy games have been exposed and

you just want to intimidate me . . ." She sucked in a sharp breath as his grip on her hands abruptly turned brutal. Pain shot up her arm from her ground-together knuckles. His eyes were snapping with fury and, suddenly afraid, she drew back as far as his reach would allow. She didn't know what he was capable of, not anymore.

"There is a motive, damn you," he said through clenched teeth, "and it's a pretty fucking compelling one, too. Morrison gave you his word that he wouldn't sell smack."

"You're crazy," she whispered. But it made sense. It made an awful sort of sense. Mick didn't respond and she again tugged against his grip. "Let go, Vinicor. You're *hurting* me."

"I'm sorry," he said stiffly and released her, watching her rub her sore knuckles. He was hanging on to his professional persona by his fingernails already, and the resentful set of her full lower lip as she stared back at him made him lose his grip. "I can't believe you think I'd deliberately try to intimidate you!" His hands curled into fists on the tabletop. He knew that what she'd discovered this afternoon was pretty incriminating, but hadn't these past weeks counted for anything?

Her mouth dropped open. "I can't believe *you'd* believe I'd think anything else! I thought I was living with one person and it turns out I'm living with someone entirely different. How the hell did you think I'd take it? My God, you have a suitcase with a false bottom, you own a gun, you electronically *eavesdropped* on my personal conversations. You even stole my underwear." She shuddered. "That's so perverted. And those are just the things I know about. I feel so . . . dirty . . . like I've been violated, and I didn't even recognize some of that stuff in your case." Her eyes widened in horror as an awful thought suddenly occurred to her. "Oh, please, Mick," she whispered hoarsely, "tell me you don't have me on film somewhere, too." That thought led to something even worse and she whimpered as her eyes darted involuntarily to the bed.

"No!" He reached out for her, but she drew back sharply and he brought his hands up to roughly skin his hair off his forehead instead. "I wouldn't do that to you, Sasha," he avowed, staring at her. "I swear to God I wouldn't. I *love* you!"

"Don't say that!" She shot to her feet. "Don't . . . you . . . say that to me. Not now, when I can't believe a word you say. Oh, God." She looked around wildly. "I've got to get out of here."

"I'm sorry; I can't let you leave. Not until it's time to go to the arena. Go take a bath or something. I'll give you some breathing space." He stood also, and suddenly he was the stern authoritarian once again. "It's uncertain at this stage just who's so determined to see Lon Morrison recruited again. So I'm cautioning you against speaking of this to anyone. It's to be discussed with no one, do you understand?"

Sasha gave him a look of acute dislike. "As if Connie would ever be involved in the sale of drugs."

"You discuss it with *no one,*" he repeated flatly. "Do you understand?"

"Yes," she said through clenched teeth. "I understand."

"Good. Keep it to yourself."

The first thing she did when she reached the line women's locker room that evening was drag Connie into a corner, pour out everything that had happened in the past few hours, and then burst into tears.

"That *snake.*" Connie pulled her into her arms for a comforting hug, turning them so Sasha's back was to the room. "Damn all men, anyway. You can't live with 'em and you can't shoot 'em."

"He said I wasn't to tell an-anybody—that it could be d-dangerous for me if I did. And I want so badly to think that's just another one of his damn lies, but, oh, God, Connie, I'm so afraid he might be right."

"You know I won't tell a soul."

"Yeah, I do, and I just had to talk to you about it or bust." Sasha stepped back and swiped the tears from her face with her fingers. Taking a deep breath, she gave her friend a shaky smile as they started to walk back to the lockers. "God, I must look such a mess—I'm probably gonna need a bigger trowel than usual to put on my stage makeup tonight." Then her weak attempt to smile gave way. "What's the matter with me, Connie?" she asked in a miserable little voice pitched so low only her friend could hear. "Why can't I find a man who doesn't spend all his time lying to me?"

Connie gripped her by both arms. "There's *nothing* the matter with you," she insisted fiercely. "Not a damn thing. It's them—it's because they *are* men." At Sasha's impatient movement, she said, "What? You think I'm kidding?" Raising her voice, she queried of the room at large, "Ladies, how can you tell if a man is lying?"

"If his lips are moving," promptly called back a line skater from across the room and Connie arched one eyebrow at her friend. "See? It's in the genes."

"Yes," Sasha murmured and her lower lip, which still had a tendency to tremble, firmed up. *"Yes,* you're right. It's got nothing to do with me at all. Men are just egg-suckin' dogs."

She must have said the last sentence louder than she realized, because a line skater some feet away set down her lipstick brush and looked at Sasha with incredulously raised eyebrows and a pitying smile that curled up one corner of her mouth. "Good grief, honey," she said in amazement, "don't tell me you're just now figuring that out?"

SIXTEEN

Karen wondered how difficult it would be to acquire a gun. It couldn't be all that troublesome, she reasoned, for it had always been her experience that one could generally obtain just about anything, given a little patience, a judicious bit of subtle question asking, and a discriminate use of sexual favors. Indeed, when it came right down to it, it was all a matter of knowing where to look . . . and if one wasn't quite sure where that might be, well . . . one simply began with a man.

She slept with three before she found out what she needed to know.

Men. They were such treasures . . . and so incredibly easy to manipulate. The one and only male who had ever challenged her was Lon Morrison, and if she ever truly put her mind to it she could readily manage him, too.

When it came to the average male, the barest essentials needed to obtain whatever knowledge she sought were so obvious it was laughable. She had her body and skillful hands and lips and an ingenuous way of asking a billion question while she was driving her prey wild demonstrating just how skillful her body parts could be. It was merely a matter of doing what she did best until all his brains were throbbing in his little head; then she slipped in the one question she really wanted answered. And if he had the solution, it was hers.

Men. Dear Lord, you had to love them. It was a rare day

indeed when one of the little darlings even realized they'd been asked for specific information.

Lon was different. And ever since they'd first rejoined forces following his release from prison, she had been more or less faithful to him. He was exciting and a formidable opponent, and the rush of exerting her influence over any other man just seemed so pale compared to the vibrancy she felt whenever she scored off Lonnie.

However she'd been *forced* to stray in this instance, and, really, it was *his* fault that she had. Him and his oh-so-precious little Miss Miller. Good gravy, was the tiny twit made out of spun glass or something?

One could only assume so, given the way Lon came running every blessed time she had the teensiest problem.

Karen and Lon were in the arena before the show, in a poorly illuminated alcove off a remote back corridor. She ran a tapered fingernail lightly up and down the thigh seam of his costume and reveled in the power that pumped through her veins. Reveled in the risk they took of being seen together, when usually they were so cautious. And in the knowledge that she was shortly going to have him right where she wanted him, smack in the palm of her hand.

Finally.

"So," she said casually. "Are you in the mood to earn a little spending cash?"

She'd known for a couple of weeks now that he was more than ready, but it had amused her to keep him dangling. She had been half tempted to wait until *he* broke down and asked her, but what the heck . . . she could be generous.

Recognizing her obvious manipulation for what it was, Lon's stubbornness and pride reared up onto their back legs now, but he knocked them to their knees and shrugged. He'd already made the decision; so let her believe it was her machinations that had convinced him if it made her happy.

What the hell difference did it make in the long run? "Sure," he agreed indifferently. "Why not?" Then he felt a little sick. Jesus, what had he done? This was all wrong.

"Okay, then," she said crisply and cannily kept all of the smugness she felt out of her voice. "Here's the way it will be . . ."

She had barely begun her recitation of how she wanted the buy handled when footsteps passed by. Karen simply drew deeper into the alcove and dropped her voice into a whisper, not bothering to ascertain the passerby's identity.

Which was a mistake. For, one moment she was laying down the arrangements, directing Lon's future movements, and the next she was speaking to thin air. Lon had dashed out of the alcove. "Saush," she heard him say. "Wait up."

The footsteps halted and Karen seethed. Over the tenderness in his voice when he inquired, "Are you okay? I saw you go by and you looked so pale." Over the knowledge that Lon would risk exposing *their* relationship if it would save his darling Sasha a millisecond of discomfort. Good grief, it was sheer luck alone that Miller didn't see her lurking here in the alcove. And then Karen's resentment burned nearly out of control over the way Lon's voice hardened when he demanded, "It's that bastard Vinicor, isn't it? I knew he was no good for you."

Karen was getting sick and tired of this nonsense. And stuck in the alcove fuming while *her* lover fawned over another woman, she began to wonder just how difficult it would be to obtain a gun.

Mick knew damn well as he slid into bed beside Sasha that he wasn't going to get away with it, but he thought it was worth the attempt. What the hell—you never knew until you tried. He didn't really expect that she'd welcome him. Neither did he expect that she'd threaten his life. But as he rolled toward the center of the bed and reached for her, that was precisely what she did.

"Get out, Vinicor." Her hand splayed out against his bare chest to hold him off and Mick, ready to snake an arm around her waist to pull her to him, felt a tiny smile flick the corners of his mouth. If she thought that was going to discourage him . . . Then something cool and very, very sharp pressed against his neck. He froze, his very breath suspended mid-lung.

"I might be forced to stay in the same room with you," she said in a gritty, furious voice, "but I will be *damned* if I have to put up with you in my bed as well."

Slowly and cautiously, Mick rolled onto his back and reached for the switch on the bedside lamp. Flicking it on, he turned back and saw its light reflecting off the skate blade Sasha held in her hand. It was one of a pair she kept protected by blade guards in a felt sack in her skate case, and he knew its finely honed edges were more than capable of slicing his throat from ear to ear. "Jesus Christ, darlin'," he said incredulously.

"Get out."

"Yeah. Yeah, all right, I'm going." He slid out of bed and climbed to his feet, where he stood and stared down at her.

Sasha stared back. Her hand, clutching the blade by the heel mount plate, was shaking badly, and she steadied it on her updrawn knee as she scooted her rear against the wall and leaned her back into the headboard that was mounted directly to the wall behind her. "You've got regular balls of steel, haven't you, *Special Agent* Vinicor?" she said through stiff lips, and then wished she'd used a different anatomical feature to describe his gall. He was naked as the day he was born and she longed desperately not to be aware of it. "Did you think you could just climb right in and cuddle up as if nothing had happened?" she demanded indignantly.

Mick shrugged. "It was worth a try," he said. "You must have thought I would, too, or you wouldn't have come to bed prepared with that." He watched her carefully. "Come on, Sasha, the room's only got one bed and it's cold in here."

"Tough." She flung a pillow at him, which he caught in one hand and then didn't even have the decency to hold in front of himself. It dangled at his side. "Put some clothes on," she suggested. "And there's an extra blanket in that bottom drawer." God, the arrogance. The sheer, unmitigated arrogance of the man.

She turned off the light and then lay stiffly alert, attuned to every little rustle he made in the darkness as he settled down on the floor. She didn't fool herself into thinking for an instant that he couldn't take the blade away from her if he were truly inclined. Her defenses were feeble compared to his capabilities, but using the blade as a deterrent was the only thing she'd been able to think of. She remembered well the night of Amy Nitkey's accident when she'd been uncertain whether she could trust him and how he'd promised to keep his hands to himself. She also remembered the pack of lies he'd fed her the next morning and had known for a fact that given the slightest opportunity, he'd climb right in and make himself at home tonight just as he had then if she didn't do something to prevent it.

Damned if she would allow him to get away with that again.

He turned over suddenly and she knew, even though the darkness was nearly impenetrable, that he was staring up at her. Her hand tightened on the mount plate and she grew tense, waiting for him to make a move.

"I really do love you, you know," he said in a low, intense voice. *"That* was never a lie."

"I thought it would be a walk in the park to just move in, trip you up, and haul your pretty butt off to jail," his voice said in the darkness a few nights later.

Sasha tensed. Damn him. It had been like this ever since

the first night. During the daylight hours he was all business, coolly authoritative and just the slightest bit remote. But come nightfall . . .

Last night his voice had risen up from the floor and the theme had been, "Why I Fell in Love with You." They were in a new town now, and in accordance with her wishes Mick had seen to it that the room they shared contained two beds. But it seemed to make little difference to the sense of intimacy that permeated their hotel room like a musky perfume, because night after night his voice crossed the small space that separated them and wrapped itself around her, wormed its way inside her, did its damnedest to seduce her.

"But I sure wasn't prepared for you," it was saying now, and against her better judgment Sasha rolled onto her side to face him. It didn't matter that she couldn't make out more than a dim outline of wide shoulders in the dark; his voice drew her in.

"God, I wasn't prepared for you," Mick repeated hoarsely. "You weren't at all what I was expecting, and you got to me. First, with your looks and your laugh and your skating. Then all of you: your sweetness and your sense of humor. Your integrity. It all just sort of crawled into my gut, grabbed hold, and wouldn't let loose."

"Yeah, right," Sasha snapped with patent sarcasm. "I bowled you over so much you tapped my phone and stole my underwear." Then she could have kicked herself for breaking the bitter silence she'd been stonily maintaining.

For Mick it was the first tiny bit of encouragement he'd encountered. He'd been talking himself hoarse for three nights straight, but she hadn't before given so much as one indication she'd heard a word he was saying. And this was the first time she didn't have her back stiffly turned his way.

Words had always been his most productive tool, but when it came to gauging their effectiveness during the past several nights he was completely in the dark. Now, when it mattered more than it ever had in his life, he feared his best asset was failing him dismally.

"I was afraid I was allowing myself to be led around by my dick," he admitted in a low voice. "All the preliminary evidence stated you had to be guilty. But because you're so pretty, I thought it was causing me to make excuses for why you didn't seem to fit the profile." He took a deep breath and lay there for a moment, his cheek resting on the biceps of his updrawn arm, straining to see her. His night vision was pretty good, but still she was little more than a shadowy outline. "And the panties . . . Sasha, I didn't set out to take them. They just kinda . . . ended up in my pocket."

Silence.

"I know you seem to envision me performing all sorts of sick rituals with the damn things, but the truth is I took them on impulse and I didn't subject them to any perverted usage."

She didn't respond and Mick moved restlessly for a moment before he forced himself to stillness. "Okay." He exhaled a resigned sigh. "So, eventually I figured out that it wasn't just my hormones talking, that you really weren't what I kept telling myself you must be. But heroin had hit the streets when Morrison was still in jail; junkies had died, and if it wasn't his old partner passing the same shit that had been missing ever since his arrest, then who was it?" He paused, hoping she'd respond, but again she held her silence. "I requested a list of anyone currently employed by the Follies who was also around back in Miller and Morrison's amateur circuit days."

She had a hundred questions, demands, sarcastic one-liners, but she bit down on her tongue to keep from uttering any of them. He was just trying to soften her up for some reason known only to himself, and she was *not* going to fall for it.

She turned her back on him and stared with burning eyes at the faint chink of light coming in through a minute gap in the draperies.

Shit! Mick rammed his hand through his hair. He wanted to get out of this frigging lonely bed and climb into hers; he wanted to force her to deal with him; he wanted to make her *talk*. Instead, he took several deep breaths to calm himself. Finally, he said in a voice made low and raspy with restraint, "I'm an excellent liar, darlin'—have been all my life. I can't deny it comes in real handy in my line of work. But the minute I said I love you, I quit telling lies. And I'll never lie to you again. I swear that to you on my mother's life."

"What the hell's the deal with you and Vinicor?" Lon demanded out of the blue, and his voice was so loud and cantankerous in the vast, empty arena it echoed.

Sasha looked up from unlacing her skates. "I thought you came along with me because you wanted to skate, Lonnie."

"That's right, I did. And we've skated." He rolled his shoulders uncomfortably beneath the weight of her protracted, level-eyed stare, but then met her gaze head-on. "That doesn't stop me being curious, though. I don't get this relationship of yours at all. You wouldn't tell me anything the other night—"

"Shouldn't that have been your first clue?"

"—And everyone's talking about the way—"

"My God," she interrupted with some bitterness. "Everyone's talking about Sasha Miller. Big news flash."

"Come on, Saush; you gotta admit the relationship is odd. The two of you barely speak to each other in public these days; yet he watches you skate every night like a hemophiliac watches his last pint of blood, and you're still living together."

She stilled, her hand on the towel around her neck arrested in mid-pull. "He watches me skate?"

Lon snorted skeptically. "Right. Like you're not aware. What is it, anyway, some sort of esoteric foreplay?"

"I *wasn't* aware, Lon." Her hands gripped the towel tightly. "Tell me how he watches me."

"Jesus, what are we . . . in junior high school? You're dodgin' the question here. Why are you still living with that jerk?"

Knowing he wasn't going to satisfy her curiosity about Mick, she sat up smartly and looked him straight in the eye. "Why are you still selling drugs when you told me you'd quit that for good?" she shot back.

Lon went very still. "What? I'm not selling." But he couldn't quite hold her gaze.

"Preparing to then." Sasha shrugged the semantics aside. His look of incredulousness was just a shade too overdone to be plausible and it made her lose patience. "Don't insult my intelligence, Lonnie. I've learned the hard way to know when you're up to something, and either you're selling or you're getting ready to sell. It's sure as hell one or the other." She tugged off her skates, wiped them off, and put them in their case. Wiggling her feet into flats, she ignored him for a few moments in the interests of getting a pressing feeling of betrayal under control. Dammit. She'd thought she could be cool about this, but it was a losing proposition. Ultimately she gave up the effort and straightened, facing him head-on. "Damn you to everlasting hell, Lon Morrison. You gave me your word."

"Yeah, and I haven't broken it yet, either," he retorted hotly.

Rising to her feet, chin thrust up at a belligerent angle, she stood nose to nose with him. "Do you deny you've been planning to?"

"So maybe the thought's crossed my mind. But thinking ain't doing, sweet thing."

She stared up at him furiously for a few silent moments. Then her gaze grew thoughtful and she abruptly inquired, "Who got you started selling this stuff anyway?"

He was patently unprepared for the question and took a step back. "Huh?"

"What part of the question don't you understand, Lon?" she demanded testily, then with strained patience clarified, "Originally someone must have approached you to feel you out on it. Who was it?"

"Uh, no one you'd know."

She knew he was lying; he didn't even have the grace to do a halfway decent job of it. "I see," she said through her teeth. "You were on the fast track to a promising career, but a complete stranger managed to see past the successful facade to a guy who was hungry for more. And having made that determination, he looked you up on the off-chance you'd like to make yourself a little fast cash."

"Something like that, yeah." Lon shrugged.

"Uh-huh. And is that same stranger encouraging you to get back into it now?"

"Maybe."

"Who is it, Lon?" When he stared at her stonily, maintaining his silence, she wanted to cry. "Is your drug connection more important than your future, then? Is that what it finally comes down to? God, Lonnie, don't you know you won't get away with it a second time? You'll end up back in jail as a two-time offender, and when you get out next time, there'll be *no* one left waiting for you."

He held her gaze with a lack of expression that made her long to smack him. She continued to talk instead, for in the past Lon had been known to dig his heels in during a quarrel, only to go off and give serious consideration to the other side of the argument once he'd cooled down. She could only hope that would be the case in this instance.

"I love you," she told him softly. "But people died because of what you did. Somehow I've always managed to ignore the truth of that in the past, but I can't do it anymore, Lon." She faced him squarely, took a deep breath, and reiterated, "Addicts died expressly because of a drug that you supplied them with. Perhaps they weren't the most productive citizens in the world, but they sure didn't deserve that. And who's to say more won't die if you start supplying it all over again?"

She'd briefly considered telling him about Mick's involvement, which in essence would give Lon fair warning that the consequences of his actions could be dire and swift. But in the end she held her tongue. She wasn't his keeper. If his word to her meant so little, then she failed to see where it was her responsibility to make him aware of the repercussions. He had to know, if he chose to resume selling, that the heroin he'd be passing was tainted and therefore likely to kill again.

She was so tired of slogging through the morass of everybody's pretenses. They all played her false. Mick pretended he wasn't really an agent for the Drug Enforcement Administration and that he loved her. Lon pretended he was going to give up this high-risk venture into drug sales. Both of them lied. Everyone seemed to have a hidden agenda and it was clear that she wasn't a high priority for any of them.

She gathered up her jacket, shrugged it on, and reached for her skate case and purse, slinging straps over her shoulder and gripping handles in her hands. "It's not too difficult to see that laying my reputation on the line for you—and what the hell's gonna become of it if you get caught selling again—doesn't enter into the equation," she said coolly and headed for the exit, bags banging off of hip and knee. Stopping at the exterior door, she turned back with one hand on the bar then pushed it open. "But maybe you'll consider this. I've still got a soft spot on my head from having a blade that had no business doing so come off my skate. Amy Nitkey got struck by a hit-and-run driver while wearing *my* coat. You didn't by any chance tell your 'stranger' that you'd given me your word you wouldn't sell again, did you?"

Neither expecting nor waiting for an answer, she shoved through the door.

* * *

Sitting cross-legged next to the bed on Connie's hotel room floor, Sasha attended to the boots of her skates. Using an alcohol-soaked cotton ball she scrubbed at the spots that marred them. "From now on," she said grimly, "I depend on no one but myself."

"And me," Connie said. "You can depend on me."

"Yes. And you." Sasha looked up. "But not on Mick or Lonnie." She returned her attention to the clean leather, eyeing it critically. "Good enough. Hand me the polish, will you?"

Connie passed over a bottle of white polish and held her peace as Sasha carefully applied a fresh coat to her skate, laying it on with smooth, even strokes. Saush had burst in on her fifteen minutes ago, up in arms and jittery as a cat. For lack of a better idea Connie had set her to caring for her skates. It was the first thing to pop to mind when she'd seen the extent of sheer undirected energy that had set her friend to pacing a restless, agitated circuit through the room while she filled her in, with clipped, furious sentences, on her afternoon.

When both boots were done and Sasha was waiting for them to dry before applying a second coat, Connie inquired gently, "Are you absolutely certain you can't depend on Mick?"

"These days I'm not absolutely certain of my own name," was the glum reply. Sasha applied the second coat. "Everything's so upside down. He talks to me every night from his bed, Connie, and according to him it's everything he always wanted to say but couldn't say before. But is that the truth, or is it more blarney from his silver tongue? He says he loves me. And, God forgive me, I believe him at the moment he's saying it."

Her hand stilled over the boot and she tipped her head back to stare up at Connie on the bed above her. "But is that because I actually hear the ring of sincerity in his voice or just because I desperately want to?" Replacing the swab in the polish bottle, she silently handed it up to her friend to tighten the cap. Her eyes lowered once more to the skate that was turned upside down over her fist. "I'm all screwed up," she admitted.

Connie passed her the black polish. "Careful, it's open," she warned. When her friend simply held the container in her hand and sat staring at it, she said, "You've got good instincts, Saush. What do they advise you to do?"

Sasha snorted. "They're horny. Who can trust anything they recommend?" Carefully she put black polish on the soles and heels of first one boot, then the other to waterproof them.

"So they want to trust him, huh?"

"They" want to marry him and have his babies. *I'm* never trusting another man as long as I live."

"It sounds as if he was right about Lon using his promise to you as an excuse to hold off this partner who wants him to start selling again."

Sasha made a noncommittal noise.

"And you have to be happy knowing Lon has been trying to avoid selling."

That snapped Sasha's head up in a hurry. "Didn't you listen to a word I said, Connie? He stonewalled me this afternoon. I gave him every opportunity to tell me he'd give this mad idea up and he didn't say a word." She glared up at her friend. "That as good as told me he's going to do what he damn well wants to do . . . and to hell with me."

"You backed him into a corner."

Sasha stared at her, her jaw agape. "So it's *my* fault?"

"No, it's a male thing." At Sasha's impatient movement, Connie leaned forward and said seriously, "Listen, Saush, I've got four brothers; I know what I'm talking about here. There's this male-ego-pride thing that drives men. If you demand they do something that needs to be done, nine times out of ten they'll wait for enough time to elapse so they can feel they're doing it of their own free will. Even when they plan to comply with whatever it is you want them to do. And God help us if we 'nag,' because then they feel they have to wait even longer." She deepened her voice. "Ain't no woman gonna pussy-whip *me*." Her voice resumed its normal pitch. "I'm telling you, kid, the male ego is a wondrous thing."

"Yeah, well, you can make all the excuses for Lon you want. As I've already said, I'm depending on myself from now on. Period."

"In a way it's too bad you can't bring Mick and Lon together."

That startled an involuntary little huff of unamused laughter out of Sasha. "Oh, God, I can see that." She tested the heels of her boots. "I think these are dry but do you have a newspaper or something I can lay them on?"

Connie hopped up and went over to the table. She was back in moments with an empty department store bag, which she handed to Sasha. "I'm serious, Saush. Lon hasn't actually done anything illegal yet and he's the only person who knows who this other guy is. If Mick had that information not only could he better protect you, he could save Lon from making the biggest mistake of his life."

"Why are you so damned concerned with Lonnie all of a sudden? I thought you said he was a no-class jerk."

"Yeah. He is." And politically incorrect as it was, she had to stifle a little pulse of sexual yearning every time she ran across him. There was something so bone-deep unhappy, so reckless and restless about him, that it just sort of . . . got to her. That day in the cafeteria he had disgusted her. Yet, if she were to be honest, she'd have to admit he had also excited an impulse deep inside that she didn't care to contemplate. He'd . . . But she was getting off track here. After a brief hesitation to gather her thoughts, Connie said gently, "But he's also your oldest friend." And she knew very well that counted for a lot in Sasha's book.

Sasha pulled her knees into her chest and wrapped her arms around her shins, clutching herself tightly. "I'm so angry, Connie," she admitted in a low, intense voice. "With both of them. God, I'm so angry!"

"I know you are." Connie slid off the bed to sit on the floor next to her friend, wrapping an arm around her stiff shoulders.

"All my life, I took it," Sasha said bitterly. "Year after year, I was lied to and I just let it roll off me. Lonnie nearly destroyed my career along with his own, but I picked myself up and rebuilt it from scratch. And I forgave him, because I knew he hadn't deliberately set out to hurt me, that I probably hadn't really even entered into it at all. But maybe that's the problem." She turned her head to look at Connie. "I don't seem to enter into anyone's considerations, ever, and I'm so sick of it."

Connie stroked her hair and remained silent. The pressure of a resentment contained for far too long built and it boiled, and finally Sasha burst out, "Why is my job to save Lonnie from himself? Because of him I may be in danger and I don't even know from whom. Why doesn't he save *me* for once? And Mick? Good old highly sexed, fast-talking Mick? Do you have any idea how it felt to read that report that gave all my old enemies in Kells Crossing yet *another* opportunity to agree on what a slut I am? He might charm me right out of my panties, and he could probably convince me that black is actually white without running short of breath." She looked at her friend and Connie saw the bitter resolution in Sasha's gray eyes. "But no matter how much I want to believe him when he whispers it in the night, he'll never convince me he loves me when he can turn right around and commission something like that to be done."

"Dammit! This is impossible." Sasha tossed aside the sheet of paper and stared out the hotel room's third-story window through eyes glazed with tears.

Her fist opened and closed on the tabletop; her chest rose

and fell rapidly while she struggled to get a grip on her emotions. Finally she sucked in a deep breath and slowly expelled it. She swallowed a sip of her diet cola, never noticing it had gone warm and flat, and, gritting her teeth, reached for the paper once again.

It was Mick's list of names of the people who had been on the amateur circuit at the time of Lon's arrest.

God, this was so hard. She didn't want to believe any of these people were capable of wanting to hurt her, yet she had to consider each and every name. But really, Dave DiGornio? Jack Berensen? *Karen Corselli?* Come on.

She tried to block out what she personally felt for the individual as she came to his or her name on the list. The only way this would ever work was to make the assessment based solely on the facts. Okay. Dave DiGornio. What did she know? He came from a monied, warm, and generous family. Jack Berensen. She didn't really know much about his background, but she liked him. Karen. Yeah, right. Sasha balled up the list and threw it across the room.

This was impossible.

SEVENTEEN

Lon watched Karen during her "Lord's Prayer" number. She skimmed the ice lightly, sweet as an angel in her trademark silver, blond hair in its prim bun shining under the cool blue spotlight that followed her around the rink as she swooped and spun.

You didn't by any chance tell your "stranger" you'd given me your word you wouldn't sell again, did you?

He shook his head. Sasha was crazy; Karen wouldn't hurt a fly.

Would she?

Well, sure, she was a bit of a control freak. And she lived for power, no doubt about that. But attempted murder? Karen-Mind-Your-Language-and-Don't-Take-the-Lord's-Name-in-Vain-Corselli?

Come on.

Yet the uneasiness that had sprung to life at Sasha's words persisted. How consistent, when it came right down to it, was Karen's piousness with her red-hot aptitude for sucking the chrome right off a trailer hitch? The disparities in her personality were the very things that had always sort of excited him about her, but he had to face it, she definitely acted like different women at different times.

Still.

There was a huge difference between giving an excellent blow job and trying to *hurt* someone. The woman *prayed* all the time, for God's sake. And what the hell made Saush believe that what had happened to her and Amy Nitkey was anything other than accidental anyway?

Still.

Karen did seem to crave knowledge of every little detail of Sasha's life, no matter how trivial. She also recognized that Sasha had the power to sway his behavior. And Karen didn't like anyone having more power than she did.

Still.

He watched her, all grace and fragility on the ice. And made a rude noise.

One of the stagehands raised his head, looking Lon's way. "You say something, Morrison?"

"Nah." Lon turned away and went to join the line skaters lining up to go on next. "Except that Sasha Miller is stone crazy."

Mick stood watching Sasha during her "Playing with Fire" routine. Man, you'd think he'd be used to it by now but it still made his mouth go dry every time he saw it. Aware of someone joining him in the arena entrance, he reluctantly pulled his gaze away from the ice and looked down. Standing beside him was Connie Nakamura and she didn't even glance at her friend out on the ice. Her black, almond-shaped eyes, beneath heavy theatrical makeup, were staring up at him assessingly.

He returned her look for several moments, then blew out a deep, disgusted breath. "Ah, shit. She went and told you, didn't she?"

Connie gave him her best imitation of an inscrutable smile and raised both eyebrows inquiringly. "I'm sure I don't know what you're talking about, Mr. Vinicor."

"Don't jerk me around, Nakamura. She *told* you. I warned her not to talk about this to anybody."

"Oh, that's just perfect, Vinicor." Connie dropped all pretense of not understanding. "My God. You men really do take the cake. You've turned her life upside down, but she's just supposed to take it on the chin?" Her voice, although pitched low for privacy, was charged with fury, and the look of pure contempt she directed at him was not in the least bit diluted by makeup that stood out garishly beneath the harsh backstage fluorescents. "Hey, it's not as if anybody seems to give a rat's rear end that she's suffering," she said sarcastically. "Let's just all be sure that she has the decency to suffer in silence."

She hadn't heard language the likes of which slipped through the barrier of his gritted teeth since the day she'd first laid eyes on him in that hotel hallway in Sacramento. Her eyes widened and she instinctively drew back when he leaned aggressively close to bring their faces to a more equitable level.

"I don't like it that she's suffering at all, damn you," he said in a hoarse whisper. His blue eyes burned with a host of indefinable emotions, and his big hands knotted and unknotted into hard fists at his sides. "You think I *wanted* things to turn out this way?"

"Oh, I'm sure it wasn't in your game plan to get caught."

"I didn't want her to be hurt! That's the last thing I wanted. But what the fuck was I supposed to do, Connie? I was sent here to do a job, and I was doin' it. At the same time I was busting my hump trying to keep from falling in love with her. Well, I screwed up on both counts, okay? Man, she was there, getting to me, every damn time I turned around, and I didn't *want* to believe she could be the one peddlin' this killer shit, but all the evidence seemed to point right at her."

Forcing his fingers to uncurl, he thrust both hands through his hair and stare down at Sasha's best friend. "I swear to God I didn't sleep with her until I was convinced of her innocence, but of course she doesn't believe that now." His own memory was a bit convenient but the bottom line was that the *only* reason he'd slept with her was because he wanted her. Not because he needed information to make the case, not because of her secrets . . . it was *her.* "She thinks I was only looking for a piece of ass and hers was the handiest."

"Well, can you blame her, Mick?" Connie saw the very real anguish in his face as Sasha's performance out on the ice drew his attention away from her, and some of the indignation she'd been harboring on her friend's behalf faded. "And did you really imagine this house arrest thing is going to further your cause?" she inquired in a more temperate tone. "That's the weirdest damn arrangement I've ever heard of, and if it's the least bit legal I'll eat that big wooly patch I bought Saush right off her damn jacket."

His attention snapped back to Connie with antagonistic intensity. Hell, no, it wasn't legal. That, of course, was one of the very reasons he hadn't wanted Sasha telling anyone about it. "You planning on tellin' her that?" he demanded.

It was difficult not to react to the hostility in his voice, but she forced herself to stand still and simply gaze back at him without speaking.

Mick scraped his hair back off his forehead again, then let his hands drop to his side. He sighed. "I guess it's no secret she's furious with me, and she's got a perfect right to be, okay?" he said in a voice that was strangled by the moderation he forced into it. "I screwed up big time; I admit it."

Then he suddenly seemed to grow taller in front of Connie's eyes. He shook off the role of penitent and was imbued with that air of command he carried so naturally as he stood there looking down at her. "I screwed up," he repeated, then added grimly, "But do you honestly want her running all over creation on her own? I didn't warn her that she could be in danger merely for the chance to save our relationship, Connie—although I plan to do exactly that. I told her because I'm convinced she *is* in danger. At least this way I've given myself an opportunity to protect her a little better."

The sheer arrogance of his proclaimed intention to redeem his relationship with Sasha almost made Connie smile. The guy had done absolutely everything wrong; he'd lied to Sa-sha, he'd spied on her, he'd stolen her damn underwear, for heaven's sake. Yet he harbored no doubt he could get her back. Beautiful.

Out of the blue he inquired, "What made you say, 'you men.' "

"Huh?"

"A few minutes ago you said, 'you men take the cake.' " Personal considerations were abruptly submerged and he was suddenly one hundred percent cop again. "You didn't say, '*you* take the cake'; you said, 'you *men*.' I want to know why."

"Oh, give it a wild stab, Vinicor. I'm sure you can figure it out."

He looked at her in frustration for a moment, then suddenly scowled. "Morrison? Did Morrison do something to hurt her?" He took a step closer. "Is she okay? I'll kill him—what'd he do?"

A snort of laughter escaped her. "I take it back—you really do take the cake. Hands down and all by yourself."

"Save your lip for another time, Nakamura. What the hell did Morrison do to hurt Sasha?"

"I think you'd better take that up with her." She eyed him consideringly. "Or better yet, why don't you compare a few notes with Lon himself? It's not inconceivable that the two of you could arrive at a satisfactory solution to this situation if you tried putting your heads together. And that would make everybody happy." She blinked. "Well, more or less."

"Don't think I haven't considered it," Mick snapped. He looked around, saw that nobody was nearby, and leaned closer. "But what the hell happens if he says, 'kiss my ass' and then tells his partner I'm a narc?" he demanded in a soft voice. "The risk to Sasha could multiply a hundredfold, and there's simply no way I'm gonna put her in that kind of danger."

"I can't believe Morrison would ever put her in that kind

of danger either," Connie retorted, but Mick was no longer paying attention to her.

His entire focus had reverted to Sasha as she arrived in the wing and prepared to climb off the ice. He snatched her jacket up off the floor and carried it over to where she was balancing on one skate as she fit a blade guard to the other. As she straightened he draped it around her shoulders and pulled it closed with his fists, effectively pinning her arms to her side and holding her prisoner. He leaned down and pressed a quick, fierce kiss to her lips. Pulling back, he demanded, "What's Morrison done to hurt you this time?"

"Oh, very tactful, Vinicor," Connie murmured. She pursed her lips, rolled her eyes, and beat a hasty retreat, knowing Sasha was not going to be thrilled with her for saying even the little bit that she had.

Sasha leaned back from the waist and regarded Mick through narrowed eyes. "Let go of me," she ordered in a low voice. She hated the way all her hormones stood up and screamed for more after that single too-brief contact with his mouth.

He loosened his grip on her jacket, brought his hands up to tunnel beneath her hair at her nape and freed it from inside her collar, spreading it out carefully over the wool and leather of her jacket. Then he stepped back. "You're not going to tell me what Morrison did to upset you, are you?"

She stared at him without speaking.

"Wonderful. The silent treatment again." He regarded her with frustration. "Dammit, Saush, I'm sorry, I'm sorry, I'm *sorry,* all right? How long are you going to make me keep paying for what I did?"

He realized later that when she still refused to speak to him, he should have simply turned around and removed himself from the situation. But it wasn't his infamous street smarts that whispered with the cool voice of reason into his ear; instead, hot emotion took control. For the past week he'd been wrestling to cope with a massive vulnerability, the power of which he'd never even dreamed could exist, and her continued refusal to speak to him proved to be one blow too many for his pride to gracefully take in stride.

He wanted to yell, to shake her 'til her teeth rattled. What he did instead was take a step back and say with cool arrogance, "Then the hell with you, lady. I've had it up to my back teeth with groveling."

His eyes traveled over her from the topmost curl of wayward black hair to the tips of her skates in a slow and deliberately insolent appraisal, as if to say, "And frankly, I don't even know if you're worth it." Then, executing a smart about-face on his heel, he rapidly strode away without a backward glance.

Sasha took her own sweet time navigating the deserted fourth-floor corridor. She'd spent as much time in the bar and then in Connie's room as she dared, but as much as she'd been tempted to spend the night with her friend, she had in the end been too chickenhearted to attempt it, afraid Mick would show up to haul her back to his room. It was true that he was apparently quite fed up with her. But his damn job was something he took very seriously indeed, and if she failed to show up for "protective custody" bed check she wouldn't for a moment put it past him to come banging on doors until he found her. At which point he would probably drag her away by force.

She was strolling past room 426 when 428 suddenly opened up and Lon stepped out into the hallway, softly closing the door behind him. Sasha felt her jaw literally drop open as she stopped dead in her tracks. That was Karen Corselli's room.

The look on his face when he turned and saw her standing there might have been comical at any other time, but at that precise moment she was still too stunned to give it the appreciation it deserved. Resisting the urge to shake her head like a punch-drunk boxer, she set herself in motion once again.

Swearing softly beneath his breath, Lon snagged her by the upper arm when she came abreast of him and hustled her slightly ahead of him down the hallway to the elevator. He had stubbornly refused to give credence to Sasha's speculations that his partner wished her harm because of a promise he'd given to her, but all Lon knew for certain at this moment was that he didn't want Sasha anywhere around if Karen should suddenly decide to stick her head out into the corridor. He didn't draw a complete breath until the elevator doors had slid shut behind them, enclosing them inside.

"Oh, my God," she said in a faint voice and had to quell a sudden, adolescent urge to giggle. "It's true then what the guys have been saying about Karen? That she . . . that she, uh . . ."

"Likes the horizontal boogie?"

"Karen *Corselli?*" Sasha demanded incredulously and shook her head. "I've heard rumors to that effect of course, but I gotta tell ya, Lonnie, I'm still having a hard time believing it." She eyed him speculatively. "And *you* and Karen? Boy, there's a combination I never in a million years would have figured." She was silent then as the elevator descended, gazing at him as if answers to all the questions percolating in her mind would emblazon themselves across his forehead if she only looked hard enough.

They didn't. "So," she finally inquired as the doors slid open at the lobby level. "What's she like then?"

Lonnie looked a little beleaguered. He rubbed at the side of his neck and looked around. Then, taking her by the elbow, he escorted her off the elevator and across the lobby to the lounge. "Come on. If you really think it's necessary to hash this all out, the least you can do is buy me a drink."

"As long as you hold up your end of the bargain and spill your guts," she agreed, surreptitiously checking the denomination of the one bill left stuffed into the front pocket of her jeans and then following along amiably in his wake. It was a ten; that ought to buy a couple of drinks.

"A coke for the lady, and I'll have a Heineken," Lon told the cocktail waitress moments later, and she nodded and started to turn away.

"Miss?" Sasha stopped her. "Make that a Smith and Kerns instead of a coke will you?" She'd already had several drinks this evening and probably shouldn't have another. But really . . . Turning to him when the waitress had departed, she said dryly, "I'm not twenty years old any longer, Lon. You seem to have a difficult time remembering that."

And that, she thought, was probably their basic problem in a nutshell. From the moment they'd reunited he'd acted as if she'd been wrapped in cotton batting and left on a shelf somewhere for the past five and a half years. He seemed to think she was exactly the same as the last time he'd seen her, regardless of the years that had passed or the experiences she'd gained in that time. Sasha looked at him across the table and said evenly, "While you were in stir, I was busy growing up."

"Yeah, okay. Sorry." He rolled his shoulders uneasily. If Vinicor was an example of one of the ways she'd grown up, then frankly, he didn't much care for it.

On the other hand there wasn't anything he could do about it, so he supposed he might as well learn to live with it.

"So, tell me about Karen," she invited. "How long have you two been"—she twirled her hand—"you know."

"You know?" The smile he gave her was slanted by irony. "I'd say the growin' up process has a ways to go if you're still calling sex 'you know.' "

"Nice dodge, Morrison. But I'm not budging until I get some answers. How long have you been sleeping together?"

"A while," he said gruffly. "And Karen's okay. She can be bossy, which you probably already know, but she's also sexy and sometimes there's a real vulnerability about her."

"Really? Give me a for instance." Vulnerable would have been the last characteristic Sasha attributed to her.

"Well, she's deathly afraid of—" He broke off suddenly and drilled Sasha with an intent stare. "This is just between you and me now, Sasha, y'hear me? All of it—my relationship with her, what I'm about to tell you. It's not to go any further than the two of us. And that includes Lover Boy."

As if she said one word more than necessary to Special Agent Vinicor these days. But she couldn't tell Lon that without a lot of dreary explanations she had no intention of getting into, so she merely nodded. "Gotcha."

"Gotcha don't cut it, Sweet Thing. I want your word."

"You have my word," she assured him impatiently. "Now spill!"

"She's afraid of the dark. No, more than afraid. *Terrified.*"

"You're kidding." Sasha blinked. "Do you know why?"

"Your guess is as good as mine, babe. She has this little night-light she is never without. I was with her once when the thing burned out and, Saush, the woman went ape shit. I'm not talking a little bit upset, here, I'm talking totally, one hundred percent freaked out."

"Poor Karen," Sasha commiserated with ready sympathy. "She must have had a horrible experience with a dark place at some point in her life. Maybe she got lost as a kid in the Carlsbad Caverns or something."

"I really couldn't say." Lon shrugged. "But Saush? The point I'm trying to make here is that Karen is more than just the one aspect of her personality that you've seen." Man, was *that* the black belt of understatement. "And I don't want to see her embarrassed by the knowledge that you know I'm sleeping with her."

Not to mention that if Karen possessed even darker aspects than he'd previously suspected, he didn't want Sasha put at risk.

"My God, just what is it you think I'm planning to do, Lon?" Sasha inquired indignantly, "go up to her and start

singing, 'Lon and Karen sitting in a tree, K-I-S-S-I-N-G'?"
She glared at him across the table. "You might find my tendency to say 'you know' instead of 'sex' a little on the ju-
venile side, but I assure you I do comprehend the basics on
how to conduct myself like an adult." She dug the ten out
of her pocket and threw it on the table, then started to slide
out of the booth, but she was hemmed in by the sudden
arrival of the waitress with their drinks. By the time the
woman had counted out her change and left, Lon had reached
a hand over to stay her.

"Calm down, calm down now; that's not what I meant at
all," he said, stroking her fingers soothingly. She was taking
a deep breath to do exactly that, feeling ridiculous for over-
reacting, when he opened his mouth again and ruined the bit
of progress he'd made by adding with a trace of male con-
descension, "You've really been tense lately, Sasha. Maybe
you oughtta take a little time out to get a firmer grip on your
emotions."

Leaving a dollar bill on the table, Sasha pocketed the rest
of her change, picked up her drink, and slid out of the booth.
"Thanks for the advice, chief," she said levelly, looking
down at him. "I'll be sure to keep it in mind."

She strode from the lounge, thinking unkind thoughts
about mankind in general and two men in particular. Too
angry to pay attention to the woman crossing the lobby toward the doorway she had just exited, she marched straight
past Karen Corselli without ever seeing her.

Mick looked up when the door slammed closed. His shoulders lost the rigidity they'd been plagued with for the past
hour and a half, and his stomach finally stopped pumping
out a steady stream of acid. He hadn't known what the hell
he was going to do if Sasha decided to park her pretty little
butt in her friend's room for the night.

Connie had already called his bluff on the protective custody scam. His take on her attitude had been that even armed with the knowledge that it was nothing more than smoke and mirrors on his part, she was tacitly agreeing to let him get away with it for the time being. He sure as hell couldn't count on her remaining so forbearing, however, if he attempted to pack Sasha off. Not, at any rate, if Sasha expressed an adamant wish not to be packed . . . and he certainly had no reasonable expectation she'd do otherwise.

Legs stretched out in front of him, Mick lounged indolently on an overstuffed chair and watched her storm into the room. Given the way she'd been pretending he was invisible ever since she'd discovered the truth of his employment, he fully expected to be ignored. That was how it usually went down these days, and after cursing at her earlier he naturally assumed he was in for more of the same. He was therefore caught unprepared when she marched straight up to him, slammed her half empty drink down on the table, planted her hands militantly on the arms of the chair he sat in, and leaned forward, getting right in his face. The scent of liquor wafted on her breath as she declared furiously, "Men are . . . *pond scum.*" Her chest heaved once, twice, her eyes burned with rage. "And I detest every last one of you."

It was the wrong time to attack him. "Well, stop the presses," he snarled right back. "What a news flash." Snapping erect, he thrust his face aggressively forward to swallow up the fraction of an inch of space she'd left between them, lip curling nastily when she jerked back in reaction. If she wanted a fight, he was more than ready to accommodate her. He'd tried being a New Age sensitive guy and look where that horseshit had gotten him—the proud possessor of way too much frustration. "This might come as a big shock to you, sister, but women aren't all they're cracked up to be either."

"Oh yeah? Do they lie and spy and act like condescending jerks?"

"Hell no, that'd be too mature. They sulk and pout and expend so much energy feeling sorry for themselves that they don't have anything left over to occasionally look at things from someone *else's* point of view."

"Feel sorry for themselves?" Sasha's voice rose several octaves and she lost all control, those words reverberating in her skull like the high-pitched scream of a table saw. He thought she was feeling *sorry* for herself? How dare he reduce her feelings to some petty little pity feast, as if he'd merely spilled a drink on her blouse and she was childishly refusing to get over it.

She came up swinging.

Mick was caught patently flat-footed and she got in two solid punches before he grabbed hold of her forearms and wrestled her arms down to her sides. He jerked her forward to knock her off balance.

She landed partly on his chest, one knee planted in the chair cushion between his legs, her other leg out from under her as her thighs sloppily straddled one of his. She was in no position to fight but she nevertheless bucked and pitched with such fierce determination he half expected at any moment to feel the sick sensation of her kneecap slamming his scrotum up to meet his backbone. He slid out of the chair onto his knees, which effectively put her knees out of commission as well by the simple expedient of dragging her down right along with him.

Sasha's breath whistled in her throat and escaped in sobs as she attempted to fight free, twisting and jerking and calling him words he would have sworn she didn't even know, or at least never in a million years would have said out loud. Mick was astounded that such a little body, even if it did belong to an athlete in her prime, could put up so much resistance against his own overwhelmingly greater strength.

He'd grown accustomed to butting his head up against the solid wall of her cool dignity—it was that very imperturbability that had made him feel about two inches tall all week long. This total loss of a discipline he'd believed to be impenetrable shook him up and drained him of his anger. He wrestled her down onto her back on the floor and lay on top of her, his hands stapling her wrists to the carpet, his heavy thighs pinning hers into immobility beneath him. Still she struggled in a blind rage, trying futilely to throw him off.

"Shhh, shh, shh, shh," he soothed. Using his chin to push her hair out of his way, he pressed his open mouth against her ear, breathing into it a medley of nonsensical sounds whose sole purpose was designed to calm her, to neutralize her rage. "Hush now, darlin', shhhhh." He buried his nose in the fragrant hair behind her ear and planted kisses on the skin just in front of her hairline, then shifted over her, stringing a line of kisses down the side of her neck. And all the while he crooned soothing words. "I'm sorry. Ah, shh, baby, shh. I'm sorry."

Little by little her struggles ceased. Where restraint alone had failed to subdue her, the combination of his soothing voice, his soft kisses, and the heat and weight of his body surrounding hers slowly penetrated the red mist of rage that fogged her alcohol-impaired control. Except for intermittent shuddery little exhalations, she was soon lying quietly beneath him.

Sasha was aware he was aroused; that rigid length lying against her inner thigh was unmistakable. But he made no overt movement to force awareness of his stimulated state on her—he didn't move his hips, he didn't even press it against her, and his lips moving up and down her throat traveled with a gentle lack of threat against her skin. It was in any case her own body's response to the knowledge of his arousal that unnerved her. "Let me up," she said in a thick voice. Clearing her throat she added, "Please."

Mick stilled; then he slowly lifted his lips away from her throat, released her wrists, and pushed up off the carpet with his hands and feet, shifting his weight to the side. Sasha slid out from under and he lowered himself again, lying on his stomach with his pelvis thrust forward, pressing his erection against the floor to afford himself the modicum of relief he hadn't dared risk taking from her. He turned his head to look at her, drawing in deep breaths through his nostrils and exhaling them silently through his teeth.

"I'm sorry," she said primly, drawing her knees up to her chest and wrapping her arms around her shins. "There's no excuse I can give for such violent behavior—"

"Oh, for Christ's sake, Sasha," he interrupted impatiently, "the real surprise here is that you haven't cracked before now." He rolled to his side, propping himself up on one elbow and staring at her intently. "I wish you'd just vent it all, until every last bit of it is out in the open—then maybe we'd have a chance to move on."

"Yeah, well. Don't hold your breath."

"No, I've learned not to do that." He studied her features one by one. "Can you at least tell me what precipitated this little brouhaha?"

"What else? If it wasn't you, then by process of elimination that naturally leaves—"

"Morrison."

"Yeah, Lonnie. Don't ask me for specifics, though, because I simply cannot talk of him to you . . . or of you to him, for that matter."

"And that's the biggest shame of all, isn't it?" He jammed his fingers through his hair. "One of the things I loved best about living with you was the way you and I could always talk about anything under the sun. I don't think there's another person on earth I've experienced that with."

"Yeah, well," she said bitterly, "the search will just have to continue, I guess, because it's not likely you'll ever experience it with me again. I tend to lose my ability to express myself freely when I discover that everything I believed to be true was actually a lie."

Mick observed her stiff posture and wary eyes, remembered how different she had been just seven short days ago, and shook his head for what he'd helped to destroy. "Morrison and me . . . we're making your life a misery, aren't we?"

She quit avoiding his eyes for the first time since he'd lifted himself up off of her and raised her chin, meeting them squarely as she said in a low voice, "About as miserable as it can possibly be."

"For what it's worth, darlin', I'm truly sorry. I know it probably doesn't help a damn thing, but I am sorry."

"Thank you," she said quietly and pushed herself to her feet. She looked down at him, wanting desperately to believe in the sincerity she saw in his eyes. Then she shrugged the desire aside. She had learned the hard way that wanting something like that wasn't a smart thing to do.

"That's nice of you to say," she said in a cool little voice, "but is it truth or is Memorex?" She shrugged impatiently. "And even if it's true, you're right, you know. It really doesn't help a damn thing."

EIGHTEEN

Lon kept one ear attuned to Karen in the shower as he
rapidly riffled her dresser drawers. He felt like a perfect fool
and did *not* expect to find anything worth getting excited
over.

And yet . . .

The truth was he hadn't liked the look in her eyes last
night when she'd tracked him to the bar. She had to have
passed Sasha; there was no way in hell she could have missed
her storming out. However, not only had she failed to cross-
examine him in her usual inimitable Perry Mason style, Sasha's name hadn't even so much as crossed her lips. That
was very un-Karen-like, so much so that it caused those short
hairs at the back of his neck to stand on end.

He had yet to figure out how the hell she had known to
come looking for him in the lounge in the first place—bars
weren't exactly Karen's usual milieu. Did she possess some
damn sixth sense or something that sent forth a signal every
time he and Saush got together? Life with this woman was
turning out to be too fucking weird for words.

His hands slid deftly between slippery layers of underwear
and he pushed the drawer closed just as he heard the shower
being turned off. Crossing over to the bed, he gave it an
assessing look, remembering his favorite place to hide his
stash of skin magazines from his mother's eyes back in his
teenaged days in straight-laced Kells Crossing. Keeping a
sharp look out on the short hall that led to the bathroom, he

flipped up the comforter and slid his arm between the mattress and boxspring until it was buried up to the armpit. Mouth twisted in distaste, thinking a cynical, *God, this is asinine,* he made a wide sweep, starting at the head of the mattress and working his way toward the foot.

He was midway down when his fingers encountered the unmistakable shape of a handgun.

Connie checked to make sure no daylight would find a chink through the tightly closed draperies, then passed Sasha the cold pack she'd rigged up with ice from the machine downstairs and a washcloth from the bathroom. She settled herself in the chair opposite her friend. "So what's your next move going to be?"

The derisive sound that issued through Sasha's nose on an exhaled huff of breath was nonverbal but nonetheless expressive. "Besides swearing off drinking for the rest of my life, you mean? God, I wish I knew." She applied the ice pack gingerly to her right temple. "You think there's a snowball's chance in hell of this thing wearing off before tonight's show?"

"Oh, it should; we've got a lot of hours yet. And if it doesn't," she continued with a cheerfulness that Sasha considered callously indifferent to the pain she was suffering, "you'll get through it somehow. I've never heard of a hangover yet that was terminal."

"They just feel that way, I guess." Sasha blew out a disgusted breath. "I feel like such an idiot. I didn't even realize I'd had so much to drink until I went ballistic on him." She transferred the cold pack to her left temple and gazed unhappily at Connie. "Lord, more than anything I wish there was something I could do to find a solution to this predicament myself. I hate sitting around like a good little victim while Mick hunts for the person responsible for landing me in this mess."

"But what can you do, Saush?" Connie regarded her with alarm, not in the least thrilled at the idea of her best friend plunging blindly into a situation for which she patently had not the slightest preparation.

"Yeah, that's the problem, isn't it; what can I accomplish on my own? It's not as if I'm qualified to do a damn thing except skate." Shifting the ice pack to the top of her head, she clamped it there with the fingers of both hands and planted her elbows on the table, squeezing her temples between her forearms. Silent for several moments, she finally raised her chin, peering through slitted eyelids at her friend across the table. "I'm fairly intelligent, I think, but I don't have the foggiest idea how one goes about detecting a drug dealer with a penchant for violence."

"So leave it up to Vinicor."

Sasha did not take kindly to her friend's advice. Her head was pounding, her stomach felt on the edge of revolt, her life seemed increasingly beyond her control, and the sensation of helplessness did not contribute to the sweetness of her nature. "I can't just sit here and do nothing, Connie," she snapped testily. "I mean, there must be *something* I can undertake on my own behalf. I don't wanna be saved by some man."

"It's not some man you object to, Saush; it's Mick."

Sasha's mouth developed a mulish slant. "Okay. Fine. I don't want to be saved by Mick." She was furious with Connie, with herself, with the world in general. None of which was a legitimate excuse for the snotty tone she used to inquire, "Is that better? You happy now?"

"Don't you take your hangover out on me, Miller." Connie shoved back from the table and stood up. She saw the stubborn expression on Sasha's face and rolled her eyes. "Listen, I know you feel wronged by Mick, and, yeah, okay, you've got a perfect right to your feelings," she said quietly. "You've had a lot of cruddy things piled onto your shoulders lately. But the bottom line here is that he knows what he's doing when it comes to this drug stuff and you don't. So stay the heck out of that part of it."

Sasha tried indignantly to interrupt. "He—"

"Yeah, yeah, yeah." Connie rode right over her. "He screwed up in a major way. He's a pig; he's a dog—I've heard it ad nauseam. But you know what, Sasha? I believe he genuinely loves you. And I *know* he'd do damn near anything to ensure your safety. Now you can hang on to your hurt and refuse everything he has to offer, including his professional expertise." She paused to drill her friend with a hard look. "Or you might want to try growing up."

Feeling misused and maligned, Sasha assured herself it was merely pain induced by the door slamming behind Connie that caused her to squeeze her eyes shut against the scalding rise of tears.

"Shit!" Mick crumpled the fact sheet into a ball and hurled it across the room. Digging the heels of his hands into his scorched eye sockets, he strung together the foulest combination of obscenities his fertile vocabulary could conjure. Damn it anyhow; he'd really liked the idea of Jack-the-bus-driver as Morrison's elusive partner. But was life about to cooperate by being that simple? Hell no. The latest missive from the home office listed several dates and facts that made Jack as his man an improbability at best.

He was right back at ground zero.

Well, screw individual liberties then; he was requesting more equipment. The time had come to saturate. There were nine more names on the list of candidates and he was tired of doing them one at a time. He would pick out the likeliest and tap the person's room with the gear he had on hand as soon as they arrived in Denver. In the meantime he'd make noise the likes of which the suits had never heard until they sent him more electronics. Then he was bugging every damn name on the list, no matter how unlikely.

He used to have a reputation as the best street hump in the business. It was time he stopped acting like a lovesick amateur and started earning it once again.

Leaving the gun where he found it, Lon tucked the dislodged bedding back into place, twitched the comforter straight, and backed away until his calves bumped into a chair, whereupon the lower body muscle power keeping him upright abruptly dissipated. He sat down hard and, elbows digging into his knees, he buried his face in his hands. Jesus. Ah God, Jesus. What was he going to do?

An image of Vinicor taking command at the DiGornio home the night Amy Nitkey was struck by the car—*Ah, Christ, Karen, was that your doing too?*—flashed into his mind, and for a moment he was tempted to take this whole sorry mess and lay it out in front of the guy. Surely they could put aside their personal differences long enough to . . .

Nice dream you dumb shit. But this is real life. Lonnie's bark of bitter laughter was muffled by his hands. Hell, who was he trying to kid? Like Vinicor would ever believe a word that Morrison-the-Convicted-Drug-Dealer had to say about Karen Corselli.

The Saint.

Ah, man, he was screwed. No matter which way you looked at it, his back was to the wall. And he'd thought he was so clever. Oh, yeah; he had just known he was smarter for sure than your average guy on the street—the rules, after all, didn't *apply* to him.

Well, he wasn't so friggin' smart. No, he really wasn't very smart at all.

What he most likely was, in fact . . . was a dead man.

Sasha let herself into their room. Her stomach felt much better but she still had to hold her head with extreme care and to avoid at all costs making any sudden unwarranted movements.

Mick was growling and swearing into the phone, and she went to the closet to pull her suitcase off the shelf. The bus was leaving Cheyenne for Denver in about an hour and a half and she still had to pack. Going into the bathroom, she shook out three aspirin, swallowed them with a glass of water, and began to gather up her toiletries.

She heard Mick hang up the phone in the other room and her hands went still, her face lifted to gaze at her reflection in the mirror. She'd given some reluctant thought to what Connie had said. And maybe, just maybe, she had a point insofar as taking advantage of Mick's professional expertise went.

But the idea of applying to him in any way, shape, or form was abhorrent to her.

Taking a deep breath, tidying her flyaway curls as best she could, she assured herself that she would nevertheless do just that. No one was going to have an excuse to tell her again that she needed to grow up.

Carrying her toiletry bag, her diffuser blow dryer, and a nightgown she'd discovered hanging on the back of the bathroom door, she walked out into the hotel room. Efficiently packing them into the open suitcase on her bed, she then turned to the nearest dresser, pulled open a drawer, and reached inside for the stack of clothing inside.

Mick lounged in a chair by the window watching her, his hands laced over his flat stomach, long legs extended in front of him and crossed at the ankle, one size thirteen shoe wagging slowly from side to side. "How's your head?" he inquired.

He could tell by the way she swiveled her entire upper body in his direction, instead of merely turning her head to look at him, that it was far from all right, but when she not-too-surprisingly said, "Fine," he shrugged and let it go at that. He had a brand new agenda, which was to accomplish what was accomplishable, not to head-bang with cement walls.

To reinforce his decision, he pushed to his feet and went to get his own suitcase. Tossing it on his bed, he worked the hidden locks and flipped open, not the suitcase portion, but the false bottom. He felt rather than saw Sasha stiffen.

"I've been an agent since I graduated college," he said in a quiet voice as he ran an unnecessary check over his equipment. He looked up at her, standing erect and white-faced next to her bed, and wondered if the day would ever come when the wanting would stop. "I genuflect to your honesty," he said hoarsely. "But, baby, trying to emulate it in this business would have bought me a pine box six feet under years ago. A DEA street hump either lies . . . or he dies." He shrugged.

"You don't want to believe me when I tell you that once the words 'I love you' were said I gave up fabricating stories for you. So I'm not gonna bother you with my assurances any more. From now on I'm going back to doing strictly what I do best." His face was closed and stern as he watched her across the small distance that separated them. "I'll get you out of this mess," he said with complete authority. "And then I'll get the hell out of your life. You have my word on it."

It was what she'd wanted ever since she'd learned who he really was. She nodded coolly in acknowledgment and went with quiet dignity around the room gathering up the rest of her personal items. She set aside a clean set of clothes and efficiently packed the rest. She dug out her diffuser dryer and makeup case once again.

Then she went into the bathroom, turned on the shower, slid down the wall, and sobbed beneath its pounding, concealing spray until the water ran cold and her tear ducts finally ran dry.

* * *

The stolen key was all but burning a hole in his pocket where it rested next to his thigh as Lon strode purposefully down the hallway. He cursed himself the entire way.

Christ, he was stupid! He'd had the gun right in his hand, but had he pulled the damn thing out of its hiding place between the mattresses long enough to see what he was dealing with? Hell, no, that might have offered the opportunity for a solution and Lon Morrison never did *anything* that constructive. There was a certain amount of damage control, he'd realized after the fact, that could be done to make a handgun inoperative. None of it would do a damn bit of good, however, if he didn't even know what the friggin' make was.

Consequently, as a direct result of his earlier panic, he now had probably seventeen to eighteen minutes tops to safely get himself in and out of Karen's room before she realized her key was missing and linked it to him. And that sure as hell didn't bear contemplating. Put the key's disappearance together with his inability to get it up for her this morning and it didn't take a genius to figure out the sort of conclusion she was going to draw.

He had the key in the door when room 424 down the hallway opened. Hastily extracting and pocketing the key he stepped lively to the center of the corridor and took ground-eating strides away from 428. He nearly tripped over Connie Nakamura as she awkwardly maneuvered her way out the doorway, an ungainly collection of luggage in both hands and under one arm. Believing in the attack-is-the-best-defense school of self-preservation, he made a small production out of checking his watch.

"Well, send up the rockets, Nakamura's gonna make the bus on time." Not offering to help, he lounged against the wall and watched her struggle with a sliding shoulder bag, a hat that had a tendency to tip over one eye, and three various-sized pieces of luggage. She had such an expressive face he could simply look at her all day long . . . but then he recalled his time constraints and shoved away from the wall, reaching out to relieve her of the largest two pieces.

"What are you doing up here, Morrison?" she demanded after a small, ungracious struggle. Collecting her dignity around her like a ragged cloak, she hitched her purse up onto her shoulder, straightened her hat, and grabbing the remaining suitcase, marched down the hallway to the elevator. Lon ambled along in her wake, grinning at the rigid set of her back. God, she was so easy to rile. By the time they'd arrived at their destination however, he'd recalled the seriousness of his predicament, and it had effectively wiped the smile from his face.

He looked at her levelly when she turned to face him at the elevator. "What am I doing? Well, I'll tell you, my little China Doll," he said and reached out to touch her hair.

And promptly got his hand slapped away. "I'm Japanese, you jerk." Connie's eyes flashed and her chin went up. "Or maybe it's all the same to you. Maybe you're one of those people who think we all look alike?"

"No." Lon stepped closer. "Shall I tell you what I am, my little Japanese Doll? I'm a dead man. And the little details tend to slip by dead men." The elevator arrived and Lon slid Connie's bags inside. She stepped into the car and he followed, turning to punch the door-open button. Turning back, he trapped her against the back wall, hemming her in by the simple expedient of placing his hands flat against the wall on either side of her head. "And since I'm probably not gonna live out the week anyway, I may as well get the answer to something I've been wondering about for quite some time now."

He slid his hands into her hair, tilted up her face, lowered his head, and kissed her to within an inch of her life.

And she let him. She let him break the seal of her lips with an easy twist of his own. Let him explore her mouth with a hot, supple tongue. Let him move in close and surround her hips with his thighs, flatten her tiny breasts with his chest. For maybe a minute, she allowed him to do it all.

Then she came to her senses. Nipping sharply at his tongue, she shoved him away.

Lon straightened and stepped back. Watching her intently, he saw her scrub at her mouth with the back of her hand. He also saw that her nipples poked at the soft surface of her sweater where nothing had poked a minute ago. He touched his tongue to the back of his hand and smiled. Disconnecting the door-open button, he punched the floor for the lobby and stepped back out into the hallway. She watched him the whole time in silence, tracking his movements with uncertain ebony eyes.

"I knew you'd taste that good," he said quietly just as the door was closing. Then he shook himself out of the minor spell she'd put him in, turned, and loped back down the hallway to Karen's room. Kneeling by the side of the bed moments later, he carefully studied the pistol in his hand.

He had to struggle briefly with the temptation to simply make off with it. But if she'd got ahold of this one she could get ahold of another, and better the devil you knew, as they said . . .

Using the bedspread, he removed any possible prints from the grip and returned it to its resting place. He reviewed the options open to him as he climbed to his feet and let himself out of the room. And allowed himself a small smile.

Maybe, just maybe, there was a slim chance after all that he'd live to torment little Connie Nakamura again.

There were odd, disquieting rumblings in her head. Subliminal disturbances she couldn't quite put a finger on. With the sweet, demure smile she had perfected years ago, Karen shunned all offers of company, sitting instead in a small pocket of isolation amidst the babble of different conversations surrounding her. She ignored the fluctuating noise level as she stared blindly out the window of the bus.

Her reflection was a dim, wavery shimmer in the rain-streaked glass and it drew her attention over and over again from the dreary, waterlogged scenery beyond. If she could only capture what she saw mirrored there, if she could only study it, dissect it, she felt as if it would perhaps provide her with the answers she sought. Repeatedly, she attempted prayer, but her concentration was fractured and the words kept slipping away.

There was a conspiracy stirring; she understood that much. She could smell it. Lonnie, who was supposed to be *her* soldier, thought he was man enough to plot against her with that mealymouthed little Sasha Miller. Against *her*. It was laughable and if he thought for one moment that she'd allow him to get away with it, he was sadly deluded.

There was a sharp pain in her head and Karen briefly squeezed her eyes shut in an attempt to alleviate the escalating pressure. Pressing her forehead against the cool windowpane, she focused on the words of the Twenty-third Psalm, fighting to string them together amidst the rumbling and mumbling in her brain. Bit by bit she felt the pain recede and her power restore itself.

The Lord is my shepherd; I shall not want. He maketh me to lie down in green pastures: he leadeth me beside the still waters.

She had thought Lon was someone she could count on. Yes, he'd had his reservations; and yes he'd had his hesitations; but she had led him so gently, so seamlessly, to the path upon which she had wanted to see him place his feet. The path he'd trod for her once before. By rights he should be doing her bidding, marching to her orders, but instead that woman-child kept nagging at him and distracting him and . . .

He restoreth my soul: he leadeth me in the path of right-

eousness for his name's sake. Yea, though I walk through the valley of the shadow of—

"What?" Karen turned her head to address the person muttering in her ear. She had to make a conscious effort to erase the scowl from her face, but for heaven's sake she *detested* it when people failed to speak clearly. And regardless that the individual words were too indistinct to discern, she didn't appreciate the vaguely menacing tone one bit either.

No one was there.

She glanced around. *The Lord is my shepherd; I shall not want.* Oh, God, oh God. *He maketh me to lie down in green pastures: he leadeth me beside the still waters.*

This wasn't the first time lately she'd thought she'd heard a voice speaking in her ear. It was Sasha Miller's doing. She'd never had these problems before little You-Promised-Me-You-Wouldn't-Sell-Drugs-Miller started her whispering campaign in Lon Morrison's ear. *Her* Lon Morrison.

Before she'd poisoned Mick Vinicor against her. And just what *was* the story behind that relationship, anyway? One day they were this big, hot item—it was enough to make you retch—and the next they appeared to be on the outs. Yet Miller still checked into his room with him in every town they came to, and he still watched her like a lover. But like a frustrated lover, Karen didn't think Sasha was supplying him with sex.

Well, no matter. After Denver, Karen would be more than happy to do that for him. She'd show him what a real woman could do.

She knew now what her Lord wanted her to do. It was a direct contradiction to the Commandments that guided her life, and it was that, she thought, which had at first confused her. But hers was not to question—the answers would be provided in His own good time. In the meantime she was a Christian Soldier and she would do what she was bid.

Then everything would be hers.

Both men, the drugs, the power.

Everything.

A tiny smile tilted up one corner of Karen's mouth as she returned her attention to the scenery beyond the rain-streaked glass as they left Wyoming and crossed the border into Colorado. *The Lord is my shepherd; I shall not want.*

NINETEEN

As soon as Mick handed her the key to their room, Sasha veered away from the line awaiting room assignment and went looking for Connie. She found her in a secluded corner of the Denver hotel lobby where she was standing all alone gazing off into space. Coming up silently behind her, Sasha gripped her friend's shoulder with gentle fingers and leaned around to murmur into her opposite ear. "You still talking to me?" she asked.

Connie jumped and whirled around. "Holy shit, Sasha," she said testily when she'd caught her breath. "Announce yourself next time, will ya? You about scared me to death." Then, "Sure I'm talking to you," she responded, but her voice was stiff and she found it difficult to hold her friend's gaze. The image of Lonnie as she'd last seen him in the Cheyenne hotel elevator flashed through her mind, and she found herself in the unexpected position of feeling uncomfortable in Sasha's presence.

God. How did she handle it? Only a little over a week ago she would have made an immediate beeline for her friend to regale her with every single detail of the encounter and talk out all the confusion that Lon's actions ultimately caused.

She bit back a nervous laugh. Not much chance of *that* now. Sasha was way too volatile these days to make it a viable option. Not that Connie blamed her, exactly—she didn't. Hell, she'd be volatile too if half the stuff that had happened to Saush happened to her. But that didn't make it any easier to tell her that Lonnie, Sasha's oldest friend and most recent adversary, had kissed Connie silly in the elevator. It was just all so awkward.

To say the least.

"I only wondered," Sasha continued doggedly, picking up on Connie's tension if not the reason behind it, "because it feels as though nobody's talkin' to nobody anymore."

"Well, hey, whose fault is that, Saush?" Connie's tone was unconsciously defensive. "I'm not the one who went and sat with the techs in the back of the bus."

Quick tears rose in Sasha's eyes, and pride being the only thing she felt she had left to her, she averted her head to prevent Connie from seeing, quickly dashing them away with a surreptitious wipe of her fingertips. God, hadn't she run out of the damn things yet? Feeling isolated and estranged from everyone who'd ever mattered to her, she turned back, tilted her chin up, and said with stiff dignity, "I won't keep you, Connie. I merely wanted to apologize for my attitude earlier. As you quite rightly pointed out, there was no excuse for taking my hangover out on you." She turned on her heel and walked away.

Connie caught the sheen of tears in her friend's gray eyes as she turned and reached out a beseeching hand to Sasha's departing back. "Saush, wait," she said unhappily. This was ridiculous; they were the best of friends. The hell with awkward.

She took off after her.

But it was too late. She called out as the elevator door began to close, but Sasha either didn't hear or chose not to respond. Her face was austerely composed, her eyes fixed with unblinking attention on the lighted number panel above her head, as the doors that separated them slid silently closed.

Lon's fingers were stiff with the need to hurry. One by one he picked live ammunition out of the bullet chambers and tumbled in blanks in their stead. He'd only had time to exchange two-thirds of them when he was interrupted by the sound of the bathroom door opening.

Whispering a curse under his breath, he shoved the gun back into its hiding place, swept the live ammunition off the comforter into his palm and tossed it, along with the box of blanks, into the pocket of his jacket on the chair next to the bed, hoping to hell he wasn't going to clatter like a baby rattle when he put the damn thing on. He threw himself onto his back in the middle of the bed, stuffing his hands behind his head in a pose of nonchalance he was far from feeling just as Karen strolled into the room.

And immediately knew he was in trouble. She looked just as beautiful, just as desirable, as ever. His heart was thumping double-time, adrenalin was pumping through his veins, danger was in the air, and there was a woman in front of him wearing next to nothing. He should have been hornier than a sailor on shore leave. Yet, he looked at her and knew that there was no way in hell he was going to be able to perform for her.

Ah, Jesus, this was just what the situation called for. First this morning and now *again*. If he didn't get aroused, her suspicions sure as hell were going to be. He'd never been fussy before—if it was warm and wet, he was its man. So why did his damn dick have to pick *now* to develop a conscience?

Karen sat down on the bed beside him and reached out a hand to stroke his hard stomach. There was a little half smile tugging at the corner of her lips and he could see she was on the verge of speaking. But before she could say a word he'd shaken her off and rolled to his feet.

When in doubt, pick a fight.

Pacing restlessly, he prowled to the window, pulled back the drape, and looked out. Dropping the curtain, he turned back to face her. He shoved his hands into his pockets and rolled his shoulders. "Let's go out."

"Don't be ridiculous." Karen frowned at him. "There's not enough time before tonight's program."

"Bullshit," he said testily and prowled the circumference of the room. "We've got a few hours yet before we have to be at the arena. Time enough."

She didn't like being contradicted but she took a deep breath and humored him. "Okay. Then how about this? You know we don't dare be seen together."

"Oh, screw that, Karen."

"Lon," she began, but he cut her off impatiently.

"Dammit to hell," he snarled. "I'm sick of being cooped up in here. If I'd wanted to have this many restrictions placed on my life I coulda stayed in jail."

"I have been trying to be patient," she said in long suffering tones, "but I've had quite enough of your foul language." Then the strained tolerance in her voice disappeared and she added in her usual autocratic manner, "You will refrain from swearing in my presence."

He was across the room in two strides to loom over her. Grabbing her chin in his hand, he jerked it up and leaned down until they were eyeball to eyeball. The muscles in his jaw jumped erratically. *"Don't* tell me what I can or cannot say," he snapped. "Now, grab your friggin' coat and let's go."

"No," she stated adamantly. "We can't be seen together."

"Have you rented your car yet?"

"Yes, but—"

"Drive it two blocks to the north and pick me up there," he instructed her crisply. "And that takes care of that problem. We'll go to the other side of town where no one on earth is gonna know us." Releasing her chin, he turned away.

And spotted a bullet in the carpet beneath his jacket, whereupon he nearly had a heart attack. But glancing back at her face, he realized her attention was fixed too intently upon him to have noticed it as well. He casually crossed to the area and holding her gaze, he picked up his jacket, sat down, and lounged on his spine. He hooked the neck of his jacket over the arm of the chair, which allowed the bottom edge to puddle on the carpet over the gleaming bullet, and beneath its cover, dangled his arm over the side and swept the bullet into his hand. He slid it into the pocket and raised an eyebrow at her with all the insolence he could muster.

He'd been pretty sure her incessant need to maintain control would make it impossible to take a direct order from him. To his gratification, he discovered he was correct. Karen's chin went up.

"I'm the one calling the shots here, Mr. Morrison," she reminded him coolly. "Not you. You seem to have a problem remembering who's in charge. Now, it's too dangerous to be seen together and I'm *not* going anywhere with you."

"Then I'm outta here, baby." He looked her up and down. "You sure you don't want to change your mind and come along with me? This is your last chance."

She crossed her arms over her chest and regarded him coldly. "I believe you know what you can do with your last chance."

"Fine." He slapped the chair's arms, gathered up his jacket, and rose to his feet. "I guess I'll just have to go rustle up someone who's a little more fun than you. That should take about ten minutes."

He heard something hit the door seconds after he closed it behind him, making him wince. It probably wasn't especially bright to piss off a woman with a gun. But at least he was spared having to come up with an excuse for why he was once again unable to perform.

Sasha stood in the shadow of a piece of scenery and watched Mick. She couldn't have said why, precisely, but then she hardly recognized herself or any of the things she did these days. Full of pain and anger, she tried to remember the last time she'd laughed, couldn't, and wondered if she'd ever laugh again. The soundtrack the music director had made mocked her night after night as she glided into the spotlight. Most likely the big phoney smile she worked to paste in place fooled no one either.

She tried to keep her eyes on the set mover in his big rubber boots, but her gaze kept sliding past him to the man with whom he was speaking. Mick. Dammit, what was wrong with her? For over a week now he had been trying to talk to her, to get her to forgive him, and she had turned a deaf ear to it. Now that he'd stopped, now that his words were impersonal and he looked at her with the same polite courtesy he'd accord his maiden auntie, she wanted to make up. God, it was so crazy, but she wanted to hear him say "I'm sorry" just one more time and wanted to say in return "yeah, okay, you're forgiven; just, please, *please* don't lie to me ever again. And hold me. God, Micky, hold me, I've missed that so much." She'd never known how safe his arms had made her feel until it was taken away.

But those words were never going to be said. Mick was leaving when this whole mess was over and she had too much pride to try to convince him to stay.

There was a concerted groan from the audience and Sasha knew whoever was on must have fallen. Whose performance was this? By concentrating on the music for a moment it came to her. Oh, sure, Karen Corselli. She shrugged. It happened to all of them at one time or another.

It took her by surprise when Karen sought her out at the conclusion of her own performance. She was walking down the back hallway on her way to the line skaters' locker room to change into her street clothes when the blond skater fell into step beside her.

"Hi."

"Hi, Karen." Sasha racked her brain for something further to say, but she really didn't know the other woman all that well and with an inward shrug finally gave up the attempt.

"I suppose you know I fell tonight," Karen said glumly.

"Afraid so. I didn't see it, but I heard the crowd. I'd tell you 'it happens' but since I've never been able to shrug it off lightly myself . . ."

"Exactly. Thanks anyhow." *I'd like to tell you it happens,* Karen mimicked with silent viciousness. *To you, maybe. As for me, I did it on purpose, you namby-pamby little incompetent. And don't think the necessity didn't gall me, either.* Her thoughts hid behind guileless eyes as she turned toward Sasha. "Um, I've got a favor to ask."

"Fire away."

Karen almost laughed. *Oh, I shall, eventually.* "Would you stay after the show and go over the ice with me? I know you always check these rinks out thoroughly."

"Oh, Karen, I don't know—"

"Please," Karen put a soft hand on Sasha's forearm and looked earnestly into her eyes. "If I'd simply fluffed it on my own, I'd shrug it off as bad luck and walk away. But there was a divot in the ice and I want to mark the spot in order to avoid it for the rest of the engagement. I know you know where every flaw is located. Please, Sasha." Abruptly her head turned aside. "What?"

"Beg your pardon?" Taken aback, Sasha craned her own head in an attempt to see what was going on.

"Huh?" Karen turned back to her. Then a flush climbed up her throat and onto her face. "I'm sorry, you must think I'm such a fool. I thought I heard somebody say something." She turned redder yet, scared by the voices that kept whispering in her ear and lethally furious that Sasha Miller of all people had been a witness to her witless behavior. "So will you?" she forced herself to plead sweetly. "Please? You don't have to worry about catching the bus; I've rented a car."

Sasha really didn't want to, but it was the blush that got to her. Karen had always struck her as such a chilly and composed woman that to see her all flustered like this was kind of disarming. She grimaced. What the heck—what would it hurt to give her a half an hour of her time? Besides, she could use the time herself since her hangover had prevented her from going over the ice this afternoon.

And it wasn't as if anyone was holding his breath waiting for her to get home. Stopping at the door to the locker room she shrugged and said, "Okay then. Sure."

"Thanks, Sasha." Karen gave her a smile of surprising warmth. "I'll see you in the rink after the bus leaves."

Sasha stood with her hand on the door handle and watched her walk away. Then, with a little smile and a shake of her head, she turned the handle and pushed the door inward.

"Saush! Wait up."

Hesitating, she looked down the corridor. Connie was jogging down the hallway toward her, her hands on the skate boots slung around her neck keeping the laces pulled taut to prevent the boots from banging against her chest with the motion. Sasha let the door close once again.

Breathless, Connie skidded to a halt in front of her. "Why was Karen Corselli getting so chummy—she wanna be your new best friend?"

"No, she just wants me to—"

"Never mind; forget about her," Connie interrupted. "She's not the reason I tracked you down." She took a deep breath and blew it out. "Saush, I'm sorry about this afternoon. I've had something on my mind that I'm having a hard time getting a handle on, but I didn't mean to go all Joanie Junior High School on you."

Sasha's mood elevated instantly. "Yeah, you really oughtta learn to be more mature." She nudged her friend's shoulder with her own. "Like me."

Connie grinned. "I'll take that under advisement," she said. "So, how's your head?"

Sasha touched it gingerly. "It's going to stay on, I think."

"And has your love life improved since we last talked?"

"I wish. Oh, Connie, it just keeps on getting messier."

"Well, mine has taken a twist."

"Yes?" Sasha perked up. It had been about eight months since Connie had had a boyfriend. "Tell me."

"I'll tell ya on the bus, but you have got to give me your word you won't go ballistic on me."

Sasha waited for her to elaborate and when she didn't, said indignantly, "You can't just say something like that and then leave me hanging. Come on! Tell me now."

"I can't Saush. You hotshot headliners may be all finished for the evening, but the rest of us peons still have another number to do, remember? I've got to be back on the ice in—what?—seven minutes? I'm going to need longer than that to talk to you about this, 'cause it's complicated. I'll tell you on the bus."

"Then at least give me a little hint to hold me until—ah, no, *damn!*" Sasha thumped the door frame with her fist. "I'm not going to be on the bus, Connie." She flapped her hand in the general direction that Karen Corselli had exited. "That was what Karen wanted. She asked me to go over the ice with her so she doesn't land on her butt tomorrow night like she did tonight. Ah, dammit anyway, I didn't particularly want to do this in the first place."

Connie nodded in understanding. "Because she's one of the 'possibles' on Mick's list?"

"Uh, well, no," Sasha replied and grimaced. "I sorta forgot about that, to tell you the truth." Then she made a disparaging noise and waved it away. "Nah, c'mon, can you honestly picture Karen Corselli mixed up in a drug ring?"

"Our Lady of the Perpetual Snow? Hey, really, why not? Drug dealers must come in all shapes and sizes. It's true I can't quite see Miss Squeaky Clean in the role, but what do you suppose a typical dealer *looks* like, anyhow?"

"I don't know. Some skinny Columbian with a pock-marked face and patent-leather hair?" Then she sobered. "I shouldn't joke about this, because when it comes right down to it what the hell do I know? I mean, let's face it, Connie, I never would have picked Lon as a pusher either."

Connie didn't have the time to pursue that particular avenue right then. "If it wasn't the list thing, then why weren't you hot to help her out tonight? I mean, I know she's not exactly a bosom buddy, but you're usually such a sport about that sort of thing."

"Well, it's just . . . I feel sorta awkward knowing she's been sleeping with Lon . . ."

"What?" Connie's voice came out in a strained whisper.

An expression of guilt flashed across Sasha's face. "Oh, great, so much for my word that I wouldn't tell anyone, huh? I guess I've got brass calling Mick a liar at every turn—at least he knows how to keep a secret."

Connie grabbed her arm. "Beat yourself up some other time," she said through gritted teeth. "I wanna know how you know about Lon and Karen."

"I caught him coming out of her room last night." Sasha took in the paleness of her friend's face and nodded. "I know, it's kind of a shocker, isn't it? No matter how many rumors have been circulated about her, it still about knocked me off my feet."

"A shocker," Connie said with some bitterness as she loosened her grip on Sasha's arm. "Yeah. That's one way of putting it."

Sasha looked at her closely. "Am I missing something here?" It was beginning to occur to her that Connie's distress went deeper than the situation seemed to merit.

"No. Look, I've gotta go, Saush." Connie couldn't seem to draw a complete, to-the-bottom-of-the-lungs breath, and she had to remove herself before she did something really stupid . . . like started to scream. "I'm gonna be late."

Sasha was disconcerted by the abruptness in her friend's voice but said gamely, "Okay. Listen, I'll see you as soon as we finish up here, okay? What room are you in? I'm dying to hear your news."

"Oh, God," Connie said with a strangled laugh. Then without answering the question she turned on her heel and fled, leaving Sasha to stare after her in bewilderment.

Mick glared at the charts he'd compiled. Dammit, the answer had to be in here somewhere. He'd eliminated a few names on the basis of who had been in the crowd immediately following Amy Nitkey's hit-and-run. Dave DiGornio, for example, had been easy. He'd been talking to his father and Cathy on the patio when Amy was struck; ergo it wasn't possible that he was the driver. One name off the list. Two others weren't quite as cut and dried but they were close enough. Mick recalled seeing them within a time frame in which he thought unlikely that the driver could have ditched his car and blended back into the crowd.

Presuming he'd bothered to blend back in at all.

He tapped his pencil on the next name on the list. Karen Corselli. Huh. Doubtful. All the same, he didn't write anybody off without compelling evidence, so give it some consideration. What did he know about her?

She preached at the drop of a hat. She set his teeth on edge. She was uptight, easily offended, and tight assed.

But not so tight assed that she'd hesitated to grab him by the balls.

He threw down his pencil and sat up straighter. What with one thing and another he'd forgotten about that. Jesus. It was an anomaly that should have jumped out at him right off the bat, but he'd been preoccupied with Sasha. It was for reasons such as this that surgeons didn't operate on their own family members and cops should never get personally involved with women on their cases. He rolled his shoulders. Well, he couldn't do a damn thing about it now, so concentrate on what he knew. Karen Corselli. Dainty, mealymouthed, and devout. Okay so far, but . . . Militant about stamping out offensive language, but not an iota of shyness when it came to glomming onto the crotch of some guy she hardly even knows and obviously doesn't like? Fondling him, inviting him up to her room, while simultaneously chastising him for taking the Lord's name in vain?

This was not the profile of an entirely reasonable personality.

Mick shoved back from the table and went to the closet. Pulling out his suitcase, he opened the false bottom, pulled out his ID and gun, then kicked the suitcase aside. He checked the clip, snapped it into place, and shoved the gun into his waistband, pulling his sweater down to cover it. Sliding his identification into his hip pocket, he picked up his keys and left the room.

It was time to stop playing games.

Two minutes later, he was down on the next floor, pounding on Morrison's door. He waited a moment, pounded again, then turned away. Damn. Okay, think. Where else might he be?

Corselli's room? Alerting a possible suspect by pounding on her door wasn't exactly recommended procedure, so he went down to the lobby and used the house phone to dial her room.

No answer.

Swearing viciously under his breath, Mick banged the receiver into its cradle and crossed the lobby to the lounge. He stuck his head in the door and looked around, not expecting much by this time.

Morrison was sitting by himself, nursing a beer at a table in the corner.

Mick walked over, pulled out a chair and sat down. He dug his ID out of his hip pocket, but a waitress materialized before he had a chance to show it to the other man. "Club soda," he said without taking his eyes off Morrison.

"I'm set," Lon told her. He crossed his arms over his chest and lounged back, eyeing Mick sourly as she walked away. "To what do I owe the honor, Vinicor?"

Mick flipped open the ID and slid it across the small tabletop. Lon sat up and leaned forward to read it, squinting to make out the words in the dim lighting. Suddenly, he swore and snapped upright. "DEA?" he said hoarsely. "You're fucking DEA?"

"That's right." Mick snapped the wallet closed and slid it back into his pocket.

"Does Sasha know about this? Ah, hell yeah, of course she does . . . and I know to the *day* when she found out. You son of *bitch!*" Coming out of his chair, Lon lunged across the table at him. Grabbing a handful of sweater in both fists, he started to haul Mick to his feet, but Mick brought his hands up under Lon's wrists and snapped them wide, breaking the hold. Gripping Lon's shoulders, he surged to his own feet, using the momentum to shove Morrison back into his seat. Leaning across the minute cocktail table, he thrust his face into the other man's and said between gritted teeth, "Sit the hell down and shut up!"

"You *used* her, you—"

"And you *didn't?*" Mick's fists twisted in the material of Lon's shirt and yanked, hauling him halfway to his feet. They stood nose to nose hunched over the table. "Don't get sanctimonious on me, you sorry son of a bitch. You got a job here by using her. She vouched for you and you were willing to destroy everything she's put together since the *last time* you fucked her over by going back to doing the same old shit that got you tossed in the pen in the first place. You think that won't affect the way the people she works with regard her?" Breathing heavily, he loosened his grip and flicked the backs of his fingers disdainfully against the material. "Between the two of us we're chipping away at her life piece by freakin' piece, but you aren't any more fit to lick her goddam shoes clean than I am, so don't talk to *me* about using her."

Lon sank back into his seat. He picked up his beer, drained it, then set the glass carefully back within the same condensation ring on the tabletop. He looked up at Mick, saw the fury and the anguish. "She's gonna dump you, isn't she?"

"Yeah, the minute I get this case solved." The look Mick gave him was bitter. "That should make you happy."

"I guess that depends on whether you love her or if this was all just a game or a job or whatever to you."

"I love her all right, but it doesn't matter to her. She's tired to death of being lied to."

"Oh, I imagine it matters a whole lot more than you think. And if it makes you feel any better, you're right about me. I'm a loser and Sasha's better off without me. But you got one thing wrong. I haven't sold since I was sprung. I'll admit I considered it when I got out and discovered that everything had changed, that Saush had you and Nakamura and didn't need me—that she'd grown up and got on with her life. But I couldn't quite bring myself to do it, Vinicor."

"But you do have a partner who's pressuring you?"

He gave an unamused snort of laughter. "Oh, yeah."

"Who is it?"

Lonnie plowed his fingers through his hair. "Ah, man, you wouldn't believe me if I told you."

"I will if you say it's Karen Corselli."

Lon's head jerked up. "You *know?*" A short, sharp bark of incredulous laughter exploded out of his throat and he leaned forward on his forearms, pinning Mick with a look of such intensity it made Mick blink.

"Jesus," Lon said hoarsely, "I didn't think there was a person in the world who would give a lick of credence to the word of an ex-con over that of a Bible-thumping, upstanding citizen like Miss Corselli. How did you figure it out?" He waved the question away. "Never mind; it doesn't matter." He got right down to business. "She's got a gun, Vinicor. I found it this morning before we left Cheyenne. I bought some blanks as soon as we hit town, but I only had time to replace about three-quarters of 'em."

"Does she suspect you?"

"No." Lon shook his head. "But that's not going to last because I haven't been able to . . . uh . . . perform. Not this morning and not this afternoon, either. At least that time I picked a fight to disguise the fact that I wasn't getting it up, but she's not stupid—she's going to put two and two together sooner or later."

The waitress came up with Mick's club soda and he waved her away with an impatient, authoritative gesture. Turning back to Lon he demanded, "Give me a profile on this woman."

"She's a control freak. A power junkie. And she's the most accomplished woman in bed I've ever met. That's how she reeled me in originally—with the promise of riches the likes of which I'd never seen on the west side of Kells Crossing and sex that I thought only existed in wet dreams. Some of the stuff she could do? Oh, man . . ." He shook his head dreamily, then sat up straighter, shaking off the memories. "You know something, though, Vinicor, I don't think she really likes it. Most women who are good in the sack, it's because they truly love sex or there's a real strong chemistry with their partner or both. But with Karen . . ." He shrugged. "I think it's a power thing, but she's so damn good you don't notice for the longest time."

Mick got a brief flash of Lon as he must have been as a randy, small-town twenty-one-year-old, and he had to purposely block it out. He didn't want to feel empathy for the man. "You want her off the streets?" he demanded coolly.

"Yeah. Sometimes I really like her, and there's something about her at times that I almost feel sorry for, but . . . yeah. I want her off the streets."

"Would you be willing to wear a wire?"

"If you think it would help Saush."

"Okay, then," Mick leaned forward to lay out the plan, but he'd barely said three words when they were interrupted by the waitress determined to serve the drink he'd ordered. The instant she walked away, both men immediately became involved in the details of the plan. More alike then either was willing to acknowledge, they passed ideas back and forth beneath the hum of surrounding chatter.

A furious voice suddenly interrupted them. "There you are, you two-faced, lying jerk," it said with low-voiced venom, and both men's heads snapped up. Connie Nakamura stood beside the table, hands on her diminutive hips, and she was the picture of outraged fury as she glared down at Lon Morrison.

TWENTY

If looks truly could kill, Lon would have been the dead man he'd yesterday informed Connie he was. She drilled him with her eyes, and they glittered with unleashed temper. There was no doubting her very real willingness to annihilate him where he sat.

Intrigued with her as always, Lon sat up and gave her his undivided attention, but Mick barely gave her a second glance. "Not now, Connie," he said impatiently and flapped a hand at her.

"Butt out, Vinicor," she snapped. "No one was talking to you."

That got his attention but hers had already reverted to Lon. "You are some piece of work, mister," she said with low-voiced bitterness. "Where do you get off coming on to me when you're sleeping with Karen Corselli?"

Both men snapped upright. "How did you find out about that?" Mick demanded at the same time that Lon snarled, "Goddammit! Sasha gave me her word she wouldn't—"

"Oh, that's beautiful." Slapping both hands down on the tabletop, Connie leaned her weight on them as she glared down at them. "You guys really are two of a kind," she said, drilling them with a look filled with contempt. "When all else fails, I guess you can always put the blame on Sasha."

She knew she was being unfair but didn't care. Leaning down she thrust her face aggressively close to Lonnie's and said through clenched teeth, "I do not accept other women's leavings, Morrison. This may come as a big surprise to you, but I . . . don't . . . have to."

"To the contrary, my fragile little cherry blossom, that doesn't surprise me at all."

"I am *not* your little *anything!*"

"Much to my dismay." Then Lon dropped the bantering and said soberly, "Look, Connie, it isn't what it seems."

"Oh, right." Her laugh was bitterly unamused. "You weren't really coming from Karen Corselli's room when I first saw you."

"Well, yeah, I was, but . . ."

"And you didn't actually go right back the minute my elevator departed for the lobby."

"Well, okay, I did, but . . ."

"Listen," Mick interrupted irritably. "Could you two carry on this conversation some other time? We've got more important matters . . ."

"Butt out, Vinicor!" Both parties snapped in unison, but then Lon said to Mick in a more reasonable tone, "Look, just give me a minute here, will ya? I'd do the same for you if it was Saush you needed to straighten things out with."

"Like hell you would," Mick mumbled under his breath but nevertheless climbed to his feet. He gave them both a disgusted look and snapped, "Ten minutes, Morrison. I'll be up in my room." Tossing a bill on the table, he strode away. Connie watched him go, then turned back to Lon.

"Well, aren't you two cozy all of a sudden," she snarled, feeling a sudden vulnerability now that it was just the two of them with no third party to act as buffer. Then her backbone snapped her erect. Oh, no; no more. He was through getting away with making her feel that way. "I won't keep you," she said with hard-won dignity. "I just stopped by to let you know that I'm on to you, and to tell you to keep your damn distance."

"Well, I'll tell ya, Connie," Lon said. "I sure wish I could oblige you, but I've got a little problem with that."

"Yes?" she challenged coolly. "And what might that be?"

Lon shrugged. "I don't want to keep my distance," he said. Lightning fast his hands whipped out and wrapped around her forearms, jerking her onto his lap. She instinctively started to struggle but he exerted upward pressure with the thighs she sat on, downward pressure on the arms he firmly held, and put his lips next to her ear to murmur, "You can continue to do that, of course, but this table has already provided the entire bar with a whole lot of entertainment this evening and I gotta warn you, you're only adding to the show."

Connie glanced over her shoulder and saw that the lounge patrons were indeed watching them with unconcealed amusement. She stilled, straightening her spine and sitting with rigid dignity upon his knees. "So, when did you and Vinicor get so chummy?" she demanded quietly, determined to maintain her dignity no matter what this clown subjected her to. And if her position here on his lap caused her heart to beat just the tiniest bit faster, well, that would be her secret. "I thought you hated each other's guts. Isn't that one of the weapons you've both been using to twist Sasha's guts into knots?"

Lonnie winced. "There's not a whole lot I can say in response to that, is there?" he answered equitably enough. "Except perhaps to say that after we've taken care of another problem we're working on, maybe we can do something to rectify that." Then his eyes narrowed on her. "Just how much do you know about Vinicor, anyway?" he demanded.

Connie looked him straight in the eye. "Enough to know that you could alleviate a lot of Saush's danger by telling him the name of the person pressuring you to resume pushing drugs."

It belatedly occurred to Sasha that she probably shouldn't have allowed herself to be manipulated into a situation that left her stranded with someone on Mick's list of possible suspects. She considered herself a reasonably intelligent woman under ordinary circumstances, but let's face it, circumstances had been far from ordinary for some time now and this wasn't the shrewdest decision she'd ever made.

It wasn't that Karen was doing anything overt to make her nervous; there was just a hint of menace that she sensed. It was not a feeling she could quite pin down, and it certainly wasn't rational. Nevertheless, it stuck with her, fueling a little kernel of unease.

She cast a sidelong glance at the woman beside her, taking note of the gleaming hair and the translucent skin that glowed beneath overhead lights. Karen turned her head and caught her eye, giving her a sweet smile. *Talk about your imagination running amok, Miller. What next, conspiracies involving Salvation Army bellringers?* This feeling was most likely nothing more than the realization that some of her own reasons for being here were a bit more convoluted than she cared to admit.

She took such pride in her own honesty, in her refusal to fool herself. Yet she had to admit, as she skated with Karen slowly over the ice, that a desire to take an action diametrically opposed to whatever she thought Mick or Lon would deem acceptable had probably played a role in her decision to stay behind tonight with a woman she didn't particularly like. It might not have been a consciously acknowledged desire, but it was one that most likely had guided her as surely as her inherent willingness to lend a hand to a fellow skater. Just one of her dirty little secrets, she thought wryly, and having exposed it to the light of day, had to wince. *Good God, Saush. How immature can you get?*

A slight smile pulled up the corner of her mouth. *Oh, trust me. Much more immature than this.*

Karen mumbled something at her side and Sasha's smile dropped away, her unease returning. This wasn't the first time Karen had said things that sounded as if she were responding to an unseen third party, but where she'd displayed a sort of endearing embarrassment about it earlier, now she didn't even seem to notice. It was almost as if she were perhaps just the slightest bit out of touch with the real world.

"Here's the spot that probably tripped you up," Sasha said, pointing to small hump of ice and dropping an orange pylon over it to mark the spot for the crew to take care of tomorrow afternoon. "The rest looks pretty good." Testing the last quadrant, she executed an unambitious single lutz that ended with her gliding back to Karen's side. "That should do it," she said. "You ready to go?"

"Yes." The little smile that played around the corners of Karen's mouth was chilling. "Oh, yes, indeed. I would say that it's definitely time."

Sasha's return smile was wary. Why did she get the feeling they were speaking on two different levels here? Well, never mind. With a shrug she skated up to the balustrade, hauled herself up, and swung her legs over to the spectator seating side. She began working her skates off. With luck, they'd be back at the hotel in ten minutes and she could put this entire eerie little episode out of her mind. It was probably just the poor lighting in here that was making her so jumpy.

The only real illumination in the otherwise dark and cavernous arena came from the overhead lights directly above the ice. Gloom edged the peripheries where they sat and except for a weak bulb burning down by the end of the corridor where they would exit, total darkness encompassed the back hallways and the wings. Wiping off her blades, Sasha slid on their guards and tossed the skates into her case; then she pulled on a pair of thick socks and her old Weejuns. She was aware of Karen doing the same next to her. Easing off the balustrade, she efficiently straightened her skate case, closed it up, pulled on her jacket, and turned back to Karen, who was still sitting cross-legged atop the railing that divided gallery from rink. "Ready?" she started to inquire.

But the word died with a froglike croak deep in her throat.

Her eyes widened and then refused to look away as Karen's hand came up and leveled a pistol straight at her chest.

Where the hell was she? Mick paced his hotel room, pausing to listen whenever he heard someone pass by in the hallway.

When he'd first arrived to find their room empty, he hadn't even questioned Sasha's absence, so accustomed was he to being avoided by her these days. But after a few moments it had occurred to him that when she wasn't safely ensconced with him he could count on her being in Connie Nakamura's company. And at this very moment Connie was downstairs in the lounge with Morrison.

Sans Sasha.

The hell with this waiting business. That had never been his style and he saw no reason at this late date to go changing methods that had worked for him in the past. Mick picked up the room key and stuffed it in his jacket pocket, heading for the door. In any case, the ten minutes he had granted Morrison were up.

And he wanted to know, if Sasha wasn't with him and she wasn't with Connie, then just where the bloody hell was she?

The barrel of the gun pointing at her chest looked big enough to drive a train through. Sasha stood very, very still. She found it necessary to lock her knees to prevent them from audibly knocking together, but she was proud of the calmness of her voice when she spoke. "This is a joke, right?" she demanded. "Karen, put that thing down. You're making me nervous." It was a wonder her voice functioned at all, never mind managed to sound so coolly incredulous. Her hands gripped each other by her waist. She might find the situation incomprehensible, but she knew in her gut that it was no joke. Her instincts had been trying to tell her otherwise for the past hour.

Karen wasted no time in letting her know that assumption was a valid one. "No joke," she replied coolly. "And you should be nervous, Sasha. Very . . . very . . . nervous."

"You mean that thing is *real?*" She took several steps backward but there was really nowhere to go. The backs of her knees came up against the front row seats and she halted. "I've never done anything to you, Karen. So what have you got against me?"

"Aside from your personality? Not a blessed thing." Karen looked Sasha up and down and the examination ultimately resulted in a smile that was fleeting and cold. She shrugged. "Don't take it personally, dear. You just got in my way."

Lon hooked his foot around the leg of the nearest chair and dragged it forward. He transferred Connie off his lap onto it. "You know that someone's been pressuring me to sell again." It was flatly stated, not a question. "Sasha was the one to tell you, I assume."

Connie bristled. "She had to have someone she could talk to who didn't have an agenda of their—"

"Don't get all defensive on me," Lon interrupted. "I'm just trying to clarify the situation in my own mind. Where *is* Saush tonight anyway?"

"She stayed at the arena with Karen Corselli to go over—"

"Jesus Christ." Lon shoved his chair back from the table with such abruptness and force it toppled to the floor. He surged to his feet. "Tell Vinicor," he commanded hoarsely and took off at a dead run for the doorway.

"Lon!"

He checked briefly, turning back. "The person pressuring me?" he called softly. "It was Karen, Connie. Tell Vinicor." Then he was gone.

Connie went into an immediate panic. Oh God, oh God.

Karen was the source of danger to Saush? She had to get Mick—Mick would know what to do. Grabbing her purse, she ran from the lounge. Lon was nowhere in sight as she crossed the lobby to the elevator, and she danced in place in front of the doors, her finger exerting continuous pressure on the floor-call button. The elevator finally arrived and she had already stepped inside the car before it struck her that she didn't know Mick's room number. She *always* knew what room Sasha was in, always . . . except that this afternoon when the rooms were assigned, she and Saush were in the midst of their argument and never quite got around to sharing that information.

Swearing, she stuck her hand between the closing doors before they could shut entirely. They bounced a few times in their tracks but then reluctantly reopened, allowing her to step off. She ran up to the desk clerk, rudely pushing in front of a woman who was in the midst of either checking in or out.

"Excuse me!" the woman said with shrill indignation.

"I'm sorry, I'm sorry, it's an emergency." Without awaiting a response, she turned to the clerk. "Quick! What room is Mick Vinicor in?" she demanded.

"I'm sorry," he said, "I'm not allowed to give you that information."

"Dammit, it's an emergency! I need his room number!"

"And I'm telling you that it's against hotel policy to give out information that breaches the privacy of our patrons," the clerk reiterated. "If you'll go to the courtesy phone over there, however, I'd be happy to ring his room for you." He waved at a white phone next to the bank of plants.

"Yeah. Yeah, okay. That's good—that'll work." Turning to the indignant woman still crowding up close behind her, she said, "I'm sorry lady," then raced over to the phone and picked it up, waiting in an agony of impatience for him to punch the number. It began to ring.

And ring. And ring.

"C'mon, Mick, c'mon. Pick it up. Pick . . . it . . . up!" There was no answer.

"Shit!" Connie slammed the receiver into the cradle and stood there chewing on the cuticle of her index finger as she stared wildly about. What now?

The ding of the elevator caught her attention and she stared at the white overhead light that indicated the car was about to arrive. Fat lot of good that would do her. What was she supposed to do, go floor to floor until she found Vinicor? The police! Of course! She could at least call the police. She pushed upright and was about to pivot in the direction of the public phones when the elevator doors slid open. Mick stood framed in the opening, looking big, menacing, and thoroughly ill tempered.

She'd never seen such a pretty sight in her life. *Oh, thank you, God, thank you!* Her voice, loud and desperate, rang out across the lobby. *"MICK!!!"*

"It's nothing *personal?"* Sasha stared in sheer disbelief at the woman holding the weapon on her. "Well, excuse me, Karen, but when someone sticks a gun in my face and tells me I should be nervous, I tend to take it very personally indeed."

Karen stared at her consideringly for several nerve-wracking moments, long enough for Sasha to reconsider the wisdom of having spoken her mind without first giving it some thought. Finally, the other woman bent her arm at the elbow, raised the gun up until it was aimed at the ceiling, and crooked the index finger of her free hand at Sasha. "Come here," she said.

Sasha stepped forward apprehensively, then stood cautiously still in front of her. There was an aura about Karen she found volatile. And perhaps it was nothing more than the fact that Karen was still perched cross-legged on the balustrade, which put her head on a higher level than Sasha's, but she suddenly seemed much taller to her.

Abruptly Karen lashed out, striking her with the butt of the gun. Sasha cried out at the pain that exploded in her left cheekbone and staggered as the blow knocked her backward. Catching herself on the armrest of the seats behind her with one blindly flung-out hand, her other hand flew with reflective protectiveness to cup her wounded cheek. Her knees threatened to crumple beneath her, but she stiffened her arm to prevent herself from falling to the floor and edged her rump onto the seat before her legs gave out entirely. She looked up at Karen warily.

"You'll keep a civil tone in your voice," the blonde instructed her coolly. "I dislike back talk."

Sasha pulled her hand away from her cheek and looked at it. It was covered with blood. "What do you want with me?" she asked in a carefully neutral tone. "I don't understand this at all."

Then suddenly she did. Oh, dear God. Lonnie's silent partner.

The partner who had messed with her costumes, fiddled with the screws holding her blades to her skates, run down a woman wearing her coat.

The partner Lonnie had informed he would no longer sell drugs for whenever she commanded because he had given his word to Sasha.

You got in my way. The words reverberated in her head.

"Ah, I see you're beginning to understand."

Sasha looked up at her. "It was you? You're the one who got Lonnie into this whole convoluted mess with the heroin?"

"Well, I don't know that 'mess' is the word I'd choose. I prefer to think of it as an opportunity," Karen replied. Sagely, she nodded. "Yes. A golden opportunity for Lon to make some serious spending cash. He was very hungry in those days. He wanted it all, he wanted it immediately, and I showed him a way to obtain it."

"It's rather remarkable that he never breathed a word to implicate you when everything blew up in his face," Sasha marveled quietly, and for the first time since she'd looked up to find Karen pointing a gun at her she saw the other woman's expression soften.

"Yes, Lon is extremely loyal." Then her mouth hardened. Loyalty to her was one thing; loyalty to this woman something else, something not to be tolerated. "Too bad you had to get in the way of that." She leveled the gun at Sasha once again.

"Lon is my oldest friend—"

"You used your influence with him to undermine me."

"I didn't even know about you! I was just trying to prevent him from going back to prison." Sasha's cheek was throbbing wickedly and she concentrated on the pain to stave off the sheer terror that was threatening to engulf her reasoning powers. She hadn't been discerning enough to be frightened before; even being pistol-whipped had seemed sort of fantastical. However she wasn't totally lacking in intelligence or good sense. It was beginning to occur to her that in Karen's eyes this situation could only end one way.

With her permanently out of the way.

Oh, God, Mick, where are you when I need you most? Where are you with your bloody fast talk and your skill with a gun? Yet, who was to blame for that, truly? She'd picked up snippets of information here and there this past week and quite consciously had made the decision to share none of it with him, a punishment for breaking her heart. She'd showed him, boy; it should be some hot comfort indeed to take with her to her grave.

No, the hell with that: she wasn't going down without a fight. If she couldn't talk her way out of this, then she'd simply have to run for it and hope to heaven Karen was a lousy shot. Shakily, she climbed to her feet. "May I ask you something, Karen?"

Karen made a "be-my-guest" gesture with her gun hand. If her expression was anything to judge by, the power she held over Sasha was according her a wealth of enjoyment.

"You're a devout woman," Sasha said carefully. "So, how do you justif"—*bad choice of words, Saush!*—"um, that is, reconcile your obvious faith to the fact that you've caused the deaths of so many people?"

Karen had had years to justify the disparity to herself. "To a man," she informed Sasha with cool arrogance, "they were sinners whose time had come to meet their Maker. I simply assisted them to a better world where they can walk with Jesus."

Well, what did you expect, Sasha wondered bitterly. *That Karen would suddenly throw down her gun and repent her sins?* She edged toward the aisle. It looked as though running was going to be her only option after all.

A new voice boomed out from the backstage entrance. "You just couldn't resist grandstanding, could you Karen?" Both women's heads turned sharply toward the entryway. There stood a shadowy figure dimly backlit in the opening.

"You've really done it this time, honey." Lon stepped forward into the light. "Your incessant thirst for power is finally going to land the both of us right smack-dab in the slammer."

TWENTY-ONE

Connie had never seen a man galvanized into action with quite the ruthless efficiency Mick Vinicor displayed. His face exhibited an utter lack of expression as she stuttered through an explanation of what she'd learned and a recitation of what she feared. But his eyes burned and a muscle in his jaw jumped rhythmically.

"Nothing's gonna happen to her," he growled. Then he was gone, loping with long-legged strides down the stairs that led from the lobby to the banquet level. After a second's hesitation, Connie ran after him.

She saw him pushing through the exterior door out into the parking lot behind the hotel just as she hit the bottom of the stairs. When she arrived in the lot seconds later, it was to find him going rapidly from car to car, stooping slightly to peer into each one. Suddenly he grabbed the driver's-side handle on an older model Ford sedan. It didn't open and he swore. He glanced at Connie when she ran up to him.

"Go get me a coat hanger," he commanded. "And hurry."

She ran back into the banquet floor and located an empty cloak room. Grabbing a hanger, she tore back out into the lot. Mick dropped the rock he was about to heave through the window and rapidly straightened a piece of the wire hanger she handed him. He inserted it where window met door frame and jiggled it up and down. There was a faint snick and he tossed the hanger aside, reaching once more for the door handle.

Connie had run around to the passenger-side door by the time he'd slid in and reached for keys that had been left dangling in the ignition. Her rap on the window was nearly drowned out as the engine roared to life. "Let me in," she demanded.

"Forget it, Nakamura." Mick spared a single glance for her anxious face peering in at him through the murky glass. "No civilians." He jerked the gear shift from park down to reverse.

"You let me in, Vinicor," she shouted, "or I'll grab the first cab I can find to take me out there. That'll add just one *more* civilian and God only knows how that might screw everything up."

Ignoring the threat, Mick backed the car from its slot, reversing in a quick, straight line. Connie ran alongside, banging her palm against the window, and he glared at her persistence. He pressed the brakes and had the gear shift slammed into drive before the car fully rocked to a halt.

"You open this damn door!" she screamed at him.

He let loose a string of obscenities. "No! Now let go of the handle or have your goddam shoulder dislocated!"

"I won't!" She trotted faster, her breath sobbing in her throat. But she didn't let go of the handle.

"Shit!" He stomped on the brakes and reached over to unlock the passenger door, swearing a blue streak as Connie ripped it open and dove into the front seat. Mick had the gas peddle to the floor before she could retract her nose from where it pressed into the cracked upholstery next to his thigh. "When we get to the arena, you'll stay in the car," he snapped. "You can make yourself useful by wiping it free of our prints or something." He took his eyes off the road only briefly to glare over at her. "What you will *not* do is pull another stunt like this to try to gain admittance to the arena. You get in my way, Connie, and I won't wait for Karen to take a shot at you. I'll shoot you myself."

She picked herself up and fumbled for the seat belt. It was

an old-fashioned lap variety but better than nothing, she fervently hoped. At a rough guess she'd say Mick was averaging seventy miles an hour, pressing his palm to the car horn and screaming through intersections whether the signal lights were red or green. The next time he turned right, cornering practically on two wheels, Connie grabbed for the flapping passenger door and slammed it shut. She hunched down in her seat, peering at Mick's grim face.

"Oh, God, I hope we're in time," she whispered to herself. "Please, please, let us be on time." She looked up to find herself pinned in place by fierce blue eyes. In the next instant, the intense gaze was removed, his eyes once again watching the road.

"We will be," he said violently. "Nothing's gonna happen to her. You hear me? *Nothing.*"

Sasha was never so glad to see anyone in her life as when Lon Morrison walked into the arena, but the feeling was not a long-lived one. He walked past her without so much as a glance and went straight up to Karen. "You're thinking with your ego instead of your head," he told her brusquely. "And that's not like you. If you had put some thought into this, you'd realize she was bound to tell her plans to Nakamura, who luckily for you brought them to me when she began to get worried—instead of taking them to Vinicor."

"Lon?" Sasha said uncertainly, climbing to her feet.

He turned to her. "When I have something I want to say to you, Miller, you'll know it," he snapped. "Until then shut up and sit down!" He immediately turned back to Karen. "There's still time for damage control but you've got to get your story down cold."

Shock reverberated through Sasha and she collapsed back into her seat. He wasn't here to save her butt; he was here to prevent Karen from getting caught disposing of her body.

Watching the exchange between Miller and Morrison, the

corners of Karen's mouth curled up with pleasure. Well, it was about time.

Then she frowned. She'd messed up. The increasingly vocal voice in her head had interfered with her normally razor-sharp ability to plan, and she hadn't plotted; she'd only reacted. Sasha had got in her way one time too many and she'd grabbed at the opportunity to get rid of her once and for all without planning beyond that moment. Praise the Lord for Lon's intervention.

On the other hand, she hadn't come this far without questioning every single situation. She regarded him with inborn suspicion. "Why don't you just take a few steps back there, big fella," she suggested coolly, waving him away with her gun hand and exercising caution insofar as keeping it beyond his reach. "You expect me to believe you're suddenly willing to sacrifice your precious little Sasha?"

"I don't see why not." Lon shrugged with careless disregard. "Saush's appeal is a short-lived thing. Just ask Vinicor."

Betrayal upon betrayal; it was just one more in a long line of too many. But it was the determining one. Sasha felt something give way deep inside and she surged to her feet, impelled by a hot rush of fury. Emitting a sound like a wounded animal, she charged Lon, shoving him with all her might and crashing him into Karen who toppled over backward onto the ice. She used the impetus she'd gained to hurl herself over the balustrade, landing painfully on one knee upon the ice, but driving the other squarely into Karen's stomach. Grabbing the other woman by the hair, she banged her head against the ice, once, twice. The gun skittered out of the Karen's hands.

Then Karen's nails were raking at her face, clawing at her hair. Sasha jerked back reflexively when a fingernail gouged the already fiercely painful wound on her cheekbone, and Karen used the brief cessation to her own advantage. Pulling her shoulders off the ground, she joined her hands together and swung them like a club at Sasha's head.

The blow cracked across the same cheek that had been pistol whipped, causing her head to turn with a vicious twist and knocking her from her uneven perch atop Karen's stomach.

Yellow dots swimming before her eyes, nausea climbing her throat, Sasha lay curled on her side gasping for breath and watched helplessly as Karen scrambled for the pistol. Finally she forced herself up onto her hands and knees, head hanging and breathing deeply, trying to see her way past the sickly white mist that swirled in from the outer edges of her vision. Please, she couldn't faint now. If she fainted now she was a dead woman. Another deep breath, and it began to recede, the narrow tunnel that comprised her eyesight expanding back to normal. She was so grateful to have it restored and to feel her nausea abate back to a manageable level that staggering to her feet in time to see Karen reach the gun seemed almost anticlimactic.

Until Karen snatched it up, swung around on her knees, and pointed it straight at her.

Panting for breath, swaying in place, Sasha eyed the other woman with a growing feeling of alarm. To see a woman normally so rigidly controlled disintegrate right in front of one's eyes was a terrifying sight.

Karen's neat hair was a wild tangle around her face, her normally sanctimonious demeanor sunk without a trace. Breath sawing audibly, chest heaving, her lips were pulled back from her teeth in a feral grimace as she glared at Sasha with feverish eyes. In an abrupt move, she whipped her hair back from her forehead with the forearm of her gun hand, but then immediately reaimed the firearm at Sasha, steadying the wrist bearing its weight with her free hand. "You," she gasped between breaths, "are about to meet Jesus."

"But not here, Karen," Lon's voice crooned soothingly

and Sasha jerked in shock. She had forgotten all about him but now he was right behind her.

"Yes," Karen contradicted him. "Right here, right now."

"No, Karen, *think,*" Lonnie urged. "They'll trace it right back to you."

"Not if you give me an alibi," Karen argued coolly and her eyes left Sasha briefly to give him a challenging look. "And you *will* give me an alibi won't you, Lonnie?"

"Yes, of course, but I still want you to think about this—"

"I'm through thinking," Karen snapped and Sasha watched her finger tightening on the trigger with a fatalistic lack of surprise.

Hard hands suddenly clamped down on her shoulders and she was swung dizzily around and released, flung toward the seating area. "Run!" Lon shouted simultaneously with the deafening report of a gunshot. She stood frozen in place, and after muttering something that sounded like, "I'll be damned, the blanks worked," he spared her a brief glance. "Goddammit, *run* I said!"

She ran. Behind her lay a mad cacophony of high-pitched shrieks, the thunderous report of gunshot after gunshot, and most incongruous of all, Lon's laughter in the aftermath of each shot. Ahead lay a solution that might save them both. She blessed all those mornings spent in all those arenas across the western portion of America as she located what she sought. Hands grasping the long silver handle, she threw first one switch then another.

Several things happened at once. The ice arena was plunged into total darkness. The gun blasted off one more shot but instead of hearing Lon's crazy laughter, which she didn't understand at all but which she'd already come to expect, there was a grunt and then silence. And she heard an exterior door down the corridor open and Mick's voice roar out her name. Heart in her throat, she ran in the direction of his voice.

Mick heard someone stumbling down the concrete hallway, saw the shadowy outline of a woman, and assumed the stance, figuring if it were Sasha she'd be screaming her head off in response to his frantic call. "Halt, or I'll shoot," he warned.

"Micky?" Her voice was a whisper and Mick swore, lowering the gun. She ran straight into his chest and his arms wrapped about her.

"Jesus Christ, baby, you don't run at someone in the dark like that. I nearly shot you." He tipped his chin into his neck trying to see her in the gloom. "Are you okay? She didn't hurt you did she? Where the hell is she anyhow?"

"Oh God, oh God, Mick, I think she shot Lon. He shoved me away and told me to run but they're back there in the arena. You've got to help him. I turned off the lights because he told me once she's terrified of the dark, but you've got to get him out of there; she's so crazy." Her teeth began to chatter.

"Okay." Mick stepped back and pressed a card into her hand. "You go find a phone and call 911, and then this number. Ask for an ambulance from the first and give my name and your location to the second. Then you stay in the office until I tell you otherwise, okay?"

"I want to go with you."

"No. Do as I tell—"

"I want to go with you!" Hysteria edged her voice and he hugged her to him again, wondering just when he'd lost command of the old authority he had always taken so much for granted.

"Okay, okay," he soothed. "But you'll stay behind me and do exactly what I say, when I say it, *without question,* you hear me? That means if I tell you to drop to the floor, you don't ask 'how come,' you drop, got it?"

"Uh-huh."

Shit. He was knee deep in mule-stubborn civilians; he'd be lucky if they all weren't killed. But grasping her delicate wrist, he pulled her along behind him as they made their way back to the arena entrance.

Darkness within the rink was absolute and they became aware of an odd keening sound as they approached the entrance. Mick stopped, let go of Sasha's wrist, and brought up his gun. "Stay here," he whispered and stared hard at her until he saw her nod. Leaving her where arena met backstage, he eased up the stygian tunnel that divided the spectator seating.

He heard the ragged whistling sound of someone hyperventilating and a voice, modulated at an unnaturally high pitch, pleading, "Turn on the light, Daddy; I'll be good, I'll be good. Just don't leave me in the dark again—please, Daddy? *Turn on the light,*" she screamed. Then the ragged, whistling attempt to breathe again, and she repeated herself word for word, starting off with a whimpered plea, culminating in screaming demands. Three times she reiterated her plea while Mick selected his position.

"Karen Corselli!" he called out and she screeched. There was a scramble in the dark, then the high-pitched, asthmatic *hee* of a woman trying to draw in enough breath.

"Turn on the lights," she whimpered. "Please? Turn on the lights?"

"Throw down your gun, Karen."

"Turnonthelights turnonthelights turnonthelights!"

"Throw down your gun!"

Another struggle for breath, then, "I lost it. Please, won't you turn on the—"

"Sasha!" he hollered. "Turn the lights back on."

There was a pause, during which he had to listen to Karen's repetitious litany for illumination. Finally, amidst a distant metallic clangor the overhead lights sprang to life. Mick squinted against the sudden glare, then cautiously picked his way over the ice to the woman crouched mid-rink with her arms crossed over her bent head.

The gun was several feet away and he detoured to slide a pen through the trigger guard, picking it up without touching it and working it into his own holster. Then sliding his belt from its loops, he approached Karen.

"The Lord is my light and my salvation, whom shall I fear?" she mumbled. "The Lord is the strength of my life; of whom shall I be afraid?"

He hunkered down and grasped her wrists in his hands, pulling them down and behind her back where he secured them with his belt. "Sasha!" he yelled and noticed that Karen didn't so much as flinch. She continued to stare down at the ice and talk to herself. "You can make those calls now." He looked back over at Karen.

". . . mine enemies and my foes, came upon me to eat up my flesh, they stumbled and fell," she murmured. "Though a host shall encamp against me, my heart shall not fear; though war should rise against me in this I will be confident . . ."

Clearly she was in no frame of mind to have her rights read to her at the moment, so he left her and went in search of Lon. Finding him crumpled in the middle of the tunnel where Mick had entered the arena, he thought it was a wonder he hadn't tripped over him on his way in.

Lon was facedown on the floor and there was blood on his back and pooled beneath his chest and face. Mick squatted down and placed a hand on the fallen man's shoulder, gently palpating until he located the entrance wound. Lon groaned.

"Well, I'm glad to hear you're still among the living," Mick said. "Can you move your feet?" There was a moment of inactivity, then first Lon's left foot then his right foot shifted fractionally.

"Good. And your hands?"

The same pattern was followed.

"Okay, good. I know you're not supposed to move a victim until a professional can look you over, but I'm more concerned about your blood loss than the chance of paralysis, which I feel is pretty slim. If you agree, I'm going to turn you over now so we can see the extent of what we're dealing with."

Lon grunted and Mick took it as assent. He rolled him carefully onto his back. Lon sucked air through his clenched teeth. "Ah, Jesus, that hurts!" he said weakly.

The sound of running feet echoed down the corridor and Sasha skidded to a halt next to them. "The aid car and the DEA should be here any minute. And there's somebody outside pounding at the main door." She sucked her breath in at the sight of all the blood on Lon's shoulder, neck, and face and squatted down for a closer look. "My God. How many times did she hit you anyway?"

"Just once," Mick answered for him and then said, "Sasha, get me something to make a compress with, will you? Then you'd better go let Connie in. She must be freezing her butt off out there in the parking lot."

Sasha had already risen to her feet and turned away, but she stopped, staring back at him over her shoulder. "Connie's in the parking lot?"

"Yeah. I imagine that's her you heard at the door." She gave him a look and he said, "It's a long story, darlin'; I'll tell it to you another time." Or maybe not, he thought, suddenly remembering the promise he'd made to get out of her life once the danger to it was eliminated. He became all business. "Get me something to stop this bleeding."

She got her bag off the seat where she'd left it and brought it back to the tunnel. Squatting down, she pawed through the contents and came up with a pair of leggings. Mick folded the legs into small squares and pressed the makeshift compresses against both entrance and exit wounds on Lon's upper chest. He applied direct pressure while Sasha stuffed her "Skate the Dream" sweatshirt beneath Lon's head.

Then she rose to her feet. "I'll go get Connie," she said.

Mick looked up at her. She had run to him, had flung herself into his arms. This was probably his one chance to win her back.

If he didn't mind breaking his word to her yet one more time.

"Good idea," he said with apparent indifference. "I imagine you'll want to stay with her tonight. Now that you're no longer in danger." Sasha stiffened and turned to stare down at him, her expression as blank as his own. "If I don't see you," he continued, then hesitated, because how did he complete that sentence. If I don't see you, what? Have a good life? Be happy? *Damn you, release me from my word!* "I'm sorry, Sasha," is what came out. "I never meant to hurt you."

She just stared at him, then finally blinked, turned on her heel and walked away.

He grit his teeth, staring after her as he continued to apply pressure to the bleeding wound on Lon's chest. When he finally looked down again, it was to find Morrison regarding him through narrowed eyes. "You sorry-ass dumb shit," Lon said when he saw he had Mick's attention.

"May be. But I gave her my word."

The arena was filled with people. Paramedics took over Lon's care and men in dark suits demanded Mick's attention. They stood in their slippery soled shoes, cautiously balanced on the ice in a huddle around Karen Corselli. Sasha watched from the sidelines as long as she could stand it. Finally, she made her way out to the group in the middle of the rink. She cleared her throat to gain Mick's attention.

"You've got to get her off the ice," she said when he looked down at her.

"Young woman," a middle-aged man began with officious impatience, "I'll have to ask you to leave. You don't belong here." He reached out with the clear intention of grasping her arm to hustle her away, but Mick stepped between them.

"Shut up," he bluntly advised him and turned his attention back to Sasha.

"You've got to get her off the ice, Mick. She's already been sitting there for—what?—more than ten minutes. She can't continue to sit directly on the ice like that without risking frostbite."

"My enemies speak evil of me," Karen said. "When shall he die and his name perish?"

"Come on, Corselli." Mick reached down to haul her to her feet. The belt he'd used for restraints was replaced with regulation handcuffs and he guided Karen over to the stands. He turned back to Sasha, who along with the suits had trailed after them. "How's Morrison?"

Karen gave him a sharp look in which he glimpsed the first glimmer of rationality he'd seen out of her. "Yea, mine own familiar friend, in whom I trusted, in which did eat of my bread, hath lifted up his heel against me," she said fervently. Then her eyes clouded over again.

He rolled his own eyes impatiently and then turned back to Sasha, lifting a hand to hover over the gash on her cheekbone. The very tips of his fingers gently brushed the flesh beginning to swell and bruise around it. "You go with Morrison to the hospital and have this looked at," he instructed her crisply. Then his attention was claimed once again by the men in the dark suits.

She watched him for several long moments, wondering if he would just disappear without a word sometime during this long night to return to his lonely, covert world of lying and spying.

The thought of it hurt horribly somewhere deep inside. Yet she said nothing in an attempt to convince him otherwise. She crossed the arena, talked to the paramedics, and climbed into the ambulance behind Lon's stretcher.

Knowing his last excuse to have her stay with him had just been removed, Mick turned his head to watch as she followed the paramedics out of his sight. He continued to stare at the empty tunnel for several silent moments. Then, his face expressionless, he went back to doing his job.

* * *

"Miss Miller?" Both Sasha and Connie stood at the doctor's approach.

"How is he?" Sasha asked anxiously.

"He's fine. Quite lucky, actually. The bullet missed his lung by about half an inch. Made a bit of a mess exiting, but it bypassed all the important arteries, and except for losing some blood he's in remarkably good condition." The doctor squeezed the bridge of his nose between thumb and forefinger and yawned. "Sorry," he said and then straightened. "He'd like to see you. I want him to rest, but he made such a production of it I felt it was better in the long run to let him have his way. He has to remain in the ER until they have a room ready for him in any case, but don't let him wear himself out."

"I won't." Sasha squeezed Connie's hand and then followed the doctor to the cubicle. Letting her in, he beckoned the nurse out and then closed the door behind them. Sasha crossed to Lonnie.

"How're you feeling?"

"Higher 'n a kite." He looked up at her. "They pumped me full of some power painkillers." Bringing his hand out from beneath the blanket covering him, he fumbled for hers. "I'm sorry I dragged you into this mess, Sasha. I really didn't have any idea Karen was so out of control. I mean I knew she was kind of screwed up, but I never thought of her as dangerous."

"Nothing is ever all black or all white, is it, Lon?" She pulled a chair over to the bed and sat down on it, resting her elbows on the mattress and holding his hand in both of hers. "I wanted to hate her, you know. I really wanted to despise her for everything she's done. But I can't. Not since I heard her begging her daddy to turn on the lights." She blew out a breath, her eyes seeing something far away. "I guess there's no one alive who's really just all good or all bad, is there?

We're all put together out of bits and pieces of our experiences."

Lon had a feeling it wasn't Karen she was talking about now. "Saush, about Vinicor . . ."

"I hear you've been putting the moves on Connie," she interrupted him. "There's a combination I never would have guessed."

"Yeah, it's pretty damn unlikely, all right. Like I've got anything to offer someone like her."

Sasha studied him soberly. "Lon, are you truly once and for all finished selling drugs?"

"Yes."

"And this won't change even if I someday find somebody to love, or if you find something you just have to own right this minute?"

"I've accepted that you can love both me and Vinicor at the same time, if in different ways—"

"I'm not talking about Mick—"

"—and if I find something I can't live without, then I'll do what everybody else does. I'll make payments to a charge card for the rest of my natural life."

Sasha smiled slightly. "Then I really don't see where you have less to offer Connie than any other man."

"Except that I'm an ex-con who might not have a job tomorrow."

"Karen wasn't your responsibility."

"Maybe. Maybe not. If nothing else, though, this shoulder is going to put me out of commission for a while. What's to stop the powers that be from using it as an excuse to dump me? I'd do it in their position."

"Well, I won't let them. Have a little faith. We've survived Kells Crossing. The Follies is a piece of cake compared to that." She hesitated, then squeezed his hand. "Lonnie, I'm sorry I doubted you tonight. You saved my life."

He gave a bitter laugh. "I damn near cost you your life."

"You're my oldest friend, you know. Nothing will ever change that."

He perked up. "We can say anything to each other, right?"

"Yes. Anything."

"Good. Then about Vinicor . . ."

Sasha rose to her feet. "I've got to go," she said. "The doctor wants you to get your rest."

He didn't relinquish his grasp on her hand, although his strength was depleted to the point where she could remove it without much effort if she really made the attempt. His voice, however, was firm. "Sasha," he said with authority. "Sit down."

TWENTY-TWO

It was early morning by the time the DEA finished collecting evidence in Karen Corselli's hotel room and Mick was finally free to seek some rest in his own. Letting himself in, he closed the door behind him and then leaned back against it, running a weary hand through his hair.

He was exhausted but didn't know if he'd be able to sleep in that empty bed by himself. Which was sort of ironic, really, considering he hadn't actually slept in the same bed with Saush for a while now. But he'd at least had the sound of her breathing and her physical presence to soothe him to sleep each night. There had still been a chance then; he hadn't been leaden with the knowledge she was gone.

Pushing away from the door, he walked into the main body of the hotel room, pulling his sweater off over his head as he walked. A chair by the table across the room creaked, a minute, telltale sound that caused him to freeze, his arms still crossed over his head, half in and half out of the garment, the sweater stretching from his nose to his elbows in the air, blinding him. Wrestling it free, he threw it to the floor and was reaching for his gun in one swift, continuous movement before he recognized the person rising from the chair.

"Sasha?"

She started across the room to him, silent except for the whisper of her old-fashioned white lawn nightgown brushing her legs. Then the sound of running water in a distant room broke the spell that had held him in place, and Mick made a sound deep in his throat and took two giant strides forward. He intercepted her in the middle of the room.

Fingers digging into her sides, he lifted her into the air, leaving her feet to dangle above the carpet as he kissed her with a rough lack of control. His mouth was voracious, forcing hers wider, reaching deep with his tongue, restlessly changing the angle of his mouth from one second to the next in an attempt to get closer. Sasha wrapped her arms around his neck and kissed him back. Kicking her legs free of voluminous folds of nightgown, she wound them around his waist.

Mick snarled deep in his chest at the feel of their bodies so close yet not close enough, and took the two steps needed to bring them to the table. Sweeping it free of clutter with one arm, he lowered her roughly onto its surface, his body plastered to hers, hands tracing down the sides of her body to the hem of her nightgown where it bunched around her thighs. He raised his hips up just enough to push the material up to her waist and then reached between them to rip himself free of his fly. In the next second his hands were gripping the backs of her thighs, pulling them high and wide apart and he was plunging deep inside her.

Sasha cried aloud with pleasure and drove her hips up to meet each powerful thrust. His mouth came down to cover hers, swallowing cries that grew stronger with every plunge and withdrawal. Then suddenly she was screaming with the force of the orgasm that exploded inside her.

"Oh, God, *yes!*" Mick lifted up enough to watch her. "I love you, I love you, I love you, I love—" His words broke off and his lips pressed into the side of her neck beneath the force of his own abrupt and violent climax. A low, animal sound forced its way up his throat with each shuddering pulsation that transferred his seed into her body. Then he collapsed atop her.

For several moments it was silent except for the sound of their harsh breathing. Then one of Sasha's feet slid from

Mick's buttock and hit the tabletop with a small slap. He pushed up on his palms to look down at her.

The first thing that registered was the nasty swelling of her cheek. It was puffed out and fiercely bruised, bristling with three black sutures. Self-recrimination hit him like a two-ton truck. "Jesus." He pulled out and pushed to his feet, staring down at her sprawled across the tabletop. Snatching the spread off the bed, he shook it out over her and then scooped her up off her uncomfortable perch, setting her swaddled in yards of hotel bedspread in the nearest chair. He stepped back and stared at her, hands fisted at his side. "I'm a real piece of work, aren't I? You were nearly killed tonight. You're black and blue, most likely in pain . . . and I'm all over you like a goddam animal."

"Yeah, and I liked it." His face was such a marvel of incredulity she had the urge to laugh. But it had faded by the time she'd fought her way partway free of the comforter. "Micky, don't leave me," she whispered. She cleared her throat and then said more strongly, "Please. If the only reason you're going is because you gave me your word that you would, then you've gotta stay. I don't want that promise, Micky; I want you. I don't think I could stand it if you left—"

Mick snatched her out of the chair and held her in a grip that even through the comforter threatened to crack a few ribs. "I want us to get married," he said in a low voice.

"Okay."

"The only thing is"—sitting down in the chair, he arranged her in his lap—"you'd, uh, be marrying an unemployed man."

"You're kidding!" She sat up indignantly. "They *fired* you?"

"No, that was what they were going to do when I refused to manufacture a case involving you. They *love* my ass now. Karen provided them with even bigger and better headlines than you would have. The truth is . . ." He studied her closely for her reaction. "I quit."

"Oh. Well. That's okay, then." She settled back against his chest. "Mick, do you think you could find me the little envelope of pills you swept to the floor with the rest of the stuff on the table? My cheek's starting to throb something fierce."

Ten minutes later they were curled together beneath the blankets on the bed. "Why'd you quit?" she asked out of the blue and raised her uninjured cheek up off his chest to see his face. "Not that I object, mind you. It's just . . . I was under the impression your work was—I don't know—like your entire life."

"It was; that's the problem." He stroked her hair. "Once upon a time it was exciting and I felt like I was contributing something. Truth is, though, I've been growing disenchanted the past couple years, but it *was* my life and I didn't have anything to replace it with." His shoulder moved in a shrug. "The War on Drugs is not being won, Sasha—it's being turned into a political platform, a tool for the grandizement of suits and politicians. I'm tired of hanging out with lowlifes . . . and believe me, darlin', this is a life form that's prevalent on both sides of the law in this business." He tucked his chin in to peer down at her. "Are you worried how we'll get by without my salary?"

"Not really. I've got a little money set aside."

"So do I, darlin', but I doubt we'll need to live on it. First thing tomorrow I'll talk to Dello about a little contract work. He could use my expertise cleaning up the rest of the Follies' drug problem. Karen may have been the most dramatic example, but the extremes she took it to notwithstanding, you know as well as I do that she's not the only one. There's plenty to keep me busy until the hiatus when the show closes. We can decide our next step then, but I don't want you to worry. My experience in this field can be transmuted in about a dozen different directions. I doubt I'll ever be short of work."

"When are we getting married?"

He shifted her onto her back and rolled to his side, propping his head in his hand to smile down at her. "Ah, now, that depends. You got any preferences how you want it handled?"

"Something small and simple."

"No huge church and guests by the hundreds?"

"I don't even know a hundred people. A little church, Ivan to give me away, Lon, Connie, a few friends and your family would be nice."

"Which kinda brings us around to what I've been thinkin'." He grinned and wagged his eyebrows at her. "How 'bout Billings, the Saturday following the last show? My mom can get everything ready."

She stared up at him incredulously. "Mick, for pity's sake, you can't just dump this in your mother's lap and expect her to pull it all together in a few weeks. Weddings are a lot of work—even small weddings."

"Yeah, and they're right up Mom's alley. Nothing that woman likes better than organizing the hell outta stuff."

"But she doesn't even know me and you expect her to just drop everything to do the work I should be doing myself?"

"Ah, man, she's gonna love you."

"Not after we dump this in her lap, she's not."

"No, I'm tellin' ya, darlin'. You're bringing home her baby boy—getting him outta that dangerous drug work. I promise, you present her with a grandkid or two somewhere down the road and the farm's yours." He licked his lower lip and watched her intently. "So whataya say?"

"Oh, I would really love that, Micky." Seeing his smug smile, she hastened to add, "But only if she agrees. And you don't go browbeating her into this, you hear me?"

Mick laughed. "The man hasn't been born can browbeat my mom into doing something she don't wanna." His hand slid out from under his ear and his head flopped down onto his biceps as he stared at her. "I can hardly wait to take you home." He hesitated a moment and then said, "Darlin'?"

"Umm?"

"What made you come to me tonight?"

"Well, Lonnie said—" she started to explain.

"No," he protested, bolting up to a sitting position. He gripped his knees in both hands and stared down at her. "No, no, no, no, *no.* Tell me I don't owe this to him!"

"I'm afraid you do. I was gonna let you go, Mick, because I thought that's what you really wanted. It hurt so much I couldn't bear to talk about it, but Lon made me sit down and listen to him anyway. He said the only reason you were cutting me loose was because you'd given me your word you'd get out of my life once this mess with Karen was over. Said I'd be a fool to let you go."

"Ah, shit." Mick dropped his forehead onto his kneecaps and sat silently for a few moments. Finally, he raised his head. "I refuse to be beholden to that man."

"He saved my life, Micky."

"I know he did, honey, and for that I'll be eternally grateful. But that doesn't mean I have to like the guy. I know! I'll talk to McMahon, see to it his heroics are publicized. The news can even be slanted in such a way it'll throw doubt on his prior conviction." He grinned, pleased with himself. "He'll be the hotshot sensation of the moment. That oughtta make us even."

"You can do that if you like. But Lon's always going to be a part of my life, Mick—get used to it."

"Damn."

He sounded so disgusted that Sasha had to smile. "Admit it," she said, giving him a little poke. "You don't dislike him nearly as much as you pretend." He made a rude noise. "You don't. I think you actually harbor a little fondness for him."

"Don't be ridiculous. I could maybe get used to him." He slid down under the covers once again and gathered her into his arms. "But I don't wanna talk about him anymore. Have I mentioned how my much folks are gonna love you?"

"I'm"—a huge, jaw-splitting yawn was hurriedly hidden

behind politely raised fingers—"gonna love them, too," Sasha replied sleepily.

Mick laughed. "Okay, okay. We'll talk about it tomorrow. I'm a little wired, but I s'pose I could be talked into winding down—now that I know we've got a future."

"Oh, we've got a future, all right," she replied around another yawn. Snuggling up to him, she listened to his heartbeat beneath her ear. And she smiled. "Brightest damn future you've ever seen."

Thrilling Suspense from
Beverly Barton